The Men and the Medium

Lyn Behan

BEHANPUBLISHING

First published by AIA Publishing 2018

Cover design: Velvet Wings Media

Paperback : ISBN 978-0-6456587-4-3

The protagonist, Lily Bancroft, did not fit the mould of a conventional woman. She wanted to go to university and study to become a doctor; she also wanted to visit Egypt and pursue her fascination with that ancient civilisation. Sadly, she achieved neither but she did lead an extraordinary life. Born in the 1880's, she was determined to live her life exactly as she wished, though first she needed to escape the confines set by her parents and so married the first eligible man who came along. Endowed with a gift for healing and obsessed with the occult, she found success in healing others and holding seances where grieving people could reach out to those who had passed.

Lyn cleverly weaves the fabric of Lily's lifestyle around the traumas of the two world wars. Her deep involvement in her work mean that relationships take second place in her life and she often hurts those who are closest to her.

The book is a page-turner and Lyn is to be congratulated on creating such a captivating heroine, only revealing at the end (spoiler alert!) that Lily is her grandmother.

Dell Brand – Author

PROLOGUE

POOLE, DORSET 1961

Leslie took off his hat and bowed his head as the coffin was lowered into the grave. The undertakers looked at Ena for a signal, then, eyes lowered, shuffled backwards until far enough away to be able to turn and walk back to the hearse.

Leslie and Ena stood alone at Lily's graveside. Ena pulled a rose from a wreath, leaned over and let it fall onto the simple coffin.

'It doesn't feel right to just leave her here with no proper ceremony, and only us to mourn her,' Leslie said, his eyes filling with tears.

Ena looked up at him, then took his arm.

'It's what she would've wished. Her spirit has gone.' She picked up a handful of the freshly dug earth and scattered it over the coffin. 'Let's sit down for a while on that bench over there. It's unusual to have a sunny day for a funeral.' She led him to the seat, and they sat in silence.

Leslie brooded over Lily's three husbands. None of them had attended her funeral. Percy had passed, so, of course, he wouldn't be there. John had sent flowers, lovely red roses with a card: 'To my darling Lily. Rest in Peace, John.' As for Richard, well, what could anyone say! Two of her three sons had sent wreaths.

Ena turned to him. 'Thank you, Leslie, you've been so good and loyal to my mother all these years.'

He wiped his eyes. 'She was the love of my life.'

'It's so peaceful here,' she paused. 'Tell me how you first met her, you've never mentioned it.'

Leslie sighed and tried to smile. 'I used to hold séances in my house when I first became interested in spiritualism. Lily started to come to the meetings. I loved her from the very first moment I saw her. She had some kind of radiance that made me feel I was worthwhile and loveable. I just wanted to be near her.' He blew his nose. His eyes filled with tears again as the memories came back.

The grave diggers approached.

Ena stood and took his arm. 'Darling, Leslie, perhaps we should go.

CHAPTER 1

LONDON, NOVEMBER 1903

Leslie regarded himself in his bedroom mirror. He didn't like what he saw: a tall, lanky man with jacket loose on his bony frame, a nondescript face topped with unruly, sandy coloured hair which flopped into pale blue eyes. He took his late father's velvet smoking jacket from the wardrobe and exchanged it for the tweed he wore. Hmm. That looked worse, made him look older than his twenty-four years. He changed back, then took his fob watch from his waistcoat and checked the time. Better get a move on, Mrs Snelling would be arriving soon.

He took a deep breath. Today was the day he'd decided that after the séance he'd ask Miss Bancroft if he could walk out with her.

He took some Macassar oil in his hands and rubbed it over his hair, carefully made a parting in the middle and combed it to the sides. It lay flat and neat. He wondered if a moustache would improve his appearance, but the only time he'd tried to grow one it had sprouted in little tufts. He turned his head from side to side, looked at his image one last time and grimaced. It would have to do.

Downstairs, he arranged the dining-room furniture ready for the séance and propped the notice in the window. Mrs Snelling knocked on the door. He let her in and took her to the breakfast room. She liked to spend some time meditating before the session.

People began to arrive. He welcomed them and showed them into the dining room. It was nearly time to start the séance, but Miss Bancroft still hadn't appeared. He paced up and down the hall. The hall mirror caught his reflection; damn, that hair was sticking up again! He smoothed it down, with his hands. Blast it, now his hands were all oily. Hearing voices outside, he quickly wiped his hands on the seat of his trousers, then peered through the hall window. Lily was coming up the steps. His heart leaped. But what was this? There was a man behind her ...

***

Percy left Tom with the noisy crowd at the Adam and Eve Music hall, turned and followed a quiet road behind the hall. The fog muffled the sounds of the horses and cabs.

He walked for a while and then, unsure of where he was, stopped to get his bearings.

'Are you going in?' said a voice from behind him.

He turned to see a young woman in a maroon-coloured cloak with dark, curly hair escaping from a little hat perched on top of her head. She pointed to a sign in the front window of the house where he'd stopped. He hadn't noticed it, but he glanced at it now, not registering the words. His eyes were drawn back to her face, and he opened his mouth to say, *No, I'm just passing by*, but those words didn't come out, and, instead, he found himself nodding. He stood back to let her go up the steps before him, then he followed her through the open door.

She turned and smiled at him. Suddenly breathless, he managed to smile back.

'Ah! Miss Bancroft!' a voice said, 'I thought perhaps you were unable to come this afternoon. I'm so pleased to see you. We were just about to start.'

Percy dragged his eyes away from Miss Bancroft. The owner of the voice, a tall, thin chap, took her cloak from her and carefully hung it up. She took off her gloves and placed them on the hallstand, then unpinned her hat. Some of the curls from her elaborate hairstyle escaped the pins and fell down her back. She seemed not to notice.

'I'm so sorry, Mr Carter. I do hope I haven't delayed the meeting?' She smiled.

'No, no, not at all.' The man turned to Percy. 'Oh, I'm sorry,' he said and held out his hand. 'Leslie Carter.'

Percy dragged his eyes away from Miss Bancroft and looked up. 'Percy Hedgecock.' They shook hands.

'Are you a friend of Miss Bancroft?' enquired Leslie Carter, a note of anxiety in his voice.

Percy shook his head. 'No,' he mumbled. 'I was just ... I mean, I saw the sign.'

'Excellent!' Percy heard relief in Carter's voice. 'Well, hang up your coat and come into the séance room.'

Percy did so, and was about to take off his scarf when he remembered he was wearing Saturday's shirt and no collar. He hastily put his scarf back around his neck and followed them into a gloomy room, dominated by a big circular table. Several people sat around it. Some of whom looked up and nodded in his direction.

Leslie Carter pulled out a chair for Miss Bancroft, then indicated an empty chair next to her. Percy blushed and sat down, thankful that the room was too dim for her to see. He smelt something, incense perhaps. The heavy atmosphere made him feel disorientated.

Leslie Carter placed an armchair on the other side of the table, lit candles, drew the heavy brocade curtains and sat down. The sound of a door opening from the opposite side of the room made Percy look up. A tall, thin woman in a flowing dress with a long chain of beads around her neck drifted in. She sat in the armchair, waited for a few moments, then took several deep breaths, closed her eyes and intoned:

'Joining hands with each other we summon the Spirit.'

The person on his left gripped his hand. Then he felt Miss Bancroft's little hand slipping into his right hand. His heart thumped.

'Beloved spirits of the past, be here with us today, be guided by the light of the world.'

Nothing. Only the soft breathing of the participants could be heard. The medium repeated the command.

A long silence. Then: 'I can feel you are here. Please rap the table to say you will join us today.'

One side of the table moved, followed by the distinct tap of a table leg.

'Are there any messages today?'

Again, another tap of the table leg. Yes.

The fact that he was in a séance now registered with Percy. He'd been so focussed on Miss Bancroft that he hadn't paid attention when Carter mentioned the séance room. Séances were all the rage these days. It was a hoax; he was sure. Someone in the group must be moving the table with their knees. He tried to concentrate. The medium asked a question and then said each letter of the alphabet. The table leg tapped after each one and then stopped.

It seemed there was a message for someone called Beatrice. A woman made a muffled sound, said she was called Beatrice and then asked, 'Was the message from Herbert?'

Percy found it difficult to concentrate and soon stopped paying attention. Instead he dwelt on the image of those smiling eyes, and that slim, curvaceous figure that had preceded him into the room. He felt hot around his neck, but didn't want let go of her hand to loosen his scarf.

The man on his left had such a firm grip on his other hand that he felt unable to let go.

The session seemed interminable. He felt confused, his palms sticky. Would she think he was a ragamuffin with his scarf and sweaty hands? He wanted it to end; he couldn't breathe. No! He didn't want it to end, he wanted to hold her hand for ever. Whatever was the matter with him? These stupid thoughts!

At last the medium announced that the spirit was tired, and the session ended with a prayer, thanking the spirit and the medium. Reluctantly Percy relinquished Miss Bancroft's hand. She turned to him and smiled.

Leslie Carter stood up, pulled back the curtains, blew out the candles, and then approached Percy. 'Have you been to a séance before?' he asked.

Percy shook his head.

'Hmm,' said Leslie Carter. 'Well, we usually have a cup of tea together afterwards, but first let me introduce you to everyone.'

He led the way out of the séance room and into what looked like a breakfast room with cups and saucers and a big teapot set out on a table. A woman picked up the tea pot and started filling the cups. Most people seemed to know each other and chatted as Leslie took Percy around and introduced him.

'Of course, you have already met Miss Bancroft.'

Much to Percy's annoyance, Leslie Carter bypassed her and went on to introduce him to someone else.

People began to leave, saying their goodbyes, then Miss Bancroft came over and smiled at them. 'Goodbye, Mr Hedgecock, Mr Carter,' she said over her shoulder as she went out of the room.

'Goodbye,' Percy echoed, then he turned to Leslie Carter. 'Goodbye, and thank you.' He hurried after Miss Bancroft.

'We hope to see you again next week,' someone said to him.

He looked back to the speaker. 'Yes, thank you, I certainly hope so.'

He reached the hall, but Miss Bancroft had already taken her hat and cloak from the hall stand. She tucked the recalcitrant curls back into her hat, smiled at him, then disappeared down the steps.

Bemused, Percy retrieved his hat and coat and ambled down the steps into the thickening fog. He looked back at the house. Number twenty three. At the end of the road he looked for the street sign, just able to make it out in the deepening gloom. He had to remember the name so he could return the following Sunday to see her again.

***

Lily Bancroft hurried home, unsettled by the meeting that afternoon. Her parents didn't know about the séances. She'd told them she was going to meetings of the National Union of Women's Suffrage, campaigning for women to have the right to a parliamentary vote. Her parents didn't approve of this but thought it was harmless enough. She did go to NUWS meetings during the week, but she'd come across Leslie Carter's spiritualist meetings and started attending. She could learn a lot from Mrs Snelling.

Now she wondered about Percy Hedgecock. He had a good aura. Well, so did Leslie Carter, but Percy Hedgecock had made her heart race.

She smiled to herself at the thought.

***

When the participants in the séance had left, Leslie tidied away the tea things, went to the parlour and sat down in front of the fire. Watching the flames, he brooded over the events of the afternoon. He had a bad feeling about this Percy Hedgecock fellow. Oh, he was probably a nice enough person, but the way he'd looked at Miss Bancroft ... and did he detect something in the way she'd looked at Hedgecock? Or was it his imagination? He felt annoyed. With this Hedgecock person there, and having to introduce him to everyone, he hadn't had the opportunity to ask Miss Bancroft if he could walk her home.

He sighed. When he was near Miss Bancroft, he felt strong and happy and just wanted to be with her. Oh, well, it seemed nothing was going right for him lately. The setback with the electromagnetic radiation project he'd been working on had taken him a while to get over. He'd been using some of Oliver Lodge's discoveries, but then an Italian named Marconi had forestalled him. He sighed again, then brightened; an idea had come to him during the séance. He picked up the latest copy of *The Model Engineer and Amateur Electrician*.

I'll write another article for them, but next Sunday, I'll definitely ask Miss Bancroft.

***

Percy was in a daze at dinner that evening, managing only to nod as the other lodgers came to the table. The boarding house, in a small terrace with three floors, had only six lodgers. Mrs Hodges the Cockney landlady was a plump, genial widow who had a soft spot for Percy.

Preoccupied with thoughts of Miss Bancroft, Percy hardly registered what he ate.

'Hey! Perce!' Tom called from the end of the table. 'I thought you was a vegetarian. You're helping yourself to roast beef.'

Startled, Percy looked up. He blinked, then realised that he'd been in such a trance that he'd automatically taken the serving fork. It fell out of his hand with a clatter.

Mrs Hodges interposed: 'Yew kin 'ave some roasted beef, Mr 'edgecock if yew like.'

'No, no; thank you. Sorry,' he said. 'I was dreaming.' He blushed and hurriedly applied himself to his meal.

On his way to his room after dinner, Tom caught up with him. 'What ho, Perce, you're not yourself this evening; what's up? Not feeling well?'

Percy blushed again, kicking himself mentally for showing his feelings so readily.

'Come on, Perce, come up to my room and tell me all about it; somefink's troubling you.'

Percy shook his head. He wasn't in the mood for idle chat with Tom. Also, Tom's room on the top floor didn't have a fireplace, and the night was chilly. As a junior clerk with the same firm, he didn't earn as much as Percy.

'Nothing to tell,' he replied, pausing at the foot of the stairs.

'All right then, why are you acting so strange?' Tom asked.

'Nothing to tell, really,' Percy repeated, loath to describe his afternoon.

However, he did feel a need to talk about Miss Bancroft. 'Well, on my walk this afternoon I stopped outside a house.' He started up the stairs, uncertain how to explain how he'd got into the house. 'I wasn't sure where I was, and then this girl came up and asked me if I was going in.'

'And you said, "Yes."' Tom grinned.

'Well, yes. And it turned out to be a séance.'

'Ah, so you got a message from the other side?'

'No, but this girl ...'

'Ah hah! Go on.' Tom listened eagerly.

'Well, she's beautiful.'

'And?' Tom said. 'Come on, tell me more.'

Percy struggled to find words, he rubbed his nose, trying to think. 'She took off her hat and these curls ...'

'Yes? And?'

'Well, her hair was all done up, but some of it fell down.'

'That's the latest ladies' fashion! The Pompadour hair style, all up on the top of their heads.' Tom looked pleased with his superior knowledge.

Puzzled, Percy looked at him. 'How do you know these things?'

'I read the ladies magazines. You've got to keep abreast of the Ladies Fashions, so you can talk to them about it!'

A wink from Tom. 'So? What colour?'

Percy thought. 'Brown, all shiny and curly. Like a chestnut.'

Tom remained silent for a moment, then laughed. 'You're in love, old chap! When do you see her again?'

'I suppose next Sunday,' Percy said slowly. 'I'll have to go back again.'

'Well, you had better luck than me. All the best girls were taken.' Tom grinned ruefully. 'There was one there with another fellow, she gave me the eye and smiled, but her man was keeping her close. Maybe I should come to your séance with you next week.'

Preoccupied, Percy scarcely heard what Tom said. 'Better go,' he said at last, reaching the top of the stairs. 'See you tomorrow.'

His small room was simply furnished with an iron framed bed, a dresser, wardrobe, writing table and two chairs. Percy pulled one of the chairs in front of the tiny grate and warmed his hands before the glowing embers. A few lumps of coal still remained in the scuttle. He carefully placed them around the embers and blew on them. Soon the small room looked more cheerful in the glow of the fire. Seven more days to wait.

Percy usually enjoyed his work as a commercial clerk in a stock broker's office, but in the following days he found it hard to concentrate. His thoughts kept going back to Miss Bancroft. He willed himself to stop thinking about her.

***

Lily stared out the drawing-room window, feeling bored. She looked around the room—a gilded cage with rich-gold velvet curtains from floor to ceiling. Her life was so restricted. Yes, her parents were fairly liberal in that they let her pursue her archaeological studies at the British Museum and go to meetings of the Suffragist movement, but she wanted more than that. From the window she could see the carriage being brought around to the front of the house by the groom, and then her father coming out of the house and getting into it.

If only Father would allow me to go to University and study to become a doctor.

But he was so old fashioned. She had a burning desire to heal and felt she already knew more than her brother, James, who was studying Medicine. She'd secretly read all his text books when he'd brought them home from University. *It's not fair! How can I get away from my father? And what could I do?*

***

The next Sunday afternoon, Percy tried to arrange his cravat around his neck so that it hid his collarless shirt. Pleased that Tom seemed to have forgotten about going with him, he arrived at the séance house early, eager to see her again. He walked in the open front door and hung up his hat, coat and scarf.

Leslie Carter came out of the séance room. 'Good afternoon, Mr Hedgecock; welcome back. I do hope you enjoyed our session last week?'

'Oh, yes, very much,' Percy replied, looking around to see if she was there.

'You're the first today.' Leslie Carter said, following his glance. 'The others will be here soon. I'm just arranging the table and chairs in the séance room. Come in and sit down.'

Percy sat at the table. Each time he heard footsteps in the hall, his heart jumped. A man came in and nodded at him, then sat beside him. And then a woman came and sat on his other side. At last he heard Miss Bancroft's voice greeting Carter. She came in, smiled at everyone and sat down at the table, on the opposite side to him. *Good; that's even better. Now I can see her without having to turn my head.* He smiled at her, and his face grew hot. He couldn't concentrate on the séance. Instead he kept worrying about what he'd say to her after the meeting. That was if she even spoke to him. He wished he'd asked Tom a bit more about how he managed to engage girls in conversation.

Mrs Snelling, the medium, drifted in and followed the same procedure as the previous week, but it seemed to go on longer.

Across the table from him, Lily grew restless. An anxious frown on her pretty face deepened as the session dragged on. Was someone waiting for her somewhere? Parents, perhaps. As soon as the meeting finished, not stopping for tea, she jumped up, took her hat and cloak and left, waving a brief goodbye to everyone. Disappointed, Percy watched her disappear out the door.

That night at dinner, Tom winked at him, and afterwards said, 'I looked for you this afternoon, but you must have slipped away. How did the meeting go?'

'The same,' Percy replied, 'I didn't get to speak to her, and she left straight after the meeting.'

Tom pulled a face. 'I suppose you have to keep going and see what happens. How're you going with the spirits?'

Percy shrugged. 'I don't know, I don't really have any time for it, but it passes a Sunday afternoon.'

Tom nodded. 'Yes, not much to do around here, unless you go to the tavern or the music halls, but you're not inclined ...'

'No,' Percy said, and then, 'Tom?'

'Hmm?'

'What do you say to girls when you meet them?'

Tom grinned. 'Oh, you tell them you like their hairstyle, or their dress or hat or whatever, and smile at them, but you mustn't be too bold with it. More like, "If you don't mind me saying so, I do think you look lovely in that dress." Or, "Is that the Pompadour hairstyle? It's very fetching." Something like that anyway.'

Percy blinked. He didn't think he'd ever be able to say such things to Miss Bancroft. 'What did you say that hairstyle was? The latest one?'

'Oh! The Pompadour. After the French courtesan, Madame la Pompadour.'

Percy nodded. 'Thank you; I'll try and remember that.'

He wandered up to his room, saying over and over to himself, 'Pompadour. Pompadour.'

Each week he hoped to get to know her; however, she always disappeared so quickly after the meetings. Sometimes he thought he'd seen her getting into a horse-drawn carriage, but the winter afternoon gloom made it difficult to be sure.

***

Leslie spent Christmas Day alone, as had been the case since his elderly parents had passed several years ago. He ate the Christmas dinner which Mrs Wilson who 'did' for him brought over. Then he sat in front of the fire with a glass of brandy and brooded over his life. *My life is dull. I'm dull. My projects are going nowhere*. His love for Miss Bancroft was unrequited. He was beginning to lose hope of ever getting the chance to speak to her. And that Percy Hedgecock kept coming to the séances and making sheep's eyes at her. He didn't have a good feeling about him.

He needed to get out more. Since his parents had left him well provided for, he didn't need to work. But if he were to marry Miss Bancroft would he have enough to support her and maybe a family? Perhaps he should look for some kind of employment? Attend one of Oliver Lodge's lectures; ask Oliver Lodge for employment in his factory? He put more coal on the fire, refilled his glass and sat thinking about Miss Bancroft and what it would be like to have her sitting beside him, warm and cosy, in front of the fire. He sighed and went back to the book on Electromagnetism he'd been reading.

***

Percy spent Christmas with his widowed mother in Dover but looked forward to getting back to London after the short holiday. Anxious to see more of Miss Bancroft, he returned to the séances, but apart from smiling at him, she seemed always in a hurry to leave.

Tom kept asking him how his romance was going, but as he kept getting the same answer—nowhere—he soon stopped asking.

'Can't believe you're still going to that place,' he said one Sunday evening. 'Do you honestly think there's something in this spiritualism stuff?'

'Not really,' Percy replied, 'But Oliver Lodge and Arthur Conan Doyle believe in it, you know, so there must be something to it.'

He didn't want to let Tom know that he had no time for it at all, just for one person. He now despaired of ever getting to know Miss Bancroft and, increasingly skeptical of the whole procedure, grew bored with the séances. It did seem like the table moved, but he couldn't be bothered trying to follow the messages and was sure the medium made them up. By late March he still didn't even know Miss Bancroft's first name.

He made a sudden decision to make the following Sunday his last séance. He was just wasting his time.

However, that very Sunday afternoon, after a lot of table tapping, Mrs. Snelling announced that the last spirit message was from someone called George London.

'Does anyone know a George London who has passed?' she asked.

Percy blinked and came to attention. His father's second name was London. A very unusual name, George London Hedgecock.

More tapping.

'George London says to tell Sarah Ann to take care.'

Percy frowned. He didn't know what to think. His mother was called Sarah Ann, but that was a common name. Had someone found out his father's name? It seemed unlikely. But they must have. He hadn't seen his mother since Christmas. Yes, he'd wasted far too much time with these séances and mooning over Miss Bancroft. It must be all a hoax. He gave himself a mental shake. This would definitely be his last séance, and he would stop thinking about her.

After the séance Miss Bancroft came over to him. 'I feel that message from George London was for you,' she said.

Thrilled that she was talking to him, he managed to say, 'My mother's name is Sarah Ann.' He paused. 'And my late father's name was George London Hedgecock.' He frowned. 'Perhaps I should go and see her next weekend. She lives in Dover.'

'That will be nice for her,' Miss Bancroft replied, and then, 'We'll miss you.' She put her hand on his arm.

Percy's eyes widened, and his heart seemed to jump. He just stared at her, suddenly dumbstruck.

'I don't have to hurry home today, so I'm walking. Perhaps you'd like to walk with me?' She smiled up at him.

Percy felt his face getting hot and his heart thumping. He tried to keep his voice even. 'That would be most pleasant.'

Impatient to leave, he hurriedly donned his coat, but she said goodbye to everyone. At last she took her hat from the hall stand and tucked up those curls, which always seemed to be escaping from her elaborate hair style. She seemed to take forever. He took down her cloak and held it for her, thrilled to have contact.

When they got outside, Percy put his hand on the small of her back and gently moved her so that he walked on the outside of the pavement, to protect her from any splashes from passing cabs. As they strolled along she put her hand on his arm. He didn't know what to say. If only he were more like Tom and able to chat charmingly to women. What was the name of that hair style? Pomp something. In trying to think of it, he missed what she'd just said.

'I beg your pardon?' He inclined his head to her.

'I said, I'd like it if you would call me Lily.'

A bubble of joy crept up his chest. 'I'd like that very much.' He tried to keep his voice steady. 'Perhaps you would call me Percy?'

'I do hope you'll find your mother recovered, Percy.'

'I hope so too, Lily,' he said, feeling the word 'Lily' roll off his tongue. So that was her name: Lily!

Lily chatted away, asking Percy if he was interested in Theosophy.

'Yes, but I don't know anything much about the subject.'

'It's very interesting, I'll lend you some books if you like.'

Entranced, Percy wracked his brains for something to say. Curses, what was the name of that hairstyle? Then he remembered. He turned to her.

'I do admire your hairstyle; The Pompeii, isn't it?'

She frowned. 'I've no idea, my maid does my hair.' Her eyes lit up. 'But Pompeii! So you're interested in archaeology, too? How wonderful! I would so like to go there and see it.' She prattled on about ruins.

He recovered from his blunder. Luckily, she didn't seem to have noticed.

All too soon they reached her house.

'This is where I live.'

Percy looked at the imposing house. Wide steps rose to the entrance door, and more steps led down to a basement. Carriage doors, closed at the moment, sat off to one side. Lily's parents must be rich to have a carriage and horses.

'Goodbye, Percy,' Lily said, drawing his attention back to her. 'I hope your mother will soon be better and that you'll be coming back to the meetings.'

'Yes, of course,' he managed to say. 'Goodbye.' He gave a slight bow. His feelings were mixed; on the one hand he felt like jumping in the air with joy, and on the other, disconcerted at the obvious show of wealth that the house displayed. *I'm not good enough for Lily! But I can't stop seeing her!* He took a deep breath and walked briskly back to his lodgings.

***

Leslie watched the way Hedgecock looked at Miss Bancroft. He was sure the man only came to the meetings just to see her. And now he'd overheard her inviting Percy to walk her home. He bitterly regretted not having asked her for that honour weeks ago, but she probably would've only accepted out of kindness. He sighed and started to clear away the tea things left in the breakfast room. He felt so dejected ... Anyway, why would she bother with a dull, boring chap like him?

***

Percy wrote to his mother that he'd be coming to see her at the weekend. The following Saturday afternoon, on the train to

Dover, he went over and over in his mind the last meeting with Lily. What exactly had she said about hoping he'd be coming back to the meetings? Had she known that he'd made up his mind not to come back and was intending to stop thinking about her?

He arrived at his mother's to find her in the drawing room, lying on a sofa with her right leg resting on a pillow. The room seemed gloomy with the curtains closed.

'Mother! What happened?

'Oh, Percy, dear,' she replied, 'how lovely to see you. It was such a silly thing, I somehow tripped and fell down the stairs.'

He gave her a kiss on the cheek and frowned. 'That ankle looks very swollen.' He went to the window. 'May I pull back the curtains? I can hardly see.'

Percy knew very well that his mother would refuse any treatment, she believed that proper food, fresh air, exercise and the power of thought would cure any ailment.

He sat beside her and took her hand. 'Please take more care of yourself, Mother.' As he said the words, he remembered the séance. Had that been his late father's spirit warning him to tell Sarah Ann to take care?

A shiver went through him as he recalled Lily's words, hoping his mother would be well. He'd been so thrilled with her asking him to walk with her and call her Lily that he hadn't paid much attention to what she'd said about his mother.

He was afraid that his mother's ankle was broken, but he knew she wouldn't see a doctor. She had fixed ideas about lots of things: vegetarianism, votes for women and so on. He wondered how she'd get on with Lily and then had a pleasant reverie about living with Lily and all that entailed ... until Sarah Ann brought him back to the present.

'You seem a bit preoccupied, my dear. Is your work very hard and worrisome?'

On the train back from Dover, he went over and over in his mind everything that Lily had said. She'd hoped his mother would be better soon, yet he'd said nothing about his mother not being well, why had she said that? And then she'd said that she hoped he'd be coming back to the meetings. Had she guessed he was thinking of not coming back? Why had she suddenly asked him to walk with her? Told him her name? Put her hand on his arm?

Was she psychic? Was there something to all this spiritualist business after all?

Such thoughts kept him occupied all the way back to London.

***

At the end of the week Percy received a letter from his mother to say that she was much better, the swelling had gone down, and there was no necessity to come again before Easter. Percy smiled to himself. *That's good, and it will mean I can see Lily again on Sunday.*

No messages came from George London at the next séance. Lily came early and sat next to him at the table. Her beauty took his breath away.

'Will you walk me home afterwards?' she whispered.

He nodded and smiled, and felt his face go hot. He looked up to see Carter studying him with a steadfast gaze that made him feel uncomfortable. The session seemed endless, and so did the chatting afterwards. Outside, the air smelt fresh after the stuffiness of the séance room.

He stood at the edge of the pavement and offered his arm. Lily took it and looked up at him as they walked. 'Your mother is well?'

'Yes, much better, thank you.'

She smiled. 'I did some distance healing for her.'

Percy blinked, taken aback. 'How did you do that?'

'I hoped you wouldn't mind.'

'Of course not,' he exclaimed, 'but how did you do it?'

'I think I might have a gift for healing; I sat and concentrated and visualised a lady called Sarah Ann, who might look something like you, and I felt her getting stronger and the bone in her ankle healing.'

'But how did you know it was her ankle?'

'I could feel a sensation in my right ankle.'

Percy was stunned. He didn't know what to say.

'I've always been interested in the occult,' she continued. 'Since I was very young I saw spirits, and I often see auras. But I don't talk about it because it's too confronting for a lot of people. My parents got annoyed with me when I was small and talked about it.' She gave a sigh and then smiled.

'When you first came to the séances, I knew by your aura what kind of person you were.'

Percy frowned, what on earth did all this mean?

Lily gave a reassuring smile. 'Don't be alarmed, dear Percy! Your aura is good; a gentle golden glow is the only way I can describe it. It means you are a warm, generous person.'

Just being near Lily gave Percy a warm gentle glow. *There she goes again, voicing my thoughts and feelings! I hope she isn't reading my mind and my body.*

Lily squeezed his arm. 'Relax, Percy; I'm not a mind reader.'

He felt a sudden frisson of alarm.

'Next week I'll bring you some books on Theosophy,' she continued.

Percy remembered that was a subject in which his mother was interested. 'Thank you,' was all he managed to say.

The following week, on their way to her house, Lily presented him with a package. 'It's the books I told you about,' she said.

He didn't like to tell her that after working five days a week from eight in the morning until after six at night and all Saturday morning, he had little time for reading, apart from his text books.

***

Every Sunday for the following few months, Percy walked with Lily back to her house if the weather was fine. When wet he got a cab and took her home. Seeing Lily on Sunday afternoons became the focus of his week. On the way back to her house she talked about Theosophy, Women's Suffrage, the occult and Egyptology. Percy hardly listened, he just enjoyed the sound of her voice, her hand on his arm, the admiring glances of other men when they saw Lily. The way to Lily's house passed a pretty park, and sometimes they walked around it with all the other couples and families taking the air.

Of course, Tom noticed the change in Percy. 'You're looking rather chipper these days, Perce,' he remarked one Sunday evening. 'How is the romance going? Any progress?'

Percy blushed. 'I'm walking her home most Sunday afternoons.'

Tom whistled. 'Phew! That's some progress! No wonder you look like the cat that's got the cream.'

Percy smiled with satisfaction. 'Yes.'

One Sunday afternoon as they walked, Percy was enjoying the air and the mere fact of being with Lily when he became conscious of her saying something about marrying. He snapped to attention.

'... and my parents want me to marry Dudley Earnshaw; he's the son of one of my father's business acquaintances, but—'

'What did you say?' he asked, interrupting her.

Lily looked up. 'My parents want me to marry Dudley Earnshaw.'

'Wh ... what?' he stuttered. 'Are you engaged to be married?'

'Oh, no. I've known Dudley since I was small. I think my father and his always had the idea that we would marry. Dudley's a nice man, and very rich, but his aura is dull, and he's boring, I'm not attracted by him.'

Percy breathed a sigh of relief.

They walked in silence for a while until Percy stopped. 'Lily,' he said.

She turned towards him.

He took a deep breath. 'I love you,' he said, surprising even himself. 'I want to marry you.' He paused, uncertain what to say next. 'I'd go down on bended knee and propose, but it's too muddy.'

Lily burst out laughing. 'Oh, Percy,' she exclaimed, 'ever the prosaic! How could I refuse you?'

Percy felt confused. Was she laughing at his proposal? Was it so laughable? He'd heard the word 'refuse'. Or was she laughing at his foolishness? The dismay must have shown on his face.

Lily kissed her gloved index finger, stood on tiptoe and pressed her finger against his lips. 'I *will* marry you, Percy Hedgecock,' she said

Elated, Percy felt as if he walked on air all the way back to his lodgings. He sat in his room and thought hard about marriage until the time came for his evening meal. Afterwards he got out pen and paper and began to plan a budget, then realised that he knew nothing about the costs of housing or feeding a family. He needed to find out all these things.

***

That very same Sunday afternoon David Bancroft was coming home from visiting a sick friend when he looked out the window of the carriage and saw his daughter walking towards their house arm in arm with a man. He leaned forward to shout at the driver to stop the carriage in order to confront them, but by the time he'd found his voice, they had gone past and Lily and her escort had turned into a park.

He burst in the front door and called out to his wife. 'Melina! Melina!'

Melina Bancroft came out of the drawing room in a fluster. 'What on earth is wrong, David dear?'

'I just saw Lily, walking along with a man!' he spluttered.

'Come and sit down.' She took his arm and led him to the drawing room. He was a tall well-built man and he stomped into the room and started to pace around. His wife, a slender woman of great beauty, was dwarfed by his bulk.

'Come! My dear! Please, calm down. Now. Are you sure it was Lily?'

'Of course I'm sure! I thought she was at that idiotic Suffrage nonsense meeting she said she was going to.'

'Well, I'm sure she was, and maybe someone was escorting her back from the meeting.'

'This is the last straw! She's twenty, time to be married! We'd better get onto the Earnshaws and get the wedding organised! No more of this going to ridiculous meetings and wanting to go to University!' He sat simmering, drumming his fingers on his knees. 'Where is she? What's keeping her?'

After a few minutes he stood up. 'I'm going to my study. When she comes in, send her to me!'

Melina sighed. 'Yes, dear.'

CHAPTER 2

When Lily arrived home, she went straight to the drawing room, where her mother was busy as usual with her sewing.

'Mama!'

Her mother stood up. 'Lily. Your father wants to see you. He's in his study.'

'Mama, I've met the man I want to marry,' Lily burst out, not hearing what her mother said.

Melina Bancroft frowned, taken aback by this sudden announcement. 'Whatever do you mean, Lily?' She put her embroidery aside. 'My dear, your Papa saw you today walking with a man. He's very angry. You must go and see him at once. You know we're very keen for you to marry Dudley Earnshaw! He's a nice boy and would provide well for you. And it would help your papa's business interests too.'

Lily frowned. 'I don't want to marry Dudley! He doesn't appeal to me. And I don't want to spend my life buried in the country!'

'My darling girl, appeal is not what counts in a marriage, one has to look at how well one's husband will provide for you and your children, and love will follow.'

'I don't want children!' Lily clenched her fists. 'And you and Papa married for love!'

Melina sighed. 'Yes, that is true; I was only sixteen, and your Papa was so handsome ...' she continued dreamily. 'But he was also quite a wealthy man, so my parents were very happy.' Then what Lily had said sunk in. 'My dear! You don't want children! Whatever do you mean?'

'I want to be free to study medicine and pursue the occult. Percy is very understanding and is interested in Theosophy and Egyptology as well. He wouldn't want me tied down by children. Anyway, I don't like babies or children.'

Melina looked horrified. 'You have discussed not having children with him?'

'No, of course not,' indignant, Lily continued, 'but I know Percy feels the same way as I do about everything.'

Flustered, her mother demanded, 'Who is this Percy, anyway? Where did you meet him?'

'He comes to the Sunday séances; I met him there. He's been walking home with me sometimes after the meetings.'

Melina's eyes grew even wider. 'Sunday séances? What Sunday séances? I thought you'd been going to one of your Suffrage meetings on Sunday afternoons!'

'Oh, I knew you wouldn't approve, so I told you I was going to the Suffrage meetings, but actually I was going to séances.'

Melina's face flushed, and her eyes narrowed. 'How long has this been going on?'

'I've been going every Sunday for about eight months,' Lily confessed. 'But Percy has only been coming for about six months.'

'Six months! You've been walking out with a man for six months behind our backs! And an occult type! Who is he, what does he do?'

'I don't know; I think he said something about working in an office.'

Melina clasped her hands to her breast. 'A clerk!' she exclaimed. 'There is no way your father will allow you to marry a clerk. You'd better go and see him. He's very angry.'

Lily shrugged. 'Papa is always angry about something! But I love Percy. He's so charming, so handsome, and so understanding; he really listens to what I say. I feel I want to spend the rest of my life with him. He's my soulmate.'

'Soulmate!' her mother echoed. 'That's not enough. You're too young to make those kinds of judgements.'

Lily fell silent. Then, jutting out her chin, she replied, 'I'm nearly twenty. Legally I can marry. But I need your consent, and I would so much like your approval. And anyway, he has proposed to me and I said *yes*!' With tears in her eyes she stormed out of the room.

Melina took a deep breath. She carefully put away her embroidery and tried to regain her composure. Distressed and angry, she stood to go after Lily. The slamming of Lily's door made her change her mind. Little point in trying to talk to her. Reluctantly she went to her husband's study.

David Bancroft had calmed down somewhat by the time Melina came in to his study. 'Where is she? Has she come home?'

'Yes, darling. She's gone to her room.'

'Did you ask her the meaning of this?'

'Yes. She told me she has met her soulmate and she wants to marry him.'

'Soulmate!' David Bancroft banged his fist on his desk, making the ink stand rattle. 'What on earth does she mean? What nonsense is she on about?' He scowled.

'I think she means soulmate as in her spiritual soul,' Melina replied gently. 'He's called Percy and is a clerk, apparently. They met at a séance.'

'What!' He was speechless for a moment. 'A clerk! A séance! Why did you allow her to go to a séance!' He almost choked.

'Darling, I didn't know she'd been going to séances! She told me she was going to Suffrage meetings for votes for women as she knew we wouldn't allow her to go to séances.'

'So, she's been lying to us as well!' His face mottled with rage. 'And these ridiculous ideas of Suffrage and votes for women.'

'Actually, I think women should have equal rights with men,' Melina glared at him.

'Humph!' was all he managed to say. He stood and put his hands on his desk to steady himself. 'I won't allow it! This is utter nonsense!'

He paced around the room, muttering to himself until he calmed down. 'We'll send her down to my sister in Hampshire. She can stay there until she sees sense. There'll be no séances and nonsense down there! Yes! That's the best plan. We don't want the Earnshaws to get wind of this Percy.'

'I don't know.' Melina hesitated. 'She might run away.'

'Unlikely, if she has no money, and I'll stop her allowance immediately. Yes! I'll write to Patricia straight away. Don't tell Lily anything about this until I hear back; I don't want her running away with this man. He's probably a gold digger. Once she's away and he realises he won't get a penny from me, it will all blow over. You know Lily and her fads. Pretend nothing until I hear back from Patricia.' With a grunt of satisfaction, he sat down and took up his pen.

***

To Lily's surprise her mother and father made no mention of Percy at dinner or the next day. Mama can't have told her father yet. Perhaps her mother had come around to the idea and was waiting for a good moment to tell him.

Four days later, she came in from a séance and found her maid in her bedroom, packing.

She frowned. 'What are you doing, Alice?'

'Madam told me that you would be going away and to pack enough for several months ...' Alice faltered to a stop when she saw Lily's face.

Lily stormed out of her bedroom and went in search of her mother. She found her in the drawing room at her desk, writing. 'Mama, what's going on? Alice is in my room packing my things! She said she'd been told to pack enough for a few months!'

Melina looked up from her writing. Calmly, she wiped her pen nib and blotted the letter. 'Yes, my dear. Your papa thought it would be a good idea for you to go and stay with your Aunt Patricia for a while, until you get over this marriage nonsense.'

'Stay at the Porter's! Why, there's nothing to do there, only hunting and fishing! You know I'm not interested in either of those things, and it's *not* marriage nonsense!'

'They have a very comprehensive library, my dear. And your cousins will be there for company.'

'Ethel and Ruby! Oh, Mama, you know very well, they are just too boring. All they can think of is riding and clothes and finding a husband with money, and Adrian will be away at University, like James!'

Melina studied her. 'My dear, your father has quite made up his mind. He will go down with you in the carriage on Saturday.'

'I'll run away.'

Melina raised her eyebrows. 'Darling, where will you run? And your father has stopped your allowance.'

Speechless, Lily glared at her mother. 'Stopped my allowance? How will I be able to buy the things I need?'

'I think he'll give money to your Aunt Patricia, and she will give you what you need.'

'Oh! This is so ridiculous! I'm to be kept like a prisoner! I'll run away and get a job.'

Melina shook her head. 'Doing what? As a governess? That's all you'd be qualified for.'

Lily paused. She wasn't keen on children. She'd go crazy if she had to be with children all day. Her anger flared again. 'Well, if you'd allowed me to go to University, I would've been able to qualify as a doctor or an archaeologist!'

Her father came into the room and overheard her last few words. 'An archaeologist! Do you think I would spend good money to send my daughter to university, only to have her grovelling around in the dirt, scraping at old bones and rocks?'

Lily stared at him. 'At least I would've been able to work!'

'Humph!' David Bancroft looked at her and shook his head, and then said gently, 'My dear Lily, I only want to protect you. Your head is filled with nonsense. Young Dudley Earnshaw is a suitable husband for you, not this clerk your mother tells me about, who is only after you for your money.'

Lily's eyes narrowed. 'Percy is not "after my money" as you put it. And now you've stopped my allowance, I don't have any money. Percy is a good man; he has a good aura.' She stopped, realising at once that she shouldn't have mentioned auras.

'Aura! Aura! Lily, enough of this occult nonsense. I'm taking you down to Hampshire in the morning, and there you will stay until you have seen the error of your ways and are prepared to give up this marriage nonsense.' That said, he stalked out of the room.

Lily shot a venomous look at her mother and then, turning abruptly, she went to her room without a word.

I'll write to Percy; he'll rescue me.

She got out her writing materials, sat at her little writing bureau, dipped her pen in the inkpot and put her pen to the paper. She closed her eyes. *Oh, Percy! When will I see you again?* After a few minutes she realised her hand had been moving. She opened her eyes. Scribbles covered the paper. She was about to tear it up, but when she looked closely she realised it looked like a foreign script. Her heart beat loudly as realisation dawned: it must be automatic writing! Thrilled, she decided to go to the British museum the next day with the page; then she remembered that her father was taking her to Hampshire in the morning. *I must tell Percy*, she thought, picking up a fresh sheet of writing paper.

Dearest Percy,

I think I can do automatic writing! I have just covered a sheet of paper with writing and I am enclosing it with this letter. I won't be able to go to the British Museum with it as my father is taking me to stay with my aunt in Hampshire tomorrow. He is very angry because I want to marry you. If you have time please take the script to the British Museum, or perhaps ask Mr. Carter if he knows what it says.

Don't write to me here. I don't think any letters will be forwarded to me.

Write to me at my aunt's,
c/- Mrs Patricia Porter,
The Oaks
Little Steadingham,
Ringwood

Hampshire
I love you darling Percy.
I know we will be together soon.
Your ever-loving Lily.

She put the letter and the sheet of automatic writing in an envelope and then realised she didn't know the address of his lodgings. She frowned. His mother lived in Dover, and her name was Sarah. Hedgecock was an unusual name, surely the postman would find her. She wrote on the envelope:

Mr. Percy Hedgecock, c/o Mrs Sarah Ann Hedgecock, Dover, Kent.

She'd get Alice to post it in the morning. She just hoped it would reach his mother and then him.

It's unfair. My brothers can study and go to University. I've read all James' medical text books. I know as much as he does. I'd make a good doctor. I can heal people. I know I can. I like archaeology, but I'd love to be a doctor and heal people. And now it seems I might be a medium.

She stood and paced around her bedroom. *Marrying Percy will allow me to be free to practise healing and become a medium.*

***

The carriage drew up at the front entrance of the Porter's big estate near the New Forest in Hampshire. Although imposing, the main part of the mellow sandstone house seemed settled in the landscape and inviting. Lily had been here before so she was familiar with the surroundings of sculptured parkland, an artificial lake and fine elm trees.

Lily's father turned to her. 'Lily, my dear,' he said gently. 'We only want the best for you. You are young, later on you will thank us for this.'

Lily smiled at him. 'I know, Papa. Thank you.' It was easy for her to say kind words. She and Percy would be together before too long.

Appeased, her father helped her down.

Ethel and Ruby—pretty, fair-haired girls; Ruby the same age as Lily, and Ethel a year younger—rushed to the door as the carriage drew up. Their mother, a tall, handsome woman, her fair hair caught in a bun at the nape of her neck, followed them out.

'Oh, Lily, you must come and see my new pony!' Ethel exclaimed, her eyes alight with excitement. 'She's a little chestnut mare; I think she'd be the right height for you, too! I hope you brought your riding habit?'

Ruby interrupted: 'No, Ethel, Brandy would be too high for Lily!' She looked Lily up and down. 'I thought you would've grown since we saw you last.'

Lily had been fourteen the last time she'd met her cousins, so she didn't think she would've grown much. She smiled. 'Don't worry about a mount for me; I'm not really interested in hunting.'

Ruby and Ethel just stared at Lily. 'Not interested in hunting!' Ruby spoke for both of them.

Their mother intervened: 'Come now, girls, let Lily have a chance to change and say goodbye to her father. Did you bring your maid, Lily?'

When Lily shook her head, Patricia turned to her daughters. 'Girls, show Lily to her room and ask Joan to unpack for her.' She smiled at Lily.

When the girls had gone, Patricia Porter turned to her brother. 'Come in and have some refreshment, David, dear.'

'Thank you, Patricia, but I mustn't linger; I have to get back to London before dark.'

She led him into the large drawing room, sunny and bright, with crimson velvet curtains framing the French doors overlooking the park. As she rang the bell and asked the maid to bring tea and sandwiches, David strolled to the windows and looked out at the horses being exercised. He grunted and turned to his sister. She smiled at him. 'I'm sure Lily will soon settle down; we're so pleased to have her stay. But what is the problem, David? You didn't say much in your letter.'

'Lily has a notion to go off and marry a totally unsuitable man. A commercial clerk!'

Patricia frowned. 'Where on earth did she meet a commercial clerk?'

'At a séance, apparently.'

Patricia's frown deepened. 'A séance! Why did you allow her to go to a séance for goodness sake!'

'We didn't! She told her mother she was going to a suffrage meeting. She knew we wouldn't let her go to a séance! She's just got completely out of hand. She is supposed to be marrying Dudley Earnshaw—a very suitable match.'

His sister nodded. 'She sounds very headstrong, but she's turned into a very beautiful young woman, you know.'

David Bancroft grimaced. 'Yes. And she's very clever, always wanted to study medicine, like her brother. But I just don't think it's a ladylike profession, dealing with sick people. All manner of unsavoury diseases, you know.'

Patricia considered this. 'Perhaps she has a calling. Maybe let her go nursing. She has probably read about Florence Nightingale and thinks it's romantic. That might take her mind off marriage.'

Unimpressed by that idea, David Bancroft shook his head. 'I don't like the idea of her nursing uncouth soldiers and the like. She should be more dutiful and marry young Dudley Earnshaw.'

'Well,' Patricia replied, 'my girls only seem interested in their horses and dancing. I'm sure Lily will settle down and forget her ideas once she goes out riding and to balls with the girls. Don't worry anymore about her.'

Her brother smiled. 'Thank you, dear Patricia. I knew I could count on you and Cecil. Give him my regards, by the way. I'm sorry I've missed him, and sorry I can't stay the night. I'd better get going now. Goodbye, my dear, and thank you.'

***

The following Sunday, Lily's absence from the séance dismayed Percy. He worried all the way through.

Leslie came over to him after the meeting. 'I see Miss Bancroft didn't come today, I hope she isn't poorly?' He raised his eyebrows.

'I hope not,' Percy replied.

Leslie looked sad. 'I trust we will see you next week.'

Percy nodded and hurried off, wondering what to do; then he realised he was heading towards her house. When he got there, he didn't quite know what to do. He walked up and down a few times. No black ribbon decorated the door, so no one had died. No straw lay on the street to muffle the sound of the horses' hooves, so no-one was sick. He thought of ringing the bell and asking for Lily. But what if she'd changed her mind and didn't want to see him anymore? Self-doubt filled him. His shoulders slumped. Dragging his feet, he walked back to his lodgings.

The following Sunday was the same: no Lily. He worried, not knowing what to do.

Again Leslie Carter came over to him afterwards. 'Miss Bancroft didn't come this week, either,' he said.

'No,' Percy replied with a frown.

'Have you heard anything from her?'

'No, afraid not.' He moved away to get his coat. 'Goodbye.' He didn't want to stay and chat. Carter made him feel uncomfortable.

That night at dinner Tom noticed his preoccupation and caught up with him after the meal. 'You all right, Perce?'

'Oh, yes; thank you Tom.' Percy made to go upstairs to his room.

'Perce. You're not all right. Tell me what's wrong.'

Percy's knuckles showed white as he clutched the newel post. He turned to Tom. 'It's just that Lily hasn't been to the Sunday séances for the last two weeks. I don't know what's wrong. I haven't heard from her.' He started up the stairs.

Tom thought for a moment, then shouted up the stairs after Percy, 'Well, write and ask her, then!'

Percy turned to him. 'Of course. Why didn't I think of that? Thank you, Tom. I'll do so at once.' He smiled and bounded up the stairs.

Tom shook his head and smiled.

Percy wrote his letter, asking Lily was she well, was she ill. He tore up that letter and started again. He hoped she was all right, as he had missed her at the meetings. He put his lodging's address on the back of the envelope and went out to post it.

He heard nothing.

He wrote again after a few days. Perhaps the previous one had been lost in the post.

No reply.

As the days went by with no news from Lily, he became more and more heartsick. He went to the séances, always hopeful that she would be there, and came away more and more downcast when she didn't turn up. He began to think she didn't love him, that she'd changed her mind about marrying him and didn't know how to tell him, so was just keeping out of sight.

I don't blame her; I'm a dull, boring person. Not like Tom, able to talk easily to people. Oh, Lily, I'll never stop loving you.

CHAPTER 3

Percy wasn't the only one distraught by Miss Bancroft's non-appearance; Leslie also worried that she might be ill. She was so tiny and fragile! A puff of wind could blow her away. Not robust at all. And he hadn't seen her at any of the other spiritualist meetings he frequented. She seemed to have just disappeared. He'd casually asked another lady at one of the spiritualist meetings that Lily had occasionally attended if she'd seen Lily lately, and she'd shaken her head and said, 'No.'

He'd thought there must be something between her and Hedgecock. With a heavy heart he'd watched them walking away from the séance every week. Now it appeared that Hedgecock didn't know anything, either. He found it hard to concentrate on his projects.

***

Lily decided to try her best to settle down in Hampshire. She felt sure that Percy would soon come for her or arrange something.

The Porter's had an extensive library, so she spent most of her time there, reading. When she tired of that, if the weather was clement, she went for long walks.

She politely refused to go riding with her cousins, trying hard to be gentle with them.

'Thank you, but I don't enjoy bouncing around on the back of a horse—unless it's the only means of transport, of course.'

One day she noticed something disturbing—an ominous grey shadow around her Aunt Patricia's abdomen.

What should I do? I could tell her and try and heal her. But would she listen to me?

That night at dinner, Patricia turned to her with a smiled. 'Lily, have you read much about Florence Nightingale?'

Lily smiled back. 'Yes, Aunt. She is very interesting. A mystic, as you know.'

'Oh.' Taken aback, Patricia tried to think of something to say.

'Of course, a lot of her ideas were spurned by the medical establishment,' Lily continued.

'Oh! Really?'

Ethel chimed in, her eyes shining: 'She is so romantic! I think I'd like to train as a nurse and care for wounded soldiers.' She clasped her hands together and cast her eyes upwards with an angelic expression.

'Don't be silly!' her sister exclaimed. 'It would be horrible; you'd have to wash the soldier's dirty wounds and ... and other unmentionable things!'

Patricia tried to bring the conversation back to Lily: 'So, Lily, dear. If you don't like horse riding, what do you like to do?'

Lily's eyes brightened. 'I like to study Egyptology and the sciences. I'd like to go to University and study medicine. I'd like to heal people.'

'That's very commendable,' her aunt replied. 'But not exactly suitable for a refined young lady.'

Lily merely shrugged.

Her cousins' eyes widened. 'Medicine! You would have to cut up dead bodies!' Ruby exclaimed, clearly horrified by the thought.

Again, Lily just shrugged.

'Do you like to dance, Lily?' Patricia asked, eager to change the subject. 'There is a hunt ball next week in the Assembly Rooms. The girls are going. I think you would enjoy it.'

'Thank you, Aunt.' Lily smiled.

Although she liked to dance, she found the ball and the men who took her out onto the floor dull and boring. But there was no lack of partners. Lily was so small in stature that she only came up to most of the men's arm pits. They had to bend over to hold her, as if she were a child. Percy was just the right height, she thought with a sigh. She stood four feet, eight inches high, and Percy must be about seven or eight inches taller than her. That would make him about five feet, four inches. Dreamily she wondered what it would be like to dance with Percy.

'Wasn't the ball splendid?' Ethel asked on their way back home in the carriage.

Lily made a polite murmur. *Another ordeal over.*

'Next weekend there's a fox hunt; shall you go, Lily?' Ruby asked, eager for Lily to enjoy her stay. 'You may borrow my old habit; I've grown out of it, so it would fit you.'

'No, thank you. I don't agree with fox hunting.'

Her cousins blinked, dumbfounded. Eventually Ethel found her voice: 'Why ever not?'

'It's cruel.'

'But foxes are vermin!'

'Perhaps, but they could be caught and killed in a more humane way, rather than mauled to death by a pack of dogs!'

The sisters sat in silence the rest of the way home.

At breakfast the morning after the ball, Lily watched her aunt, Patricia. *She's a very kind person. I wish I could help her.* Her aura showed that there was time.

Later, before lunch, Lily went into the morning room and found her aunt lying on the chaise longue. Patricia made to get up when she saw Lily, but Lily raised her hand.

'Dear Aunt, please stay and rest; I think you are tired.'

'Just a bit, my dear; I think it's my age,' she blurted, and then pursed her lips, appearing to regret her words. Lily supposed it wasn't the sort of thing one would normally say to a young girl.

'Please let me sit with you, I think I can help you.'

Patricia blinked. 'No, no, my dear, it's nothing. I should go and see cook now.'

Lily put her hand on Patricia's arm and looked her straight in the eyes. 'Please! I do this for Mama; just lie back and close your eyes.' That was an untruth about her mother, but Lily felt it was warranted.

Patricia suddenly lost her resistance. She lay back and closed her eyes.

Lily held both her hands over Patricia's abdomen. With her eyes closed she focussed on the grey shadow and felt a tussle, as if the mass was fighting her will. Eventually she sensed it getting weaker.

After perhaps ten minutes she withdrew her hands and opened her eyes. Her aunt was asleep, breathing gently.

Lily crept out on tip toe and went to wash her hands. She felt drained, but curiously elated. *Was that my first real healing?* Percy's mother didn't count, as that had been distance healing and so not certain. She sat in her bedroom with an anatomy book she'd found in the Porter's library on her lap, staring into space. A smile lit up her face. She stood and stretched.

Yes, this is my destiny; I'm certain. I can heal. When I marry I'll be able to hold healing sessions in my own home. My life will be worthwhile. Energy and resolve filled her.

Later, at lunch, Patricia looked at Lily and smiled. 'Forgive me, Lily, I must have fallen asleep while I was talking to you this morning. Most rude of me.'

Lily returned her smile. 'I think you were just very tired, and perhaps I'm a very boring conversationalist. Mama has the same problem, she tends to doze off when I'm talking.' She picked up her knife and fork. 'But I trust you are feeling more rested now?'

'Yes; thank you, my dear.'

Her cousins looked at them, bewildered.

'Are you not feeling well, Mama?' Ethel asked.

'I'm very well,' her mother replied. 'Now, what are you planning to do this afternoon?'

Ruby shrugged. 'It's pouring with rain, and windy.'

'Yes,' Ethel said, 'it wouldn't be pleasant to go riding.'

Patricia's eyes lit up, as though she'd thought of something which might please Lily. 'Have you seen an Ouija board, Lily? Adrian brought one for the girls the last time he was down. They haven't tried it yet.'

Lily brightened immediately. 'Oh, have you really got one? I've heard of them but haven't seen one.'

Patricia smiled, apparently pleased that she'd found something to interest Lily. 'I'll get it for you after lunch,' she said.

Surprised by this turn of events, Lily thought that her aunt must think that the Ouija was some kind of board game, like draughts.

After lunch the girls settled in front of the fire with the Ouija board on a card table.

'How do we play, Lily?' Ruby asked.

'Um, see how the first thirteen letters of the alphabet are written in a semicircle with the remaining letters underneath, and then numbers one to ten and zero?'

'Yes,' Ruby said slowly.

'What's this?' Ethel asked, holding up a tear-shaped piece of thin wood.

'I think it's called a planchette. We sit with our fingers lightly on it and ask a question. The planchette moves around and points to letters or numbers in reply. And look, here is Yes and No.'

'Ooh, how exciting!' Ruby exclaimed as they each placed two fingers of their right hands on it. 'What will we ask?

Lily wanted to ask when she'd see Percy again, but as his name had not been mentioned since she'd arrived, if she asked the question, Ethel and Ruby would want to know all about him. She didn't want to discuss him with them.

'Will it snow?' Ruby asked suddenly.

The girls gasped as they felt the planchette move to point at 'No'.

'Oh, my goodness.' Ethel's mouth dropped open.

They looked at each other, then Ruby asked, 'Will I meet my future husband at the next hunt ball?'

The planchette moved to 'Yes'.

'What's his name?' Ruby gasped.

The planchette moved around to spell out the name 'Harry'.

While the planchette moved Lily had a clear vision of a young officer and his death from a war wound. She heard a faint voice saying, 'Poor Captain Langton.'

Ruby jumped up and looked at Ethel and Lily. 'You're doing it, Ethel! You know I'm sweet on Harry Langton!'

'I didn't! I swear I didn't!' Ethel protested. She glanced at Lily. 'Lily! Are you all right? You've gone deathly pale.'

Lily took a deep breath. 'Perhaps I am a little tired,' she said. 'I might go and lie down. You two continue to play.'

Her cousins' expressions fell, clearly disappointed.

'Perhaps, after you've had a rest we can play again, as long as Ethel behaves,' Ruby replied.

Lily nodded.

Ethel pouted. 'I honestly didn't move the planchette,' she muttered.

Feeling confused, Lily went to her room and lay down. What did this mean? It seemed she could heal and do automatic writing. Was she a medium too? She felt sorry she'd sent the sheet of paper with the automatic writing on it to Percy. It was probably lost! Or else he was upset by it and that was why she hadn't heard from him. Maybe he'd had it translated, and it said something rude or inappropriate!

She got up and paced around her bedroom. She felt like going for a walk, but the rain was too heavy. *I know! I'll try the automatic writing again.* She hadn't really paid much attention to the previous text.

***

Lily managed to repeat her healing with her aunt several times after her first attempt. She became artful in ways to suggest that her aunt lie down. Once she asked if she might talk to her about a problem she had.

'If you'd lie down on the chaise longue I'd feel more comfortable talking about my problem. Especially if you just close your eyes,' Lily said. 'I get a bit nervous if someone watches me closely.'

Surprised, Patricia lay down as Lily suggested. 'You don't strike me as being of a nervous disposition,' she remarked. 'But as you wish my dear.'

Lily spoke in a soft monotonous tone about her wish to study medicine. At the same time, she held her hands over Patricia's abdomen. She let her words trail off and focussed on healing.

When she'd finished and she opened her eyes, she found her aunt asleep and gently snoring. Lily smiled. She thought she'd better rouse her, or her aunt might be distressed to think she'd fallen asleep once more while talking to her.

She put her hand on Patricia's shoulder. 'Dear Aunt,' she said, giving Patricia a gentle shake.

'What ...?' Patricia rubbed her eyes and sat up.

'Dear Aunt, you've been so helpful, letting me talk so much. I feel happier now.'

Patricia frowned, probably unable to recall one word of what Lily had been talking about, but then her expression lightened, and she smiled. 'Oh, that's good! Whenever you feel the need to talk to me, my dear, I'm so happy to help.'

***

Eventually Percy decided he must put Lily out of his mind. He'd go down to Dover and visit his mother the following weekend.

Percy's appearance shocked his mother.

'Whatever has happened, Percy? Are you sick? You look so thin and pale.'

'No, no, mother,' he tried to smile. 'Just busy at work. And this dull weather doesn't help.' He waved towards the window. A grey drizzle blotted out the view of the houses opposite.

As they sat down to dinner, Sarah remembered something. 'Oh! A letter came for you a few weeks ago. I thought it a bit strange as it didn't have a proper address on it, so I didn't bother sending it on to you.'

She got up from the table, went to the bureau and handed him an envelope.

He opened it and unfolded the two pieces of paper. Only scribble covered the first. He frowned and then looked at the second sheet, scanning it quickly. The colour rushed to his cheeks, and he laughed with delight. 'Oh, Mother! Thank you!'

She looked at him with curiosity.

He took a deep breath. 'It's from someone I thought I'd lost contact with.'

She still simply looked at him.

'Well, it's from someone special,' he confessed. 'A lady. How lucky the postman was able to deliver it.'

Sarah nodded. 'Perhaps you'll be able to eat and sleep now,' was all she said.

'I must write back, Mother, if you can give me some writing paper after dinner.'

He couldn't wait to write. Lily must wonder why she hadn't heard from him. He forgot all about the paper with the hieroglyphics on it.

***

Six weeks and still no news from Percy. Lily began to despair. She had read all the books that interested her in the Porter's library. Her aunt's tumour had disappeared, and her aura was now good. Lily felt thrilled at her success, and she ached to heal more people. Her cousins were only interested in riding or clothes and going to dances and meeting eligible bachelors. She went to one more dance with them and then made excuses not to go again.

After that all the eligible bachelors in the county came to visit her, and all were dismayed to find Lily polite but aloof. Rather than send them away, however, this seemed to add to her attractions.

One day while out walking, she heard a voice: 'Lady! Lady!'

She looked around. By the hedgerow a bent old woman, who looked like a bundle of rags, tried to stand with the help of a hawthorn stick. Lily thought she must be one of the gypsies camped across the fields. Half afraid, she was about to walk on when the old crone spoke again:

'Lady, you have the gift! Can you cure me?'

Lily turned back, studied the woman for a few moments and then shook her head. 'It's too late.' A black aura surrounded the woman. 'However, I can try to relieve your pain and make your passing easier.'

She walked over to the old crone, closed her eyes and passed her hands around the woman's body for several minutes.

'Bless you!' muttered the woman. She grabbed Lily's right hand and peered at it. You'll be loved all your life,' she said, 'You have a great gift. Use it wisely.' She let go of Lily's hand and stumbled back towards the gypsy camp.

Pensive, Lily walked slowly back to the house. *I have a great gift. I always knew it. I must use my healing talent! When I marry Percy, I shall be free to use my healing gift.*

Inspired, she quickened her pace.

***

Patricia Porter thought it time for her niece to go back to London. Lily spent all her time either in their library, reading, or walking around the countryside on her own. She was not supposed to go walking on her own. She didn't seem to be eating much, either. Patricia worried about her. Wandering off like that, anything could happen. And apparently some of the young men in the area had got wind of Lily's lonely rambles and had ridden past and stopped to engage her in conversation. She'd had to instruct one of the young gardeners to keep a lookout for Lily and discreetly follow her to make sure she came to no harm.

When the gardener told her about the gypsy episode, she re-solved to ask her brother to take Lily back to London. She'd become very fond of Lily, and she really was no trouble, but she could see that Lily was unhappy. When a letter came for Lily, she hoped it would cheer her up. She gave it to her at breakfast.

When Lily saw it, the colour rose in her cheeks, and her eyes sparkled, but she said nothing. Though curious, Patricia didn't want to press her. The girls chattered on, and Lily put the letter casually to one side. 'Thank you, Aunt.'

Soon after, she excused herself from the breakfast table. 'I think I will go for a walk, it's such a nice morning.'

Patricia just nodded and smiled, glad she wouldn't be without the watchful eyes of the gardener.

When Lily got to her room, she tore open the envelope. She'd known instantly that it must be from Percy, and she'd pushed down her excitement in order to appear calm and noncommittal. When she read that Percy had written to her at home, she realised that her parents must have destroyed his letters. Anger rose at this realisation, but she fought it off. Anger wouldn't help her situation.

She tucked the letter into her bodice and put on her outdoor shoes, fumbling with the button hook in her haste. She set out along the lane, trying to compose her thoughts.

The first thing would be to reply to Percy. As soon as she got back from her walk, she wrote telling him that she missed him and loved him, but didn't know what to do. Her father thought that Percy only wanted to marry her for her money.

She put her letter in an envelope and addressed it to Percy's lodgings, then went downstairs and left it on the hall table with the other letters ready to be posted.

***

When Percy got her letter, he was overjoyed, then horrified to read that her father thought he only wanted to marry Lily for her money. For two days he wondered what to do, then finally made a decision. He had to see her father and disabuse him of the notion that he was after her money. He wrote to Lily's father, asking if he could meet him.

***

David Bancroft sat at the breakfast table and smiled at his wife. He spread his napkin on his lap and helped himself to bacon and eggs. He started eating then opened his letters. He nearly choked over his breakfast when he read Percy's letter.

Melina Bancroft looked up. 'What is it my dear?'

'A letter from that young pup that wants to marry Lily! The hide of him,' he exclaimed. 'He asks if he could meet me! Well, he certainly can. I'll give him a piece of my mind and send him packing! The cheek! The hide!' His face turned red with indignation. 'I'll write and tell him to come and see me on Saturday afternoon. I'll soon put a stop to all this nonsense.'

Melina filled his coffee cup, then said, 'David, darling. I've had a letter today, too. From Patricia. She thinks it's time Lily came home. She says she loves having Lily to stay, that she is such a lovely girl.' She looked at her husband with a quizzical smile. 'But she says she's worried that Lily seems to be wasting and might become ill.'

He looked at her, frowning and only half listening due to rehearsing in his mind what he'd say to that young pup. 'What?'

She repeated what she'd said, then continued, 'I've been thinking, darling; you know how headstrong and impulsive Lily is, how she gets carried away with new ideas. Perhaps this man is just a passing phase. Probably she'll be bored with him after a few months. But if we forbid her to see him, well, that would only make him more desirable in her eyes. Next year she'll be twenty-one and legally able to marry him.'

David Bancroft put a forkful of bacon in his mouth and chewed as he mulled over what his wife had said. 'Hmm, yes, I see your point. Perhaps we should arrange for him to come and visit. Almost as if we approved of him. It seems like she's against anything we want her to do, so if we make too many objections it will only make her more determined to marry him.' He drank some coffee. 'Then she's likely to run off to Gretna Green or do something equally stupid.' He thought for a moment. 'What you say makes sense.' He smiled at her. 'My clever darling!' He got up from the table, dropping a kiss on her head. 'I'll write back to him at once.'

***

The cordial letter from David Bancroft surprised Percy; it invited Percy to meet him the following Saturday afternoon. Percy immediately wrote telling Lily this news. Things were working out!

However, he became more and more nervous as the Saturday afternoon approached. What exactly should he say? It'd all sounded logical when he'd first had the idea and wrote to Lily's father. Now he just felt apprehensive.

Eventually Saturday afternoon came. He shaved and dressed carefully, then went out, feeling sick with nerves. Luckily the weather was fine. It wouldn't do for him to arrive all wet and bedraggled.

He stopped at the entrance steps. The house was so big, his mother's house had three stories, but it was in a narrow terrace. This house was twice as wide and the carriage entrance must lead to stables at the back.

He took a deep breath, straightened his shoulders and raised his chin. *Lily loves me and I love her. I can't give her the luxury she has had all her life, but I can take care of her, and I know she doesn't care for outward show.* He tried to reassure himself.

He stepped up to the front door and rang the bell.

The door opened and a maid appeared. He took a deep breath and said, 'Percy Hedgecock. Mr Bancroft is expecting me.'

The maid nodded. 'Please come in; may I take your coat?'

'Thank you, yes.' He took it off and handed his hat and coat to her.

'Come this way, Mr. Bancroft is in his study.' She led him through a hall whose walls were lined with what looked like family portraits. Reaching the end, she knocked on a heavy wooden door.

'Yes?'

She opened the door. 'Mr Hedgecock to see you, Sir.'

A tall, well-built man stood and walked around from behind a mahogany desk. 'Ah! Mr Hedgecock! How nice to meet you.' He held out his hand to Percy and with a smile that didn't quite reach his eyes and said, 'Sit down.'

Percy was completely taken aback. He'd expected an irate father angry at Percy's presumption.

They shook hands, and Percy sat down at the desk facing Lily's father.

'Can I offer you a drink? A cigar?' he asked.

'No, thank you Sir.'

David Bancroft lit a cigar and looked at Percy. He seemed a bit surprised. He'd probably been expecting a slick, man-about-town fortune hunter. 'Now! What did you want to see me about?' he looked at Percy expectantly.

Percy took a deep breath. 'I'm not sure if Lily has told you, but we've been seeing each other for several months. Well, that is, I've been escorting her home from the Sunday séances ...' He swallowed nervously.

'Go on.' David Bancroft leaned forward across the desk, studying Percy intently.

'The thing is ... you see ...' Percy didn't know how to put it. He swallowed again then burst out: 'I love Lily. I want to marry her.' When David Bancroft just kept looking at him, he went on, 'I'd like your permission to court her.' He faltered to a stop.

David Bancroft nodded. 'Hmm. May I ask if you are in a position to support a wife and family?'

'Well, I work as a commercial clerk with Swanton and Symonds the Stockbrokers ...' again he stopped, uncertain how to continue. He took another deep breath. 'My late father was a partner in a company of solicitors in Dover. He left my widowed mother well provided for, and he also left me a small inheritance which will come into effect upon my marriage. My annual income is £1000, which should rise each year.' He paused, conscious that he'd been gabbling. When he received no response he continued, 'I believe I will be able to keep Lily very comfortably.'

Lily's father's eyes narrowed—he looked as if he had doubts about that. Taking another puff on his cigar, he said, 'So, you've known Lily for about six months, but apparently only briefly when you've escorted her home from these so-called séances. I would suggest that you don't really know her at all. Are you aware of her association with the Suffragettes and the Women's Social and Political Union? Not to mention Annie Besant and her theories about educating women how not to procreate?'

Percy blinked, taken aback. 'Well, we haven't discussed procreation ...' he stammered, and then blushed at the implications of the word "procreation". 'But we have discussed Theosophy.'

David Bancroft sighed. 'You mean Lily has lectured you about Theosophy and women's rights.'

Percy realised that that was exactly how it'd been. 'It's all very interesting, and Lily has strong ideas about these things.'

David stood up. Percy did the same.

'Well, Mr Hedgecock. Neither her mother nor I think that Lily is ready for marriage. We have decided it would be a good idea for you to get to know her and our family before we talk of courtship. Mrs Bancroft is thinking of organising a little dinner party next week after Lily has returned from her sojourn in Hampshire. Perhaps you would care to join us then?'

Percy couldn't believe his ears. His ordeal was over. And he hadn't been thrown out of the house! 'Certainly, Sir. That would be most pleasant.'

'I'll ask my wife to invite you.' He rang the bell. When the maid came in he said, 'Please show Mr Hedgecock out.' He put out his hand. 'Nice to have met you.'

'Thank you, Sir.'

Percy left the house in a daze. So Lily would be coming home. He'd see her again! He thought his heart would burst and almost skipped down the street.

Meanwhile in the house, Melina Bancroft waited in the drawing room for her husband to come and tell her all about the interview. 'What kind of man is he?' she asked when he walked in.

'He seems pleasant enough. I told him you would be inviting him to dinner next week.'

'Oh, that's a good idea.' She folded her sewing. 'Shall I invite the Earnshaws as well? Dudley will show up this Percy!'

'No, I don't think that's advisable. In fact, well, I didn't mention it before, but old Earnshaw told me a few weeks ago that he didn't think Lily would be a suitable wife for Dudley after all. He must have heard about her exploits. He thought she wouldn't settle down to married life in the Midlands.' He grimaced. 'He's probably right.'

***

At dinner at the boarding house that night, Tom noticed the change in Percy. 'You're looking happy tonight, Percy!'

Everyone around the table looked up and at Percy. His face reddened with the sudden attention.

'Yes, you do look well, Mr Hedgecock,' Miss Heatherby said in her trilling voice. 'If you will forgive me for making a personal remark.'

He smiled at her. 'Not at all, Miss Heatherby.'

Everyone waited to hear why he'd changed from the sad, silent man who'd merely picked at his meals the last few weeks, into the bright young person now heartily eating. When no explanation came, they shrugged and turned back to their plates.

The following Monday Percy received a letter in the post:

'Dear Mr Hedgecock,

My husband and I would be honoured if you would consent to join us for an informal dinner on Saturday 16th October at 7.30pm

Yours sincerely,

Melina Bancroft (Mrs David Bancroft)'

Percy wondered what the etiquette was when first dining with the parents of the woman you wanted to marry. Was there time to write to his mother and receive a reply before Sunday? If he wrote and posted the letter that night, she would receive it on Tuesday, and if she replied straightaway he should get it by Friday.

First he wrote a letter to her parents accepting their invitation, and he had the two letters written by the time he went down for the evening meal. Then he had an inspiration: Old Miss Heatherby had been a governess to several wealthy families. He could ask her - or maybe not – she would want to know everything.

He waited until everyone at the dinner table had sat down, then as his landlady served the meal, he smiled at Miss Heatherby and said, 'I expect there were lots of dinner guests when you were a governess in wealthy homes.'

The other boarders looked up in amazement, no doubt wondering what on earth Percy was thinking. They were all tired of hearing Miss Heatherby going on and on about 'young Master Harold' and 'little Miss Marjorie' and how clever they were and what a lovely establishment it was where she'd worked. Not that great, though, they'd all thought, because, after being with them for many years, they'd dismissed her with a small gift of money.

Only by giving the occasional piano lessons did she manage to have enough money for her board and lodgings.

Miss Heatherby went pink with pleasure. 'Oh, yes, Mr Hedgecock, I remember one party for Master Harold's eighteenth birthday ...' and off she went.

Percy tried a few times to interrupt. His chance came as she put a forkful of food in her mouth. 'When Miss Marjorie's fiancé first came to dinner, did he bring anything?' he asked innocently, then saw Tom giving him a wink. Percy felt his face go hot and knew he'd gone bright red. No doubt Tom would corner him after the meal to find out what had prompted these questions.

Miss Heatherby became so occupied with her memories that she ate slowly, and so the meal took forever, but Tom called to him as soon as they rose from the table. 'Hey, Perce!'

Percy had to stop and wait.

'Come for a stroll?' Tom said.

'Yes, all right; I have letters to post.'

They fetched their coats and went outside.

Tom lit a cigarette. 'So, what's going on, then? Is it the same girl you met at the séance that's caused the change? I thought that had all gone quiet.'

'I've been invited to dinner with Lily and her parents next week.' Percy smiled, unable to hide his delight.

Tom whistled. 'That's excellent. I thought something was up when you asked old Miss H. those questions. So do you have the answers?'

'Well, no,' Percy admitted. 'I'm not sure if I should take anything. I've written to ask my mother about the etiquette.'

'You know what?' Tom said. 'Don't worry about it; you're a damned nice chap, and her parents will think you're highly eligible.'

'Hmm, not really; I don't have any income apart from what I earn, which isn't a lot, and her parents seem quite wealthy.' Percy sighed.

'Cheer up, old boy; lucky you—beauty, money and intelligence! And old Miss H. is always going on about what a lovely young man you are, just like Master Harold ...' He made a face. 'You'll knock'em for six!'

Percy wasn't reassured.

'I'm going for a beer; join me?' Tom asked

'No, thanks, I'll post these letters and then go back.'

***

On Monday as he dressed for work, Percy suddenly thought about what he should wear on Saturday night. He owned four shirts and seven collars. The collars fastened with collar studs at the nape and the front of the shirt. On Sunday nights after his bath, he gave his landlady his dirty linen to wash. On Tuesday nights when he got back from work, three clean shirts hung in his wardrobe, and six starched collars lay in the top drawer of his dressing table.

All week he worried about not having clean linen for Saturday night. He finally resolved to keep his Friday shirt as clean as possible by rolling up the sleeves to keep the cuffs clean during the day and wear his Friday collar on Saturday morning, then wear the clean Saturday collar that night. Puzzling over the logistics gave him the beginnings of a headache. Hopefully the Bancrofts still had the softer gaslight and not the new electric light.

When he got back from work on Friday, he found a letter and a parcel from his mother waiting for him. The parcel contained a linen dress shirt and collar, and his father's gold cuff links and collar studs.

The letter read:

'My dear Percy,

I thought that perhaps you would find this shirt and collar appropriate to wear to dinner. They belonged to your father.

I cannot give you any advice about the dinner party, for, as you know, your father and I rarely entertained, and your father was already a friend of the family and a frequent visitor to the family house. When he asked for my hand in marriage, an occasion such as you describe did not arise.

But you have been well brought up, and if there is anything that this lady's family think is lacking in you, then I think she is not worthy of you.

You have my blessing, dear son.

Your ever loving

Mama

Percy smiled. Dear mother! Her gifts were perfect.

Feeling less anxious, he hung up the shirt and put the collar in his top drawer. He had two suits, one for work and one for special occasions. He would follow Tom's advice and not take anything to the dinner, but maybe some flowers for Lily's mother? Yes, he thought, maybe a small posy for Lily and one for her mother.

On Saturday evening he dressed with extra care. His mother would be proud of him. His heart raced; he hadn't seen Lily for nearly three months.

In the hall he met Miss Heatherby on her way to the boarding house dining room.

'Oh, Mr Hedgecock!' she trilled, 'please forgive me for making a personal remark, but you do look ever so handsome.'

Percy's faced reddened. 'Thank you Miss Heatherby,' he mumbled.

'Are you going somewhere special?' She followed him along the hall towards the front door.

'Yes, I'm going to dinner with some friends, Miss Heatherby, and I think I shall be late if I don't look sharp. Good evening!' He hurriedly closed the front door behind him and hailed a cab to take him to Lily's.

The maid let him in and took his hat and coat, then led him to the drawing room. She tapped on the door and then opened it. 'Mr Hedgecock,' she announced.

His eyes went straight to Lily. *Oh, my darling Lily!* He wanted to rush straight to her, but he paused, unsure what to do.

Lily jumped up. 'Mama, this is Percy.' She caught his hand and led him forward.

He bowed to her mother. 'How do you do, Mrs Bancroft.'

She smiled. 'How do you do, Mr Hedgecock.'

Percy saw where Lily's beauty came from; her mother was beautiful, too, but with dark curly hair, where Lily's curls were coppery red. They had the same enormous grey-blue eyes fringed with impossibly long lashes, and rosebud mouths.

Percy shook hands with her father. 'How do you do, Sir.'

He received a firm, 'How do you do,' from her father.

'Please sit down, Mr Hedgecock,' Lily's mother said. 'But may we call you Percy?'

'I would like that,' Percy replied, blushing.

'Now, Percy, please tell us all about yourself,' Lily's mother said. 'Lily hasn't told us much at all, except that you met her at her séance meetings. So, you are interested in Spiritualism and Theosophy too?'

'Um, well, I'm still learning about it; I don't really know much about those subjects,' Percy replied, floundering.

By the time the maid came to announce that dinner was ready, Percy felt quite wrung out.

Lily gave him a smile and squeezed his hand as they went into dinner.

Mr Bancroft offered Percy wine.

'No, thank you, Sir.'

He offered his wife and daughter wine, and when they both shook their heads, he filled his own glass.

Soup was served, and Percy was relieved to see it was vegetable. When the main course came he politely refused the meat.

Mrs Bancroft raised her eyebrows. 'Do you have a dislike for lamb?' she enquired.

'I don't eat meat,' Percy replied, flushing. He'd not thought to tell Lily.

'I'm so sorry.' She turned to Lily. 'Why didn't you tell us that Percy was a vegetarian?'

'Oh, sorry, I didn't think to tell you,' Lily said, hiding the fact that Percy had never mentioned it.

Mr Bancroft studied Percy. 'Would it be rude to ask the reason for you not eating meat?' he enquired.

Before Percy could answer, his wife interrupted. 'Yes, it would be rude, my dear,' she said with a pleasant smile. 'We do not wish to embarrass our guest and discuss these matters at the dinner table.'

Percy smiled at her gratefully.

'Tell us a bit about your work and the London Stock Exchange, Percy, if you wouldn't mind,' Mr Bancroft said.

Mrs Bancroft frowned at her husband, but Percy immediately said, 'Certainly, Sir, if it wouldn't bore the ladies too much.'

'Well, I'd like to know more about what Percy does at work.' Lily smiled at him, her eyes having their usual mesmerising effect on him.

Percy tried to explain about the gold standard and that now, with wireless telegraphy, bonds and shares could be sold instantly. 'When a client instructs a broker to buy bonds or stocks, they don't know the price at that point in time.' He paused. 'The broker buys the stock, and the client pays for them on what is called settlement day. That's usually once a month.' He stumbled to a halt, thinking he was being boring.

'So it's really like a shop,' Lily said. 'Someone needs something, they go to the shop, and if the shopkeeper doesn't have it in stock, he'll order it, and when it comes in, the shopkeeper will pay the merchant, and then he charges the customer what he paid for it, plus a little bit extra for his profit.'

Percy felt surprised that Lily had understood so quickly how the market worked. 'Well, yes, a bit like that,' he replied, feeling somewhat deflated.

Her father looked proudly at Lily.

'So,' Lily continued, 'if there were a crisis and the clients couldn't pay for the stock, a lot of brokers could go bankrupt?'

Though taken aback, Percy merely said, 'That could certainly happen, Lily.'

Mr Bancroft smiled fondly at Lily. 'Lily picks things up very quickly,' he remarked to Percy with a smirk.

Lily's mother smoothly changed the topic of conversation, and the dinner proceeded with safer talk about some of the artefacts in the Victoria and Albert Museum, and the building work presently being carried out on the establishment.

At last the dinner finished. Mrs Bancroft rose from the table, and Percy and Mr Bancroft got to their feet. She looked at her husband. 'Lily and I will go to the drawing room for coffee.'

After the women had departed, the maid removed the table-cloth and placed a bottle of port and a Stilton cheese on the table.

'Port?' David Bancroft offered the bottle to Percy.

'No, thank you.'

David Bancroft poured himself a generous amount.

'Cheese?'

Percy shook his head. He felt too nervous to eat any more.

David Bancroft took a chunk of cheese and studied Percy as he ate and drank. His silence made Percy feel anxious and unsettled. At last David Bancroft stopped eating and took out a silver cigar case.

'Cigar?' he offered.

Percy shook his head. 'Thank you, Sir, but I don't smoke.'

David lit his cigar and took a sip of his port. After an awkward half hour of trying to find common ground and failing, David Bancroft suggested they join the ladies.

With relief, Percy agreed.

They went back into the drawing room, where the Lily and her mother sat having coffee.

'Percy and I have had a very pleasant discussion, my dear,' David said to his wife, 'and we hope he will find time to call on us regularly.'

Lily's mother smiled at Percy and patted the seat beside her. 'Do sit down, Percy.'

Percy was happy to obey. Soon the time came for him to leave. He made his farewells and thanks, then walked back to his lodg-ings with relief, elated that the evening had gone successfully.

***

Later, in their bedroom, Melina Bancroft said to her husband, 'What do you really think about Percy?'

'Well, he doesn't appear to be after Lily for her money; in fact, he seems quite a nice chap, but quite unsuitable for Lily.' He paused to remove his cuff links. 'He's not the man I would choose for her. I thought he handled the meat thing quite well, he stuck to his guns. He doesn't smoke, and it seems he doesn't drink alcohol. He's probably one of those nonconformist religious types, down on everything pleasurable. Who knows?' He shrugged. 'I found it hard to talk to him, so I'm pretty sure Lily will be bored with him after a few months.'

'I thought he was very nice. I can see why Lily has fallen in love with him.' Melina brushed her hair, a faraway look on her face. 'He's very good looking; in fact in some ways he reminds me of you—that dark, brooding look.' She gave a mischievous glance at her husband, then put down the brush and got into bed. 'But he seems such a gentle person; I hope he doesn't get hurt by Lily.'

Her husband blinked. 'What on earth do you mean? '

'I think he really loves Lily, and she will soon be bored by him.' She sighed.

'Only time will tell,' David said, getting into bed beside her.

***

The next morning at breakfast, Tom looked at Percy and asked, 'Last night went off well, then, Perce?'

Everyone looked up from their plates.

'Oh, Mr Hedgecock, you said you were going to dinner with some friends?' Miss Heatherby fluttered her eyelashes.

'Yes, thank you,' Percy replied. 'It was most agreeable.'

Tom winked at him and later waylaid Percy as they left the dining room. 'So, did you come up to scratch then?'

'Well,' Percy replied slowly, 'I'm not sure. I think her father has doubts.'

Tom regarded him. Curious, he asked, 'Have you ever walked out with any other girls?'

Percy blushed. 'No, she's the first, but I loved her from the minute I saw her, and I don't think I could love any other woman.'

Tom shook his head. 'Good luck to you Perce, old boy. I suppose you'll be going to the séance again this afternoon?'

'Yes, indeed,' replied Percy as he walked into his room.

***

Leslie greeted Hedgecock when he turned up for the séance. He thought Percy looked much happier than of late and saw the reason when Miss Bancroft arrived. When she saw Hedgecock, her eyes sparkled and a smile lit up her face. They went into the séance room together, leaving Leslie feeling as if he'd been punched in the stomach. He tried to greet the other participants with a smile. *At least I know she is well*, he thought, trying to console himself.

***

After the séance, once again, Percy walked Lily back to her house.

'Oh, Percy, it's so good to be home and to be seeing you again!' Lily exclaimed. 'Hampshire was so boring!'

Percy looked down at her. 'My darling, Lily, I was distraught when I had no news from you!'

She pinched his arm affectionately. 'Silly Percy.' Then she admitted, 'Well, I felt the same way.'

When they reached the Bancroft's house, Lily said, 'Please come in, Percy, and have tea with us; Mama told me to ask you.'

He did take tea with her mama, and he went to dinner with the Bancrofts several times after that, each time feeling more at ease. David Bancroft tried to talk to him about his work and accounting practices, and eventually they found topics of conversation that interested them both.

Mrs Bancroft, being a good hostess, drew the shy Percy out and engaged him in conversation.

The weeks passed, and one afternoon after a séance, Lily bubbled with excitement. 'My brothers will be home for the Christmas holidays next week. Mama said to invite you to dinner. I know you'll like my brothers. James is the elder and at university studying Medicine, and Ernie is at boarding school.'

Percy felt dubious; he hoped they wouldn't be those superior types that would look down on a commercial clerk. He was afraid he wouldn't know how to talk to them.

'Don't worry,' Lily said, 'they're very ordinary boys, always up for a prank and fun.'

That made Percy feel even more disconsolate. His upbringing had left little time for pranks and fun. *They'll find me very staid and boring.*

***

Lily had told Percy to come early the following weekend and take tea with them before dinner. When Percy arrived James, the medical student, tall and serious, held out his hand to Percy. 'How do you do, Percy.' He smiled in a friendly manner.

Ernie, the younger, seemed like a male equivalent of Lily—bright and bubbly, with the same chestnut curls and seemingly very friendly.

James suggested a game of billiards before dinner.

'Yes, do,' Ernie said to Percy. 'Not you, Lily, we need to get to know Percy without you.'

Lily pouted but acquiesced when she noticed her mother looking at her.

'I need your help, please, Lily,' her mother said, leading her into the drawing room.

'Why do you need me, Mama?' Lily demanded.

'I don't,' came the reply. 'But I think it's good for the boys to get to know Percy on his own.'

Lily shrugged.

'Perhaps you'd like to do some needlework,' her mother suggested.

Lily looked at her aghast. 'You know I detest needlework!'

'Lily, my dear, when you are a housewife, you will need to know how mending is done. Come, I will show you this stitch.' She held out an example of some neat sewing.

'I'll give all my mending to a seamstress when I have my own home,' Lily muttered under her breath.

Downstairs in the Billiards room, Percy hesitated. 'I've never played Billiards,' he admitted.

'Really!' Ernie exclaimed. 'Well, we'd better teach you, because Lily is a crack player, and you mustn't let her beat you!'

Lily's brothers soon put Percy at ease, and he was pleasantly surprised to find that he enjoyed their company. After the game as they made their way back to the drawing room, James turned to Percy and asked, 'Have you known Lily long?'

'Quite a while.'

'She'll find it hard to settle down to married life,' James said, 'what with her demonstrations with the Suffragettes and going to rallies like the one last May in Hyde Park. The parents were extremely annoyed with her about that.'

'You mean the rally against The London Education Bill?' Surprised, Percy paused on the stairs. 'Did she go to that?'

'Indeed, yes! The parents stopped her allowance for a month, but I don't think it had any effect.'

Percy frowned thoughtfully.

***

Percy spent Christmas with his mother.

'Now, tell me all about the dinner party and this young lady you've met,' she said, pouring him a cup of tea after their meal.

Percy smiled. 'She's very beautiful and very clever. I think you'll like her. She's interested in Spiritualism and Women's Suffrage.'

'She does sound a most admirable person; I hope to meet her soon.'

Percy told his mother how Lily's father had been totally against his and Lily's engagement in the beginning and had sent Lily down to his sister in Hampshire, and hadn't forwarded his letters to Lily. 'If you hadn't kept her letter to me, I'd never have known the situation or where she was,' he said.

'Oh, that is terrible!' Sarah Hedgecock said indignantly. 'Why would he want to keep you apart?'

'I think he feels that I'm not good enough for her, just after her money.'

'What! How could he think such a thing?'

'I don't know. And I don't know what changed his mind.'

'He must have been impressed with you when you wrote and then met him.' Sarah Hedgecock smiled fondly at her only son.

'I expect he was just being protective of Lily,' Percy replied. 'She is very beautiful and in some ways very unworldly.'

'Hmm,' Sarah said. 'I doubt I'll like this David Bancroft if and when I get to meet him.'

Percy didn't know what to say to that, so he ignored it. 'Anyway, he wants us to really get to know each other before I can officially start to court Lily. And he wanted to know about my ability to support her.'

His mother nodded. 'Yes that all sounds very sensible. If either of you decide before then that you're not really compatible, you wouldn't have the issues of Breach of Contract to deal with.'

Percy smiled. There speaks the solicitor's wife, he thought to himself.

***

It became routine for Percy to walk Lily home after the meetings and then take tea with the Bancrofts. Sometimes Mrs Bancroft invited Percy to Sunday lunch, which meant they had no time for the séance meetings—not a great loss to Percy.

As the months passed Percy learned more about Lily's exploits. During the week she attended meetings of the National Union of Women's Suffrage Societies and different séances, or she went to the Library to do research on Egyptology. Her association with the newly formed and somewhat militant Women's Social and Political Union worried him, but he thought it was just a result of boredom. A free thinking, lively woman such as Lily needed something to occupy her mind. Once they were married and had a family, she'd have plenty to do and would soon settle down.

***

The months went by and it seemed that Lily hadn't become bored with Percy. David Bancroft began to think that perhaps he should agree to Lily and Percy marrying. 'Lily will be twenty-one soon,' he said to his wife one evening. 'Nothing to stop her running off and getting married. And I certainly don't want that kind of scandal. Do you think we should agree to this marriage with Percy?'

Melina looked up from her book and considered for a moment before replying, 'She still seems very enamoured of him, and I don't know who else would have patience with her. The way she lectures everyone all the time, and has such outrageous ideas. Any new fad takes her fancy. And now she's joined the WSPU, and they are so militant. I'm worried she'll be like those suffragettes, Christabel Pankhurst and Annie Kearney, and get arrested. Really, where will it end?' She sighed 'Perhaps it would be best if we get her safely married. And Percy is quite charming.'

'Hmmph.'

The following Saturday evening after dinner, when Lily and her mother had left the table and David and Percy were alone, David finished his port and lit his cigar. 'Well, Percy,' he began, 'Mrs Bancroft and I have been wondering if you are still of a mind to court Lily?'

Percy blinked, taken aback. 'Yes, yes, of course! It's my dearest wish.' His face reddened.

'Well, in that case, perhaps we will leave you and Lily alone for a few minutes so you can ask her. She may have changed her mind.' David looked sternly at Percy.

They returned to the drawing room and found Mrs Bancroft busy with her embroidery while Lily half-heartedly tried to make something out of a tangled mass of embroidery thread.

'My dear,' David said to his wife, 'would you step outside for a moment please? I think Percy has something to say to Lily.'

Lily looked up quickly, managing to stab herself in the finger with her sewing needle.

Melina got up, and with a sharp look at Lily, followed her husband out of the room.

'So!' Lily said, 'what is it that you have to say?'

Percy looked nervously at the blood on her finger and went pale. 'I'm sorry,' he said, 'I can't stand the sight of blood.'

Lily looked at the few drops on her finger, shrugged, then took out her handkerchief and wrapped it round her finger. 'Is that what you wanted to tell me?' she asked.

'No, no!' He went down on one knee. 'Lily, will you marry me?'

Lily bent over and took his face in her hands. 'Of course I will, Percy darling.' She kissed him, leaving a trail of blood from her finger across his face. 'Oh, look!' she said, 'That must be an omen!' She took her handkerchief and carefully wiped his face.

Percy took the bloodstained wisp of lacy linen from her. 'I will keep this for ever.' He tucked it into his top pocket, carefully avoiding looking at it.

'Percy, my love, I didn't know you were so romantic!' She laughed.

Mr and Mrs Bancroft came back into the drawing room.

'Mama, Papa!' Lily exclaimed, her eyes shining, 'Percy has asked me to marry him, and I have accepted!'

'Congratulations, Percy.' David walked over and shook Percy's hand.

'Dear Percy,' Melina murmured, 'welcome to our family.' She gave him a kiss on the cheek.

Percy's face went red. He appeared overwhelmed with happiness.

***

Etiquette demanded that the parents of the engaged couple should meet as soon as possible. The following weekend Lily's parents travelled down to Dover. Surprisingly, this meeting went well for both sides, and they settled on a date for the wedding.

Percy found a suitable place to rent— a three-storey detached house with a pleasant aspect and garden. The front door led into a large hall with a drawing room on one side and a dining room on the other. Further on, one came to a breakfast room, then a big kitchen and scullery. Four large bedrooms and a bathing room made up the first floor, and another flight of stairs led to attic rooms. Percy took Lily to see if she approved of it. It would be vacant in a few months.

Lily walked around solemnly and then announced, 'Well, it has a good atmosphere, and here is a room I can use for séances and psychic sittings.' She indicated the dining room. 'And there are rooms in the attic for servants, so I'm very happy with it.'

Surprised, Percy said, 'You want to hold séances and sittings here?'

'Of course.' Lily looked puzzled. 'I want to do healing sessions as well.'

Percy gave a tolerant smile, confident that once he married Lily she would settle down to a normal married life and forget all about her occult plans

'Come and see the garden. It'll be perfect for children to play in.' Percy took her arm and led her outside.

'Children? No, no, Percy. I don't want children.'

Percy, busy looking at the garden fences, didn't hear what she said.

CHAPTER 4

Lily and Percy married in 1905. Percy was twenty-three, and Lily was twenty-one. The morning of the wedding Percy gathered all his belongings and said goodbye to everyone at the boarding house. He'd arranged to meet James, whom he'd asked to be his best man, at the new house. They all wished him well and presented him with a wedding gift of a silver tray. Percy felt touched, since none of the boarders had much money.

'We shall miss you, Mr 'edgecock,' his landlady said.

'Yes,' echoed Miss Heatherby, 'such a lovely man.'

Tom gave him a wink. 'See you outside, old chap.'

When Percy got outside to the waiting cab, Tom put a small, wrapped parcel in Percy's hand. 'Think you might find this useful!' he said with another wink.

Percy felt very nervous about the wedding, but when he mentioned it to James, he only laughed at him.

'Quite common, old chap; pre-wedding nerves! You should have had a bachelor party last night to relax you, like I suggested!'

But Percy had had too much to do at work before his honeymoon. He couldn't afford to take more time off to have a party.

'Anyway, I'm here to make sure you don't do a disappearing act on Lily!' James smiled. 'Not that I'd blame you. Hope marriage quietens her down a bit.'

'I'd never leave Lily,' said Percy solemnly. 'I've loved her since the day I first met her.' He blushed at making such a statement.

James grinned. 'Come on, old boy, won't do to be late. Lily would never forgive me.'

When Percy saw Lily coming down the aisle on her father's arm, a lump came into his throat; she was so beautiful. His short speech at the reception was well received, then at last he and Lily were on the train to Brighton, their honeymoon destination.

Percy had had no experience with women. He hoped he'd know what to do when the time came. Tom's parcel had been a copy of Mrs Smythers' publication *Sex Tips for Husbands and Wives from 1894*, but he hadn't had time to read it. He'd opened the parcel in the cab, seen the title and stuffed it quickly into his portmanteau. Now, alone with her in the first-class rail carriage, he thought that perhaps he'd be able to have a quick look when Lily got ready for bed. He went hot at the thought of Lily getting into the same bed as him.

Could he get his portmanteau down from the overhead rack, get the book and pretend it was a stock-broking reference book? No. Lily would immediately want to see what he was reading. He looked at her. *My God! She's so beautiful, my wife. And she looks so serene.*

Lily paused in her reading of the latest book about the pyramids and turned and smiled at him. 'We are going to be so happy,' she exclaimed. 'Imagine, I am a wife! Mrs Percy Hedgecock; now I'll be free to do everything I want!' She took his hand, leaned over and kissed him ardently.

Percy suddenly felt less anxious.

A week later, when looking for a something to read, Lily found Mrs Smythers' book in the bottom of Percy's portmanteau. She laughed out loud when she read some of the tips in the book:

'*While the ideal husband would be one who would approach his bride only at her request and only for the purpose of begetting offspring, such nobility and unselfishness cannot be expected from the average man,*' she read. And then:

'*The wise bride will permit a maximum of two brief sexual experiences weekly during the first months of marriage.*' At this she again burst of laughing.

'Percy!' she called, 'I am an unwise bride! Where on earth did you get this book?'

Percy, who'd been shaving, came out of the bathroom with half his face covered in lather to see what Lily was laughing at.

'This book!' she said, 'where did you get it? It's so funny!'

He looked at it and blushed through his soapy lather. 'Tom gave it to me. I think it was a joke.'

'Have you read it?'

'No.'

'Probably as well,' Lily said, 'you would have thought me a terribly loose woman.' She leaned over and pulled him to her. 'Come here, soapy husband.' She wiped the lather off his face and dragged him to the bed.

'Let me finish shaving!' he protested.

Lily took the razor from his hand, put it on the bedside table and murmured, 'Mrs Smythers, you have no idea.'

***

Back in London, Percy thought the first few months of their married life idyllic. Lily's mother had employed suitable servants whilst they were on their honeymoon, so on their return, every-thing was running smoothly. Knowing her daughter, Melina had employed a trustworthy housekeeper/cook, a maid, a scullery maid and a man to do the heavy work. She'd bought linen and other essentials, and sat with Mrs Burton, the housekeeper, to organise food and household deliveries.

Lily occupied herself with organising her spiritualist acquaintances and setting up a séance room.

They fell into a comfortable routine. Percy had breakfast and went to work before Lily woke and returned at seven or eight at night. After his quick wash and freshen up, they had dinner. Lily left all the decisions about the menu and buying the food to Mrs Burton, who was also a very good cook. On a Sunday afternoon if the weather was fine, Percy and Lily went for a walk in the park or to the new Crystal Palace where Lily liked to play billiards.

However, things changed a few months later when Lily began to feel sick in the mornings.

One night as they sat down to dinner, Percy looked at Lily and frowned, 'My darling you're not eating; are you feeling unwell?'

'I think I might be expecting a baby. I've missed the curses, and I'm feeling sick!' She burst into tears.

'Oh, my poor darling,' Percy said, getting up and coming around to her. Then what she'd said sank in. Delighted, he lifted her from her chair and kissed her. 'Imagine, I'm going to be a Papa!'

He swung her round and up in the air, until he suddenly realised that this was probably unwise for a lady in her condition, especially if she were subject to vomiting. Gently he set her down. 'Why are you crying? You must be hungry; I'll ask Mrs Burton to prepare you something light for dinner.'

'No, I'm not hungry, and I feel so sick, and I'm crying because this is all happening. I don't want babies! I don't like babies! I was hoping to have some freedom as a married woman and do so many things!'

He took out his handkerchief and tenderly wiped her tears. 'You will still be able to do all those things you dreamed of,' he said. 'We can hire a nurse to look after the baby.'

She brightened at this, and Percy thought that once she held her baby in her arms, she'd be like most women and be devoted to the infant.

***

Baby Piers was born in 1906. It was a difficult and protracted birth. When Percy got home from work the evening before, the house seemed to be in an uproar. There was no dinner and he could hear Lily's screams. He ran up to their bedroom, but Mrs. Burton stopped him from going in.

'Madam is in labour, sir. Everything is going well, the midwife is with her. I've left some sandwiches in the kitchen for you. Now, don't you go coming in and disturbing her!'

Percy was distraught, 'But why is my wife screaming?' he demanded.

'It's all perfectly normal sir, now you just go down to the kitchen and have a cup of tea and a sandwich, Nurse says it will be a while yet.' And she disappeared into the bedroom.

Percy dithered around outside the bedroom door, terrified that Lily might die. He paced up and down, wincing every time he heard Lily scream. Eventually he went down to the kitchen. He looked for a kettle but they seem to have all disappeared. He managed to eat half a sandwich and drink some water and then went back upstairs.

After pacing up and down for what seemed like hours, he fetched a chair and sat outside the room, dozing and waking with each scream. Towards morning there was a silence and his head dropped onto his chest and he slept. Suddenly his head jerked up, what was that? The sound of a baby crying. His heart stopped. He desperately wanted to open the door and look in. But he couldn't chance seeing blood and passing out. He stood up and started pacing along the hall again. When the bedroom suddenly opened he jumped. Mrs Burton stood there with a bundle in her arms.

'Congratulations, sir, you have a son.'

Percy's breath was taken away by the sight of the angry red, wrinkled face that Mrs Burton tenderly displayed.

'And my wife?' he could hardly get the words out.

'Nurse is just preparing her sir. I think you can go in now.'

Percy went in to find a white-faced Lily lying in the bed, her chestnut curls spread over the pillow, damp with the effort and pain of labour.

'Lily! Oh my darling! Are you all right?' He bent and kissed her brow.

'Percy! Where is my baby? Is he all right? Percy, I never want to have to go through that again!'

He held her hand and made soothing noises.

'Where is my baby, Percy?' she tried to sit up in the bed but was too weak.

Mrs Burton came over to the bed.

'Here is your son, Madam.'

She held the baby out to Lily, but she was too weak to hold him.

'Oh Percy darling! He's beautiful!'

Percy looked again at the screwed up face, wrinkled and angry looking.. 'Um yes,' he said.

He took a little hand that had come free from the swaddling. Immediately the little hand clasped Percy's finger. Awestruck, Percy took the baby from Lily who seemed to have fallen asleep.

'Is my wife all right?' He turned to the midwife.

'Yes, sir, but she's lost a lot of blood and is very weak. I don't think she will be strong enough to feed the baby herself.'

'Can we engage a wet nurse?'

The midwife looked up from gathering her bag and instruments.

'Yes sir, I know a reliable woman who will be glad of the extra money, and she lives near. I'll send her round today.'

Percy sat on the end of the bed gently rocking his son in his arms. Then the baby's little mouth started to pucker up and a mewling sound emerged. Immediately Lily's eyes fluttered open.

'My baby! Give me my baby,' she tried to sit up.

'My darling, here he is, but I think you are not strong enough to feed him.'

'Nonsense! It's his birthright!'

She desperately tried to hold his little head to her breast but fell back with a sigh. Tears came to her eyes. 'I can't hold him, Percy,' she whispered.

'My darling, you must rest now. A lovely lady is coming today to help feed him.'

But Lily's eyes were closed and she slept.

Percy suddenly realised it was already morning. He had to get to work! But he couldn't leave Lily!

He looked up. 'Mrs. Burton, I must write some notes to my employer and also to Lily's parents. Would you find a boy to deliver them?'

'Of course, sir.'

'Um. What do I do with the baby?'

Mrs. Burton smiled and held out her arms. 'I'll take him, sir and put him in his cot. See, look how I do it.'

His letters written and dispatched to his employers and to the Bancrofts, Percy suddenly felt dizzy with relief. He went to the kitchen where Mrs Burton was busy preparing food.

'Mrs Burton! You have been up all night with my wife. Please will you go and have some rest now?'

She smiled at him. 'You too, Mr Percy, you were up all night!'

'Well, perhaps we should both have a nap.'

Percy went up to his bedroom and quietly opened the door. He crept around to his side of the bed and took off his shoes and trousers and jacket. Then slid carefully in between the sheets, trying not to disturb Lily.

He was just dozing off when the baby started to cry. Lily stirred and muttered something.Quickly he slid out of the bed and took the baby from the crib and went out of the bedroom, rocking the baby in his arms. He didn't want to wake Lily.

Then he saw Mrs Burton coming up the stairs.

'I thought I heard the baby,' she said.

Conscious that he was standing in the hall in just his underwear and shirt, Percy didn't know what to do.

Mrs Burton smiled. 'Give me the baby. You go and lie down in one of the other rooms sir.'

Thankfully Percy did as he was told. He'd get his trousers later, for now he just wanted to sleep.

***

The Bancrofts came over as soon as they received Percy's note about the baby.

Melina was thrilled with her first grandchild.

'Congratulations, Percy!' David Bancroft held out his hand to Percy.

'Thankyou sir,' said Percy, still dazed with lack of sleep as the doorbell rang and the midwife arrived with the wet nurse.

'This is Mrs. Harris, sir. She will be feeding the baby,' the midwife said as she handed Percy a piece of paper.

'This is my bill and the charges for Mrs Harris.

Percy, still in a daze, took the paper.

David Bancroft took command.

'Mrs Burton, perhaps you would take my wife and Mrs Harris up to Mrs Hedgecock then make tea for the ladies and also bring some into the breakfast room for myself and Mr Hedgecock.'

Mrs Burton bobbed her head. 'Of course, Sir.'

'Now, Percy,' David Bancroft looked at Percy as they went into the breakfast room, 'Melina and I would like to give you a little something to help with the baby,' he waved his hand at Percy, 'I know, I know, you can provide for her and all that, but she is delicate and needs extra care and we just want to help. Melina thinks you need to employ a nanny. Now don't get all proud and on your high horse, with me, my boy!' as Percy started to protest.

He took a cheque from his jacket pocket. 'Please! Let us do this!'

Percy looked at his father-in-law, suddenly realising that David Bancroft was finding it equally hard to say those words.

He smiled. 'That's most generous of you, sir. I really appreciate it.'

David Bancroft shook Percy's hand warmly.

'Sometimes it's harder to receive than to give,' he said with a grin.

***

One afternoon when little Piers, as they had decided to call him, was three months old, Lily sat watching him sucking eagerly at Mrs. Harris's breast.

Mrs. Harris looked over at her. 'It's not easy seeing annuver woman feed your baby is it, missus?'

Lily shook her head. 'What about your own baby? Do you have enough milk for her too?'

'Oh yes, missus! Mr. 'arris calls me a reglar ol' milch cow!'

Lily shrank from this coarse talk.

'An' annuver fing, while I'm feedin' babies I don't have the curses, so I can't get in the fambly way agin. Don't want no more buns in me oven!'

Lily stared at her. Then comprehension dawned. 'You mean, that when you aren't menstruating you won't get pregnant?'

Mrs Harris looked blank.

Lily tried again. 'No curses, no babies?'

Mrs Harris gave a gap toothed smile. 'Thas right missus!'

***

Percy found her in tears. He put his arms around her. 'Darling! What's wrong?'

'Oh, Percy, I feel so sad not being able to feed my own baby. I should be bonding with him. I know I didn't want babies but now he is here and I love him so much, but it's Mrs. Harris that he looks up at and smiles at when she is feeding him. I'm not a proper mother!'

'Of course you are, darling! Lots of women have the same problem.'

'I can't bear to watch him feeding!'

Percy took her in his arms. 'Next time it will be different and easier, darling.'

Lily stiffened. 'No next time, Percy! I don't want to go through childbirth again.'

He patted her back reassuringly.

'Why don't you carry on with your séances and stuff, that might take your mind off things.'

***

Lily started her séances again. She'd had some success with automatic writing and wanted to expand on it. She knew little Piers was well looked after, Percy had engaged a nanny to look after him and Mrs Harris was still feeding him. She felt a bit superfluous really, but they were happy days. On fine Sunday afternoons, they took the baby in his perambulator to the park for a stroll. Percy noticed that while the baby got admiring looks from the women of their acquaintance, Lily got admiring looks from the men. He thought that motherhood suited her; she looked more beautiful than ever.

When Lily found she was pregnant again, she couldn't believe it. *I'll have to breast feed the baby this time I can't keep having babies.* She kept thinking of Mrs Harris and her extended breast feeding to prevent pregnancy.

The pregnancy was hard, the morning sickness lasted all day and every day. But the birth of little Ena was not as bad as with Piers. Lily tried to feed her but she didn't have enough milk to satisfy the baby. Mrs. Harris was called upon again.

'No worries, missus, course you wouldn't be able to feed, look at you! A little scrap like you, youse is ony a babe yerself!'

Lily began to think she wasn't cut out for motherhood. She loved her children but she felt distanced from them. *It's because I couldn't feed them! I didn't bond with them.*

Ena was only a few months old when Lily became involved with the Women's Social and Political Union.

'The National Union of Women's Suffrage Societies isn't militant enough,' she told Percy one Saturday morning. 'I'm going to the Hyde Park rally on Sunday organised by the WSPU.'

'But they are the militants, those Pankhurst women!' he exclaimed. 'Lily dear, you must not go! There will be crowds there; you'll be crushed!'

'Nonsense! I have to make a stand for my beliefs!'

'Lily, you only gave birth to Ena a few weeks ago; you're not fit enough. Please, darling! I beg of you!'

Lily merely smiled and shook her head. 'You fuss too much, Percy darling.'

'Promise me you won't do anything illegal and get arrested. Please?'

'Percy, I have no intention of getting arrested and spending the night in a smelly prison cell. Now, stop worrying.'

He had to be content with that.

*****

By the time Percy and Lily had been married six years, they had two more babies, George and then David.

Lily had started healing sessions in the dining room as well as séances, which meant they had to use the breakfast room for all their meals. Lily seemed to be getting increasingly tired, and Percy worried about her. Their intimate life had diminished, and now, when Percy approached her in bed, she tended to push him away.

'I'm afraid I'll get pregnant again, I can't bear that sickness,' she said; 'you have no idea what it's like trying to manage a house and children and work as well while feeling nauseous all the time. It's easy for you.'

Percy felt it was all his fault.

'It's not your fault,' she said when she saw his face. 'I just don't want any more babies.' She turned on her side, away from him.

'Perhaps I should talk to James, now that he has qualified,' Percy said. 'He might be able to suggest something.'

'Bromide, probably,' was all she said.

Percy didn't relish the thought of talking to James. Discussing his and Lily's sex life with anyone would be difficult, let alone her brother, but he made an appointment with James at his practice.

He sat in the waiting room, nervously turning the pages of a periodical, not taking in any of the words. Eventually James came to the door and beckoned him in.

'Hello, Percy! Haven't seen you since little David's christening,' James said. 'And that was very interesting! How did Lily get Dame Ellen Terry to be David's godmother?'

'Oh, Lily did a healing for her, and she and Lily are very close now,' Percy coughed nervously.

'What's up, Percy? Do you have a cough? I thought you looked full of beans at the christening, and you look pretty chipper to me now, so what's up?'

Percy sat. His face reddened, and then he said, 'Lily doesn't want any more babies, and I don't know what to do.'

James studied Percy. 'I would've thought Lily would have the answers to that, with her association with the women's movement. She tried to get Phoebe to join the WSPU, did you know? Phoebe asked me what I thought, and I said it wasn't a good idea.'

Percy thought that James was lucky that the young lady he was courting was much easier to deal with than Lily.

'Anyway,' James continued, 'back to your problem; you do have choices. There is a condom for men, and also Marie Stopes is advocating a sponge soaked in vinegar for the woman. I'll give you an address where you can get the condoms.' He scribbled on a page of his note book, then looked up at Percy, who'd gone bright red with embarrassment. James laughed. 'Oh Percy, if only you knew how many men come to me with this problem. It's much better than a back-street abortion.'

Percy's eyes widened in horror. 'I could never subject Lily to that.'

'Well, I know it's illegal, but it's happening all the time.' With that he stood up and slapped Percy on the shoulder. 'Cheer up, old boy; did you know I've asked Phoebe to marry me? You and Lily seem so happy; it's a bit of an incentive to settle down.'

'Phoebe is a lovely girl,' Percy said. 'I think you and she would be well matched.'

Percy walked away from James's surgery feeling a bit more optimistic. He got out the address James had given him for the condoms, thinking that this might add some cheer to the evening. He hoped it would be a man serving him.

Tongue-tied, he showed the note James had given him to the man in the shop selling the condoms. He paid for them and was walking out when the man, with a wink, said, 'Have a good evening, Sir.'

Percy didn't think his face could get any redder.

He walked home, already anticipating the night. When he went in the front door about to call for Lily, he heard a baby screaming in the dining room. Rushing in, thinking it was baby David, he found Lily with a woman and a crying baby.

'What's going on?' he demanded.

Lily turned around. 'I'm giving healing to this woman,' she said calmly. 'She has a skin complaint, and the baby is a bit fretful. Could you ask Nanny to come and take the child while I finish the healing, please?'

Percy looked at the grubby baby. Suddenly feeling very angry, he turned to the woman. 'Please come back another day. Without the baby!' he ordered.

The woman hurriedly wrapped her shawl around herself and the baby and scuttled out of the room.

Lily turned to Percy, her eyes blazing. 'How dare you talk to one of my clients like that!'

Percy took her by the shoulders. Never in his life had he felt so angry. He half shook Lily. 'Never bring people like that to our house again,' he shouted. 'Did you see that scabby baby? And you wanted our children's nanny to pick it up? You want to expose our children to all kinds of disease and sickness?'

Lily didn't move. She just stared at him.

The anger went out of Percy. He dropped his hands. 'I'm sorry Lily,' he said, 'but don't you realise the danger to which you are exposing not only our children, but also yourself?'

'I'll find an alternative place for my healing sessions,' she said stiffly. 'Now, if you will excuse me, I will go and wash my hands with carbolic soap and change my clothes.'

Feeling shaken, Percy sat down and put his head in his hands. This was the first time he and Lily had quarrelled seriously about anything. He thought of himself as a mild-mannered man and not easily roused to anger. He hadn't realised that she was so seriously committed to her healing. He'd been too busy at work to notice the changes occurring at home. The happy evening, he'd been anticipating dissipated.

That night in bed Lily lay stiffly beside Percy. Miserably, he turned to her. 'I saw James today,' he began.

No response.

'Lily ... I love you, my dearest.'

Lily turned to him. 'Percy, you don't seem to realise how important my work is to me.'

Percy wanted to say, 'But more important than our children?' He didn't, though; he knew that would antagonise her even more. He just took her in his arms and said nothing.

A crisis had been averted, but he felt control slipping away from him.

CHAPTER 5

L eslie had tried over the years to put Miss Bancroft out of his mind. He knew that she and Percy Hedgecock had married. He'd seen the notice in the newspaper. They'd stopped attending his weekly séances and spiritualist meetings soon after their engagement. In a way that had been a relief. It had been painful to watch them together. Turning the knife. He'd tried to keep busy working on wireless radios, writing articles for *The Model Engineer and Amateur Electrician*, running his spiritualist meetings and other projects.

Then one Spring morning, while eating breakfast and opening his letters, he found an envelope with handwriting and a return address that he didn't recognise. He buttered a slice of toast and then, using the same knife, slit open the envelope. A smile lit up his face when he opened the letter and read the contents:

April 25th

Dear Mr Carter,

I expect you will be surprised to hear from me after such a long time.

I am writing to ask if you know of anywhere I could hold séances and spiritual healings.

I now have four children and our home is no longer suitable.

I remain yours sincerely,
Mrs Percy Hedgecock (née Lily Bancroft)

Lily Bancroft! It must have been six or seven years ago since he'd last seen her. He sat for a few moments, a thoughtful expression on his face. He still loved Lily; he always would. It had taken him a long time to come to terms with the fact that Lily favoured Percy Hedgecock and not him. He thought it was probably fortunate that he hadn't asked to walk her home that day when Percy first came to the meeting. A rejection would have been hard to bear.

Forgetting his breakfast, he got up and went to his writing desk.

Dear Mrs Hedgecock,

Thank you for your recent letter. I am pleased to hear that you and Mr Hedgecock have been blessed with children.

I am happy to be able to offer you my home to hold séances and spiritual healings as Mrs Snelling has gone to Italy for an extended stay, and I have not been holding any meetings since her departure.

Yours sincerely

Leslie Carter.

He went back to the breakfast table to retrieve the envelope and was just able to make out her address on the back through the smear of butter and marmalade.

A few days later his doorbell rang, and when he answered it, there she was, on the doorstep.

He blinked, stepped back and held the door open for her. For a few seconds he couldn't speak, the tide of emotions overwhelming him. 'Why, Mrs Hedgecock, what a lovely surprise! Please, do come in,' he eventually managed to say.

'Thank you, Mr Carter, it's so kind of you to offer to rent me a room.'

He took her into the dining room, which was where Mrs Snelling had held her séances, and pulled out a chair.

'Please sit down, Mrs Hedgecock. Would you like a cup of tea?'

'No, thank you, but please, do call me Lily!' she smiled at him as she took off her gloves.

His heart thumped against his ribs. She looked so beautiful. He managed to stammer, 'Please call me Leslie.'

She smiled. 'Thank you, Leslie. Now, what days would suit you? I expect Sunday afternoons would be best for the séances, and perhaps Saturday afternoons for the healings?' She inclined her head, looking at him.

He swallowed. 'Yes, Lily, that would be most suitable.'

'I've been doing healings during the week, too, but perhaps we can see how things go?'

He nodded. 'Yes, yes, of course.'

'Now, about the rent.' She looked at him. 'How much should I pay? Perhaps the same as Mrs Snelling?'

He stared at her. 'Why nothing! Mrs Snelling didn't charge for her séances, and I couldn't possibly charge you!'

'Yes, but people do offer me money for my healings. I never charge, but someone suggested I leave a donation box. If anyone is so inclined they can leave something.' She smiled. 'I've had necklaces and rings left. Some ladies have no money, but do have jewellery ...'

Leslie just shook his head.

'But you must take something; I insist.'

'Let's just wait and see how it works out, shall we? Now, please let me offer you refreshment.' He wanted to keep her there longer.

Lily rose. 'No, thank you; I must go home. So, would next Saturday be suitable to start?'

Leslie got up and smiled. 'Of course!'

He stood with mixed feelings at the front door for a long time after Lily had left. It felt so wonderful to be in her presence again. Being near her made him feel complete somehow. *As if Lily is the missing piece in the jigsaw puzzle that is me. I hope it won't be too painful to be near her when she is so unattainable.*

He shook his head. Better stop these silly thoughts.

***

Lily announced that she had found a place to hold her healing sessions. 'I wrote to Leslie Carter,' she said. 'Mrs Snelling has gone to Italy, and he will be very pleased for me to replace her.'

Percy looked crestfallen. 'That sounds very suitable,' he said.

'I can get a cab,' she continued. 'I've given the address to Mrs Burton, so if anyone comes here, she can redirect them.' She thought for a moment. 'Do you think I should put a notice in "The Light"?'

'What light?' Percy frowned.

Lily stared at him. 'The Spiritualist newspaper. The one I receive every week.'

'Oh, yes, well, I don't know, darling. Whatever you think best. Or perhaps ask Mr. Carter.'

'I will.'

***

A few months later, as they were getting ready for bed, Percy said, 'Lily darling, we hardly see you these days. I know the children miss you, and I certainly do; I think that we should keep Sunday as a day to be all together.

Lily looked at him accusingly. 'You work long hours all week, the children are usually in bed when you come home from work, and Saturday is a busy time for healing sessions; it's the only time a lot of people don't work, and that only leaves Sunday for séances.'

Percy sighed, knowing that what she said was true.

'And if you want to see more of me, you can come to my Sunday afternoon séances at Leslie's,' she continued.

Percy thought that if that was the only way they could spend more time together then perhaps he would. It wouldn't solve the issue of the children missing their mother, but one step at a time.

'Very well,' he said, 'next Sunday I'll come with you.'

Lily smiled her enchanting smile. 'It's so nice that you are taking an interest in my work,' she said.

Percy felt more optimistic after their conversation, but the following week he felt strange returning to Leslie Carter's. It brought back memories of his first meeting with Lily. He studied her. *She looks even more beautiful now.*

Leslie opened the door. 'Hello, Lily, and Mr Hedgecock, it's nice to see you again.'

Lily smiled. She removed her gloves, then took off her hat and coat and hung them up. 'I'll just go into the breakfast room and sit quietly.'

Percy took off his coat and then turned to Leslie. 'Please call me Percy.'

Leslie nodded. 'Thank you, Percy, and do call me Leslie. Now, come into the séance room, you know it, of course. People have just started to arrive.'

Percy went in and sat down. He looked around. Nothing had changed. Still the heavy brocade curtains and dark furniture.

When everyone had settled, Leslie drew the curtains and lit candles.

Percy caught his breath when Lily appeared, looking ethereal and beautiful. She seemed to glide in. He thought the séance would be similar to what he'd experienced before, but it was very different from Mrs Snelling's sessions. Lily sat, and Percy fixed his eyes on her. Suddenly she seemed to slump back in her chair. Alarmed, Percy went to jump up and go to her, but Leslie put a restraining hand on his arm.

'Don't be worried,' he whispered. 'She's in a trance'

Percy watched as Lily's voice changed such that it was unrecognisable. It seemed to be the voice of a man, speaking in broken English. He introduced himself as Eduardo her spirit guide and had a message from someone who'd passed. He said the message was from Peter and gave some details of the house where he used to live with Anna. A woman in the sitting gave a sob and said under her breath, 'My Peter!' Eduardo gave some more information and said to tell Anna that Peter was happy, and she was not to worry about him.

Then other messages came which seemed to be relevant to members of the group.

To Percy's astonishment, when Lily came out of the trance she appeared to have no recollection of what had happened. The woman who'd said 'My Peter' identified herself as Anna. This was her first time at a sitting, and she had never met Lily before.

On the one hand Percy felt pride in Lily having this gift and on the other hand, he felt alarm at this manifestation.

Leslie came over to him and said, 'While everyone is having tea, and Lily is doing a healing, please come and see my workshop in the back garden, you might be interested in what I'm doing.'

Leslie led him into what had once been stables at the end of the back garden. All kinds of equipment and wires filled the space. 'Are you familiar with the work of Oliver Lodge and Marconi?' he asked Percy, who shook his head. 'I'm working on some of the same ideas as they.'

He took Percy round the room, enthusiastically showing Percy all his equipment and telling him about his experiments with airwaves and wireless.

Percy didn't understand what Leslie was doing, but it all seemed very impressive. He tried to appear as if he understood.

Leslie sighed. 'I was close to developing a wireless transmitter, but Marconi beat me to it. That was a big blow; his method was superior to mine. There's still a lot of improvements to be made.' His expression brightened. 'I've just been asked by Herbert Musgrave to go and work with The Royal Flying Corps on their experimental projects. He's very keen on using wireless telegraphy on aircraft.'

Percy nodded. He knew nothing about the Royal Flying Corps or wireless telegraphy.

Leslie seemed eager to keep Percy longer while he demonstrated different electrical phenomena, but it was all over Percy's head. He had no real interest in electromagnetism.

As they left the workshop, Leslie suddenly stopped and took Percy's arm. 'Percy, I don't quite know how to say this, but Lily has a donation box by the front door; she said that was what she did before.' He hesitated. 'The thing is, there has been a lot of money donated, and Lily is inclined to tell poorer people to take what they want from the box. Even the poorest people will try and leave something.'

Percy regarded him enquiringly.

'What I'm trying to say is that I'm so glad that you came today as I want to give you the money.' He went back into his workshop, came out with a leather pouch and handed it to Percy. 'I've been collecting it up, and I think there is a fair amount.'

Percy looked in the pouch. His eyebrows rose in astonishment to see it filled with gold coins and some silver, there was even an amber necklace.

'She said she'd be paying you rent when she had money.' Percy didn't quite know what else to do or say.

'Yes, well, I don't like to take any, and when I asked Lily, she just said to take what I thought was right.'

'I don't know what to do.' Percy hesitated. 'It's really Lily's money, but you need to have a reasonable rent.'

The two men looked at each other.

Then Percy said, 'Perhaps you should take a percentage. What about 15%? We can sort it out now, if you like.'

Leslie scratched his head, making his sandy hair stand on end. 'No, that's far too much.'

Percy shook his head. 'I'm certain that Lily would want you to take it. You have overheads, you know.'

Leslie looked doubtful. 'I'll go on keeping it for you,' he said. 'Perhaps you could call by every so often and take it.'

Percy nodded. 'Yes, I will. Thank you. I have to admit that the extra money will be useful. You're a good friend to Lily.' He held out his hand. Leslie took it, and the two men smiled and shook hands.

'That would be a big relief to me,' Leslie said. 'Lily works so hard and gets very exhausted. When she goes into a trance or when healing, it drains her, as you know, and she gets very tired. It's only right that she should be compensated.'

Percy felt guilty. He hadn't realised that these sessions were so draining for Lily, or that she was amassing a lot of money from it. 'Let's go back to your workshop and sort this out now,' he said.

Back in the workshop Percy emptied the purse onto a bench and counted the money. 'It comes to £235, 12/6.' His eyes widened in surprise. 'That's such a lot!' He did a quick calculation. '15% would be 25 pounds, 6 shillings and 10 pence halfpenny, would you check that for me?' He counted it out.

Leslie looked stunned. 'How did you do that?'

'Do what?'

'Work that out in your head.'

'I'm used to figures' Percy replied, with a shrug. 'Now, here's £26 to make it a round sum.'

'That's too much!' Leslie protested with an embarrassed expression.

'No,' Percy said. 'That's what we agreed. I don't know what to do about the necklace. It looks valuable. If it's all right with you, I'll take it and the rest of the money and keep a note of it for the future for Lily.'

They went back to the house where Lily was saying goodbye to everyone.

As they were leaving, Leslie said to him, 'Do come again, Percy, it's so nice to have the opinion of someone from the business world.'

Percy managed to make a suitable reply and bid him good evening.

On their way home in the cab, Lily turned to him, her eyes shining. 'What did you think of the séance?' she said. 'I'm keen to try materialising spirits like Elizabeth d'Esperance.'

Percy had never heard of this Elizabeth. Lily chattered on about Arthur Conan Doyle and other people who were involved in the Spiritualist movement.

Percy wondered sometimes if he'd ever really known Lily, or if it were even possible to know her. She seemed to be spending more and more time with her séances and healing sessions, and less and less time with him and the children. He felt quite remorseful that he'd not realised why she was often home late and always exhausted. He sighed inwardly and simply took her hand and smiled.

***

In the Spring of 1914, James and Phoebe were married. At the wedding, Percy studied Lily. He remembered their own wedding and the honeymoon. Perhaps he and Lily should take a holiday in Brighton or even with his mother in Dover to try and recapture that magical time.

He sat waiting for Lily, who was helping Phoebe change her dress before she and James left for their honeymoon in France,

James came and sat beside him. 'It's good to be married and settled,' he said. 'I very much fear there will be war soon.'

'War?' Percy frowned. 'What do you mean? I haven't heard any rumours of a war.'

James stared at him. 'Surely you've been reading the papers?'

Percy had to admit that he rarely had time to read more than the financial papers.

'Well it seems it's political at the moment, a power struggle with Germany.' James shrugged. 'The Great British Empire and all that! But I have a bad feeling about it. The British army is not only under equipped but doesn't have the manpower to fight a war.' He frowned, worry lines creasing his forehead.

Percy started. 'Really? Hopefully Britain will be able to keep out of it.'

James shook his head, a gloomy expression on his face. 'I think it's unlikely.'

Percy worried about that. How would it affect the financial markets and would his family be in danger? He joined Lily and they collected the children and made their way home.

In the cab, Percy remained quiet, lost in thought. He'd better start reading more of the news in the papers, but he'd been so busy with work and the children's demands. Lily's healing sessions and séances kept her away from home more and more. However, she seemed much happier now that the threat of another pregnancy had diminished, and she was doing the work she felt she was made for. But he still thought she neglected the children. She only saw them at dinner and beyond a hug and a kiss to each of them and a *'Hello Darlings!'* she seemed to take little interest in them. He sighed.

'What's the matter, Percy?' Lily enquired. 'You seem very quiet.'

'I was thinking it would be nice to go to Brighton and have a second honeymoon.'

She squeezed his hand. 'Dear Percy, you always were a romantic.' She leaned over and gave him a kiss.

One night he brought up the subject again. 'Lily, we hardly see you these days; you are so busy; the children and I miss you.'

'Oh, phooey,' she replied, 'you're busy every day at work, and the children have their school work and music lessons and games, they seem quite happy, and anyway Piers is seven now and nearly time for him to go to boarding school. James and Ernie were eight when they went.'

Percy hated the idea of his sons being sent to boarding school. He'd been lucky in that there was a very good boys school in Dover, and he'd been a day pupil, but he'd heard what some boarders endured with bullying and homesickness and other things that didn't bear thinking about. He didn't want that for his boys.

Percy loved his children, and he felt sure that Lily loved them in her own way. Now that he knew more about Lily, he thought that the boarding school issue was a passing phase. If he could persuade her to wait until Piers was nine, she may have lost interest in the whole business of schooling.

'I was thinking that you work so hard and are so tired these days, it would be nice if we all went and spend a week or two of the summer in Dover with my mother; it would be a rest for you,' he said. 'And we could look at the Grammar School in Dover and see if it would be suitable for the boys.'

Lily's eyes gleamed with enthusiasm. 'Yes! I feel I need a rest. You have no idea how exhausting and draining it is trying to heal people and giving séances. And we must go before the war.'

Percy started. 'War?'

'Yes, darling; there will be a terrible war.'

CHAPTER 6

The news of the assassination of Archduke Ferdinand of Austro-Hungary on 28th June 1914 did nothing to cause Percy any alarm; the Balkan states had been sparring for years. He carried on with his arrangements for the family to stay with his mother in Dover in the middle of July. He intended to see them settled in and then go back to the city for a week, come down for the August bank holiday weekend and stay for the rest of the week.

By the middle of July, however, Percy felt a little unsettled at the way things were going in Europe, but they went ahead with their plans to travel down to Dover.

That week, the senior partner in his firm, Arthur Symonds called a meeting of the staff. This was an unusual occurrence.

He looked serious. 'I've heard rumours that the German banks and brokers have been selling millions of pounds worth of Austro-German securities onto the British Stock Exchange. If these reports are true then these are now worthless. Apparently, it's an attempt to smash the City of London and thus the Government.'

Shock waves went around the staff. Eric Swanton, the other partner, looked grim as he nodded his head in agreement.

'Well, it's only a rumour, but no smoke without fire, as they say,' Arthur continued.

'I suppose there isn't much we can do at this stage,' Percy said slowly. 'Let's hope the Government has it all in hand.'

A few sceptical sniffs greeted that remark.

When the time came to take his family down to Dover, Percy felt a mixture of apprehension and anticipation at the move. His mother was thrilled to see them, and fortunately her large house had room for her to retreat from the onslaught of her boisterous grandsons. Little Ena tried to organise everyone and smooth over any difficulties.

Dover seemed to be in a holiday mood. An Amusements Committee had been set up to attract holiday makers. Even though there'd been talk of an impending war, most people were too intent on enjoying their hard-earned annual holiday. Even Lily seemed carefree and happy and more loving towards the children and him. Percy felt overjoyed that they seemed to have restored some harmony to their marriage.

Percy tried to ignore the talk of war around the town and concentrate on his family and enjoying his weekend with them.

His mother took him aside one morning after breakfast. 'Things look serious, Percy,' she said. 'You may not have noticed, but there has been a lot of work going on at the Castle and the Batteries, building defences. Everyone seems nervous, and the presence of the Territorials and the fleets in the harbour doesn't help.'

Percy had never heard his mother speak in such a way before. He put an arm around her. 'Dear Mother, please don't worry about war. I'm sure it won't affect us.'

'Go and find Lily and the children and enjoy the fine weather while it lasts,' was all she said.

Percy, Lily and the children watched the constant arrival of ferries from France with holiday makers hurriedly returning home; their holidays on the Continent cut short by the threat of war. Percy went back to London on Sunday night on the last train from Dover.

'Goodbye, darling,' he said to Lily. 'I'll be back on Saturday evening.'

Things seemed fairly normal all week, busy with buying and selling shares, but when he went into work on Friday morning, Tom had already arrived and sat reading the early morning paper.

He greeted Percy with a shake of his head. 'It's looking grim, Perce,' he said, 'listen to this:' He read from the paper: '"*Austria has said Serbia isn't doing enough to apprehend the Arch-Duke's assassins and should take steps to prevent the publication of propaganda against Austria-Hungary*",' He looked up with a frown and then continued, '"*and they must stop the covert shipments of arms and explosives from Serbia to Austria-Hungary*".' He stopped reading. 'The Austrians say a whole lot of other things, and Serbia has forty-eight hours to meet all their demands or else they will recall their Ambassador ...'

Percy dropped into the chair next to Tom. 'Show me!' He took the paper from Tom and hurriedly read the article. 'This will mean war,' he said.

Tom nodded in agreement.

Arthur Symonds called an emergency meeting of the senior clerks: 'We have been told by several clients to sell their shares. Bad news travels quickly. I'm going to the Stock Exchange now to try and sell as many as possible. Please keep working normally, we must give the impression of having everything under control if any clients come to the office.' He nodded a dismissal and strode away.

However, by the end of the day it seemed no-one wanted to buy. Percy examined the balance sheets and saw that things didn't look good. Everyone was trying to sell and cash in their shares. And cash meant gold. Although bank notes and cheques were commonly used for large transactions, coins were necessary to pay salaries and for day to day purchases, and that meant gold sovereigns, silver and copper.

Percy didn't know what to do, but then came to a decision. He sent a telegram to Lily: *'Staying in city for the weekend. Crisis at work. Percy.'*

He went to dinner with Lily's parents on Sunday. After the meal, David asked Percy if he could have a word with him.

'I don't like the look of the way things are going, Percy,' he said.

Percy agreed. 'If you have any outstanding debtors, I'd suggest you try and get paid in cash as soon as possible. I doubt you'll be able to sell any shares at this stage, but withdraw as much cash as you can from the banks.'

David nodded thoughtfully. 'Most of the money I'm owed is pretty secure,' he said, 'but one never knows.'

Percy sighed. 'I'm worried. Tomorrow is settlement day when trades are matched and crossed. It means that the brokers have to make up any surplus or deficit on their books.' He paused. 'As you know, we do that by settling outstanding trades with cash.'

David Bancroft nodded.

Percy continued, 'And if prices go down dramatically a lot of brokers will be bankrupted.' He frowned. 'The European banks are calling in their loans, and some brokers are having to borrow to repay them. Interest rates look like going up. I don't know where it will end.'

As he said the words, he remembered that Lily had said something to that effect, the first time he'd had dinner with her parents.

'I'd better go home; I must be up early in the morning.' He rose and shook his father-in-law's hand.

The next day, share markets around the globe began to close. By the Wednesday of that week the atmosphere in the city was tense; several of the Acceptance Houses or short-term money traders faced insolvency. Questions were raised in Parliament about the crisis. When Austria-Hungary declared war on Serbia that very day, it seemed inevitable that Great Britain would be drawn into the war.

Percy spent the next morning at the bank trying to withdraw cash for the upcoming salaries. It was not only the end of the month, but also the Bank holiday weekend, and they needed more cash than a usual weekend. He also wanted to get cash for himself to pay his monthly bills and have money for the holiday in Dover.

When he reached the counter and presented his list of cash requirements, the bank teller, a balding, sad-looking man, frowned and said, 'Sorry, Mr Hedgecock, I can only give you your normal weekly withdrawal amount in sovereigns. I'll have to give you bank notes for the remainder.'

Taken aback, Percy demanded, 'But I need the coins!'

'Sorry, sir, but you'll have to take the bank notes to the Bank of England to change them for gold coins.'

Percy took the cash and bank notes and put them in his leather carry bag. He went back to work and informed Arthur Symonds, who told him to go straight to the Bank of England and change the bank notes for gold coins.

Percy hastened to Threadneedle Street. When he saw the queue of people going all the way from the Bank of England down the length of Threadneedle Street, he stopped. Stunned, he joined the queue, thinking that there must be at least two hundred people patiently waiting. Two women in front of him turned to him. "Ello luv' one said, 'this is a bit of an 'ow dew do, aint it?'

He nodded.

"Ow do they fink we can pay our girls wiv out coins?' the other said.

'Yes, indeed,' Percy replied and hoped they would turn their attention to the man in front of them. He turned around and saw a queue already forming behind him. He nodded politely at the man behind him and then stayed quiet, pointedly looking to the side.

Eventually it came to the bank closing time, but all those inside the bank doors were allowed to wait and be served. Percy was pleased to find himself one of them.He finally got the gold coins he wanted and went back to work, feeling more and more worried as he handed the bags of coins to Eric Swanton.

'We were getting concerned when you didn't come back,' Swanton said.

Percy told him of the situation at the Bank of England.

'Oh, dear, and we've just heard that several stockbrokers have been bankrupted. Apparently, they had business with overseas customers who've had to default on their loans. Some of them had wanted to make the repayments, but they haven't been allowed to take the gold out of Europe.'

Percy started in disbelief.

'But at least we have the cash to pay our staff, especially with the long weekend coming up,' Swanton continued.

Percy stayed late at work, balancing and reconciling the accounts, worried about where exactly his firm stood. He went home to a late dinner and bed, and after a sleepless night, he got into work early and met with the senior partners. They decided that Arthur Symonds would go to the Exchange as usual and try and sell some of the shares they considered were unlikely to perform but were more marketable.

At 11.30 a.m. Arthur returned to the office and called a meeting: 'The Stock Exchange is closed until further orders,' he announced. 'There was a notice on the door. Apparently, the Press will be notified the day before the House is re-opened, and the notice was signed by the Secretary, Edward Satterthwaite.'

The staff gave a collective gasp at the implications of this order.

'Yes, there were a lot of anxious and annoyed brokers all expecting to do business,' he continued. 'As far as I can gather, the government has ordered it to prevent the collapse of the financial markets, but I think we can still do business privately between clients. Fortunately, most of our business is based on British stocks and bonds.' He tried to smile. 'As it's the Bank Holiday weekend, I think we will now close the office until Tuesday. I'd like to thank you all for your dedication and hope you all have a pleasant long weekend.'

Tom caught up with Percy as the staff walked out. 'What do you make of all this then, Perce?'

'It's unheard of,' Percy replied. 'We shall just have to wait and see. I'm off to Dover now, and I think I can just make an earlier train if I hurry. I hope you enjoy your weekend, Tom.' With a wave he hurried in the direction of the station.

Percy got to Dover to find his sons in a ferment of excitement.

'Papa,' young Piers shouted, 'you must come down to the harbour; the HMS Bulwark is there with HMS Arrogant and all these destroyers!'

Percy smiled. 'We'll look tomorrow, but now I'm just off the train and feeling a bit tired. Where's your mama?'

'Mama has gone to a séance,' George said. 'She took Ena.'

Percy groaned inwardly. *So much for our holiday!* He sighed, guessing that Ena had probably felt she should go with her mother to look after her. He sometimes thought that Lily was so naive that little Ena had much more common sense even at seven years old. She was very protective towards her mother and seemed to mother her brothers, particularly little David.

He didn't raise the subject of the séance with Lily when she returned, but resolved to try and make the weekend and the extra few days of his holiday a happy time, especially as the weather seemed to be fairly settled, even if it was a bit cool.

His mother told him that the Port of Dover had had searchlights installed and that he should let the children stay up late to go down and watch them sweeping backwards and forwards across the harbour entrances. The children were thrilled with the luxury of a late night.

Every day the children wanted to go down to the harbour and watch the ships. On the bank holiday Monday, they watched the 'Princess Clementine' arrive, a paddle steamer with over twelve-hundred people on board happy to have left a Belgian port. Lily nudged Percy. 'Look, there's Lord Kitchener.'

Percy looked to where she discreetly indicated.

'He's here on leave, but I think he must be trying to board a steamer to return to Cairo,' she continued.

Percy looked at her in amazement. 'How do you know all this?'

She made a face. 'It's common knowledge in Dover,' she replied, a bit acerbically. 'You've been so wrapped up in your old stock market that you haven't seen what's under your nose. And we will be hearing more about Lord Kitchener while he's alive.' She gave a shiver and murmured, 'A cold watery death.'

Percy had hoped to be able to relax and enjoy his annual leave with Lily and the children, but the atmosphere in Dover was so tense that he began to think he'd be better off back in London keeping an eye on the banks and the market.

On Monday 3rd August, he read in the evening paper that Germany had declared war on France and invaded neutral Belgium

'I think I should go back to London tomorrow,' he told Lily.

Lily stared at him. 'You're always saying you don't see enough of me, and now you're going to forgo your holiday with us to go back to work!'

Percy saw her point. 'You're right,' he conceded, 'I probably wouldn't be able to do much, anyway.'

The next morning, Tuesday, he went out early to get the morning paper and read with astonishment that the Government had declared an extension of the bank holiday until Friday. There would've been no point in him going back to London.

That night at 11p.m., England declared war on Germany. The Wednesday morning papers carried the grim news. Percy shook his head as he read, dismayed at the news, but when he told Lily, she simply shrugged and said, 'Well, perhaps now you'll relax and not be so agitated; you're like a cat on hot bricks!'

Piers overheard this exchange and said, 'Oh, Papa, there will be battles in the harbour, can we go and watch please?'

Percy spent the rest of the week in Dover trying to relax and put the war out of his mind, but he kept worrying about work, how long the war would last, the children, Lily, his mother ... his mind went around in circles.

Eventually they returned to London. The Stock Exchange remained closed. Percy returned to work, but there wasn't much work to do, just a few private sales. The news of the new one-pound note which the Government had decided to issue caused some consternation; they'd been printed in a hurry and were of very poor quality.

When Tom saw them, he examined a few carefully and then laughed. 'Even forgers would find it difficult to copy these!'

As time passed, people got used to handling notes instead of gold coins, and it appeared that the exodus of gold from the Bank of England had been stopped. The financial crisis which had threatened to engulf the country had been averted. At least, for the time being.

***

In August that year, Leslie received a telegram from the Post Office. He read in bemusement:

In accordance with your wireless licence, Postmaster General requires you to remove at once all your aerial wires and dismantle your apparatus. One of his officers will shortly call upon you.

What next, he thought; do they think I'm a spy? Taking away my main interest and hobby!

***

Lord Kitchener was appointed Secretary of State for war and immediately predicted a long war that would last at least three years. He further announced that the current army was undermanned in the face of a global war and instigated a campaign to enlist men into the forces. All over the country posters appeared with recruitment slogans: 'Your King and Country Need YOU,' featuring pictures of a stern-faced Lord Kitchener pointing a finger.

One morning in late August, Percy got into work to find Tom grinning from ear to ear.

'Perce!' he said, 'I'm going to enlist. They're forming new Pals regiments, and there's a Stock Brokers Battalion; I'm going to join!'

He set off around the office enthusiastically trying to persuade other young men to enlist with him.

'It's Lord Derby's idea,' he told them, 'he thought we'd be more likely to volunteer if we could join up with our pals!'

A lot of the other young men, bored with hanging around the office with little to do, liked the idea.

Percy felt dubious. 'Tom, I think you must be getting on for twenty-seven years old, and you're engaged to be married. What about your fiancée?'

'I didn't think about her,' Tom admitted, his smile slipping somewhat, 'but look at this poster.' He showed Percy yet another poster. 'Anyway, I think she'd prefer me to be defending our country, rather than sitting here waiting for the stock market to re-open.'

Percy flinched. He nodded. 'You have a point.'

'Hey, Perce! I didn't mean you to feel bad! You have a wife and four children, you have responsibilities.'

'I know,' Percy said slowly. 'But I'm a pacifist; I don't think I could kill anyone.'

'You would if anyone tried to harm Mrs Hedgecock or the children,' Tom replied.

Percy nodded again. 'I suppose so.' He didn't like to tell Tom about his weakness of fainting at the sight of blood.

By the end of the week Tom had gone to join 'The Stockbrokers Battalion', along with several more of the staff.

In September, against Percy's wishes, Lily enrolled Piers in a boarding school, the same one that James had attended. James had spoken highly of his time there and Piers had seemed keen to go. Excelling in sport, he soon settled in, and there didn't seem to be the kind of bullying that occurred in many other boarding schools.

It became quiet at work as, one by one, the men left to join up. With scant work to do, Percy grew a little bored. He spoke to his father-in-law about it after one Sunday lunch.

'The news isn't good from the front, but I don't feel I can enlist,' he said.

'By golly, no,' David exclaimed. 'Lily and the children need you at home! Anyway, the war is supposed to be over by Christmas.' He grimaced. 'Young Ernie is talking of joining the Royal Flying Corps.'

Percy rather envied Ernie; the thought of trying to pilot one of the new flying machines had a romantic appeal.

When he told Lily that Ernie had joined the Royal Flying Corps, he could see she had mixed feelings.

'That's so dangerous! But so exciting! I hope he doesn't crash. One of my clients crashed on Salisbury Plain when they were testing a new aircraft.'

The week before Christmas, Tom came into the office, wearing his uniform and looking very smart. The few women still working in the office looked impressed.

'Just came to say Happy Christmas to you all,' he beamed.

'How's it going?' Percy asked.

'Well, not much happening at the moment, just training and moving around. I'm looking forward to seeing some action,' Tom replied.

Everyone was pleased to see him and hear about his training. It relieved the monotony of the office.

The Stock Market reopened on the 4th January 1915, and Percy hoped his life would get back to some kind of normality. With Lily busy with her healings and séances, and Piers away, it was relatively quiet at home. The other children all attended a nearby primary day school.

When the bombing of London started, Percy worried about his family. One Sunday soon after the attacks began, while gathered together at the Bancroft's for lunch, James said he had something to tell them.

'I hope he's not going to enlist,' Melina said quietly to her husband. 'It's bad enough that Ernie has joined the Royal Flying Corps.'

James announced that he and Phoebe were expecting a baby, but only Melina and little Ena seemed to be excited by this news. Talk turned to the bombing.

'I'm trying to persuade Lily to take the children to the country to be safe from these Zeppelin raids,' Percy announced.

The children started clamouring to go to the country.

'Nonsense!' Lily said, 'I'm not running away from the possibility of a few bombs; they won't affect us!'

Percy shook his head. 'My dear, I know my mother in Dover would be happy to have you and the children until this awful war is over.'

Lily snorted. 'Don't be ridiculous! Dover is likely to get more air raids than London! Dover got the first air-raid bomb of the war! No, I'm staying here. People need my contact with their loved ones who have passed. And now with all the war injuries my healing skills are needed more than ever.'

Melina looked at David and raised her eyebrows, as if to say, 'I think I was right, Lily does have the upper hand.'

Her husband simply rolled his eyes and started to say something about Lily and her healing notions, but Melina caught his attention and frowned.

James changed the subject. 'I think conscription might be introduced for single men, Percy, so it's good I'm married now.'

'But as a medical practitioner, wouldn't you be exempt?'

James shrugged. 'Who knows? They need doctors at the front too.'

***

The war dragged on. Lily did extra days healing and individual sittings at Leslie's, leaving Percy to discipline the children and see to their welfare. George joined Piers at boarding school, and they still had Mabel, the original nurse maid who'd come to work for them when Piers was born, but Percy felt she was a bit too soft on the boys. He worried about Ena, since she seemed to be always looking after them and mothering them. He felt it too much for her young shoulders.

One night, just as dawn broke, Lily woke screaming. 'Ernie, oh my God, no, not Ernie!' She sat up in the bed. Alarmed, Percy tried to take her into his arms. 'My darling! What is it?'

'Ernie just came to me and told me his plane had been brought down. He was on a mission over Belgium, bombing the German lines and was shot down!'

Percy tried to comfort her. 'It's just a bad dream.'

In the dim morning light Lily stared at him, her eyes huge in her white face. 'No, no, no, he came to tell me,' she repeated. 'Oh, my little brother!' She burst into wild sobbing.

Percy just held her. He knew better than to try and persuade her it was a nightmare. She seemed to be always right about these things. Look at Lord Kitchener. He'd drowned in the North Sea. 'A cold watery death,' wasn't that what she'd said? He shivered. Too many good men killed in a pointless war. Lily was probably right about Ernie.

He held her until her sobbing ceased, then kissed her forehead and gently rocked her.

'I must go to my parents.'

'Perhaps wait until later,' he suggested. 'They'll be informed soon enough, and if they see you like this, they'll be even more distraught.' Trying to calm her, he asked gently, 'Did Ernie say anything else?'

'Just that he was confused; he thought he saw our Grandfather Bancroft.'

'Please wait until I come home from work,' Percy begged. 'I'll finish early and go with you.' By then confirmation of Lily's dream, or vision—he didn't know what to call it—may have reached the Bancrofts.

She reluctantly agreed.

They arrived at the Bancrofts late that afternoon, and the lack of tears and sad faces made it clear that Lily's parents had not heard any bad news. Percy pressed Lily's hand and tried to indicate that she should say nothing about Ernie.

'Where are the children?' Melina Bancroft asked. 'This is a pleasant surprise; will you stay for dinner?'

'No, no,' Lily said, 'we were in a cab and thought we'd call in and see you.'

David Bancroft frowned at the lame explanation. He looked closely at Lily, noting her pale face and red eyes. He raised his eyebrows and looked at Percy, but stayed silent.

The front door bell rang and, soon after, the maid came in with a telegram. She handed it to David. His face paled when he saw the War Office insignia. He nodded to the waiting maid. 'No answer.'

Before he opened it, he joined his wife on the sofa, then read the fateful words:

'*We regret to inform you that Captain Ernest Bancroft is missing in action, presumed dead.*'

He closed his eyes and put his arms around Melina.

'What is it?' she asked fearfully. 'Is it Ernie?'

David suppressed a sob. He could only nod.

Melina stared into space, transfixed, unable to make a sound.

Lily went to her and tried to put her arms around both her parents. 'Oh, Mama! Papa!' She burst into tears.

Percy didn't know what to do. He'd been very fond of Ernie and had felt sick inside all day at the thought of Lily's words. Then he remembered James. Maybe he'd better try and contact him. It would be hard for the Bancrofts to do it.

He walked to the telephone in the hall and gave the operator James's number. When James came on the line with a cheery, 'Hello,' Percy said, 'James, this is Percy. I'm afraid I have bad news. Lily and I are with your parents. A telegram has just come. Ernie is missing, presumed dead.'

The phone went silent. 'James, are you there?' Percy asked anxiously.

'Yes. Look, I'll finish up with this patient and come straight over.'

Thankful that the Bancrofts would have both James and Lily with them, Percy went back to the drawing room. 'I've just tele-phoned James, he's coming straight over.'

David nodded. 'Thank you, Percy,' he managed to say.

Heavy-hearted, Percy left. Now he must break this awful news to the children.

***

In March 1916, when no more volunteers came forward, conscrip-tion was introduced for single men between the ages of nineteen and forty-one. This still didn't provide enough men to replace the slaughter going on in the conflict, and in May conscription was extended to married men, with just a few exceptions.

Lily's father spoke to Percy. 'I can give you a job in my company and say it's a starred job,' he said, meaning that the job was critical to the war effort and he would be exempt. James was exempt as a doctor, much to his and Melina's relief.

'I can't enlist,' Percy replied. 'I'm absolutely against this war.'

'Well, so are most people,' David said drily, 'but, what do you say about coming and working for me?'

'I'm terribly grateful for your offer, but it would be against my conscience to accept. I'll wait and see what happens with the call-up.'

Two weeks later Percy received a notice to attend the local recruitment office. He was thirty-three. His medical examination was cursory. The doctor saw his glasses, tested his eyesight, then scribbled something on a piece of paper and told Percy to join the queue at the recruitment desk.

When his turn eventually came, he gave the medical report to the enrolling Sergeant who took Percy's details and told him he'd be joining the Army Service Corps.

'Do you know how to drive a motor vehicle?' the Sergeant enquired.

'I'm learning,' Percy replied.

'You'll be signed up for driving a lorry to the front with supplies. Here, take this form and get your pass for the train to the A.S.C depot at Lee. The date and time is on it.'

Percy looked at the pass. It was for the following Friday.

He felt he'd had some kind of reprieve. He wouldn't have to kill anyone or see blood. At least he hoped so. He went back to work and told the two partners who were sympathetic.

'Don't worry, Percy, your job will be waiting for you after the war when you come back,' they told him.

If I come back!

Back home he made a list of all the things he must organise before leaving. When Lily came home he told her the news.

'Oh, Percy! I hope you'll be all right!' She put her arms around him. 'Will it be very dangerous?'

'I don't really know. I think I'll be driving a lorry with ammunition or supplies or something to the front, or driving a bus with soldiers, taking them on and off periods of duty. But, Lily, my dear, we have to talk about finances. When I'm in the army I won't be getting enough to keep this household going. I think I might get something like a pound a week. I don't know about allowances for the children, but I'm worried that you'll not have enough to live on and pay Mrs Burton and Mabel, and also the children's school fees.'

Lily shrugged. 'We'll manage. I'm getting a lot of donations from my clients. I never charge for my services, but I have a donation box, as you know.'

'Yes,' he said. 'I think that will help a lot.' He didn't know how to broach the subject of her bringing the money home and paying the bills.

Next day he swallowed his pride and went to see David Bancroft.

'Sit down, Percy,' David said.

'I've been drafted into the Army Service Corps, and I'm not sure how much I'll be paid, but I think it might be about one pound a week,' Percy said.

'One pound!' David exclaimed. 'That's not enough!'

'I know; I might get extra for Lily and the children, but even so, I don't think it will pay the bills and the children's school fees. I wanted to ask you if you would take over my finances while I'm away and pay the bills and Mrs Burton and the others' wages. Of course, if there isn't enough money in my account and you have to pay out of your own purse then please keep account of the amounts, and I'll pay you back as soon as I'm able.' He gave a big sigh and closed his eyes. He didn't think he could feel any lower.

Opening his eyes, he continued, 'Lily gets money from her sittings and healings, but I can't depend on her to manage the accounts. Even if she does get money, she's so kind and soft hearted that she'd be likely to give it out to the next needy person she sees. She has such a brilliant intellect, but she seems to have no concept of how to budget or manage money.'

David came over and put a hand on his shoulder. 'Percy, dear boy, of course, I'll be more than happy to look after things.' He walked over to the sideboard. 'Pity you don't take a drink, Percy, what you need is a stiff whiskey right now.' He poured himself a tot and sat down.

'It's probably the last thing I need!' Percy said. 'I'll go home and get all the accounts ready and bring them over tomorrow and go through them with you. I'm very grateful to you, Sir.' He got up and shook David's hand.

Early on Friday morning, Percy got up while everyone was asleep and gathered together his personal things. He took out the linen handkerchief which Lily had used to wipe the blood from his face when he'd proposed to her. His landlady had laundered it, but now, as he held it to his face, he fancied he could still smell Lily on it. *Nonsense*, he thought, *Lily never used perfume*. Reluctantly he undid the gold chain with his father's watch from his waistcoat and put them in the drawer. He took Lily's handkerchief, a note book, pen, pencil, penknife, razor, shaving brush and his money wallet, and then said goodbye to David and Ena before they left for school.

'Be good for mama, now, children,' he told them as he hugged them both. 'Tell Piers and George when they come home at mid-term that I said goodbye, and I will write home.'

Ena started to cry. 'Daddy, I don't want you to go to war!'

He hugged her. 'I know darling, but we must make England a safe place for Mama and you children to live in. Now, off you go with Mabel.' He smiled at Mabel as she took the children's hands.

'Goodbye, Sir and stay safe,' she said before leading the children out the door.

Percy walked upstairs to where Lily still slept. He went to their bed and took her in his arms.

She sighed.

'Goodbye, my darling Lily,' he murmured into her ear.

She woke with a start. 'Percy, darling! Are you going already?' She jumped out of bed. 'Oh, my darling, please take care. Remember I love you and so do the children.'

She hastily put on her peignoir and followed him downstairs to the front door. 'Take care, my darling,' she managed to say through her tears.

He eventually tore himself from her arms. 'I'll miss my train if I don't go now. Mustn't be AWOL before I even start.' With one last kiss he left.

Lily went back upstairs and dressed, ready for healings at Leslie's. He would be working, but she'd see him tomorrow at the séance. He would understand her fears for Percy's safety.

***

Leslie enjoyed his research work with the Royal Flying Corps, especially now that the law required that all amateur radio enthusiasts must dismantle their sets. He missed tinkering with his wireless transmitter at home, but now he was getting paid for doing what he loved.

He saw Lily at the weekends for her séances, and she often stopped for a chat after everyone had left. He treasured those moments.

***

Percy got the train to the Army Depot at Lee and was issued with his kit. How would all this gear fit into his kit bag? Uniform, blankets, towels, billy can, knife, fork and spoon, not to mention his few personal things. He took the rifle hesitantly. He wanted to refuse it and say he'd never be able to use it, but the queue behind him pushed him along.

Dearest Lily,

Well, here I am at the training camp in Camberwell. We had to put on the uniforms we were issued with and then pack all our civilian clothes into a bag and label it with our home address. I hope my bag arrives safely.

We had to march to our first billet which was an empty house. I don't think anyone slept. Then next day we were up at 6 a.m. and marched to the Barracks and received our identification discs. My number is DM2/208600. I thought you would think that's a lucky number 2 + 0 + 8 + 6 + 0+ 0 = 16, 1 + 6 = 7

The next day we came here by motor-bus and were assigned our lorries.

I am well, but tired. It's non-stop training, driving lessons & how to service the lorries. Then drill, marching up & down with our rifles. We have to carry rifles, I don't know why. I am not very good at the target practice. But I am enjoying learning about engines.

The food is all right. I've met a man called Harry who is a bank clerk in civilian life. He is married too & has three children, about the same age as ours.

I miss you & the children so much.

My love to you and the children.

Your devoted husband, Percy Hedgecock.

He hoped that Lily would write to him soon.

Eventually everyone was passed as fit for the job. In a convoy they drove their lorries to another camp at Blandford. This took two days, and they had to sleep in their lorries overnight at each stop where they were issued with food.

Dearest Lily,

I hope that all is well at home. I am looking forward to a letter from you.

I was inoculated last week. I think maybe for lock-jaw and typhoid fever. Some of us felt very poorly. Harry was very bad and feverish, but I was all right.

I am so pleased to have Harry for company. All the other men are much younger. We were given something called Bully Beef and Hard Tack to eat. The hard tack is like a rock-hard biscuit. As you know, I have problems with my teeth, so I didn't like to bite it, but then I saw the other men getting tea and soaking their Hard Tack in it. I gave my Bully Beef to Harry. I felt sick just looking at it.

We were in Blandford, then we went to Avonmouth docks. We had to load our lorries with ammunition and stores and then drive them onto a transport ship. There were lots of horses being loaded. I was surprised to see so many. Then we had to march to the railway station and get trains to Southampton. I thought of the time you and I went to Brighton on our honeymoon.

Then we had to board a steamer going to France, with guns and horses. I can't believe how many horses are on the boat. At high tide that night, our steamer was escorted out of the harbour by two torpedo boat destroyers. It was a rough crossing. I felt sorry for the horses. I was lucky and wasn't sea sick, unlike most of the men.

When we got to France, it seemed just like England, except for the signs. We were put into lorries and driven to a camp. We had to wait there for our lorries to arrive. It was good to see mine.

I had better go now.

Your devoted husband, Percy Hedgecock.

Percy felt quite pleased to see his lorry; it was like an old friend by now. They were each issued with emergency rations, bandages and, Percy was alarmed to see, ammunition. For several days they drove in a convoy, sleeping in barns at night. The first night, Percy felt something large run over his blanket, on hearing squeaking, he froze. Sleep was impossible after that.

They reached the railhead, loaded up the lorries with ammunition and were directed to a battery.

Percy arrived at the battery. The noise of bursting shells and gun fire was overwhelming. It seemed like organised chaos. Before he had a chance to look around, he was told to help unload his lorry and reload with empty shells. Then to call to the first aid post and bring back wounded soldiers. He and his co-driver helped to load the men on stretchers into the back of his lorry. When they arrived at the Casualty Clearing station, he helped carry the injured men into the camp. It was only afterwards that he realised that he had seen blood and not fainted.

He felt permanently tired from the non-stop routine of maintaining and cleaning his lorry, guard patrol, collecting and delivering ammunition to the batteries, returning with empty shells for shipment back to England for recycling, and the transport of the wounded. Often this had to be done under cover of darkness. At last he had a moment to write to Lily.

Dearest Lily,

It's been a while since I was able to write. We are kept going day after day. Well, day & night, really, as the enemy is constantly shelling our supply routes. During the day we are collecting the supplies & cleaning & maintaining our lorries, & then at night we take the supplies to the batteries.

Batteries are where the artillery are; I think there are about 5 officers & perhaps 200 gunners in a battery. We have to take food, water and ammunition and replacement clothes to the front. And sometimes we have to bring back the wounded when there are no ambulances available.

I'm not supposed to say where we are, but it's somewhere in north east France.

There are a lot of Australians fighting here.

It's hard work, but not as hard as for the men in the trenches.

I hope you and the children are well; I miss you all so much.

Your ever loving and devoted husband

Percy Hedgecock, September 1916

He'd been in France for several weeks before he received a letter from home. All the other drivers had received letters except him and he'd begun to worry. He ripped open the envelope.

Dear Daddy

I hope you are safe. This is Ena, your daughter, writing.

We miss you so much Daddy. I hope it is not too horrible where you are.

Mummy is going to write soon.

She took David and me to Mr. Carter's yesterday when she was doing a healing, because Mabel has left to work in a munitions factory, she said we don't need a nanny any more. And Mrs Burton had to go out to visit her sick sister.

Mr. Carter showed us his workshop and things he was doing. It was very interesting. David was very good, he didn't fiddle with any of the things.

Mr Carter gave me a parcel. He said to give it to Grandfather Bancroft the next time I saw him. I hope that is all right, Daddy?

I am going to put this in an envelope and give to Mrs Burton to send to you. I think Mummy might write something too, but if she forgets, it's because she is very busy. I know she loves you, Daddy.

From your devoted daughter,

Ena Hedgecock.

Percy sat looking at his letter for some minutes, then glanced across at Harry, who was reading his letter with a smile on his face.

'Good news, Harry?' Percy asked.

Harry looked up. 'A letter from my wife. Everything seems to be going all right. The baby is teething and keeping her awake at night. The eldest, Donald, has just started school this September and he seems to be enjoying it. Don't think that will last! And little Emily is starting to talk.' He smiled. 'How about you? Everything good at home?'

'Yes, thanks,' Percy replied. He and Harry had become good pals. Percy felt grateful to have someone his own age and with a similar background that he could talk to. Harry adored his wife, too, and was always saying how wonderful she was. She could cook and sew and was a great mother.

Unlike Lily, Percy thought. And then he berated himself for being disloyal. Lily was special; she had unique gifts and felt she had to use them. How could he ever explain Lily to anyone? Not that he would ever dream of doing so.

He sat down to write to Ena.

My darling daughter, Ena

I was so very happy to get your letter.

Yes, please give the parcel to Grandfather Bancroft. He will know about it.

We are all doing our best here to keep the world safe from bullies.

I saw something last month on my way here that made me think of you. It was a red London bus converted to a pigeon loft! The pigeons carry messages in little tins tied to their legs. When they get back to their home on the bus they land on a wire that rings a bell and someone goes and gets the message.

I am pleased Mr Carter showed you his workshop. He is very clever and working on lots of things to help the war effort. I think he would like to know about the pigeons here. If you go to his house again. Please give him my regards.

I must go now and clean my lorry. We have to do it every day, and check it out.

Please give Mummy a big kiss from me and my love to the boys. And a big kiss to you.

Your loving father,

Percy Hedgecock. October 1916

***

One night that following month, Percy's unit was returning from the front with empty shells, several gunners who were due a spell off duty, and also some wounded men, when enemy shells bombarded them. The lorry in front of Percy got a direct hit, the explosion nearly blinding him. He stopped, his heart in his mouth. It was Harry's lorry.

Percy just made out the damage in the gloom of the night. Together with the other drivers, he picked his way over to help the wounded men as best as he could. They carried them to the lorries. Then he saw that the cab of Harry's lorry had been torn apart and Harry blown sideways along the cab.

'Harry!' He bent over Harry's inert body and gently turned him over. When he saw his mutilated face, realisation dawned. He took off his greatcoat and spread it on the ground, then gently dragged Harry out, laid him on his coat and wrapped his body in it. Then he went behind the convoy and vomited. Someone came and helped lift the body into the back of Percy's lorry.

Percy never truly recovered from the sight of Harry's shattered body and the three gunners who were also killed. He kept thinking of Harry's joy when he'd received a letter from home, and his pride in his young family. The next night he realised that if they'd been going slightly faster, it would've been his lorry that would've been hit. He couldn't stop picturing Harry's family, now left fatherless. Those little children who would never see their father again. Overcome with grief, he lay sleepless, trying to muffle the sound of his crying.

Feelings of despair and anguish bogged him down, and it was Christmas before he had the will to write home again. He wondered if perhaps he should write to Harry's wife; he had the address. But he wouldn't know what to say. Perhaps Lily might be able to help Harry's wife, but she never sought out people; they heard about her and came to her. With a feeling of hopelessness, he started a letter to Lily.

Dearest Lily,

It will soon be Christmas and I shall miss not being at home with you all.

I expect you will be going to your parents for Christmas dinner.

I think there may be a special Christmas dinner planned for us here, but the fighting goes on in the trenches.

I hope you are all keeping well.

My love to you & the children.

Your devoted husband, Percy Hedgecock. December 1916

He chose not to write about Harry, thinking it might distress Lily since she was under the impression that as a driver he would be safe. He thought she imagined him driving from the railhead to the battery with ammunition and back again. He didn't want to worry her.

CHAPTER 7

L ily felt restless. She loved her healing work and séances, and thought it was what she was born to do, but she missed Percy much more than she'd thought she would. She missed their love making, the feeling of security and contentment that she felt when wrapped in his arms.

Do other wives of men at the war feel the same? Or am I a really an unwise bride like Mrs. Smythers wrote. How do other women manage?

She knew of no one she could ask. She only met women who came for healing or séances and had no close female friends with whom to exchange confidences.

At least I have Leslie. Where would I be without dear Leslie?

She felt so close to him that he seemed like a dear brother. Not like James. She loved James, but she couldn't talk to him. He didn't understand spiritualism or healing. He just scoffed at her and said that the people she healed would have got better anyway, and that the spirit messages are just pandering to what people want to hear. And Mama?

No, she wouldn't understand how I feel. She has Papa to turn to whenever she has these feelings.

Lily sighed.

At least I have my work to occupy my days.

***

Lily's children enchanted Leslie. She brought the youngest, David, and the daughter, Ena, quite often. The other two boys remained at boarding school, and Lily didn't bring them when they came home for the holidays. She said they were much too boisterous. But David and Ena seemed interested in his projects. Ena was the image of her mother. Such a sweet child, he thought, with the same lovely mischievous smile and sparkling eyes as Lily.

One Sunday, while in his workshop after the séance, he asked her if she saw her Grandfather Bancroft very often, and when she said, 'Yes', he handed her a parcel. 'Would you give that to your Grandpapa please?'

She nodded. 'Yes, of course.'

David looked up at Leslie. 'Do you go out to work?'

Ena answered for him. 'Daddy wrote that Mr. Carter is working on important things to help us win the war.'

'Is that why you're not fighting in the war?' David asked.

Ena blushed for him. 'Hush, Davey,' she admonished. 'Mr Carter is doing important things.'

Leslie laughed. 'Well, I've been working with a lot of other people to see if we can put wireless radios into aircraft. That will be very important for the airmen.'

David's eyes lit up with interest. 'And can you? How does it work?'

'Well, it's all secret at the moment.' Leslie smiled. 'Come, let's see if your mama is ready for a cup of tea before you go home.'

After they'd gone Leslie sat down in front of the fire. He loved that Lily came to his place for her healings and séances. At first, he'd been worried that it would awaken all the yearning love he felt for her. Well, it had. But it was worth it just to see her again, just to be near her. He felt as if she had a special aura which encompassed him with love when in her presence. *Stupid idiot, Leslie,* he said to himself. But she did seem to turn to him these days if something worried her. Not that she worried much about anything, he thought with a smile, only about the boys. With no father at home she found them a bit uncontrollable when they came home for school holidays. He couldn't really advise her, though. As the only child of elderly and reclusive parents, he hadn't had close friends his age, and anyway, he'd always been busy with his experiments and inventions. He knew that some people thought of him as a bit of a nutty inventor.

Apart from Lily, John Watts was his only real friend, and he'd been so involved with his job with wireless research that he hadn't seen John for some time. He should get in touch with him again.

He went back to thinking about Lily. Perhaps it helped her just to talk about things. He'd managed to persuade her to stay for a cup of tea after her healing sessions. They sat in the parlour, in front of the fire when it was cold or in the garden if it was sunny. He drifted into a pleasant reverie of Lily being permanently beside him.

Eventually he roused himself and went to heat up his dinner.

The following morning at the Royal Flying Corps, Leslie was engrossed in trying out a Short-Wave Tuner when one of the technicians came over to him.

'Heard about John Watts?' he asked.

Leslie looked up, frowning at the past tense. 'Why?'

'Well, he was training a young pilot, and the aircraft went into a tail spin. Pilot was killed but Watts survived. His legs are pretty mashed up, apparently. Poor bugger.'

Leslie paled. 'Where is he? Which hospital? I must go and see him.'

The technician didn't know, but as soon as his day's work finished, Leslie went to the office and tried to find out.

***

War-wounded soldiers returned from the front filled the hospital. Nurses and orderlies dashed everywhere, and no one stopped him, so Leslie wandered around looking at the list of names on ward doors until he eventually found John Watts. He went in, and a young nurse came over to him.

'Can I help you?'

'Yes, please.' Leslie gave his best smile. 'I'm looking for a John Watts.'

'He's in bed four.' She indicated a bed surrounded by curtains. 'But the doctor and Matron are with him at the moment; you'd better wait outside.' She hurried off to attend to another patient.

'I'll just wait near his bed,' Leslie replied to her retreating back.

He heard a man's voice asking questions and John's gruff replies. Through a gap in the curtains he could just see John's bruised face and bandaged head.

'What happened?' John asked.

'Your plane came down,' said a man's voice—probably the doctor. 'You've been in a coma for the past few days.'

'My aircraft? The BE2C?'

'It crashed,' the doctor said bluntly.

'Oh, God, what happened?' John said. 'It was a young pilot, Reggie something. We were doing target practice on Salisbury Plain ...'

'Well, I'm sorry to tell you that the pilot died, and you are lucky to be alive.'

A groan came from John. 'Young Reggie? Gone? Oh my God.' He fell silent, then: 'My legs? I can't move them!'

'We managed to save both your legs, but I'm sorry to tell you that that you won't be able to walk again, however the burns are healing nicely.'

John turned his head to the side. The nurse hurriedly put a kidney bowl under his chin and wiped the tears from his cheeks as John vomited.

The doctor pulled back the curtains, nearly falling over Leslie who quickly dodged behind the curtain nearest the wall. The doctor frowned at him as he moved off, saying over his shoulder to John, 'You're strong and healthy, you'll soon make a good re-covery.'

The Matron followed him, not noticing Leslie.

As soon as she'd disappeared, Leslie came to the bedside. 'Wattie, old chap, how are you?'

'Leslie!' John managed to splutter through the tears and vomit.

'Steady on, old chap,' Leslie said. 'I know you're in a lot of pain, just wanted to say, I'm here if you need me.'

John's face was white with shock. He looked at Leslie. 'It's coming back to me. We'd been doing a final training session, Reggie in the back piloting, and I was in the cockpit in front. I'd been throwing bags of flour over the side for target practise as Reggie flew over the targets.'

He started to retch. Leslie moved the kidney basin under John's chin.

'What happened? What did I do wrong?' His anguish showed in John's face.

'Nothing, old boy; pilot error,' Leslie said gently. 'You were thrown clear, but the fuel tank behind Reggie exploded ... try and rest now. I'll come back again tomorrow.'

On his way out, the nurse said, 'Better wait a few days before you come again.'

'Thank you,' he said. 'John is one of the best.'

The nurse nodded. 'He's a good patient.'

'Yes, I'm sure he is.' Leslie paused. 'I guessed he would blame himself. Had to see him and reassure him.'

He went home with a heavy heart.

***

The following weekend Leslie went back to the hospital and found John sitting up in bed with cradles over his legs.

'Hello, Leslie; good of you to come and visit.'

'Great to see you sitting up.' Leslie took John's unbandaged hand.

'Yes; it's the first time.'

'Can you bend your legs?'

'Um, no. Not yet. But I will,' John said in a determined voice.

'How long will you be here?' Leslie asked.

'Don't know; depends how I go.'

'With this rotten war, it's going to be hard to get into a convalescent place. You know, if you need somewhere to go until you're fit again, you're very welcome to come and dig in with me.'

'I won't need a convalescent home,' John growled, 'but thanks for your offer; that's really decent of you, old chap ... What are you up to these days?' he added.

'Same place,' Leslie replied with enthusiasm. 'But I'm working on a new project at home. Looking forward to showing it to you.'

They talked about wireless radio for a bit and then Leslie noticed that John was looking pale. He realised that talking was still a big effort for him. 'Better go, old chap,' he said patting John's shoulder.

John closed his eyes. Everything, even talking, was such an effort.

A nurse appeared and said, 'Mr Watts, I think we'll lie you down now; you've done well for your first time sitting up.'

They moved his pillows so he was lying down, then gave him more pain killers. Grateful to be lying down again, he was just drifting off into a restless sleep when he heard a familiar voice.

'John!'

Oh, dear God. He groaned. It was Victoria. He didn't feel up to facing her. She lived next door to his parents. Ten years younger, she'd been a nuisance, always pestering him and her brother to let her join them in the back shed where they built models when they were young. He opened his eyes.

'Hello, Vickie, good of you to come.'

'I had to come, as soon as I heard you were able to receive visitors,' she said.

John turned his head away from her and closed his eyes. He hadn't seen her since his last visit home over a year before. 'I was sorry to hear about your father,' he said. 'It must be hard for you now.'

'Yes.' She sighed. 'I miss him terribly, but he's out of pain now. Your parents have been a great comfort to me.'

'Good,' was all he managed to say, hoping she'd go away and leave him to sleep.

She paused, then said hesitantly, 'John, when my father was dying, his last words to me were that he could die peacefully knowing that you and I were going to be married.'

John turned his head in shock, speechless.

Vickie saw the look on his face. 'Did you tell him that?' She looked at him expectantly.

John remained silent, desperately trying to remember what her father had said the last time he'd been on leave and had called to see the dying man. He vaguely recalled Vickie's father asking him to look after her, now that her brother had been killed, she had no-one. Vickie's mother had died when she was young. What on earth was she on about—marriage? The pain killers had made him woozy; he couldn't think straight.

'Well,' he said eventually, 'I think he asked me to take care of you, but ...' Before he could continue, her brow cleared.

'Oh, that's wonderful!' She smiled. 'John, darling you have made me very happy.'

'But ... but,' he stammered, paused then mumbled, 'the doctors said I won't be able to walk again.'

Oh!' Vickie said, taken aback.

'Vickie, I'm a cripple; I couldn't possibly expect you to be tied down with me.'

'I wouldn't be tied down; it wouldn't be a burden,' she replied. 'It's so like you to think of me first, but I know we'll be very happy together. I can think of nothing I would like better.'

He didn't have the energy to find the words to tell her that he didn't return her feelings. *Bloody hell.*

She got up to leave. 'You're tired, darling John. I'll let you rest. We can talk about wedding plans the next time I come.' She bent and gave him a kiss on his forehead, then turned and went out with a little wave.

He felt confused and alarmed. Had he agreed to marry her? He couldn't recall exactly what he'd said, but she seemed to assume they would get married. The pain in his head felt worse now.

His anxious parents also came to visit him a few days later.

Thankful to find him alive and conscious, his mother fussed around him. 'John, my dear, how good it is to see you, I hope the pain is not too severe?'

He reassured them that he was coping.

'And, my dear boy! Vickie told us the good news!' They both sat looking at him with expectant smiles. When he looked blankly at them, his mother said impatiently, 'About the wedding!'

He smiled weakly and tried to explain: 'Mother, Father, it's not like it seems; I really didn't ask Vickie to marry me ...' Their expressions changed to bewilderment. 'She seemed to think I'd told her father that I'd marry her, but all I did was reassure him that I'd take care of her.'

His parents looked at each other.

'Don't you want to marry her, John?' his father asked.

'I don't want to marry anyone. I'm a cripple. The doctors say I won't walk again!'

His mother's face clouded. 'Oh, my dear boy. That is bad news. How will you be able to work and support Vickie?'

His father studied him. 'It's a bad business, Son,' he said eventually.

John grimaced. *Why does my father excel in stating the bloody obvious!*

'Well, I think it's a wonderful thing what Vickie is doing,' his mother said brightly, 'to be happy to marry you even if you are crippled. She's a lovely girl; she's been like a daughter to me, you know.'

'Yes!' John exclaimed. 'Exactly! It would be like marrying my sister!'

'Oh,' his mother said. 'I hadn't thought of that ... but she isn't, so it will be all right in the eyes of the church! Anyway, we can go into details later, and when you're ready to be discharged from hospital, you must come home, and Vickie and I can nurse you!'

Bloody hell! He kept thinking over and over to himself. *Over my dead body. That's all I need, Mother and Vickie fussing over me and treating me like a baby.* With relief, he suddenly thought of Leslie's offer.

'I've already made arrangements,' he said. 'You remember me talking about Leslie Carter? I don't know if you ever met him? Well, I'm going to stay with him for a bit; it's closer to the hospital for treatment.'

'Oh,' his mother said, clearly disappointed. 'Well, I suppose that makes sense. It's not easy getting up and down to Kent.'

His father looked at him. 'I think we'd better go. You look a bit tired, all this talk of marriage has exhausted you.'

'I'm not going to get married!' he said, but his mother wasn't listening.

'There, there, dear, you'll feel better after a nice sleep, and then you'll see what a good idea this marriage is.' She patted his hand.

His father sighed. 'Better give in, Son,' he said. 'Once these women get an idea in their heads there's no stopping them.' He looked after his departing wife and continued vaguely, 'It won't be so bad. You get used to it.' He gave his son a nod, then wandered out after his wife.

John felt angry and impotent. Trapped in bed and unable to move without the help of nurses. *Bugger this. As soon as Leslie comes again, I'll ask him if his offer still stands and get out of here.*

A week later Leslie returned.

'Leslie,' John said, with a grin. 'It's so good to see you!'

'And good to see you, old boy! Especially out of bed.'

'Yes, they got me up two days ago. I'm on the mend apparently.' He held up a scarred hand. 'Look, no bandages!'

'That's the stuff,' Leslie replied. 'So, when will you be discharged?'

'Well, actually, they're sending me to another hospital, more a convalescent home, in Norwood. It looks like it'll be a while yet before I can be discharged. Apparently, I have to be able to get around on crutches first.'

'Ah!' Leslie smiled. 'Well, once they have you there, perhaps I'll be able to get you to my place. Norwood isn't far from me. I have it all worked out.'

John grinned. 'You're a pal, Leslie, but I can't impose on you until I've mastered getting around on crutches.'

'We'll see,' Leslie replied, then changed the subject.

When Leslie was about to leave, he said, 'So what's the address of this place where you'll be going?'

'Princess something. I'm not sure.'

'I'll ask on the way out. Good to see you on the mend, old boy!'

'Thanks, Leslie; you're a tonic!'

***

Three weeks later Leslie managed to find the time to visit John in the convalescent home. He looked around the bright and airy building. It seemed like a nice place.

'How are you going, Wattie?' he asked his friend when he found him on the veranda.

John grinned. 'All the better for seeing you, Leslie!'

They chatted for a bit, and then Leslie announced, 'Right then. I think it's time for you to come and dig in with me.'

John frowned. 'It's too early, Leslie. Much as I'd like to, and try as I might, I still can't get these crutches to do what I want.'

'I think it would be good for you to come on the weekend, so put all the discharge stuff in place, and I'll fetch you on Saturday afternoon.'

John stared at him. 'That's impossible. How will I get out of here? I can only manage about three paces with these crutches.'

Leslie smiled again. 'I have a plan. Just organise it from your end.' He stood. 'All right. See you on Saturday afternoon. Have your bag packed!' And with a wave he was gone.

Bemused, John shook his head in disbelief. *But what have I got to lose?* He rang his bell to call the nurse.

***

Leslie introduced the burly man to John. 'This is Mr Wilson. Mrs Wilson, his wife, 'does' for me.'

Mr Wilson gave John a gap-toothed smile. 'How dew do, guv.' He held out his hand, then saw John's hand and just waved at it.

'So, are you ready?' Leslie looked at him. 'All packed? Can't delay; I have a Hackney cab waiting for us.'

Puzzled, John frowned.

A nurse came over to him. 'All ready, Mr Watts? I have your discharge papers here. Mr Carter assures us he will take care of you and bring you back for a check-up in six weeks.' She handed the folder to Leslie.

Before he knew what was happening, a hospital orderly and Mr Wilson had put a hand under each of John's armpits and carried him outside to the waiting cab. They installed him in the back. Leslie appeared, carrying John's bag, the folder and crutches.

'I feel like I've been kidnapped!' John said, a bit dazed.

Leslie and Mr Wilson bade goodbye to the nurse and the hospital orderly, then got in the carriage and sat facing John.

'All under control,' Leslie said with a triumphant grin on his face. Mr Wilson also looked pleased.

'That wuz easy, Guv,' he said to Leslie.

Twenty minutes later the cab drew up outside a modest terraced house.

With the help of his crutches, Mr Wilson and Leslie, John managed to get up the steps to the front door. Mrs Wilson must have been watching out for them because the door opened as they approached. She stood back and tut tutted as John came in. He nodded in her direction.

'Through here, Sir. The parlour is all prepared for you.'

Two big armchairs, various small tables, a bookcase and a writing bureau furnished the large room. Though a bit gloomy with its heavy brocade curtains, the fireplace and a bed against one wall made it seem cosy.

Leslie frowned as he put John's bag near the bed. 'I haven't changed the room since my parents passed. Well, apart from moving a bed in here.'

'It's perfect,' John said as he looked around.

Mr Wilson touched his forehead and looked at Leslie. 'Goodbye then, Sir.'

'Thank you, Mr Wilson, you've been a great help. I'll see you tomorrow.'

'I'll bring round some dinner for you later,' Mrs Wilson said as the couple went out.

Leslie looked at John. 'I expect you'd like to rest for a bit after all that excitement, and then I'll show you around.'

John smiled. 'Can't thank you enough, old boy.'

'But first I want to show you what I've rigged up!' Leslie's face lit up with anticipation. He disappeared and then came back a few minutes later pushing a dining-room chair with arms.

'Look! I've put wheels on the legs so you'll be able to sit in and push yourself around with these sticks.' He showed John two rubber tipped walking sticks. 'Look, I'll demonstrate.'

He sat in the chair and, using the walking sticks, pushed the chair around.

John burst out laughing. 'Now I see why you were so anxious for me to come and stay! You wanted to test your new invention on me!'

Leslie gave a sheepish grin as he glided around the room and then out into the hall.

'It's perfect, old boy!' John exclaimed. 'All right, let me have a go.'

Leslie brought the chair back and helped John into it. 'I think you'll have to steady it with the walking sticks when you try and get in it,' he said.

John beamed. 'This is wonderful, Leslie. All right, show me the rest of the house.'

Leslie showed him the dining room across the hall and pointed out the staircase leading up to the bedrooms. The breakfast room and kitchen sat behind the staircase.

'Off the kitchen is the scullery and then a toilet.' Leslie opened the door to show John. 'And look, I've put a bell here in case you get into difficulties.' He indicated a ship's brass bell with a wooden handle.

John shook his head and then smiled. 'You've thought of every-thing!'

They returned to the parlour, and Leslie turned to him. 'Oh, and I forgot to mention that a Mrs Hedgecock comes to do healings here on Wednesdays and Fridays. I'll be at work. I get an early train, but Mrs Wilson will be here.'

John grinned. 'Oh, you and your hocus pocus spirits!' he said. Suddenly things seemed brighter.

***

Next morning, Leslie came into John's room with a breakfast tray and sat down beside him. 'I've just made tea and toast. I'm no cook! I've asked Mrs Wilson to get some lunch for you before she leaves. It's plain food, but good enough for me.'

John smiled. 'This is luxury compared to the hospital food. Thank you.'

'I hope you slept well?'

John nodded. 'Yes, very well, thank you.'

'Remember I mentioned Lily Hedgecock, who comes here to do healing and séances?' Leslie said through a mouthful of toast and marmalade. 'Well, I think you might benefit from her healing sessions.'

John snorted. 'Leslie, old chap, don't try and get me onto your spiritualist larks, please! You know I have no time for it. Any healing to be done I'll do it my way.'

'As you wish.' As Leslie spoke, the newly installed telephone rang. He went out into the hall to answer it.

John heard him talking. 'Yes, indeed, he is here, and who may I say is calling? Victoria? Yes, he's all settled in ... of course, you are most welcome to come up to London and see him ... any time ... it's hard? Of course, with the wartime restrictions on travel ... yes, yes, I understand. Would you like to speak to him? I'll have to get him into the wheelchair and bring him to the telephone ... You don't want to put him to any trouble? Of course, I understand ... righty ho; I'll pass on your message ... and love? Of course. Bye, bye then ...'

Leslie returned to John's room. 'That was a lady called Victoria,' he said, rather unnecessarily.

'Yes, I gathered that.'

'She sent her love. She would get the train up to see you but it's a bit hard at the moment. A lot of the London buses have been sent to France to help the war effort, so transport is a problem.' He raised his eyebrows. 'So what's going on? Sending her love? I didn't know you had a lady friend.'

John sighed. 'She lives next door to my parents. I told them I was coming to stay with you. I gave them your telephone number. Vickie and I grew up together. Her brother, Paddy was my best friend. Killed at the battle of Neuve Chapelle.' He paused and frowned. 'Now she seems to think I told her father I would marry her. I tried to tell her it was all a misunderstanding, but she didn't give me a chance! Caught me at a weak moment when I was a bit sedated from the pain killers. Now my parents think it's a fait accompli.'

'Oh dear. That's a turn up for the books. But she doesn't sound such a bad egg you know; could be worse.'

'Thanks, Leslie.' John screwed up his mouth. 'The thing is I just don't want to get married, and certainly not to Vickie. She's ten years younger than me; I haven't seen her in years and we have nothing in common. The last time I was home on leave her father was dying and asked me to look after her. I said I would, thinking he just meant to keep an eye on her.'

The sound of the front door bell interrupted their conversation.

'Oh, goodness, how the time flies!' Leslie exclaimed. 'That must be Lily and her clients. Please excuse me while I say hello, and then I'm off. I've missed my usual early train. Can't be helped! Special occasion! Mrs Wilson is usually here with Lily when I'm out.'

He went out, leaving the door ajar. From the bed, John saw a tiny, auburn-haired woman talking to Leslie, who, after the exchange of greetings, said, 'Come and meet my friend.' He brought her to the door.

'John, let me introduce you to Mrs Hedgecock,' he said.

John looked at Lily, suddenly breathless. She held out her hand. He took it gingerly in his damaged one. 'John Watts.'

'How do you do, Mr Watts.' She stood there with her hand in his. Neither knew what to say until Leslie coughed discreetly.

'I was telling John that he should have a healing session with you, Lily,' he said.

Lily looked at John. He took a deep breath. 'What a good idea.' The words just seemed to come out of his mouth. He smiled at her, and they arranged that Lily would give John a healing session two days later.

He watched her swing around and disappear into the room she used for healing. People started to arrive. They sat on chairs in the hall, waiting patiently to see Lily. John couldn't get her out of his mind.

When Leslie left, closing the door behind him, John pulled back the bed covers and looked at the ugly sight of his mutilated and burnt leg muscles. The left one, even worse than the right, had hardly any flesh left. His knee joints seemed to jut out of nothing. He practised trying to bend his knees, but the excruciating pain stopped him. He was determined not to give in, however. How could he possibly show his legs to Mrs Hedgecock? His heart sank, and remorse overcame him. At least he was alive. Not like poor Reggie.

***

Lily went straight home after her healing sessions that day. Sometimes if Leslie came home early they had a cup of tea together and talked about any interesting cases she'd helped, or Leslie told her about things at his work—not the secret stuff obviously. But today she felt strange, her body tingling. She'd felt an instant attraction to John Watts. Perhaps she shouldn't give him a healing, after all. Maybe refer him to another healer she knew. But she couldn't go back on her word. And she did want to see him again.

***

The morning of John's healing appointment with Lily, he managed to get into the wheelchair with Leslie's help before Leslie left for work. He felt such a mixture of emotions that he thought of cancelling his appointment.

Mrs Wilson appeared and, with a cheery, 'Hello,' wheeled him into Lily.

Lily sat at the dining room table. She stood as he entered. John found it hard not being able to stand in the presence of a woman. The habit was ingrained in him.

'Hello, John.' She raised her eyebrows. 'If I may, can I call you John?'

He nodded.

'And please call me Lily.'

He swallowed. He couldn't take his eyes off her. He indicated his legs and mumbled something about burns.

She smiled. 'I don't need to see your injuries, John. Now, there's no need to be apprehensive. Just sit back and try and relax.' She came over and stood beside him.

He watched as she positioned her outspread hands, with palms facing downwards, just over his legs without touching them. Then she closed her eyes. John felt a strange warmth in his legs. Dizziness overcame him and his eyes closed. His whole body relaxed, but he was conscious of his heart beat, and his pulse seemed to speed up. He wasn't sure how long she remained with her hands there. When he half opened his eyes, he saw that they'd moved up his body and hovered over his lower arms and hands. He suddenly felt overwhelmingly tired. He closed his eyes again, and was just drifting into sleep when a gentle voice pierced his consciousness:

'John, how are you feeling?'

He opened his eyes.

Lily made sweeping motions with her hands from his head to his toes, then she flicked her wrists before walking over to a bowl of water on the sideboard to wash her hands.

'I'm not sure,' he replied, 'but I feel so very tired.'

She dried her hands and walked back to him. 'Yes, that's quite normal.' She smiled again, a smile that lit up those amazing eyes. 'I'll call Mrs Wilson to take you back to your room.'

She disappeared out the door and returned with Mrs Wilson, who said briskly, 'Come along, Mr Watts, we'll get you back into bed for a rest.'

John didn't even murmur a protest, but allowed himself to be pushed to his room. When he got himself seated on the bed and Mrs Wilson went to lift his legs up and onto the bed, he was amazed to find that he was able to bend his knees a little without as much pain as before.

'Thank you, Mrs Wilson,' he said as he drifted off into a deep sleep, the best sleep he'd had in several months.

At their dinner that night, at the kitchen table where it was easier for his chair to fit, John looked thoughtfully at Leslie. 'Do you happen to have two more walking sticks?'

Leslie's eyebrows rose. 'Is there something wrong with the ones you're using to propel your wheeled chair?'

'No, they're fine, but I have an idea. I'll need two more.' John grinned.

Leslie's eyes lit up. 'I'll buy some tomorrow.' He laughed. 'We're like two school boys,' he said. 'Tell me what you have in mind; I'll get a pencil and paper and you can sketch out a design.'

Next evening in Leslie's workshop they came up with a prototype: pincers attached to the end of each walking stick and a metal rod going up to the handle with a levered hinge.

'Now to the test bed.' John smiled, happy to be busy again after so long. He lay on the bed, and Leslie lifted his legs onto the bed and removed his slippers. 'Now pass me my trousers from my bag.'

John took the trousers and attached a pincer to each side of the waistband. Then he extended the walking sticks so he could wriggle his feet into the trousers. Gradually he manoeuvred the trousers up his legs until he was able to reach the waistband with his hands. It was a tense moment.

'One problem,' Leslie remarked, hiding a smile.

'What!'

'The fly is facing the wrong way...'

They both laughed, easing the tension.

John rested his elbows on the bed and managed to lift his hips and wriggle into the trousers. He took a deep breath; it'd been an effort. 'Well, at least I'll be able to get myself dressed now. I'm sick of this dressing gown!'

'I would've been happy to help you. You're just too bloody independent,' Leslie replied.

The two men looked at each other and grinned.

***

Lily felt as if a magnet was drawing her towards John. She should stop the healings and refer him to another healer. *He'll soon be well and go out of my life. I don't need to stop seeing him. I'll keep our relationship on a professional basis.* But she knew John was attracted to her and that thought pleased her. *Stop it!* She told herself. *Think of Percy and what he's going through!*

***

Every few days, John had a healing session with Lily, and after a month he could bend his knees without pain. She usually left him until the last of her clients, as most of them had taken time off work to see her. Leslie put some of the dining room chairs in the hall for them to sit on while waiting.

'Leslie,' John said one evening, 'I've been thinking about making a splint that will allow me to stand up again; let me show you my design and see if you can improve on it.'

The two men spent several evenings making a wooden splint with wires and supports. Now that John had more movement in his knees, he thought the next step in his recovery would be to stand up out of the wheelchair. He showed Lily the apparatus one morning after a healing session.

She laughed. 'Well, it looks impressive. Well done.'

Pleased by her approval, John felt more optimistic than he had since the accident.

'Let me demonstrate.' He bent over and strapped the supports to his legs, then wriggled out of the wheelchair and tried to stand. He let go of the wheelchair and crashed flat on his face onto the floor.

'Oh, dear, I think you were not supposed to try those callipers without Leslie,' Lily said with a small smile. 'I'll call Mrs Wilson to help you up.'

Together she and Mrs Wilson managed to get him up and back into the wheelchair. Only his pride was bruised. He smiled at them both. 'Thanks; sorry about that. I think I need to make a few modifications to my design.'

John couldn't believe how much his legs had improved. He had to admit that Lily had some kind of healing gift. After every session with her, the pain had lessened and he'd regained more movement. Also, astonishingly, it seemed some of his leg muscles had started to regenerate.

By the time he'd been with Leslie for three months, and with the help of his walking contraption, he managed to walk the length of his room. Victoria, who'd been telephoning him every week or so, decided it was time to pay him a visit.

'Oh, dear man. Look at you,' she exclaimed when she saw him get up from his chair to greet her. 'You're standing up.' With a few strides she went over and took his arm.

He sat down again. 'Getting there.'

Vickie's expression dropped, seemingly disappointed. 'So good to see you're on your feet, but you won't need a nurse!' She then went on to tell him she'd decided to join the VAD as a nurse, so she would be able to care for him. After an hour of listening to everything about the Voluntary Aid Detachment, what the training involved, her uniform and how his parents were, John felt exhausted. He thought she'd never depart.

When Vickie finally left, his thoughts went to Lily. She was everything he wanted. Not Vickie. He'd tried to push thoughts of Lily aside. But now he realised that he was in love with her. He'd never been in love before, had never thought he could feel this way about a woman. He wanted to spend his life with Lily, to care for her, to love her. Not Vickie. No! Never with Vickie.

*****

That night after dinner, Leslie said, 'Let's go to your room and have a glass of wine, old boy; it seems your visitor has left you a bit ...' Leslie hesitated.

'Downcast? Dejected?' John offered.

'Well, not your usual self, shall we say. I'll fetch glasses and a bottle.'

He returned to the parlour bedroom. John already sat in one of the comfortable wingback chairs. Leslie poured them each a glass of wine, lit the gas lamps, drew the curtains and sat down in the other chair.

'Thank you, Leslie.' John studied his glass.

'So, what's happened to put you in such a sombre mood?' Leslie asked.

John frowned. 'Oh, just Vickie. How can I get out of marrying her, Leslie? She bores me to tears. We have nothing in common, and I don't feel attracted to her.'

Leslie drank some wine. 'Don't know, old boy, not my field of expertise.'

John looked at Leslie. He'd sometimes wondered about Leslie's sexuality; he seemed such a gentle soul, not effeminate by any means, but ... now he said hesitantly, 'Have you ever had a lady friend, Leslie?'

Leslie considered his glass of wine. 'Well, I did start walking out with a lady I met at a Spiritualist meeting, but then ...'

'Then?'

'Well, then Lily started to come to the séances I was holding at my house. When I saw her, I knew that was it.'

'It?'

'That I could love no-one else. It was hard trying to tell this other lady that I'd have to discontinue our walking out together, but I think she was secretly relieved. She probably found me a boring stick of a fellow. She soon found someone else and was married the following year.' He sighed. 'I've loved Lily ever since. That was before she'd even met her husband.'

The two men fell silent.

'That must have been hard for you.'

'Yes. Sounds stupid but I was heart-broken.'

A pause, and then John asked, 'What's he like, her husband? Have you met him?'

'Yes. Like I said, I used to hold séances here years ago. Lily came. A Mrs Snelling was the medium. Althea. You may have heard of her?' He raised his eyebrows. John shook his head. 'Well,' Leslie continued, 'Percy started coming to those séances. That's how they met. After they were married she started to hold séances at her own house, and then Mrs Snelling went to Italy for a year, and I didn't bother with another medium. When Lily contacted me to ask if I knew of anywhere suitable for her to hold séances, I suggested she come here. That was several years ago. If I remember correctly, it wasn't convenient for her to hold healing sessions at their place because of the children.'

'She has children?' Surprised, John looked up.

'Yes, four; you'd never think it, would you?'

John took a gulp of his wine. He said nothing, just frowned into his glass.

'But Lily's husband ...' Leslie eventually said. 'Well, he, Percy, came here a few times to Lily's séances. It was before the war. Um, he isn't the kind of man I would've expected Lily to choose.'

'In what way? Maybe it was an arranged marriage.'

'I don't think so, but I would've expected him to be more ... I don't know, a bit more dynamic, outgoing. I don't know. No,' he continued slowly, 'he's very quiet, reserved, gentle ... he seems a very nice person. I don't know how else to describe him, a bit academic, perhaps?'

'Handsome?' John asked.

Leslie smiled. 'Well, I'm not much of a judge of men's looks, but I think he must be because most of the women at the Spiritualist meeting seemed to swoon over him. Dark and brooding.'

'Hmm.' John sat in thought. He looked up at Leslie. 'Why didn't you make a move with her? Sorry, old boy, but if you knew her before she met her husband ...'

Leslie laughed wryly. 'I was waiting for an opportunity to ask if I could walk out with her, but I left it too late. Just when I'd plucked up the courage, Percy came on the scene. I haven't had much to do with women, you know. I was an only child, and my parents were elderly when I was born. I was a surprise.' He smiled ruefully. 'Well, I didn't quite know how to approach her, dithered a bit,' he paused, 'top up your glass?'

John nodded. 'Thanks.'

They sat in silence.

Still thinking about Lily, John suddenly asked, 'Her husband, what does he do?'

'Percy told me he worked as a Commercial Clerk in a Stockbrokers, which seemed so mundane for our lively Lily.'

'Yes, too boring by far.'

'He seems clever, especially with numbers. Now he's been conscripted. The Army Service Corps, apparently, as a driver.'

'Humph.' John almost sneered. 'Ally Sloper's Cavalry, a bit of a comedown, heh? He'll find that hard, after pen pushing all his life.' Ally Sloper was a popular cartoon figure always trying to get out of paying his rent by disappearing down back alleys. 'Sorry, Leslie. That wasn't a nice thing to say, the wine has loosened my tongue. Not used to it anymore. ... Oh, God, why is my life such a mess!' he burst out suddenly. 'It should have been me, not Reggie!'

Leslie got up. 'None of that talk,' he said briskly. 'Hmm, this bottle is empty, I'll get another.'

John lay awake that night, thinking about what Leslie had said. He realised now he'd been trying to ignore his growing enchantment with Lily. And Leslie loved Lily too. And why did everyone call Leslie, Leslie and not Carter or Les, or some nickname? His mind roamed all over the place. Now Vickie had appeared in the picture. How could he marry her when he loved Lily? And only wanted to be with her ... And Lily has four children! Four! Why did four make more difference than one? How could he get out of marrying Vickie? And all this spiritualist nonsense. Lily was an intelligent woman; why did she believe it? Leslie too. He, John Watts, wasn't a teenager! He'd had women, but now they held no appeal; he only wanted Lily... Perhaps he should leave Leslie's, go back to his old digs ... But he wouldn't be able to manage on his own ... go home? ... God, no, not with his mother fussing around him, Vickie bobbing in and out, practising her nursing skills, and his father shuffling around trying to smooth things over with his constant platitudes and stating the bloody obvious ... His mind went around in circles. Near dawn he eventually drifted into a restless sleep.

He woke up grumpy and with a headache. *Too much wine. Not used to it.* Better shave and get ready for his treatment with Lily.

She arrived with a small boy. 'I hope you don't mind,' she said. 'This is my youngest son, David. Our housekeeper had to go to a funeral, so there was no-one to take care of him.'

John looked at the boy. A pair of brown eyes solemnly regarded him. Apart from the brown eyes and the colour of his curls, he was the image of Lily.

'This is Mr. Watts,' she said. 'He was in an air plane that crashed.'

'How do you do, Mr. Watts,' David said. 'My mama will make you better!' He smiled with Lily's smile.

John was enchanted. He'd had no contact with small children—apart from Vickie, he thought ruefully—but this little boy was a heart stealer. 'I know she will,' he replied.

Little David looked up at him. 'May I stay with you while Mama does her healings? Please?'

'Of course.'

'Are you sure?' Lily smiled, then looked at David. 'Only when I'm healing other people,' she said. 'When I'm with Mr. Watts, you must stay with Mrs. Wilson.'

'Yes, Mama,' he replied and sat down at the end of John's bed.

When Lily went out, John said, 'How old are you, David?'

'I'm six,' he replied, 'and how old are you, Mr Watts?'

John smiled to himself at the way David was trying so hard to be polite, not realising that it wasn't the done thing to ask an adult his age.

'I'm thirty-three.'

David nodded sagely. 'That's a very nice age.' He paused. 'My friends call me Davey. You can call me Davey, Mr Watts, if you like.'

John found it hard to keep a straight face.

'If you don't mind me asking, Mr. Watts, how did your air plane crash? Were you on a mission?'

John found it easy to talk to this little boy, who seemed to understand and be interested in everything he said. Before he knew it, Lily was giving a little knock on the door.

'May I come in?'

David jumped up and opened the door. 'Oh Mama, I've had such a nice time with Mr. Watts! May I come again?'

Lily smiled. 'We'll see. Now, go to the kitchen and stay with Mrs. Wilson.'

'Yes, Mama. Goodbye, Mr. Watts; thank you for a lovely time.' He skipped out of the room.

John smiled. 'Thank you, Davey. It's been a pleasure.'

Lily closed the door and looked at him shrewdly. 'You look tired.'

'Yes, late night. Leslie and I were up talking.'

'I have to talk to him,' she said. 'Now that my husband is away, and my older sons are at boarding school, I think I will resume my sittings and healings at my house. He has been so good letting me have his dining room, but I don't want to impose on him any longer.'

John felt like his heart had stopped. He just looked at her. She looked at him.

'Dear. John,' she said warmly, 'of course I will still come and give you treatments here, but I think that once a fortnight will be sufficient from now on.'

His emotions flew all over the place: relief that at least he would still see her, and wonder as to why she said this now. Her husband had been conscripted months ago, according to Leslie. Was she psychic? Did she know that he and Leslie had discussed her? And only once a fortnight? Could he last that long without seeing her?

Was it because she was attracted to him and wanted to put more distance between them?

'Please relax, John; I can't do a healing while you're so resistant.'

He tried to relax. As usual, she worked her magic.

***

That evening he said to Leslie, 'Why do you think Lily has suddenly decided not to hold her treatments here anymore? Is it anything to do with me?'

Leslie sighed. 'Don't know, old boy. Perhaps she feels she needs to give me back my own space.'

John considered this for a while. 'Hmm,' was all he said.

Lily had told her clientele her new locale for healings and sittings, so when she came to see John, usually no-one else was around. Now Lily always brought little David. Sometimes an old client arrived, and Lily saw them first. During that time David talked to John. When Lily healed John, David stayed in the kitchen with Mrs Wilson.

John became very fond of David and looked forward to his visits, but he suspected that Lily brought David as a kind of buffer between them.

Without Lily coming every few days, his life seemed to lose meaning and momentum. He felt bored and wanted to get back to work. Reminding himself that there was a war on, he worked away at his walking with solid determination, until he was able to go without the callipers and just use walking sticks.

'I think I can return to the RFC now,' he said to Leslie one morning at breakfast.

Leslie looked at him. 'You're bored and unsettled now you're mobile again. My projects aren't enough for you. Probably a good idea, if the Flying Corps medicos will give you the all clear.'

John smiled. 'Yes, I'll telephone for an appointment after breakfast; if that's all right with you.'

'Of course!' Leslie seemed pleased to see John enthused and happy.

The doctor who'd treated John consulted his notes and frowned. 'I can't believe this is you. This patient,' he tapped his notes, 'could never have recovered as well as you have. Certainly not in this amount of time.' He shrugged. 'Oh well. I won't waste time wondering about it. I can see you're fit to work in a non-combative role.'

John ended up doing aircraft pre-flight inspections and on ground training of new pilots. He tried to put Lily out of his thoughts, but on the occasions when he met up with Leslie, he always managed to nonchalantly ask if Leslie had seen anything of Lily.

Leslie usually told him about the Spiritualist meetings where he sometimes saw Lily. 'She seems very well,' he would reply. 'Tired, of course, as we all are with this war.'

CHAPTER 8

Percy felt he might never see his family again because of this interminable war. The thick gluey mud that had been everywhere before Christmas turned to hard-packed, dirty ice. The solid tyres of his lorry skidded over the ice. The lorries had no windscreens, and his hands and face ached with the pain of the biting cold. He kept telling himself that it was worse for the boys in the trenches, but it didn't make him feel any better.

After the main Somme offensive, their unit moved, but everything was the same: going to the railhead, collecting ammunition and stores, delivering to the battery, guard duty and cleaning and maintaining the lorries.

The letters from home were sparse: some from his mother and the odd one from Lily. Ena corresponded most regularly.

Dear Daddy,

I hope you are safe. This is Ena, your daughter, writing.

We miss you. I am doing well at school.

Mabel came to see Mrs Burton last Sunday. She is well. She looks yellow.

Mummy saw her and was worried. She said Mabel is being poisoned and she should stop working at the munitions factory. People are calling the munitions workers Canaries! Because of their yellow colour. But Mabel said she is doing her duty for the country.

Mrs Burton says she feels tired these days, so I try and help her. And when the boys are home from school, George likes to help in the kitchen.

Mummy is well.

We love you Daddy. Come home soon.

Your daughter, Ena Hedgecock. January 1917

His letters back were almost standard: Hope you are well. Miss you. I am well. The weather here is rain/snow/sleet, and then as winter became spring and then summer, very hot. He couldn't understand why he'd not been granted a leave pass. Maybe something had happened and his name had been misplaced. When the Americans joined in the war effort, he thought he might be released for a ticket to Blighty, but it was late December in 1917 before he got leave. He knew he was a changed man from the one that had left all those months ago.

He hadn't been sure what train he'd be able to get or what time he'd arrive after getting off the boat. When he got off the train with his kitbag, he was lucky to get a cab. Night was falling by the time he knocked at his front door.

It opened, revealing a young girl. Percy dropped his kit bag and exclaimed, 'Ena!'

She took a few steps back and then said tentatively, 'Is that you Daddy?'

He smiled and she ran into his arms. 'Mummy, Davey, boys, it's Daddy!'

Voices instantly filled the hall. The children gathered around and bombarded him with exclamations. 'What a lovely Christmas present!'

At last, over their heads he saw her. 'Oh, my darling, Lily,' he sobbed.

The children let him go and hung back when they saw his tears, unsure of this father that they hadn't seen for a year and a half.

He saw the shock on Lily's face and realised that he must present an objectionable sight. He tried to pull himself together. 'I'll be better after a bath and a proper shave,' he managed to say.

Ena took charge. 'Piers, fire the gas geyser for hot water. George, please take daddy's kit bag to the scullery. David, go upstairs and get his dressing gown and slippers.'

They scuttled around, dismayed at the sight of their father crying.

'How long is your leave for?' Lily asked as they went through to the scullery. She thought it best for him to take off his clothes there; she'd heard talk of soldiers bringing back lice.

'Three days.' He wiped his nose on his sleeve, then took a deep breath. 'I'm sorry, Lily, I'm just tired from the journey; please forgive me.'

She managed a smile. 'It's all right, darling. It's such a lovely surprise. We didn't know you were coming.'

'Neither did I until the day before yesterday. Oh, Lily, my darling, I've missed you so much.'

'Come, the water in the tub in the scullery will soon be hot, and you'll feel better after a good scrub. I'll let Mrs Burton know there'll be an extra special person at dinner tonight.' She gave him a kiss on his stubbly cheek.

George watched anxiously. 'Do you need anything from your kit bag, Daddy?'

Percy smiled, amazed at how his children had grown since he'd been away. 'Yes, my razor, if you would fetch my shaving bowl for me, please, George.'

'Yes, Daddy, and then can I go and help Mrs Burton in the kitchen?'

Percy didn't know how to respond.

Ena came back with clean towels. 'George loves to help Mrs Burton with the cooking,' she said.

'Now children, leave your father to wash in peace,' Lily said, shepherding them out of the scullery.

Suddenly he was alone. It felt so strange.

Dinner seemed a lavish feast compared to what he'd been eating. Mrs Burton did an amazing job with the food. Lily had always eaten meat and encouraged the children likewise, so he found the trouble to which Mrs Burton had gone in producing a vegetarian meal for him rather overwhelming.

'Welcome home, Sir.' She smiled as she put a dish on the table in front of him.

'Thank you, that looks delicious.'

The children kept stealing surreptitious looks at him. His build had always been slight, but now he looked gaunt and haggard.

He and Lily had a long-awaited reunion that night. Early in the morning when Lily woke up feeling cold, she suddenly remembered that Percy was home. She put her hand out to feel for him and cuddle into him for warmth, but felt nothing. Then she heard gentle snores coming from the side of the bed and found him rolled in a blanket, asleep on the floor.

'Percy!' she said quietly, 'why are you on the floor?'

He stirred and looked at her, then got up and back into bed, pulled the blanket over them and took her in his arms. 'I'm so used to sleeping in my lorry; this feather bed is too soft. My back was hurting.'

'Silly old thing,' she said fondly, then kissed a trail down his neck.

Next day they went to the Bancroft's for Christmas dinner. Lily hadn't told them that Percy would be joining them, so no-one was prepared to see him. He tried to be bright and cheerful, but he couldn't stop thinking about Harry's family. They'd be spending their second Christmas without their father.

***

Mrs Burton cleaned and pressed Percy's uniform, so when he returned to the front, he looked a bit more presentable than when he'd left.

As he climbed into his lorry the first day back, he thought to himself that perhaps it would have been better not to have gone on leave. It'd been so short and made it harder than ever to leave Lily and the children.

That night he tried to think of something cheerful to write.

Dearest Lily,

I hope you & the children are well.

It was hard to leave you all.

Tell the children there are lovely dogs here that are trained to find wounded soldiers. I think that some of them were family pets that people gave for this work.

The weather is very bad & cold. We have to drive our lorries at night & it's hard going in the mud, & with the rain in your face it makes it hard to see where you are going.

Your devoted husband, Percy Hedgecock

February 1918

He thought it didn't sound very cheerful, but he was too tired to think of anything else.

The arduous routine of moving stones for road work, carrying ammunition to the front and bringing back spent shells and wounded men continued, until March, when the German Spring Offensive began. The ASC were told that any men deemed fit enough would have to take up their rifles and join the fighting, while the ASC men's place would be taken by soldiers who'd been wounded but were still able to do some driving duties. And so Percy had to take up arms. By now, he felt so demoralised that he didn't even think about it. He just did as he was told, trying to ignore his principles of nonviolence.

An exhausted and starving German Storm trooper was the first and only man he killed. The Storm trooper had his bayonet raised and came straight towards Percy. He could kill or be killed. He hesitated for a second, then raised his rifle, closed his eyes and fired. The German fell onto Percy, and his bayonet went through Percy's calf, pinning him to the ground. The German's blood covered Percy's face. He tried to push the body off of him, but everything went black.

Sometime later words filtered through the pain.

'This one's still alive by the look of it, quick pull the Hun off 'im.'

Percy groaned.

'The bugger's lucky; the weight of the Hun stopped him bleeding to death.'

The First Aid men managed to pull out the bayonet and compress the wound. Percy passed out again with the pain.

It didn't matter how often he told himself it had been him or the German, he still couldn't forget the German's eyes. Blue grey. Like Lily's. He had recurrent nightmares of him killing Lily, from which he woke screaming. When his leg had healed he was sent back to his driving duties.

The nightmares continued.

The war dragged on. He kept going, driving his lorry and doing whatever was required.

***

November 11th 1918. Armistice. The end of the war.

Lily sat at her dressing table brushing her hair in readiness for her morning healing. Thoughts jumbled around in her head. She yearned to see Percy again. She couldn't wait to go to bed with him. Oh, it was so hard being without him! She looked in her bedroom mirror. *Do I look much older? More tired? Will Percy still desire me?*

***

At the end of November John paid one of his rare visits home to his parent's place.

His mother beamed with delight. 'You've come at such a good time! Vickie arrived home two days ago for a weeks' break!'

Vickie still had the house next door to his parents, and she came to visit as soon as she heard John was home.

'John! You naughty boy; why didn't you tell me you were coming home for the weekend?'

'It was a spur of the moment decision. I knew they'd tell you,' he replied weakly. 'Um, how are you?'

'Tired,' she replied. 'I've been nursing soldiers returned from the trenches. A lot have been sick with something called the Spanish influenza; it's been pretty grim.'

John made sympathetic noises.

'Your parents have invited me to dinner,' she went on, 'but perhaps we can go back to my house afterwards?' She gave him a coy look.

He groaned inwardly. The last thing he wanted was to be alone with her. 'I'm pretty tired, actually. The legs are still giving me a bit of grief,' he replied, relieved that he had an excuse.

'Oh. Oh. Of course. I didn't think. Maybe tomorrow you can come around and we can talk about the wedding. I was thinking that we can live in my house after we're married. It became mine after poor Daddy died.' She looked sad for a moment, and John felt he'd been mean.

'Good idea,' he said unenthusiastically.

Vickie brightened. 'Good oh! After breakfast, then?'

John immediately felt cast down. How could he get out of marrying her? She'd had so many losses in her life, and she wasn't such a bad egg, but he simply didn't want to marry her. If he told her bluntly that he'd changed his mind, she might go like her mother and become suicidal. There, he'd acknowledged it. He was sure her mother had killed herself. He must try and broach it with his mother.

Dinner over, he said politely, 'Vickie, perhaps I should escort you home.'

'Oh, yes. Please!' She put down her napkin and stood up.

He took her to her front door. She opened the door and went in, beckoning him to follow. He quickly gave her a pat on the shoulder. 'Goodnight, Vickie. Bit tired, see you tomorrow.'

He saw the disappointment on her face, but ignored it. He returned to his parents, wanting to know the truth.

His mother was clearing the dinner table, and his father was trying to help, but getting in the way.

John waded straight in. 'Dad? What happened with Vickie's mother?'

His mother stopped stacking the plates. 'What do you mean?'

'Well, she wasn't sick, and if I remember she died suddenly. Paddy never spoke about his mother after she died, and I can't recall her ever being mentioned. In fact,' he continued, 'if ever her name came up, the subject was quickly changed.' He looked enquiringly at his parents.

His mother carefully placed the plates back on the table and sat down. 'After Vickie was born, Matilda changed,' she said slowly. 'She used to be a bit like Vickie, bright and bubbly, but then she just got sadder and sadder. The doctor said it was a kind of melancholy that sometimes happened to older women after childbirth.' She became silent.

John waited. 'And?' he prompted. 'I need to know the truth, Mother.'

His mother sighed. 'Apparently the doctor had given her tablets to help her sleep, and she saved them up and took the whole bottle. She never woke up.' Her eyes filled with tears. 'It was so sad for Peter and poor Paddy and the baby'.

'All happens for a reason,' his father said.

John closed his eyes. *God give me patience*. He felt trapped. If he called off the wedding, what might Vickie do? He didn't want her suicide on his conscience. But then, he told himself, Lily was out of bounds, anyway. She was happily married. But what if her husband was killed? It happened in the ASC. But the war was over. The ASC were still in France. Maybe Lily was already a widow. What if he married Vickie and then found out Lily had been widowed? He became angry with himself. 'I think I'll have a drink,' he said. 'Any spirits, Dad?'

His mother looked disapproving, but his father brightened. 'I think there is some brandy for medicinal purposes; I'll get two glasses.'

Next morning when he went to Vickie's house, she peered around the door in her dressing gown. She looked pale and hardly able to stand.

'You'd better not come in; I think I've caught this Spanish influenza.' As she spoke she closed her eyes and crumpled into a heap on the floor. Though a tall woman, John managed to lift her up. He carried her into the living room and lay her down on the sofa.

'What can I do?' he asked helplessly.

'Nothing,' she managed to say. 'I don't want you to catch it, just bring me some water and then leave.'

John brought her a glass of water and then went back to his parents' house.

'Mother!' he shouted up the stairs. 'Vickie seems to have this Spanish flu. She said to leave her alone. I don't know what to do.'

His mother ran down the stairs. 'Oh no! We'd better bring her here; she'll need looking after. You'd better get her. I can put her in the spare bedroom.' She ran back up the stairs. 'I'll make up the bed now.'

John went back to Vickie's house. She still lay on the sofa. He told her what his mother had said. 'What do you need?' he asked.

'Nothing,' she muttered. 'Just to sleep.'

He managed to pick her up and carry her next door and up the stairs to the spare bedroom where his mother had just finished making the bed. The effort and her weight made his knees ache. 'I'll have to sit down for a bit, Mother, then I'll help you.'

His mother looked at him. 'John, dear. I know you were planning on staying another two days, but I think you should go as soon as possible. You still haven't recovered your strength after the accident, and you're not strong enough to fight this awful influenza.'

'I had planned to call in and see Leslie Carter on my way back,' he said 'and I'm sure he won't mind me arriving a couple of days early.'

Busy settling Vickie into bed, his mother had stopped listening.

He walked downstairs to find his father hovering around in the kitchen.

'Cup of tea?' he asked John. 'Nothing like a good old cuppa to make things better!'

'No, thanks, Dad. Mother said it's best if I leave as soon as possible so I don't get this rotten influenza.'

'Probably for the best, Son.'

'I'll get my stuff.' John went upstairs, packed his bag, then put his head round the door of the spare bedroom. 'I'm going now, Mother,' he whispered.

She looked up from the bed where Vickie lay. 'Take care,' she mouthed.

***

Pleased to be away from Vickie and his parents, John got an early train to London and arrived at Leslie's just as Mrs Wilson was leaving.

'Hello, Mr Watts! How nice to see you again! I know Mr Carter is expecting you, but not until the day after tomorrow. He'll be pleased to see you. A lovely surprise. I'll let you in.' She paused on the step. 'I'd better go home and make a dinner for you; there won't be enough for two.' She hurried away.

Eventually John heard Leslie's key in the lock. The front door opened, and he called out, 'Hello Leslie, it's John! I've come a couple of day's early, hope you don't mind!'

Leslie joined him in the parlour. John stood to greet him and they shook hands. 'Delighted, old boy!' Leslie said with a smile. 'Good to see you. Let me get my coat off and we'll have a drink.' He frowned as if he'd had a sudden thought. 'Oh, we'll have to share my dinner; Mrs Wilson only makes enough for one meal, but there's probably some bread and cheese in the pantry.'

John smiled. 'The good Mrs Wilson has it all under control. She was just leaving as I arrived, or I would've had to wait for you to get home. All a bit sudden.'

Leslie poured them each a glass of whiskey. He raised his eyebrows. 'An emergency?'

'Yes, I went home yesterday evening. Vickie came to dinner last night, and seemed all right, but this morning it seems she's been struck down with this Spanish influenza. My mother thought it best that I didn't hang around; she seemed worried that I would catch it.' He smiled. 'So, I was very happy not to have to face Vickie and the marriage questions.'

Mrs Wilson arrived with an extra meal. 'Just need to pop it in the oven at six o'clock with Mr Carter's,' she said.

After she'd left, John said, 'I hope that Mr Wilson won't have to go without dinner because of me!'

'She's an amazing woman, can make a meal out of nothing,' Leslie replied. 'I'd be lost without her. Now, tomorrow is Saturday, and I don't work so what would you like to do? I hope we'll soon get permission to resume building radios again.'

Keen to start work building a crystal radio set, the two men had a pleasant evening making plans for the weekend. But on Sunday evening, John got a severe headache and felt too unwell to eat dinner.

'Sorry, Leslie, but I think I'll have to lie down. I hope it's not this Influenza, but I don't feel well at all. Should be fine by morning,' he said.

The next day, however, John had a fever and vomited several times. Leslie called the doctor who confirmed that he had the Spanish influenza.

'The hospitals are full,' the doctor said, 'Just monitor him, bathe him with wet towels to try and keep his temperature down and try and get him to drink lots of water.'

Worried, Leslie immediately telephoned Lily. 'Lily, John Watts is here. He's pretty bad with this Spanish influenza. What should I do? Mrs Wilson has made him some lemon juice, but he's not keeping it down. She's with him now.'

Lily's heart seemed to miss a beat. She'd resolutely put John out of her mind. 'I'll come as soon as I can,' she replied. 'But I don't think my healing will be effective on ailments like influenza.'

Since the time Percy had got angry with her about the woman and the baby with scabies, Lily had been very careful around anyone that might be infectious. She always kept several large men's kerchiefs with her. Now, when she got to Leslie's she got one out and tied it around her nose and mouth.

'I'm so glad you've come,' Leslie said. 'I don't know what else to do. I think he's reaching some kind of crisis point. He's incoherent and has red spots on his cheeks; his skin looks blue and he can hardly breathe.'

Lily entered the room and heard a bubbling sound from John's chest. She went to him and took one of his hands. 'It's Lily,' she mumbled through the kerchief, then raised it so she could speak clearly. 'John, darling, it's Lily.'

Leslie gave a small gasp at hearing this.

She leaned closer. 'Don't leave me,' she murmured, trying to keep her voice low so that Leslie wouldn't hear. Leslie brought her a chair, and she sat beside the bed, holding John's hand for over an hour.

Gradually his breathing eased, and the blue colour disappeared.

Leslie brought her a cup of tea. 'I think the crisis has passed,' he whispered.

Lily nodded. 'I hope so.' After using all her power and mind towards healing John, she felt physically and emotionally drained. And she now acknowledged that she had some kind of affinity with this man she hardly knew. She felt shaken. What could it mean? Was John her real soul mate?

Leslie raised John, and Lily wet his lips.

After another hour, she rose. 'I think he might be able to sip some water now, Leslie,' she said. 'But I must go home. Do you think I might wash my hands?'

'Of course, my dear. In the bathroom. I'll find you a clean towel.' He went out and called her a cab.

A week later John's breathing had become easier, and he could sit up and drink from a cup.

Although Lily had visited him every day, he hadn't been well enough to talk.

Now he smiled. 'Lily,' he managed to croak through his cracked lips. 'Oh, Lily, my dearest!'

Lily froze. 'Don't say that.'

John looked puzzled. 'Lily, I've been so ill, but I'm sure I heard your voice calling me your darling.'

Lily sat with downcast eyes. 'I call everyone darling; hadn't you noticed?'

John lay back on the pillows. 'Lily, I know I've been very ill, but today I'm feeling much better, and I'm certain I heard your voice saying, "Don't leave me now, darling". Please, look at me, Lily.'

She raised her eyes.

'Lily, tell me. You did say that, didn't you?'

Lily slowly nodded.

John's face lit up. He opened his arms to her.

She stood. 'John, please stop. I'm married and the mother of four children. And you are engaged to be married, so Leslie told me.' She paused. 'I cannot hurt my husband and my children, and you cannot hurt your fiancée. We must stop this now and never see each other again!' She started to cry.

John opened his arms and she went into them. It seemed so natural and right.

Lily was the first to break away. 'Oh, John, no! I must go before Mrs Wilson comes in, or Leslie comes home from work.' She gathered her things and walked towards the door.

'Lily! Please don't leave!'

But she was gone.

John collapsed back in the bed. He felt so feeble, physically unable to go after her. He hadn't been able to get out of bed for a week. His mind whirled. What should he do? He knew she was right. Vickie would be devastated, and so would Lily's husband. Not to mention her children. And if the others were like little David! It didn't bear thinking about. He thought he'd never felt so down. On the other hand, the thought that Lily loved him filled him with joy.

He lay on his sick bed, wondering how one woman could have such power over a man. It wasn't just her beauty, she had some kind of magnetism. He shook his head. Enough! It wasn't to be.

It took him several weeks to recover his strength. He ached with longing to see Lily again, but she resolutely kept away. He didn't even know her address! He couldn't ask Leslie. He didn't feel like talking it over with him, knowing that Leslie loved Lily, too.

As soon as he felt well enough, John went back to work. His work with the Air Force had come to an end, and the Associated Engineering Company offered him a job. During the war they'd had an assembly line operating and had built many buses and lorries for the war effort. He tried to put Lily out of his mind and concentrate on engine design and assembly line construction, but he often went to see Leslie, always hoping that Lily would be there.

***

Dec 1918

    Dearest Lily,

    The war is over, but there is still a lot for The Army Service Corps to do.

    Our C.O. told us all that there are over 2 million troops on the Western Front & about half a million horses & they all have to be fed and supplied with water, during a strategic withdrawal. It is impossible to get those men & horses back home quickly. Transport to the railheads has to be organised & then health checks, trains & shipping. And we still have to deal with the armaments & ammunition. So I think it will be the New Year before I get home. And a lot of men have this Spanish Influenza. So far, I am all right.

    I hope you all have a lovely Christmas.

    Give my love to the children.

    All my love

Your devoted husband, Percy Hedgecock.

Percy arrived home, exhausted and pale, in mid-February 1919. He started to shake and then collapsed just inside the door. Lily called Mrs Burton, and the two of them managed to get him up the stairs and into bed, where Lily removed his clothes to wash him. She was horrified to see him just skin and bone. No wonder it hadn't been difficult to carry him up the stairs.

A scrap of linen fell from his vest as she took it off. She picked it up. It looked vaguely familiar, a lacy edge—then she saw the stain on the corner. She closed her eyes. 'Oh, Percy darling, this was the handkerchief I used to wipe the blood off your face the day you proposed to me!'

Overcome with guilt, she thought of that embrace she'd exchanged with John. *How can I love two men? Percy is the father of my children. I must stay true to him.*

Tenderly she washed him and dressed him in a clean nightshirt. She sat with him through the night, wetting his lips with a damp cloth and using all her powers to heal him.

After two days, he could sit up and take some bone broth Mrs Burton had made.

He looked at Lily. 'Lily, darling. I've been so ill. But you've been with me. Thank you, my darling,' He took her hand. 'I love you so much, Lily.'

'I know you do, darling. And I love you. Now you need to sleep and eat until you get your strength back.'

He sank back into the pillows, and as soon as he fell asleep, she crept out of the room and down to the kitchen.

Mrs Burton looked up. 'Now, Mrs Hedgecock. It's your turn to rest. You're exhausted. Mr. Hedgecock will be fine now. I've put the geyser on to get a bath ready for you, and then off to bed with you!'

Lily smiled gratefully. 'I don't know how on earth we would have managed all these years without you, Mrs. Burton. You're a treasure, and we all appreciate you.'

Mrs Burton nodded. 'It's a pleasure to have been with such a lovely family.'

***

David had joined his brothers at boarding school. Only Ena remained at home with Lily, and she'd instructed Ena to stay away from her father and to take her meals in the kitchen with Mrs Burton until they were sure that Percy wasn't infectious.

Percy slowly recovered, and the boys came home for the Easter holidays, delighted to see their father. They clamoured to know about the war and the lorries that Percy had driven.

On Easter Sunday everyone gathered at the Bancroft's for lunch. Percy got the chance to see his father-in-law and thank him for looking after his affairs.

'I don't know if I should tell Lily about the money from her healings,' he said.

'Not necessary,' David replied. 'Ena's very smart; she gave me the money quietly. She understands her mother. Which is more than I do!'

Although he was still very frail, a week later Percy went back to work.

He'd been afraid there might be no job for him, but the partners seemed pleased to have him back. He looked around the office. Little had changed since he'd left nearly three years ago. The partners looked a lot older, and there were new faces amongst the women.

'What happened to Tom?' he asked.

Eric Swanton's mouth drooped. 'He was killed on the Somme.'

Another waste of a good man, Percy thought sadly.

Seeing the thin and pale Percy, Arthur Symonds suggested he only work two days the first week, to get back into the way of things, and Percy felt grateful for that. The two new women who'd been doing his work seemed a bit resentful at him taking back his old job. But it didn't last because Percy was so appreciative of how they'd kept his books.

'What you've done is splendid,' he said after looking over the records. 'I think perhaps it would be better for you two to keep working on them, and perhaps Mr Swanton could find me other, less important accounts to work on.'

He was so gentle and unassuming that they both said simultaneously, 'Oh no, Mr. Hedgecock, that wouldn't be right!'

Still feeling quite weak and emotional after the influenza, ready tears came to his eyes. He coughed and swallowed. 'Thank you, ladies.' He gave a little bow of acknowledgement.

'Let us get you a cup of tea,' one said, looking at his eyes filling with tears. They hurried off to the little tea room.

Eric Swanton, having watched all this from his desk at the other end of the room, just smiled.

But the war had changed Percy. He'd always been a quiet and reserved man, but now he seemed quieter and even more introspective. The nightmares about the German he'd killed kept occurring and he still couldn't get Harry out of his mind.

***

Lily didn't know what to think or do. Percy was no longer the cheerful man she'd married. They hadn't resumed their lovemaking, and he didn't respond to her advances. One evening when

Percy sat reading a book, she watched him out of the corner of her eye. He hadn't turned a page for some while.

'Percy, darling. Are you feeling all right?' she asked gently. 'You don't seem to be yourself since you came back from the war. Did something happen that you would like to talk about?'

Percy looked up from his book. 'Sorry, darling, what did you say?'

She repeated her question. Percy looked blank for a few minutes and then shook his head. 'No. Nothing happened to me. Awful things happened to other men. But not to me.' He bent his head to his book.

She sighed. 'You don't seem interested in me or the children anymore.'

He looked puzzled. 'Of course I'm interested! I'm just tired.'

'Perhaps you should see a doctor. I can telephone James.'

'I don't need a doctor; there's nothing wrong with me.'

'Darling, I really think you do!'

'Please leave me be, Lily!' He turned a page of his book.

Later that night when they got into bed, Percy immediately turned over and, Lily thought, pretended to be asleep. She tried to cuddle him, tried to arouse him, but his body went rigid.

'I'm tired, Lily,' he muttered. 'Let me sleep. Please.'

'Darling, I need you to love me,' she whispered, stroking him.

'Lily. Leave me alone. You don't understand. I ... I ... I'm not able to love you. I'm sorry, darling.' He started to cry.

'Oh, Percy! My darling.' Shocked, Lily took him into her arms. 'It's all right! This will pass; it's just a reaction to the war. I wish you would tell me about it. Or tell someone.'

'There's nothing to tell. Forgive me, Lily.'

Lily lay awake for a long time.

***

Percy couldn't bring himself to tell her, or anyone that he had killed a man. He retreated more and more into himself. When he came home from work he sat and read, but the words often didn't make sense. He read the same paragraph over and over and then sat staring into space. He couldn't bear to see the sadness on Lily's face, knowing she felt rejected by his inability to make love to her. His thoughts kept going around and around. His day's work exhausted him, leaving him feeling dispirited and melancholy, and he had problems sleeping.

I should have let the German kill me, he thought one night, still awake, tossing and turning. *I wouldn't have to bear this guilt or see Lily's disappointment*. He knew he must stop these thoughts. *I have the children and Lily to think of. I must keep going for their sakes.*

Their gardener had retired, and Percy couldn't find anyone to replace him. So many men had been killed in the war. One Sunday morning, he sat listlessly looking out the dining room window and saw the state of the garden. He knew he should do something about it, but he didn't seem to have the energy. Then he felt a little hand on his arm. It was Ena.

'Daddy, what are you looking at?'

'Just thinking about the garden, darling. It looks so awful. I don't know what to do about it.'

'Why don't you and I go out and have a look at what needs to be done,' Ena suggested. 'Come along, Daddy, I'll help you.

Reluctantly he got up, and they went out to the garden shed. He'd never done any gardening before, but after moving a few things, he found a garden fork and a pair of rusty shears. He stood for a while just looking at them.

'I'll help you. Look, you loosen the soil with the fork, and I'll pull the weeds out.'

After an hour, he smiled at Ena. 'That looks so much better! Are you tired, Ena?'

'No, daddy, we can keep going.'

He found solace in the garden, and most weekends after that he spent some time there. As the days lengthened and summer came, he went into the garden in the evenings after work. It relaxed him and lightened his mood.

He began to feel better, but his relationship with Lily deteriorated. He didn't know what to say to her these days. She seemed restless and unsettled. He felt afraid to approach her in bed; he didn't want to arouse her and then not be able to satisfy her. He didn't know what to do.

Now that married women over thirty had been granted the right to vote, and the education bill had been passed, Lily had no more causes to champion. Theosophy and attending lectures still absorbed her, and she spent a lot of time at the British Museum. Her healing sessions and séances in their house ceased when Percy came back from the war. When Silvia Pankhurst was jailed for sedition, he worried that Lily would get back with the suffragettes. He didn't know whether to be relieved or worried when he found out she was spending time with Dr Marie Stopes at her birth control clinic in Holloway.

'Lily darling,' he said one night after dinner. 'You seem a bit out of sorts, lately. Is there anything wrong?'

'I'm very well,' she replied, seemingly affronted by his use of the phrase 'out of sorts'. Just feeling useless. I want to do more study and start my healing again.'

Percy thought carefully. 'What have you been thinking?'

'I would like to start séances again, and I think I'd like to start my own Spiritualist Church.'

Percy's eyes widened in alarm. All he could think to say was, 'I don't think this house is suitable for a church.'

Lily fell silent and opened her book again.

The following weekend they joined James, his wife and two children at the Bancrofts for Sunday dinner. Having the whole family around helped Melina get over the loss of Ernie, so they gathered regularly.

After the meal—a noisy affair—Ena took James's children off to play, and her brothers went down to play billiards. As they left, Lily turned to James. 'James! I was wondering if you would rent me an office in your consulting rooms to do healing sessions.'

Everyone stopped talking.

James blinked. 'I don't think so, Lily!'

'For goodness sake, Lily,' her father exclaimed. 'Can't you forget all that spiritualist nonsense? You're a mother with four children. It's ridiculous!'

Percy looked up and saw the disappointment on Lily's face. It would've been hard for her to ask this of her brother.

'Sir,' he said, 'Lily needs to pursue her healing; it's important to her.'

David Bancroft snorted. 'Rubbish! I thought motherhood and the war had knocked all that out of her.'

No one spoke. Lily sat with downcast eyes, her hands nervously twisting her handkerchief.

Percy stood. 'If you will excuse us, Sir.' He nodded to his father-in-law and then to Melina. 'I think the children are tired and we should leave now. Come, Lily.' He took her gently by the arm. 'Thank you for the dinner.' He smiled, and in the silence that followed, they went to find the children.

The boys grumbled at having to finish their game of billiards, but the look on their father's face precluded any arguments. They went home in silence.

'I'm tired. I'll go and lie down,' Lily said quietly as soon as she stepped through the door.

Percy followed her up to the bedroom. 'Darling, Lily, we'll work something out.'

'Thank you for standing up for me, Percy,' she said in a subdued voice as she sat at her dressing table. Then she burst into tears. 'Oh, Percy, I'm afraid for my father. His heart isn't good. I could see it getting blacker as he got angry with me!'

Percy put his arms around her. 'Would he accept a healing from you, my darling?'

'No, absolutely not! You heard him! I'm afraid I'll be the cause of his heart failing.'

Percy didn't know what to say. 'Lily, darling, I know that you'd like to have séances and have healings here, but I need the privacy of my home. I can't face bumping into people I don't know when I come home from work.' He thought hard and eventually said, 'Perhaps ask Leslie Carter if he would be willing for you to go back to his house for a couple of mornings a week, until we find something. And if he can't have you there, he may know of somewhere you could go.'

Lily's sobs gradually ceased. 'Thank you, Percy, I'll telephone him later when I'm a bit calmer.'

When she spoke to Leslie after dinner the next day, he hesitated, then eventually said, 'It's good you want to resume your sessions, Lily, but perhaps just two days a week, maybe Tuesdays and Thursdays would suit you?'

Lily came back to the living room with her eyes shining. With a radiant smile she announced, 'Percy, darling! Leslie said it would be all right with him, so we arranged for healings and séances two days a week until I can find somewhere more permanent, and he'll let his contacts know that I'm back healing and holding séances.' She smiled at Percy and walked over and kissed him.

He put his down his book and smiled.

'Perhaps we should have an early night?' she said.

Percy's smiled faded, and he picked up his book again., 'I'm not tired at the moment,' he muttered.

CHAPTER 9

Every time John went home to his parents, Vickie greeted him with delight, but he felt she was anxiously wondering when they would get married. Eventually, just after he arrived one Friday night, his mother broached the subject.

'John, it's time you and Vickie were married. The poor girl is getting quite worried and anxious, you know. You can't lead her on like this.'

John nearly exploded. 'Mother, I haven't "led her on" as you put it. I really don't want to get married. Peter Burgess made me promise to look after Vickie, but I never wanted or intended to marry her. She just caught me at a bad time when I was getting over the accident.'

His mother's eyes widened in shock. 'John. How can you say such a thing now, after two years of letting her think you wanted to marry her! You have to. Your father agrees. Don't you Paul?' She gave an angry look at his father.

His father blinked and looked up from the evening paper. 'Yes, dear, of course,' he replied vaguely, likely not having heard a word.

'You haven't even bought her a ring,' his mother said in an accusatory tone. 'Now, what about taking her out in the morning to choose a ring, and we can have a little celebration tomorrow night?'

John felt as if an invisible tide swept him along.

A tentative knock came on the front door, and Vickie walked in. 'I thought I heard John's voice,' she said.

'Yes, he's here; come in.' His mother stood up and beamed. 'And he's just told us that tomorrow morning he's taking you into town to buy an engagement ring!'

John felt his anger building. He clenched his fists and his muscles went rigid. *Bitch! You bloody bitch!* At that moment he hated his mother.

Vickie's face lit up. She clasped her hands together. 'Oh, that's wonderful, John!' She saw his scowling face and her expression changed to one of confusion. 'Are you all right, John?' With an effort he controlled himself. 'Yes! Of course.' He tried to smile.

His mother gave him a triumphant look.

The rest of the evening seemed like a nightmare. Vickie and his mother chatted away about clothes and rings and wedding dresses. His father hid behind the evening paper. John felt as if he'd been given a life sentence.

The next morning, he and Vickie went to buy the engagement ring. For the last few months, every time Vickie had passed a jeweller she'd stopped to look at the rings, so she knew just what she wanted. Now, however, she became a bit hesitant. 'John, dear ... I was wondering, if instead of buying a ring, I used my mother's engagement ring, then we could put the money you would've spent on a ring towards a nice honeymoon.'

Her pronouncement surprised him such that he blurted out, 'Are you sure? I'm quite happy to buy a ring.' As soon as the words had left his mouth, he regretted them.

Vickie reddened. 'Sometimes I wondered if you still wanted to go ahead with the wedding, but if you're happy to buy a ring, then it means you do want to marry me.'

Now was his chance to tell her, but looking at the childish expression of happiness on her face, he felt he'd be a brute to destroy it. Anyway, he had no chance of being with Lily. *What the hell. It could be worse.*

She smiled. 'That's settled then. We'll go back to my house—well, it's *our* house now, and get Mummy's rings.' With a little skip of joy, she took his hand.

When they arrived back with Vickie wearing Matilda's ring, John's mother gave a start of surprise.

Vickie held up her hand, smiling. 'I thought it would be better to wear Mummy's ring and use the money for our honeymoon.' She blushed at the mention of a honeymoon.

His mother raised her eyebrows and looked at John.

'It was Vickie's idea,' was all he said, just stopping himself from shrugging. He tried to put a smile on his face and pretend to be looking forward to the wedding.

Later that night after taking Vickie home, she asked him to come in.

He hesitated.

'I thought we might talk about where to go for our honeymoon,' she explained.

'I'm a bit tired,' he replied feebly. 'I'm happy with whatever you think.' Suddenly he remembered the Isle of White. Sea planes were being built there. It would be interesting to visit the factories and see what they were doing. 'What about The Isle of White?'

'That sounds wonderful! Dear John, you always come up with good ideas!' She kissed him.

He tried to respond but didn't manage any enthusiasm. 'We'd better not get carried away, Vickie. Goodnight now.' He quickly turned and left.

***

A couple of weeks before John's August wedding, he went to Leslie's for a weekend visit.

'I need a breather from these wedding plans, Leslie,' he'd said when he'd telephoned him to suggest it. 'It'll be my last weekend as a free man.'

'Wonderful, old boy!' Leslie replied. 'Look forward to seeing you. I have to go out for a few hours on Saturday morning, but I'm sure you can amuse yourself in my workshop, especially now that I've got my new radio licence. You'll laugh! Applicants now have to satisfy the Post Office that we have "some definite object of scientific value in view"! Toodle-oo!'

John arrived on Friday night to find Lily there. He hadn't seen her for nearly two years.

'Hello, John.' She smiled and put out her hand. 'Leslie told me you were coming for the weekend and that you were soon to be married, so I just wanted to call in and wish you all happiness.' But as she put her hand in his and their eyes locked, her smiled faded.

All the old emotions flooded back. He knew she felt the same incredible longing. He took a deep breath. 'Lovely to see you again, Lily. Have you been well?'

'Oh, yes, indeed.' She kept the conversation light, but when Leslie went out to make some tea, she fell silent. They looked at each other.

'Lily, please!' John said. 'I have to meet you again; please don't go out of my life!'

Leslie's footsteps came down the hall, the tea tray rattling.

Lily looked towards the door and said nothing.

Leslie walked in and placed the tray on the coffee table. 'Here we are.' He looked at Lily. 'Will you be mother?'

She reddened slightly and looked down. 'Of course, dear Leslie!'

When Leslie went out to get more hot water for the tea, John quickly said in a low voice, 'Lily, Leslie has to go out tomorrow morning for a few hours. Please come over.'

She nodded, then hearing Leslie returning, said brightly, 'So where are you going for your honeymoon, John?'

The conversation turned to The Isle of Wight and sea planes, and soon Lily had to leave.

Leslie went outside to call a cab.

John looked at Lily. 'Please ...'

She nodded. 'I'll try.'

Leslie returned, escorted Lily to the cab, and then came back inside. 'That was probably not a good idea,' he said to John, 'telling Lily you were coming this weekend.'

John shrugged. 'Oh, I don't know,' he replied, trying to sound casual.

That night he didn't sleep until dawn, his mind filled with thoughts of Lily. Would she come?

Next morning Leslie left at nine o'clock, leaving John in a fever of excitement. He paced from the hall to the dining room and back. At last, half an hour later, a knock sounded on the door.

He threw it open. Lily walked in and took off her cloak. He took her in his arms and kissed her passionately. 'Mrs Wilson doesn't come until eleven o'clock,' he managed to say.

Lily took a deep breath. 'Let's go to your room.' She led him up the stairs.

John followed in delight and amazement. He hadn't believed that this could ever happen.

The hour passed too quickly. 'Oh, my darling, how can I live without you,' he murmured into her neck.

'John,' she replied, pulling away from him. 'I don't know what came over me; this is so wrong. I have to leave now, and this must never ever happen again. I don't know what to do! I never dreamed I would be unfaithful to Percy. But I couldn't help myself! We must never meet again.' She looked close to tears, an expression that wrenched at John's heart.

He sat on the bed and watched as she dressed and tried to arrange her mass of curls. 'Lily, my dearest darling. You have made me so happy,' but as he said this, he realised the implications.

Dressing quickly, he walked downstairs with her.

'I must go before Mrs Wilson comes and sees me here.' Her cheeks flushed.

Before John could say anything, she'd opened the front door and disappeared.

His mind spun in a whirlwind. What did it mean? Would she leave her husband and come and live with him? They *had* to be together. He couldn't live without her. They *had* to meet again. Then he remembered Vickie. He groaned. 'Oh, God; What a bloody mess!'

The rest of the weekend passed quietly. He tried to stay cheerful and interested in Leslie's latest projects, but eventually Sunday afternoon came—time for him to leave.

Leslie shook his hand. 'All the best, Wattie; hope you and Vickie will be very happy.'

'Thanks, Leslie. It's only a very small, quiet family wedding, or I would've invited you.'

'Quite understand, old boy. Anyway weddings aren't really my thing! But don't forget me! Come and visit whenever you're this way.'

'Thanks, I certainly will.'

John's mind raced. He couldn't stop thinking about Lily. He began to feel resentful towards Vickie and had to give himself a mental shake. He resolved to make the best of the situation and accept that Lily was gone from his life.

***

John had agreed to all Vickie and his mother's suggestions and plans for the wedding, not caring about any of it. He just had to show up with Vickie's mother's wedding ring in his pocket. He didn't have a best man, and his father would give Vickie away. One of her VAD friends was to be bridesmaid.

On the morning of the wedding, he felt that, in all honesty to Vickie, he should call off this marriage. His mother fussed around while his father looked for his cufflinks.

'Dad,' John said, 'I don't think I should go ahead with this wedding.' Was his father listening?

'Where has she hidden them?' No, his father wasn't listening.

'Dad!'

His father grunted.

'Dad, I said, I don't think I can go ahead with this wedding.'

'Yes, yes, it's full steam ahead! As soon as I can find my cufflinks!'

'Dad! I don't want to get married!'

His father looked up. 'What? Nonsense, Son. It's just pre-wedding nerves. I was the same the day I married your mother ...' His eyes glazed, then focussed on his son. 'Too late, lad! Can't back off now, not the done thing. Ah, here they are. Now why did she hide them under my collars?'

John turned away. *Well, that was that.*

The wedding went smoothly, and he thought Vickie looked very nice in her simple white dress. He was glad when it was over and they all went to the local hotel for lunch.

John had taken their cases to the hotel on his way to the church. They went upstairs, and Vickie changed out of her wedding dress and into her going away suit. She gave her wedding dress to his mother. After lunch, they made their farewells, both glad to get into the cab which would take them to the railway station.

Vickie remained quiet in the cab, but once in the train she chattered excitedly. How lovely the wedding was: her friend, the bridesmaid; the speeches; the flowers; the service. Eventually John became so bored that he got a book from his bag and tried to read. When Vickie saw him with the book, she fell silent.

He felt a bit guilty, and after unsuccessfully trying to concentrate on his book, he closed it. Seeing this, Vickie immediately started to talk again. He tried to make allowances for her, thinking she might be nervous, and tried to be pleasant and make appropriate comments, but by the time they got to their boarding house, he felt tired and annoyed. The boarding house seemed nice and their room pleasant with a view of the harbour. He took off his shoes and lay on the bed. He felt like having a sleep, but Vickie paced around the room with excitement.

'John! Let's go for a walk and explore.'

Reluctantly, he got up and put his shoes on again. Walking still caused him a lot of pain. 'All right.'

They strolled around Cowes, and then had dinner at the boarding house. John felt the other guests' eyes on them, the honeymoon couple, and they smiled knowingly when he and Vickie left the dining room.

'Goodnight!' a few chorused, the men winking at John.

He wondered how he'd ever be able to endure the rest of his life married to Vickie. Her voice went on and on. He couldn't remember her being this bad before, but now that he thought about it, he hardly knew her. They'd only met when he came home for the odd visit. And he was ten years older than her. They didn't have much in common, he thought now.

He began to feel some sympathy for his father and had visions of himself turning out like him, just reading the paper and grunting in agreement whenever his wife said something.

His irritation built. At nine o'clock, they went up to their room.

'You go to the bathroom first,' he suggested, opening his book.

Vickie took her dressing gown, found her toilet bag, and went out and down the corridor to the bathroom. After half an hour, he wondered what on earth she was doing and was about to go and knock on the bathroom door when she appeared looking very nervous. He thought she'd done something to her hair, and she had some kind of silky dressing gown on. He got his towel and toilet bag and went to the bathroom. Ten minutes later he returned.

Vickie was sitting up in bed. The silky nightgown she wore had a high neck and long sleeves, but it was half open at the front, revealing the curve of her breasts—a startling sight.

He took his book from his bag and got into bed beside her. Giving her a conciliatory smile, he said, 'Reading helps me to relax.'

He tried to read for a while until he heard a smothered sniff. He turned to look at her. A tear slowly slid down her cheek. 'What's wrong now, Vickie?' he said, feeling guilty.

With a suppressed sob, she said, 'It's our wedding night and you're reading a book! I thought ... I thought on our wedding night, you would make love to me.'

Oh fuck! He simply didn't desire her! But he turned to Vickie, attempting a smile, and managed to get aroused. He pulled up her silky nightgown and lay on top of her. Soon after, having gained his release, he withdrew and rolled off. He went to get up and wipe himself and then saw the blood.

'Was it good for you?' she said in a shaky voice.

He looked at her and felt ashamed. 'I'm sorry, Vickie, that was a bit rough. I didn't realise you were still a virgin. Forgive me.'

Her chin wobbled. 'I was saving myself for you,' she whispered.

Oh, God! Filled with remorse, he got a wash cloth and went to wipe her.

She pushed his hand away. 'I can do it,' she said, still whispering. 'I didn't know it would be so painful.'

He tried to make amends by being thoughtful for the rest of their time in Cowes, going for walks with her, looking at the shops and even foregoing visiting the seaplane factory.

At last the week ended, and he took Vickie back to her house, then returned to his digs near where he worked. It seemed to be the best arrangement until they sorted out where to live. The first weekend when he returned to Kent, Vickie decided she'd like to come and live in London with him and let the house in Kent. His mother was disappointed; she had hoped John would get work in the area so he and Vickie would be living next door.

'I'll spend the next few weekends looking for a suitable house to rent,' he told Vickie as he left. He gave her a quick kiss.

'Goodbye, darling.' She waved goodbye. 'I'll start sorting and packing our things ready for moving.'

John spent the next three weekends looking at houses, but couldn't find anything he thought might be suitable. *No point in rushing, though.* Somehow he didn't find the prospect of coming home to Vickie every night very appealing. He thought he'd better go down to Kent the following weekend and tell her about the places he'd seen.

When he arrived, he knocked on the door and tentatively opened it. He still hadn't got used to the idea that the house was now theirs and that he could just walk in. It would always be Peter Burgess's house to him.

Vickie rushed out to meet him, all smiles. Before he could give her a kiss, she threw her arms around him. 'I have news!' His jacket muffled her voice.

'Oh? Good news, I hope?' he replied.

She stood back and looked at him. 'We're going to have a baby!' she announced joyfully.

John closed his eyes—another bond to tie him to her. 'That's certainly news.'

'Are you pleased?' Her smile faded.

'Of course, I am! It's wonderful!' He tried to put some excitement into his voice.

'I was waiting to tell you before I told your parents. I'm feeling quite sick, not just in the mornings, but all day, so it was a bit hard to hide it from Mother,' she continued. 'Now, take off your coat and come and eat. I've made your favourite dinner: steak and kidney pudding, according to Mother.'

She started calling his parents Mother and Father after the wedding—another thing that irritated him. He took a deep breath and tried to smile. 'That's lovely of you, dear.'

When they sat down to eat, he saw she ate hardly anything.

'I'm still feeling really nauseous,' she said as she pushed her food around her plate. Then she got up from the table with her napkin to her mouth. 'Excuse me,' she mumbled. 'Please keep eating; it's just the sickness.' She rushed out of the room, and he heard her upstairs in the toilet, vomiting.

Better leave her alone. He didn't feel like eating now.

She returned looking pale, and then saw his plate. 'Oh, now I've put you off your dinner!'

'It's all right,' he replied. 'It was lovely, thank you.'

She sat down and looked at her plate. 'I've been thinking that perhaps I should stay here until the baby is born,' she said quietly. 'It will be nice to have Mother next door to help. I'd love to be with you all the time, but if I continue to have this sickness I won't be much of a companion for you.'

'Hmm, that sounds sensible.' He couldn't think of anything else to say.

A few minutes later, a knock came at the front door. It opened and his mother's voice called. 'Anyone home?' She came in followed by his father. When she saw their serious expressions and Vickie's pale face, she looked worriedly from John to Vickie. 'Is everything all right?'

Vickie smiled. 'We have some news for you.' She looked at John, waiting for him to tell his mother. When he said nothing, she burst out: 'We're having a baby!'

His mother beamed with joy. His father patted his arm—almost in sympathy, John thought.

'Well done, Son,' his father said.

John rolled his eyes.

Sometimes, instead of going down to Kent, John spent the weekend with Leslie on the pretext of helping him with his latest invention. Vickie was so absorbed with knitting and sewing and preparing for the baby that she didn't seem to mind.

In 1921, just nine months after their wedding, their son was born. John wanted to name him David; Vickie wanted Peter or Patrick. They called him Daniel.

The pattern for their marriage had been established. He stayed in London during the week and went back to Kent most week-ends. He decided to buy a car; public transport was taking too much of his time. He bought a second-hand Model T Ford and spent a lot of his free time fixing it.

CHAPTER 10

In 1922 Piers turned sixteen. With the boys home from school for the Easter holidays, the house filled with noise again. Ena was thrilled to have them back.

'It's so quiet without you,' she said. 'I miss you all. And you've all got so big!'

'Yes,' Percy agreed.

He studied Lily as she put on her hat and gloves, preparing to leave for Leslie's. She'd held healing sessions twice a week at Leslie's for nearly two years now. She also gave private healings for well off people in their own homes. At first, it'd seemed that the old vibrant Lily was back, but now he felt she was slowly drifting away from him. They didn't have much to say to each other anymore, and when they did talk she soon became impatient with him. She was quick to grasp concepts and, unless it was something to do with numbers, he had to think hard to keep up.

Maybe this is what happens to long married couples. He couldn't go by his own parents. His father had died when he, Percy, was ten. The Bancrofts seemed very happy and content, and so were James and Phoebe. But then, Lily wasn't like other women.

He sighed as he made his way back to the parlour.

That evening Percy looked at everyone sitting at the dinner table and smiled. 'It's nice to have everyone here again.'

Piers looked up. 'Daddy, I want to leave school and learn about mechanics. I don't want to go to University; I want to get an apprenticeship and work on engines, or be a bus driver.'

Horrified, Lily stared at him. 'I would've given anything to have gone to University,' she said, 'how can you possibly think of getting an apprenticeship!'

'He can go to University at any time,' Percy said. 'Piers, wait until you finish this school year, it's only a few more weeks, and then you can leave. Meanwhile, we can find out about an apprentice-ship.'

For once Lily didn't argue; perhaps because Percy rarely took a stand.

Later that night, while getting ready for bed, Lily turned to him. 'Percy, I really don't like the idea of Piers doing an apprenticeship. He's clever and should go to University.'

'My darling Lily, everyone is different. He's not like you, and he has always liked building things and been interested in engines. Since I came home from the war, he has been asking me to teach him to drive, and he's always checking the engine of the car. It's important that he does something that he's interested in and enjoys doing.'

'I suppose so, but where can we find an apprenticeship for him? I don't know anyone with an engineering company.'

'What about Leslie Carter? He knows a lot of people, he might be able to suggest somewhere.'

Lily nodded. 'I'll ask him, but I don't often see him when I go to his place to do healings as he's usually at work. Mrs Wilson lets me in.'

The next evening, Lily telephoned Leslie.

'My dear Lily, how are you?' Leslie said, always pleased to hear from her.

'Dear Leslie, I have a favour to ask of you.'

'Always ready to help, my dear. I'm sorry that due to my work, I don't see much of you when you come over for your healings.'

'Well, my eldest son, Piers, wants to leave school and do an engineering apprenticeship, and we don't know of any engineering factory that would take an apprentice. Percy thought you might know of a suitable place.'

'I'll certainly do my best to find out for you,' he said. 'And Lily?'

'Yes?'

'Have you heard that Howard Carter has found the entrance to Tutankhamun's tomb?'

Silence. Then, 'Yes.' Lily gently replaced the receiver.

***

Leslie approached John with a request about a possible apprenticeship. 'It's for Lily's eldest son; he's interested in engines, and if he can't get an apprenticeship, he said he'd get a job as a bus driver. You can imagine Lily's reaction to that.' He smiled.

'Yes,' John replied. He closed his eyes, picturing Lily. 'I know that A.E.C do take apprentices, so I'll find out. What's he like?'

'Young Piers? I've never met him. He's at boarding school, and Lily rarely talks about the children.'

'Give me her telephone number, please, and if I can organise something, I can ring her.'

The thought of contacting Lily filled John with excitement. Two weeks later, he telephoned her. His heart sank when Mrs Burton answered the phone and said that Lily wasn't there, but Mr Hedgecock was and she would get him.

John didn't want to speak to Lily's husband, but Percy said hello before he had a chance to say anything. 'Hello, Mr Hedgecock,' John replied, 'you don't know me, but a friend of your wife asked me if I knew of anywhere that would take an engineering apprentice.'

'Oh, yes, that would've been Leslie Carter?'

'Yes, and I've arranged for your son to go for an interview at Associated Engineering Company in Walthamstow on Friday at 8 o'clock.'

'That's most kind of you. Lily will be so pleased. Who shall I say telephoned?'

'John Watts.'

'May I have your telephone number? I'm sure she'll want to thank you personally.'

John smiled. So, he would get to speak to her. He waited, on edge, all evening, and eventually heard the telephone ring in the hall.

His landlady answered it and knocked on his door a minute or two later. 'Telephone for you, Mr. Watts.'

'Thank you, John,' Lily said. 'It's very kind of you to get an interview for Piers.'

'I'd do anything for you, Lily. You know that.'

He heard her taking deep breaths before she spoke again: 'What does he say when he gets there?'

'Tell him report to the Works Manager and say that John Watts sent him.'

'Thank you. I'll tell him.'

'And, Lily?'

'Yes?'

'It will be very hard work, and he'll start at the bottom, making tea and doing odd jobs like a messenger boy for a few weeks before he gets sent to the different machine shops.'

'I'll warn him.'

'It will be a very good training if he can stay the course.'

'He's a determined boy.'

John tried to think of something else to say to keep her on the telephone. But she was already saying goodbye and thanking him again.

***

'That was very nice of Mr. Watts to go to the trouble of finding an apprenticeship for Piers,' Percy said when Lily went back to the parlour. 'If this interview goes well, I suppose he'd better leave school now and not go back for the summer term.'

'Yes,' Lily replied, trying to get her breath; her heart was beating so fast. 'I hope Piers won't let him down.'

Excited at the prospect of an apprenticeship, Piers went off to the interview. To everyone's delight, the Works Manager told him to start the next morning at seven o'clock for a trial week. Piers didn't seem to mind the early morning starts, getting up at half-past five to walk to the tram and then take a bus to the factory, and it was usually seven o'clock at night by the time he returned home. At the end of the week the Works Manager started him as an indentured apprentice. Piers told his parents that the manager had said he'd been impressed with Piers' eagerness to please and willingness to do whatever he was told with a smile.

'Imagine that our eldest child is out in the world and working!' Percy said to Lily that night after dinner.

'Hmm?' Lily looked up from the book she was reading.

'I said, it's hard to imagine we have a son out in the world and working.'

'Yes, I don't like to think of it. I'm getting old. I think the children should start calling me Lily, instead of Mummy.'

Percy looked surprised. 'You're not old!'

'I'm thirty-eight, Percy!'

'But you certainly don't look it; in fact anyone would take you to be twenty-five!'

Lily felt somewhat gratified by his comment, but her increasing age wasn't really the cause of her restlessness. 'But I haven't done the things I always wanted to do!' she said. 'I want to go to Egypt and see the Pyramids—you know I've always been interested in Egyptology, and now Howard Carter and Lord Carnarvon have discovered the entrance to Tutankhamen's tomb!'

'My darling, Lily, I don't think we can afford the money to go to Egypt at the moment. Perhaps when the boys are finished school, we can think about it.'

'I get money from the healings I do at Leslie's, and my private healings,' Lily said thoughtfully. 'I think he has been putting it aside for me. Of course, he has to take something for rent. I must remember to ask him the next time I see him.'

Percy frowned, probably hoping she'd forget.

***

John kept an eye out for Piers. He didn't have to wait long before the young apprentice came to him with a folder of plans from the Works Manager.

'Thank you,' John said, taking the folder. 'You're new here, I think.'

'Yes, I'm Piers Hedgecock. I've just started an apprenticeship. And I think you must be the Mr. Watts who vouched for me?'

'Yes.'

'I'd like to thank you for helping me,' Piers said.

John noticed his resemblance to Lily. 'That's all right. You should do well. Just do as you're told and work hard.'

'Yes, sir, thank you, sir.' Piers nodded and went off on his next errand.

John turned back to his work. He must stop thinking about Lily. She was married with a husband and a young family, and he had a wife and baby. But, oh God, it was hard.

***

The development of the gramophone absorbed John and Leslie the following year. They worked on various improvements, and John made a beautiful timber case to hold his gramophone and a cabinet with divisions to hold the records.

'I don't know why you're making a cabinet to hold gramophone records,' Leslie remarked as he watched John working on the oak timber. 'They'll be defunct once the radio takes off.'

'Maybe. I know with a radio you don't have to keep changing the record, but you can't listen to the music you want. With the radio, you just get whatever happens to be playing.'

Leslie nodded. 'That's true, but most people like a variety, not like you, who keeps playing Cavalleria Rusticana all the time!'

John laughed. 'Is that a hint?' Then he sighed. 'I really must go back to Kent next weekend. Little Daniel's nearly two now and very sweet; I miss him.'

'Hmm. You don't seem to go very often these days.'

Vickie's demands kept him away:

'Daniel needs a little brother or sister, John,' she'd said last time he visited.

Then his mother had started: 'We don't want little Danny to be an only child like you, John. It would be much nicer for him to have a little brother or sister, you know. Don't you agree, Paul?'

His father had looked up from his paper and grunted something.

'See, your father agrees.'

John had given an echoing grunt and then a sardonic smile. It seemed he was getting ever more like his father!

'Look how you and Patrick were so close,' his mother had added. 'He was like a brother. That's what Daniel needs.'

John sighed again. Vickie bored and annoyed him and made it hard for him to feel any sexual attraction towards her, and that made him feel guilty. He realised that his not being home very often, not seeing as much of his son as he should, compounded the guilt, and now he wouldn't do his duty and provide a sibling for him.

'That's a big sigh,' Leslie remarked. 'Look, I've put Cavalleria on again for you.'

John smiled. 'Thanks, Leslie. You're a pal.'

***

Ena, now sixteen, left school, and Piers moved to digs near his work to avoid the long travel every day.

Two restless women in the house, both beautiful and clever, overwhelmed Percy. Lily always seemed to be going somewhere. She often took Ena either to the Crystal Palace to play billiards or to a theatre or whatever was the latest craze, as well as to her séances and healings.

The initial satisfaction of having Ena to accompany her soon wore off. Percy thought Lily was a little bit jealous of Ena's youthful beauty. He guessed that the focus of attention would've been on Ena, rather than Lily.

At dinner on the boys' first night home from boarding school, Ena dropped a bombshell:

'Daddy, I'd like to learn about the stock market and broking. Could you help me to find a position?'

Lily looked up. 'Darling, Ena, I thought you'd want to go to University!'

Ena looked at her mother. 'Mummy, I mean, Lily, I really want to work and learn about finance and earn some money.'

'Earn money! When you could go to college and learn about the universe! My darling, I cannot believe you are my daughter. Why, when I was your age all I wanted was to go to university and study. First Piers has gone off to work in a factory, now you're wanting to work in an office. George, you're next. Do you want to do something low class and common as well?'

'Daddy works in an office,' Ena said quietly.

Lily ignored her remark.

Percy picked up the salt-cellar and put it back down.

George looked up. 'I want to learn to be a chef,' he announced.

Lily opened her mouth, then closed it again, speechless.

'I want to leave school. I'm fifteen now, and I want to learn to be a chef,' he repeated loudly. 'And, Mama, you're a snob!'

Percy glared at George. 'How dare you speak to your mother like that; apologise at once!'

George mumbled something that vaguely sounded like, 'Sorry.'

Percy looked at Lily. 'Lily darling, Ena and George have to do what makes them happy.'

Lily burst into tears, banged down her knife and fork, jumped up from the table and slammed out of the room, leaving the family stunned by this outburst.

Ena stood to follow her, but Percy placed a restraining hand on her arm. 'Let her go, Ena. I know she's unhappy, but I don't know what to do about it.' He paused for a moment. 'Ena, darling, you don't have to earn money, you know. I can increase your allowance.'

'Oh, Daddy, I have enough with your allowance; it's just that I want to learn about the stock market and have an income and be independent.'

He smiled. 'I'll ask around. I don't think I should ask my employers. The other ladies might see it as favouritism.' He turned to his second son. 'But George, this is something new!'

'No,' George said. 'I've always loved to cook. I've always helped Mrs Burton in the kitchen. It's just that no-one has noticed.'

'I've noticed,' Ena said, 'and Daddy, Mrs Burton does need help; she has to do everything now.'

Percy felt guilty. He hadn't thought about all the work to do in the house.

David just sat, silently watching the drama.

Eventually Percy got up from the table and sighed. 'I'd better go and see your mother.'

He went up to their bedroom where he found Lily lying on the bed gazing into space.

'Lily darling, are you all right?' He knelt beside the bed.

'Percy! No, I'm not all right! You have your work, and you spend more time in the garden or listening to music on your old phonogram than you do with me. And since the war you seem to have got quieter and more withdrawn than ever. You don't love me like you used to.'

Percy didn't know what to say. He put his hands over hers. 'I know I can't satisfy you in a lot of ways,' he said eventually, his heart sinking. 'I didn't realise I was holding you back.'

She sighed and turned towards him. 'It's not your fault, Percy. We're too different. Perhaps we should never have married, or rather, perhaps I should never have got married.'

He went cold. 'What can I do, Lily? I don't know if I can change. I don't enjoy going out and meeting people like you do, and you know I love you, darling, I just can't ... you know, anymore.'

Lily stared into space.'I don't know what is happening with my children. They all want to do common, working-class jobs. Where did I go wrong?'

Percy thought that perhaps if she'd been home more often, shown more interest in her children instead of packing them off to boarding school, they may have been different. However, he didn't say it.

'But there's still David. Maybe he'll want to go to University.'

Percy doubted it.

***

Just before Christmas, Ena started work with a stockbroker that had a good reputation. Percy had found it easy to find a position for her. He was known to be a good, reliable worker, and Ena made a good impression when she went for an interview.

It pleased Percy that Ena was standing on her own feet and doing something she enjoyed. David was a shy, diffident boy, excelling in sport and mathematics, but he hated being at boarding school, especially now that his brothers had left. Percy missed him, but Lily wouldn't hear of taking him out of boarding school.

George surprised them all. He went around to every hotel restaurant until he found one that would take him as an apprentice. He told them the news one night over dinner

Percy felt proud of him 'Well done, Son!' he said.

'I start next week. I know I'll only be washing up and cleaning vegetables for a while, but that's all right,' George beamed.

Lily just stared at him in dismay. But she soon had something else to occupy her mind.

CHAPTER 11

Just before Easter in 1925 Vickie gave birth to John's daughter. Though having another child was much against his better judgement, he'd given in to pressure from Vickie and his mother, and that made him feel like a weakling.

A new type of double decker bus with an enclosed top deck was due to be introduced on the London streets that summer. He had to work late most days and some weekends, so he didn't get down to Kent as often as Vickie thought he should.

'I can't manage Danny and the baby on my own,' became her constant refrain. 'I'm tired all the time, and it's getting me down.'

'Doesn't my mother help you?'

'Yes, but she has enough to do with your father,' she replied petulantly.

He felt a bit guilty, and the fear that she might turn out like her mother niggled in the back of his mind. Then how would he cope? 'After these new buses are operational in the summer, I should be able to get back most weekends; well that's if everything goes smoothly.'

Vickie looked at him suspiciously. 'So who else is working late at night?'

'The draughtsmen and another engineer,' he replied wearily.

She sniffed but said nothing.

By December John knew there was something wrong with baby Margaret's legs. They looked twisted. The doctor said they would straighten out once she was older. However, John wasn't so sure.

'Vickie, I think we should seek another opinion on Margaret.'

'Oh?' she looked up from breastfeeding the baby. 'What do you suggest?'

'I know a lady who might be able to help.'

Vickie's eyes lit up, and hope filled her voice. 'Can she come and see her? Or can we take Margaret to her?'

'I'll find out. She has a good reputation. I'll telephone her when I get back to London.'

The next night as soon as he got back to his digs, he went to the telephone in the hall. He felt his heart beating against his ribs. Her telephone number was burnt into his brain. He asked the telephonist for her number and waited, breathless.

Ena answered.

'Oh, hello, I wonder if I might speak to Mrs Hedgecock?'

'Yes, I'll fetch her now. May I ask who's calling?'

'It's John Watts.'

He heard the receiver being put down, then voices, and after a few minutes, Lily's voice: 'Hello, John?'

'Hello, Lily. I need your help. Our baby, Margaret has a problem with her legs. They seem to be crooked; I think it's her hips. She's eight months old now. I wondered if you'd be able to help.'

Silence. Had she put down the phone and walked away?

'Of course,' she replied eventually. 'If I can help I will. Where is the baby?'

'In Kent. I could come and get you and take you down, or bring the baby to your healings at Leslie's if that would be more convenient.' His heart beat so loudly he felt sure she'd be able to hear it.

'Yes. I can go down to Kent with you to see the baby. When?'

'I have to go back to work tomorrow. Could you make it next Saturday?'

'Yes. Do you know my address?'

She gave him her address, and they arranged that he'd be at her house about eleven o'clock the following Saturday.

John sat down at once and wrote to Vickie, telling her that a Mrs Hedgecock would be coming the following Saturday. He went straight out and posted it.

At ten minutes to eleven on Saturday morning he stood outside Lily's house. He knocked on the door, and when it opened he found her already waiting. They looked at each other. Wordlessly he opened the passenger door and helped her into his car. Once they'd driven past London he stopped the car and turned to her.

'Oh, Lily. My beautiful, Lily! This is the wrong way for us to meet again.' He leaned over to kiss her.

She tried to push him away, but with not much resistance. 'Oh, John.'

'My darling, Lily.'

'Come, let's see what we can do for your baby daughter.'

Ashamed, he replied, 'Of course,' and they drove on.

At the house he escorted her in.

'Vickie, this is Mrs Hedgecock. She's a healer.'

Vickie frowned, taken aback. 'I thought you were bringing a children's specialist.' She shrugged. 'Well, she can't do any harm, I suppose.'

Luckily Lily didn't hear this.

When she saw the baby, she went over and touched her little legs. She closed her eyes and gently stroked each one. She did this for several minutes while Vickie looked on sceptically, John's mother hovering around in the background. Then, unbelievably, the little legs seemed to twist and right themselves.

Vickie's mouth fell open.

John smiled. For some reason he felt immensely proud of Lily.

The baby looked up at Lily, smiled, and kicked her legs.

'Oh, Mrs Hedgecock! Thank you so much!' Vickie said, ecstatic. 'How can we ever repay you? How much do you charge?'

'I don't charge,' came the reply. 'People sometimes give me a donation, but it's not mandatory.'

'John!' Vickie said in a shrill voice. 'Please pay Mrs Hedgecock. But please, I'll make you some refreshment. Or Mother will.'

'Yes, of course,' said his mother. 'You've had a long journey.'

They walked into the kitchen where the kettle already simmered on the stove.

Vickie followed them with Margaret in her arms. 'I can't thank you enough, Mrs Hedgecock.' She glanced at John and frowned, catching him looking at Lily. 'How did you know about Mrs Hedgecock?' she asked him.

John shrugged and tried to sound casual. 'Oh, Lily is a friend of Leslie Carter.'

Vickie examined Lily, eyes narrowing. Perhaps she noticed Lily's stunning beauty. She turned away and sighed as if it didn't matter. 'I'm so pleased baby Margaret is all right.'

On the drive back to London, John pulled into a hotel. 'Lily, darling. Please let me buy you dinner.'

Lily smiled. 'I'm not hungry; thank you, John.'

'I am. Oh, Lily, please, my darling, I've missed you so much.'

'John. I feel the same, but you have a wife and a young boy, and now a baby. I have a husband and four children.'

'Your children are nearly grown up. They don't need you. My children don't need me either. I've never loved Vickie. I have only ever loved you, Lily.' He took her in his arms, and she couldn't resist. 'Lily, we must be together. We have to find a way.' He gave her a long passionate kiss.

She pulled away, breathless. 'John, take me home, before we do something we might regret.'

'There are lots of things I regret, Lily, but meeting you isn't one of them.'

He turned back to the steering wheel and tried to start the car. Nothing happened. He got out and tried turning the starting handle, but still no response from the engine. He cursed and lifted the bonnet. Lily sat in the car, seemingly quite happy to stay there forever. She smiled at John as he tried again to start the car.

'No go, I'm afraid,' he eventually said. 'What to do!'

They were still a long way from London. He cursed himself for even stopping. Then he saw a little secret smile on Lily's lips.

'I think we might be stranded here tonight,' she remarked.

His heart leaped.

'I'd better telephone home,' she said.

He walked into the hotel and registered them as Mr and Mrs Watts.

***

The weekend after Lily had been down and healed the baby, Vickie started to harangue John as soon as he got in the door.

'So how is your Mrs Hedgecock? Did you get back to London all right? I telephoned your digs and they said you hadn't returned.'

He sighed. 'Can't I even get in the door? The car broke down. I had a job to fix it. I was late back.'

She sniffed. 'She's quite nice looking, for her age, don't you think?'

'Who? Mrs Hedgecock? Possibly.'

'Oh, don't pretend you don't know,' her voice sounded bitter. 'I saw the way you looked at her.'

He tried not to react. 'I'll go and see Margaret.'

'No! Don't wake her! I've only just put her down.'

'Where's Danny? I'll take him for a walk to give you a break.'

'He's in with your mother,' she replied sulkily.

Grateful to have an excuse to get away from her, he started out the door again. 'I'll go and fetch him and see mother and father.'

He left quickly, pretending not to hear her say, 'That's right! Run away.'

Little Daniel was the only thing that made Christmas bearable, and seeing Margaret kicking her little legs. Every time he looked at her he thought of Lily.

The first weekend after New Year, John made the excuse that he had to work on his car and couldn't get down to Kent. Vickie wrote straight back, unimpressed, demanding that he get a job near them, that it wasn't fair on her.

He needed to see Lily. He spent Saturday afternoon working on his car, but on Sunday he just wanted to hear her voice. He went down the hall of his lodgings to the telephone, picked up the handset and asked for Lily's number, praying she'd be at home. Amazingly she was.

'John!'

'Lily, can we meet?'

'I'm just on my way out to a meeting in support of the miners.'

'Where is it? I'll see you there after the meeting; tell me where I can find you.'

Lily mentioned a hotel close to Hyde park.

'I'll meet you there.'

He waited anxiously at the hotel, and then he saw her. He had to close his eyes and stop himself from running to her. 'Lily,' he took her arm, 'come into the hotel. We can have tea.'

She smiled at him. 'That's a good idea.'

They went in, and he ordered tea.

'I'm not really hungry,' she said.

'Oh, Lily, I'm only hungry for you.' He looked at her and then said tentatively, 'Shall I get a room?'

'No, no! I must go home.'

He just sat and looked at her. 'I miss you so much, Lily; I can't go on like this.'

Lily looked down at her hands. 'John, I feel the same way, but I don't know what to do. Percy needs me, since the war he's been different. Sad all the time. The children are growing up. The older ones are settled now. Only David is still at school. I don't know what he wants to do.'

'Please, Lily, stay the night with me.'

She looked up at him. 'No, John. I can't.'

'Another night, then? Please, Lily!'

She shook her head. 'I can't carry on like this, John. I don't want to hurt Percy.'

He took her hands. 'Lily, darling, you have to live your life for you, not for others. I can't carry on like this, either. My marriage is a farce; I love only you. This is tearing me apart.'

She sighed. 'I know. I feel the same. I might be able to find an excuse to be away from home. I don't know when. I'll telephone you. Oh, John, I hate this clandestine muddle.'

John grinned, feeling ecstatic. 'I'll arrange something.' He took her hands. 'My darling! Look, this is the telephone number of my digs. Ring me there, any evening after seven. Even if we can just meet for an afternoon. Please Lily.'

The following Saturday afternoon, John met Lily at the British Museum and took her to a nearby hotel, where they had tea.

'Darling! I could book a room for us.'

Lily wavered.

He smiled. 'We would be private.'

She said nothing.

He got up and went to reception. When he returned they quickly finished their tea and then went up to the room John had booked. He took her into his arms and was about to kiss her when Lily suddenly stiffened.

'Oh, no,' she cried. 'No! Mama, no!'

John leaped back. 'What's wrong?'

'My mama! She's passed. She just came to me.' Lily's expression became distraught. 'It's a judgement on me for being unfaithful.'

John took her to a sofa and sat her down. 'Lily, calm down. I don't understand; what's wrong?'

Lily burst into tears. 'I must go home, John. I'm sorry. This is all my fault; it's a judgement.' John realised that his planned afternoon of rapture was ruined. 'My darling, Lily, I'll drive you straight home. Come now, compose yourself and go down to the lobby. I'll settle my account and meet you there.'

In his car on the way to her house, she said, 'If anyone asks, I met you at the rally, and you brought me home.'

'Of course.' He couldn't think of anything else to say.

***

Percy heard the sad news just before Lily came home. He paced up and down the hall, waiting for her, and went to meet her when he heard her coming.

'Lily, darling, I have bad news.'

'I know! She came to me and told me she'd met Ernie. Oh Percy, what happened?'

'She was hit by a runaway horse. Apparently, she fell and hit her head on the road, and never regained consciousness. Oh, Lily, darling.' He took her in his arms. 'My darling, there is something else. Your papa collapsed when he heard. He's not well. We must go to him at once.'

Lily burst into fresh sobs. 'It's all my fault.'

'How could it be your fault, Lily? It was an accident. Come, we must go to your father. I don't know where Ena is. I think she went to a dance with some friends. But there's time enough for her to learn the news. I'll ask Mrs Burton to tell her to telephone when she gets home.'

Lily and Percy drove straight to her father. They found him in the drawing room where he'd been reading the paper when the news came.

He looked deathly pale and had a blue tinge around his mouth.

'Lily,' he managed to say. 'I can't live without your mama.'

'I know, dearest Papa.' She took his hand.

'God bless you, Lily dear. You know I love you, even though we've had differences.'

'Yes, Papa, and I love you.'

He gave a weak smile and closed his eyes. 'Tell James, I love him, too.'

'Papa! You have to stay. It's not your time. We need you. Please relax and I will help you.'

She took his hands and stroked them. Then she placed her hands over his heart.

After a while his breathing became steadier, the blue tinge disappeared and a slight colour came into his cheeks. Lily closed her eyes, but she still remained with her hands over his heart.

Gently Percy said, 'Lily. I have to go out for a bit.'

She opened her eyes. 'No! Please don't leave. Why must you go out?'

He sighed. 'I have to go to the hospital to arrange to bring back your mother's body. Her maid was with her when it happened; she managed to come back and tell your father, but then she became hysterical and collapsed. I tried to telephone James, but he's in Edinburgh at the moment so Phoebe said. There is no-one else.'

'It's all my fault,' she said again.

'I'll be back as soon as I can. Darling Lily, please do as I say. The housekeeper is going to prepare a place for her. I've asked the maid to bring tea for you, and I've left a message for Ena to come as soon as she gets home. Please, darling, I beg of you.'

She nodded. 'Thank you, Percy.'

He kissed her and left.

CHAPTER 12

What a rotten end to what should've been a romantic after-noon, John thought as he left Lily at her house.

Worse was to come, however.

The following weekend he went back down to Kent and found Vickie sitting in the kitchen with her arms folded and a cold look in her eyes. A feeling of impending doom came over him.

'I've had you followed,' she announced.

Oh, God. 'And?' he said.

'You were seen going into a hotel with a woman last Saturday night.'

Taken aback, he blinked. 'And?'

'It's been going on for a long time,' Vickie spat out the words. 'I thought there was something up, the way you've been saying you had to work and not coming home every weekend. Now I have proof.' She sat hunched up with repressed anger. 'I hate you, John Watts. You've betrayed me. You've been unfaithful. I don't believe you ever loved me.'

He couldn't deny any of it.

She looked up, her eyes red and wild. 'I want a divorce,' she shouted, 'and you will never see the children again. I could kill you, John Watts.'

He wanted to say that the law didn't work that way, but her outburst stunned him so much that he just stood and said nothing.

'That's right. You can't deny it, can you?'

'I'd better go,' he said quietly. 'When you're calmer we can discuss it.' As soon as the words left his lips, he knew he'd said the wrong thing.

She jumped up and screamed at him: 'That's right! Run away; turn a blind eye; ignore me; ignore the children. Run back to your precious Mrs Hedgecock. She's a slut.'

He took a deep breath and opened the door.

'Get out of *my* house. Don't ever come back!'

He'd hardly got through the door when she slammed it behind him. He stood for a few minutes to collect himself before going back to his car.

His mother came out from next door and walked over to him. 'I heard the shouting,' she said. 'What's going on? Is Vickie all right?'

'No,' he replied. 'You'd better try and calm her down. I'm going back to London.'

His mother looked at him with dismay, but before she could say anything, he'd started his car and gone.

He stopped the car at the first hotel he came to and looked at his shaking hands. *My life is a mess,* he thought as he got out of the car and went into the hotel. *What do I do now?* He thought of Leslie and used the hotel telephone kiosk to call him.

'Leslie, old boy, do you think I could come and spend the night at your place? I'm on my way back from Kent.'

'Of course, John. Are you all right? You sound a bit strange.'

'Yes, yes, just been a rotten couple of weeks.'

'All right, drive carefully.'

He drove in a daze, numb from shock. When he finally stepped into the tranquillity of Leslie's house, he felt a surge of relief.

'Come in,' Leslie said, then he frowned as he took in John's appearance. 'Old boy, what on earth is wrong, you look deathly. Come, I'll get you a brandy.'

John accepted the brandy with shaking hands, drank it in one gulp, then had a coughing fit. 'Long story. Give me a minute,' he managed to say.

Leslie sat quietly. When he saw that John had regained his composure, he said, 'Spill the beans, old chap.'

John sighed. 'The thing is that Lily and I have been seeing each other again, well, not really, only once or twice; it all started with the baby. The baby girl, Margaret. She had a problem with her hips, all twisted. I contacted Lily and took her down to Kent and she fixed little Margaret's legs. It was miraculous! But Vickie got suspicious. The car broke down on the way back and Lily and I stayed in a hotel overnight. Together.'

Leslie pursed his lips and frowned.

John continued the story, including their thwarted afternoon together at the hotel, 'We'd just gone up to the room when something terrible happened. Lily had a psychic experience. She said her mother had appeared to her and that she must have passed. She was so distraught, just wanted to go home. So, I took her home. I telephoned the next day to find out what had happened. The housekeeper answered and said that Lily's mother had been killed, a runaway horse apparently.'

'Yes, I heard Lily's mother had passed,' Leslie said. 'I had a message to say Lily wouldn't be able to do her healings for a while and to please cancel any appointments, but I didn't know the details. Poor Lily!' He got up. 'I think I need a drink. More for you too, John?'

'Please. But there's more.' John handed Leslie his glass.

Leslie sat down again.

'Today I went down to Kent and Vickie was beside herself. She'd hired a private detective to follow me, and he saw me and Lily go into the hotel and upstairs. He managed to check the register somehow. I'd stupidly put Mr and Mrs Watts.'

'Oh dear.'

'Yes.' John grimaced. 'I'm not skilled at clandestine affairs. Anyway, today she said she wants a divorce and that I will never see the children again.'

'I'm sure that isn't the law,' Leslie said.

John sighed. 'I don't know. I just feel completely down and out.'

Leslie refilled their glasses. ' What did your parents say?'

'I didn't go to them. My mother heard Vickie shouting and came out. I couldn't stand a lecture from my mother, and my father would've just said, "Tut tut, bad business, my boy."' He put his head in his hands. 'What on earth will I do, Leslie?'

'I suppose the main thing now is to try and protect Lily from any repercussions.'

'What do you mean?' Frowning, John looked up.

'Well, Vickie may cite her in the divorce. It depends on whether this detective chappie can identify her as the woman you took up to your room.'

'Oh, my God, it's getting worse and worse. And how could anyone not remember Lily? Or not notice her? As soon as she walks into a room the atmosphere changes. Everyone in the room is compelled to look at her.' He took another gulp of the brandy. 'I'd better not have any more to drink.'

'Is there any way you and Vickie can patch things up? There are the children to consider.'

John thought. Then shook his head. 'Patch things up? Vickie would be watching my every move. My life would be hell. She was rabid with anger. I thought she was going to kill me.' He took another deep breath. 'How can I keep Lily out of this mess, Leslie?'

'I don't know, old boy. I think there was a new law brought in recently. I remember reading about it in the papers, something about a wife can now divorce her husband on the grounds of adultery, but it has to be proven.'

'Oh, that's ridiculous! I suppose I'll have to get a photographer to take pictures of me in bed with a woman.'

'Well, yes, exactly,' Leslie replied. 'Perhaps that would be the only way to keep Lily out of this. Rig up something like that and then post the incriminating photos to Vickie.'

'You're a genius, Leslie.' For the first time since he arrived, John felt slightly less distraught. 'That still doesn't solve the problem of the children, though,' he added soberly.

'One thing at a time, John,' Leslie said. 'These court cases take months, sometimes years. Perhaps we have both had too much to drink. Why don't we go out and try and get something to eat? I don't think Mrs Wilson's dinner will stretch for both of us.'

'I'm not hungry; you eat your dinner. If you have some bread and cheese that will do for me.'

***

John's news left Leslie feeling devastated. He'd tried not to show any reaction when John told him about the affair with Lily. Now, alone in his bedroom, he sat in the old armchair beside his bed and closed his eyes. John and Lily! His best friend and the woman he, Leslie, adored.

He couldn't believe that Lily would be unfaithful to Percy, or that John could be unfaithful to Vickie. The fact that John had

never wanted to marry Vickie didn't absolve him. But Lily! Oh,
Lily!

Eventually he got into bed, but sleep didn't come.

***

Percy often thought later that Melina's death was the start of
the unravelling of his life. He found the funeral terribly sad. Lily
was distraught and kept saying she was to blame. Percy tried to
reassure her, but to no avail. Several months later Spring had
arrived, but she was still cast down and not herself. He tried to
raise her spirits.

'Lily, darling, would you like to go away for a holiday somewhere? We could go to Egypt if you'd like. You've always wanted
to go.'

Lily tilted her head and frowned at him. 'No.'

'My darling, you must stop blaming yourself. Your mother's accident had nothing to do with you.'

She couldn't meet his eyes.

Her state worried him. She hadn't resumed her healing sessions
or been to any rallies since her mother's death. Not even the
General Strike had roused her from her apathy. He'd spoken
to James, but James had said he could do nothing unless Lily
came to him. He thought it possible that grief at their mother's
death had brought on an early menopause, causing her to fall into
melancholia. Percy suggested that Lily go and see James, but she
met his suggestion with a look of scorn. She shook her head, as if
his suggestion wasn't worthy of comment. He didn't know who to
turn to, but perhaps Leslie knew of someone to help her.

Percy telephoned him.

'I don't know, Percy,' Leslie said. 'As you know, she hasn't been here to do her healings or séances since her mother died. Does she have any women friends that might help? Or her daughter?'

'She doesn't really have any women friends,' Percy said,' at least she has never mentioned any, only well-known women she has healed, and I wouldn't want to ask them. Anyway, none have come to the house, and Ena doesn't have any ideas either. But thank you, Leslie. If you have any thoughts or know anyone who might help, please let me know.'

Leslie did know of someone who might be able to do something, but it might be something for the worse, not the better.

CHAPTER 13

With much distaste and misgivings, John employed a photographer to take a photograph of him and an actress in bed at a hotel in London. With the General Strike and the resulting disturbances, a few weeks passed before he posted a copy to Vickie with a note saying he was guilty of adultery with this woman, Sarah Smith on the night of Saturday 24th April.

Vickie shook as she read the letter. She told herself to stay calm, but she felt violently angry. She wanted to kill John and that woman. *Stay calm; think!* She sat and thought, rocking herself backwards and forwards, then, as she reached a decision, her rage boiled to a head. She flew next door, bursting in without knocking.

'Now look what your precious son has done,' she shouted, waving the papers in front of John's father.

Paul Watts looked up from his paper and frowned. He took the photograph and gave a start when he saw it.

'It's just come in the post! He thinks he can divorce me and be with his fancy piece, and she gets off scot-free,' she shouted. 'He's sent me this photo of him in bed with some paid tart. He thinks that will be enough for me to divorce him. Well it is, but I don't see why that slut, Mrs Hedgecock should come out of it with her reputation intact. Oh, no, but she's ruined now; I'll see to that.'

Paul Watts stood up. 'Now look, Vickie, there's no use upsetting more people than necessary. That woman healed little Margaret, and perhaps she has children of her own. Why cause more distress?'

These words inflamed Vickie even more. 'Margaret would've got better eventually anyway, the doctors said. I can't bear to think that woman touched my child, and why shouldn't she suffer? She's ruined my life,' she screamed. 'Mind the children, please, mother; I have to go to the Post Office.' She took off down the road with her apron still on.

Stunned, her mother-in-law left her ironing and went next door to get her grandchildren.

Half an hour later Vickie returned. She came into the kitchen, panting. 'I found her telephone number, and I telephoned her husband and told him his wife has been having an affair with my husband.' She banged her fist on the table, and then collapsed in tears.

Paul looked at his wife. 'Perhaps I should get the doctor.' He went to the shed to get his bicycle.

Surprised that in a crisis he was so level headed, for once Vera didn't argue with her husband. She picked up the papers and the incriminating photo. What on earth was the world coming to? She tried to put her arms around Vickie, but Vickie fought her off and hit out at her.

'Your saintly son,' she snarled.

An hour passed before the doctor came and administered a sedative. 'I think we'd better get her into hospital,' he said.

***

When Percy answered the telephone and heard a woman ranting and raving, he was about to put the receiver down when what she'd said sank in. Sickened, he quietly hung up without speaking. Unable to face Lily, he got his hat and coat and went to the drawing room door.

'I'm going for a walk, Lily.'

Without looking up Lily said, 'It's raining! Who was that on the telephone?'

'A Mrs Watts.' He turned away and walked towards the front door,

Lily jumped up and went after him, but he slipped outside, closed the front door and disappeared down the road before she had a chance to catch him.

***

Lily paced up and down, waiting for Percy to come home. Why would John's wife be telephoning Percy? Had something happened to John? But why would she ring Percy?

Eventually she heard the front door close.

She ran out to the hall. 'Percy! Where have you been? I was worried about you!'

'Were you, my dear?'

'Are you sick? Come, you're soaking wet.' She thought Percy looked pale and ill. 'What is it? Are you all right, darling?'

Percy hung up his coat on the hall stand, took off his hat and stood looking at it, slowly turning it around in his hands, then he hung it on a hook and went into the drawing room.

Lily followed him.

'It was a Mrs. Watts on the telephone. She said you and her husband have been having an affair.'

'Percy! It's not true,'

He let out a breath of relief and sat down.

Lily continued, 'At least, I, um, on two occasions, but it's all over. I haven't seen him since Mama passed.'

Percy stared at her and shook his head. He didn't seem to know what to say or do. Eventually he stood. 'I think I'll go for another walk.' He strode to the door.

Lily ran over to him. 'Wait, Percy. Wait!'

He shook her off and left the room.

Lily wrung her hands, paced up and down, and then when she heard the front door slam, went to the telephone.

***

John had only just walked in from work on that Saturday afternoon when his landlady called him to the telephone. Assuming it would be Vickie, since she would've got his letter that morning, he answered abruptly, 'Yes? Watts here.'

When he heard Lily's voice he looked around to make sure no-one was listening. 'What is it, my darling? It's so long since I heard your voice. I thought you wanted nothing more to do with me.'

'John! Your wife just rang my husband and told him we were having an affair!'

'Oh, God!' His heart sank. 'Lily, I did all I could to protect you. This is all my fault.'

'No, it's mine!' He just made out her words through the tears. 'I don't know what to do. Percy has just walked out. He's so angry.'

Can't blame him, John thought. 'Darling, can we meet somewhere?'

'No, no. I don't know what to do. Oh, John, I've missed you so, and now everything is such a mess.'

'Please! Meet me somewhere, the Museum, anywhere.'

'I won't be able to stay here; Percy will never forgive me.'

Privately John thought that Percy would forgive Lily anything, but he didn't say it. 'What will you do?'

'I don't know; it's been such a shock. I can't think straight.'

'Lily, if Percy divorces you and Margaret divorces me, then we can get married.'

Silence.

'Are you there, Lily?'

'Yes. How can you think such a thing at this point, John?'

'Because I love you and want to live with you always.' He heard the sound of a door closing.

'It's Ena, I have to go.'

Silence followed the click of the receiver returning to its cradle.

John put the receiver down, went up to his room and sat down. Would the problems never end? Perhaps it was a good thing to have it all out in the open. He should probably go down to Kent, but as he thought this, the telephone rang in the hall.

His landlady's voice accompanied a knock on his door: 'Mr Watts, telephone for you. Again.'

Damn; what now?

It was his father. 'Um, hello, Son. I think you'd better come down. The doctor's been and Vickie's been taken to hospital. I think she's had some kind of nervous breakdown.'

It took a few seconds for John to comprehend this latest disaster. 'I've just got home from work. I'll leave in half an hour. Thanks, Dad.'

***

Percy just kept walking. He didn't know what time it was, and neither did he care. *Oh, Lily, my darling, how can I live without you? How could you do this to me? I've failed you, Lily. But how could you let another man touch you? And how could you lie with another man?*

Night had fallen by the time he returned home. Ena and Lily were waiting for him.

'Daddy, where have you been?' Ena asked. 'We were worried about you.'

He looked from one to the other. Had Lily told Ena? Probably not. He managed a smile. 'Just went for a long walk, Ena, had to do some thinking, clear my head.'

'Are you hungry? You missed dinner. I'll get you something.'

Lily just looked at him and said nothing.

'No, thank you, Ena darling. I'm not hungry. Just tired. I might have an early night.' He started for the stairs.

Lily still said nothing.

'Are you all right, Daddy?'

'Yes, Ena. I'm fine. Just a bit tired.' He walked up the stairs.

Ena looked closely at her mother. 'What's going on, Mama ... I mean, Lily?'

'Nothing, darling. I'm feeling tired, too. I might have an early night.'

Ena shrugged. 'Goodnight then.'

When Lily got to the bedroom, Percy was already in bed. She sat down on the other side. 'Percy, darling.'

'Please. Spare me your apologies.'

'Percy. It just happened. I didn't mean to hurt you.'

'Lily. Please. Just leave me alone. We need to talk about this, but not tonight.'

Silently, Lily undressed and got into bed beside him. She tried to put her arms around him, but he moved away. How was it possible to love two men? She did love Percy. She'd thought he was her soulmate. Now, she still loved him, but not in the same way she loved John. *He* was her soulmate. *Oh, what a mess.* She couldn't sleep, just lay thinking. Perhaps she should leave Percy. But where would she go? She couldn't go home. That would finish her father. John lived in lodgings; she couldn't go there. She'd really messed up her life.

She thought of Leslie. No, that wouldn't work.

She knew Percy wasn't sleeping either. She wanted to put her arms around him. Dawn was breaking as she fell asleep.

Percy ached to turn over and take her into his arms, but pain and pride and the sense of betrayal held him back. And she might make overtures, and he wouldn't be able to satisfy her. Afterwards he sometimes thought that if he had, then perhaps he might have saved their marriage. He would never know.

The next night he moved into Piers' bedroom.

***

John arrived to find his parents distraught. At least little Danny was pleased to see him, and the baby gurgled and smiled at him.

His mother harangued him as soon as he got in the door, her mouth pursed with disapproval. 'How could you go off and have an affair, John, and with that so-called psychic healer woman. I can't believe it. And poor Vickie. So upset. She's lost her parents, her brother and now her husband. Can't you try and make amends? Go and see her, say you're sorry, tell her you'll never see that woman again.' She went on and on.

At last his father took a stand. 'That's enough, Vera. John's just come in after working all week and driving down here. Let him get in the door.' The effort of making this statement took its toll. He subsided behind his paper. 'Glad you're home, Son.'

'I'll take the children back home for tonight,' John said, 'and tomorrow we can talk about what to do next.'

'Yes, that would be best.' She looked at him suddenly. 'Have you eaten?'

'Not since breakfast.' The clock now read eight o'clock.

'Oh. I'll get you something to eat.'

'Just a sandwich. I'll eat it next door after I put the children to bed.'

In bed at last, he thought of Lily. What to do? Would Vickie ever be able to come home and look after the children? He wouldn't be able to cope with work and looking after them, and he couldn't afford a nanny. As it was, most of his pay went to Vickie, the rest went on his lodgings, and a small amount to cover his living expenses.

Damn and blast Peter Burgess! It was all his fault with his pressure to get him to promise to look after Vickie. He felt so tired, but sleep wouldn't come. He eventually dozed off as dawn broke. Then baby Margaret started to cry. What the hell did he do now? Was Vickie still breast feeding her? He couldn't recall. He dragged himself out of bed.

Daniel stood at the bedroom door. 'I think she'd like a rusk,' he said solemnly.

Suddenly overcome, John swept the little boy up in his arms and gave him a big hug. 'Daddy loves you, Danny! You're very clever. Do you know where the rusks are?'

He spent the next hour trying to feed the children, change Margaret's nappy and find clean clothes for them.

Daniel self-importantly helped him. 'I like having you home, Daddy,' he remarked.

John felt guilty, but he found a certain satisfaction in doing these simple chores without Vickie hovering around, telling him he was doing it all wrong.

He found a baby's bottle and the jug of milk.

'Mummy boils the milk and then you let it cool down,' Daniel instructed.

He'd just fed Margaret and put her down to sleep and given Daniel his breakfast when his mother arrived.

'I've come to give the children their breakfast,' she said.

'I've done it all. Danny helped me.' He smiled at his son, who was trying hard to get through a bowl of lumpy porridge.

'It's delishush,' Daniel managed to say.

What a loyal trouper.

His mother gave a sniff when she saw he'd coped quite well.

John turned to her. 'I think I should go and visit Vickie in the hospital now, if you wouldn't mind staying with the children.'

'Of course,' she replied, 'but make sure you tell her you're sorry and it's all over with this woman, and ask her to have you back.'

He shook his head sadly. 'It's gone past that, Mother.'

'Never too late, Son. Remember the children.'

He found Vickie in a psychiatric ward sitting up in bed, nervously picking at the bedspread. He wasn't expecting to see her so calm after hearing what had happened the previous day.

'Hello, Vickie.' He sat down by the bed.

'Hello, John.' She didn't meet his eyes and started to tremble, then she looked up. 'John, you've got to get me out of here,' she said with fear in her eyes. 'I heard the doctor talking to one of the nurses. They want to give me electric shock treatment. I saw it done when I was a VAD. Please John. I'll do anything, whatever you want, but please don't let them do that to me.'

He didn't know what to say.

'I'll do anything rather than have that.' Her eyes pleaded with him. 'Please, John. Look, I'm sorry. I've calmed down now. I've spent all night thinking things over. You're a good man, John.'

He grimaced.

'No, really. I can see now that this has all been my fault. You never wanted to marry me. It was my father who wanted it. Well, so did I. I loved you John, but I was wrong to force the issue, and I was wrong to keep on for another baby. I thought it would bring us closer together.' She gave a wan smile. 'I shouldn't have telephoned Mrs Hedgecock's husband. He was innocent, and now I've ruined two people's lives.'

John took her hand. 'I'm sorry too, Vickie. I should've been stronger and not gone ahead with this marriage. I didn't want to hurt you. I always felt you were more like a sister than a wife. I promised your father I'd look after you, but I didn't dream at the time that he meant marriage.'

She nodded. 'We have two beautiful children, John. What will we do?'

He sighed. 'I just don't know, Vickie. I love little Danny and Margaret. I know I haven't been home much to be with them. I'm not really a good father. Most weekends I was working. Truly. Things are getting bad generally. Work is getting scarce. Now with the general strike, it's a forecast of things to come. I'll always support you and the children, but I don't think our marriage can continue. I think it's best for you to go ahead and divorce me.'

She nodded sadly. 'Yes, I see that now.'

'I'll come back as many weekends as possible. Perhaps I'll be able to take the children sometimes when they're older, and I'll try and find a house to rent, instead of lodgings, so that I can have them.'

'I'll make up a bed in Danny's room for when you come home.' Tears glistened in her eyes.

'Thank you, Vickie. I appreciate that.' He got up. 'Do you think you're well enough to come home?'

'Yes. Please, John, tell the doctor you're taking me at once and that I don't need any treatment.'

'I'll see what I can do.'

The doctor looked dubious when John told him he was taking Vickie home.

'She was quite manic when she was admitted,' he said. 'I'd prefer her to stay under observation for another few days. She needs treatment. Particularly in regard to her family history.'

'I think she'll be happier and more settled in her own home with our children,' John said firmly. 'I'll take full responsibility for her, Doctor. Thank you for all your help.'

He got back to Vickie's ward to find her dressed and ready to leave.

'I was afraid you wouldn't come back,' she whispered. She was so very pale, he thought she might faint.

'Come, let's get you home.'

His mother looked delighted to see them both back. 'Everything settled then?'

Vickie gave a slight smile. 'Yes, Mother.'

John had to get back that night. He couldn't afford to miss a day of work.

CHAPTER 14

Percy found it hard to appear normal. Ena, who adored her father, immediately guessed something was up.

She found him one evening sitting in the old wicker chair he'd moved to the garden. 'Daddy, please tell me what's wrong. Have you an illness? You've hardly eaten the last few days, and you seem so down in the mouth.'

He hugged her. 'There's nothing wrong with me, Ena darling. Just a few things on my mind.'

'And Mummy is acting strangely too. Is she sick?'

'No, darling, Mummy just has things on her mind as well.'

'Is it money? I can contribute a little now that I'm working.'

He tried to smile. 'Dear Ena. No, there is really no need to worry. Now, what are you doing tonight, off to a flapper dance?'

Ena's face lit up. 'Daddy! Well, yes! I love dancing the Charleston. I bought a new dress yesterday.'

'Well, come and show me before you leave.'

The days dragged by. Percy spent most evenings in the garden. He'd pick up a trowel and wander around, not focusing on anything except the ache in his chest. He didn't know what Lily was doing. She seemed to be out all the time. When he did see her, she looked pale and exhausted. His heart was breaking. He thought that perhaps she was spending her time with this John Watts, but wouldn't he have to be at work? His own work was suffering, too. He found it hard to concentrate.

He desperately wanted to talk to her, to tell her he loved her, and perhaps they could heal the rift. Maybe go away for a holiday. They hadn't been for a holiday since they'd all gone to Dover, and that had been thirteen years ago.

Perhaps, he would talk to her, try and get her to come for a holiday with him. It might be a good idea to look into a trip to Egypt. He sighed. The garden was his only solace.

***

Leslie opened the door and smiled when he saw Lily standing there. 'Lily! How lovely to see you. Come in.' He held the door for her, then took her coat and hat and hung them on the hallstand.

Slowly she took off her gloves and put them down, then she burst into tears. 'Oh, Leslie! It's so awful!' She turned to him.

He opened his arms, and she walked into his embrace. He held her close and closed his eyes, enjoying having her in his arms. 'Lily, what is the matter?'

'Oh, Leslie, it's awful; John's wife telephoned my husband and told him John and I were having an affair! It's not true!' she sobbed.

Leslie held her so close he felt sure she must feel his heart thudding. At a loss for words, he said nothing.

'We are not having an affair, Leslie! I don't know what to do. It's terrible at home. Percy is so upset; he's ...' She sniffed, then whispered, 'He's ... moved into Pier's bedroom.'

Leslie's heart raced. She and John were not having an affair! Perhaps there was a chance for him! He felt himself go hard against her and abruptly let her go. *Oh, God; what will she think?*

But Lily didn't appear to notice. She took out a handkerchief and blew her nose. 'I'm sorry, Leslie, I've just been so distraught.'

'Come into the parlour, dear Lily. Sit down and I'll make a cup of tea.'

He went to the kitchen, but Lily followed him. 'Leslie! What shall I do?'

He hesitated, then filled the kettle and put it on the gas stove. 'Lily, my dear. You know you're welcome to come and stay with me. But I don't know if it would be appropriate. Percy might get the wrong idea, and people might talk.'

'I don't care what people might say!' Lily burst out, scornfully. 'Oh, Leslie, I don't know who to talk to. What would I do without you?'

He took his handkerchief from his pocket and gently wiped the tears from her eyes. 'Lily my, dear. Please don't cry. We'll work something out.' He longed for her to come and live in his house. To see her every day. But what would Percy say? What would John say? Did he, Leslie, care? Yes. Because they were both good men. John was his friend. No, actually, he didn't care. *All's fair in love and war.*

He poured the tea. 'Sit down, Lily.'

She took a seat across the small kitchen table, and he handed her the cup and saucer. Her hands shook as she took the saucer in one hand and the cup in the other. After several sips of tea, she calmed down.

'Thank you, Leslie. I'd better go home. I just needed to say it to someone.'

He nodded. 'I understand, Lily. But you're always welcome here, to stay, or just to talk.'

She stood. 'Thank you, darling Leslie.'

He helped her into her coat and handed her hat to her, then took a deep breath. 'Lily.'

She looked up.

'I would love for you to stay here.'

She looked down and started to pull on her gloves. 'Thank you, Leslie dear. You are my dearest friend.'

'Wait, Lily. I'll get you a cab.'

After she left he went back to the kitchen and sat at the table, trying to compose himself. He couldn't continue like this. He had to talk to someone. Althea Snelling. He'd telephone her.

'How can I help you, Leslie?' she asked after they'd exchanged pleasantries.

I should have rehearsed this conversation. 'Well, you see, I have a small problem. Well, not a problem exactly. Er, well, a personal issue.'

'Is it a health problem? A delicate health problem?'

'No, no, nothing like that.'

'That's good. So, a relationship problem?'

'Yes! That's it!' He gulped. 'You see, there's this woman.'

'You are in love with a woman, and she doesn't return your affections?'

'Yes. Oh, dear, it's very complicated.'

'What do you need from me, Leslie dear?'

'Would you give me a reading to see if this relationship will ever go anywhere? I don't know what to do.'

'Of course.'

Leslie made an appointment, but his session with Mrs Snelling didn't give him much encouragement.

'This lady is too mixed up at the moment, Leslie,' she said at the reading. 'I see children. Is she married?'

He nodded. 'Yes.'

'You'll have an ongoing relationship with her, but I can't see you having a physical relationship with her. It'll always be platonic.'

His heart sank.

'I'm sorry, Leslie. That isn't what you wanted to hear. You must put her out of your mind for the time being. She'll come back into your life at a time when she'll be able to help you adjust to a difficult situation. She cares deeply for you.'

Sadly, he got to his feet. 'Thank you, Althea. At least I know now.'

***

Later that year John had a visit from young Piers.

'Hello, Mr. Watts, could you spare me a minute?'

'Of course, Piers, what is it?' He hoped Piers wasn't going to start to harangue him about his affair with his mother.

'Well, I have a young brother, David. He's fifteen now, and he wants to leave school and do an engineering apprenticeship like me. He asked me to ask you, if you could help him, like you did for me. He'll be home from school in two-weeks' time.'

John remembered the engaging little boy. 'I'll see what I can arrange, but things are very hard at the moment. Work is getting scarcer, as you know. A lot of factories can't compete with cheap imports because of the newly introduced gold standard, blast Winston Churchill ...' He stopped. Piers was discreetly shifting from one foot to the other. He obviously had to be on his way. 'I'll do what I can. Come back next week and I'll tell you if I've been successful.'

'Thank you, sir.'

John thought there was every hope he would be successful. With the increasing use of conveyor belts and assembly lines which could be used by unskilled workers, he suspected that his company would soon be laying off some skilled men, and employing cheaper apprentices to do the work. He sighed and told himself he'd better start looking for another job as well. He was one of those higher paid engineers.

A few weeks later he managed to get Lily's son David an interview for an apprenticeship with AEC. Piers grinned with delight when John told him.

'Did you tell them he wouldn't be able to come until the school holidays next week?' Piers asked anxiously.

'Yes, Piers. Look, David must telephone this number and make an appointment.'

'Thank you, sir.' Piers hopped up and down with excitement.

Just before Christmas Lily telephoned and said she had to see him. Exhausted from trying to sort out the divorce, visit the children and Vickie, and keep his job, he felt both overjoyed and apprehensive.

'Lily, my darling; I haven't heard from you or seen you for months. I didn't know what was happening, and I was afraid to telephone you.'

'John, I can't go on living this lie with Percy. He's so quiet and sad all the time. I can't bear it. I think I should leave. Perhaps he'll feel better if I'm not around.'

John opened his mouth but didn't know what to say. She sounded so sad.

'But I don't know where I can go ...'

He smiled to himself at how she let the sentence trail off, clearly waiting for his input. *At last.* 'Lily, I'm going to find a house to rent, and you can come, and we can be together. Give me a few weeks.'

'It's Christmas in two weeks ...'

He heard voices and the receiver being replaced.

***

John found a house near his work. He'd have to get a woman to come in and 'do' for them, in the same way as Mrs Wilson 'did' for Leslie. He couldn't envisage Lily doing washing and ironing and cleaning. He hoped the basic terrace house in a not-particularly-nice area wouldn't be too much of a come down for Lily. It had three bedrooms with an upstairs bathroom, a gas geyser to heat the water for the bath, and a kitchen, scullery, dining room and living room downstairs.

By the end of November, he'd managed to arrange everything. He'd found a Mrs Tring who would 'do' for him. Before he left his lodgings, he took a chance and telephoned Lily, thinking that if Percy answered he'd just put the receiver down. However, Lily answered.

'Lily, I've found a house. It's all furnished. Everything is organised. You can come whenever you're ready. I've moved in, but I have to go down to Kent and spend Christmas with the children.'

'That's wonderful, John,' she said after a moment of silence. 'Let's get Christmas over. and I'll come to you in the New Year.'

'Oh Lily, my darling!' His heart thumped. At last they'd be together. He gave her the address. 'I hope Christmas won't be too hard for you. When you're ready I'll come for you.'

'No. I'll get a cab.'

***

When Lily told Percy she was moving out, he just stared at her blankly. 'I'm sorry, Percy, I didn't mean this to happen.'

Percy swallowed and paused before speaking: 'Lily, I sincerely hope you will find happiness.' He thought for a minute and then added, 'I think it best that you tell the children and your family of your decision.'

He got up and walked up to Piers' room, where he sat for a long time with his head between his hands, not bothering to stop the tears.

***

Though always reluctant to go down to Kent, John made the effort for Christmas. Vickie did her best to keep the atmosphere light, for the sake of the children, but he saw and felt the underlying sadness.

His mother didn't make things any easier. She always had a disapproving look on her face, and, as usual, his father retreated behind his newspaper. John sometimes wondered if he had a racy book hidden behind the paper and felt like snatching the paper away one day and exposing him, but he restrained himself.

'I've found a house to rent,' he told them. 'So later on, perhaps I'll be able to take the children for a weekend.'

'Oh, I suppose that woman will be moving in with you now!' his mother said.

His father looked up with a jolt from carving the Christmas turkey. The awkward moment passed when his mother saw the blood.

'For goodness sake, Paul. Now look what you've done. Can't you do anything right? Cutting your finger instead of the meat; now there's blood everywhere.'

She got up from the table. 'John, finish carving while I see to your father's finger.'

John looked at Vickie. A tiny spot of blood showed on the tablecloth. 'I'll give you my new address later,' he said.

***

Leslie spent Christmas alone, as usual. But this year he felt even lonelier than usual. He couldn't help thinking of Lily and John and their betrayal of their marriages. He wondered how he would've reacted if Lily had fallen in love with him and not John. Would he have been able to resist her? Probably not. *I mustn't judge them too harshly.*

He ate the Christmas dinner Mrs Wilson had brought him, but he barely tasted it, so occupied was he with his thoughts. A glass or two of brandy would be good, he eventually decided, stretching his long legs out to the fire.

***

Percy found Christmas difficult. They all went to James and Phoebe's for Christmas dinner. Everyone pulled crackers, and Percy tried to be cheerful.

David suddenly stood up. 'I've got something to say!' he announced.

Everyone looked up.

'I'm starting work as an apprentice at Percy's firm. Mr Watts arranged it for me.'

Percy looked at Lily and saw this was news to her. 'Well done, Davey,' he managed to say. *Will that man Watts ever stop invading my life?*

Everyone clapped, and David smiled broadly.

'I've got him into my digs,' Piers said.

Ena looked carefully at her mother. Percy suspected that she knew something was going on, but he doubted she knew what.

Lily got to her feet.

Percy expected her to berate David for not going to University.

'I have an announcement to make, too,' she said. 'Percy and I are separating. I will be moving out after Christmas.'

Stunned silence greeted this remark.

Percy looked stonily at his plate.

Suddenly David Bancroft thumped the table with his fist.

'What nonsense is this? Leaving Percy? You mean he's turned you out. Is there hanky panky going on? Has this spiritualist mumbo jumbo been too much for you, Percy?'

Percy looked up. He put his hand on Lily's. 'Sir,' he said. 'Lily and I have been having personal issues. We have decided to put some space between us for a while. I believe this sometimes happens in a marriage. There is hope that we will get back together eventually.'

Lily sat down, her face white, eyes downcast.

Her father made a harrumphing sound in his throat. 'Someone pour me a brandy!'

Lily squeezed Percy's hands. He knew she hated hurting him, but he hurt all the same.

After the meal, the boys quickly disappeared to play billiards, but Ena came over to her parents.

'Not, now, Ena,' Percy said. 'I'm taking your mother home. The boys can make their own way. Do you want to come with us, or have you other plans?'

She glanced from one to the other. 'I'll go home with the boys.'

***

In the New Year, Vickie surprised John with a letter.

Feb 1927.

Dear John,

I just want to let you know that I have decided to train as a nurse and go back to work. Because of my VAD work it won't take me long to qualify, and then it will be easier and you won't need to support me, just the children.'

Your mother said she would look after the children. Daniel is at school now and Margaret is toilet trained and an easy child. Your father is very good with her. She follows him around everywhere.

I hope all is well with you.

Regards

Vickie

He wrote straight back to thank her. He felt lucky things had been straightened out between them.

***

Percy found the house very quiet. Lily had gone, the boys as well. Only he and Ena remained. The garden was cold and chilly, and darkness descended early in the evenings. He wondered what to do about the house. Ena and Mrs Burton weren't able to look after this big place any more. Perhaps he should move and get something smaller ... He put a record on his gramophone and got his book. Later, he'd think about it later.

'Daddy!' Ena said, entering the room.

He smiled. 'Ena darling.'

'Daddy, I have news.'

He waited.

'I've met a man I want to marry.'

His heart sank. 'Tell me about him.'

'He's a detective.'

'You're very young, darling.'

'Not really! I'll be nineteen in August'

'Oh, Ena! Nineteen is too young.'

Ena pursed her lips.

He saw Lily in her, except for the brown eyes. He took her hand. 'Ena darling, I won't stand in your way. Why haven't I met this young man?'

'He works away a lot. When we're married I think we'll be based in Hampshire. Perhaps Bournemouth.'

He smiled sadly.

'I'm sorry, Daddy, it must be hard for you with Mama gone. You'll be all alone. What will you do?'

He shrugged. 'Perhaps move to a smaller house.'

'I'll help you find somewhere and help you move.' She remained silent for a moment, and then burst out, saying, 'Mama is so mean; I hate what she has done to you.'

'Ena, Lily is not like other women. Don't think badly of her. I'm a dull chap. Too dull for your mama.'

'That's not true. You're the best and greatest Daddy.'

He smiled. 'Now, when can I meet this man? What's his name by the way?'

'Karl. Karl Worger.'

'That sounds German.'

'Perhaps. But I must go, Daddy. I'll bring him to meet you soon.'

***

Lily moved in, thrilling John with her presence. He found the first few weeks wonderful and felt happy in the house. He had a shed out the back where he thought he'd be able to build some furniture in his spare time.

But Lily soon became restless. 'I must try and get a séance going here,' she said, one evening. 'I must find out if there is a spiritualist church nearby.'

'I don't know,' he replied. 'I haven't really looked around the area.'

'Perhaps Leslie would know. Could we go and see him this weekend?'

Reluctantly John agreed. He'd planned on getting some timber to build a dressing table for Lily.

Leslie smiled, delighted to see them. 'I'd given up on you both,' he said as he ushered them inside.

'Dear, Leslie, as if we would neglect you!' Lily gave him a hug.

Leslie stood back and examined them both. Living with John suited her, he thought. She had a glow about her which had been missing for several years. John looked well, too, though a bit strained, but maybe that was his imagination.

'Come out to the workshop, John, and see my latest project,' he said once they'd removed their hats and coats.

'Oh, you two,' Lily said. 'How boring. What am I going to do while you two moon over a few bits of timber and wire?'

Leslie walked into the parlour and took some papers from the coffee table. 'Here are the latest articles about Tutankhamen's tomb.' He turned and held them out to her.

She took them eagerly, sat on the sofa and immersed herself in the words.

John smiled at Leslie, and they went out to the shed.

***

Some months later Lily and John had a surprise visit from Piers and David.

'Hello, Mama,' Piers said. 'We thought we'd come and see you and Mr Watts.' He turned to John and held out his hand. 'Good morning, Mr Watts.'

'Oh, please, call me John.'

David gave his mother a perfunctory peck on the cheek. 'Hello, Mother,' he said, then he turned to John. 'Good morning, um, John.' They shook hands.

'I'll make a cup of tea,' John said in an attempt to break the uncomfortable atmosphere. 'Please sit down.' He retreated to the kitchen and put the kettle on, wondering what presaged the visit.

He found out when he returned with the tea tray.

'Ena is getting married,' Piers announced.

Lily flinched. 'She's too young!' she exclaimed, her eyes wide. 'Why is she getting married so young?'

The boys shrugged. 'She asked us to tell you,' Piers said.

'Why didn't she come and tell me herself?'

'I don't think she is happy about you leaving Papa.'

Lily reddened. 'So what does she want me to do?'

'I don't know!' Piers replied. 'She just asked us to see you and tell you.'

Lily frowned. 'When is the wedding?' she asked.

'May, I think ... I'll get the details.'

'Tell her I'm very happy for her,' Lily said. 'Perhaps she and I could meet one day. Will you ask her?'

John looked at David. The quiet, solemn boy hadn't said a word. 'How is work going, David?'

'Very good; thank you, Sir.'

John thought they'd never forgive him for stealing their mother away from their father. 'Have you joined the sports club?'

David brightened at the inspired remark. 'Yes, indeed, Sir. I'm on the AEC rugby team!'

'Well done! That's an achievement. When is your next home game? I'll come and watch.'

The boys drank their tea then seemed happy to make their excuses and leave.

Lily sighed as they closed the door behind them. 'My baby girl getting married! That makes me feel old.'

John took her in his arms. 'You are the most beautiful woman in England! You'll never get old.'

Lily just smiled.

John made a point of finding out when the firm played their home rugby matches, and he turned up at every match. David noticed his presence. The third time he came, David approached him after the match.

'I hope you enjoyed the game, Sir?'

'Yes, and you played very well, David.'

'Thank you, Sir.'

John's life settled down. Every second month he drove down to Kent to see his children. Lily attended a local spiritualist church, started séances and kept herself busy with research on her projects. Lord Carnarvon had requested a healing session, so she was thrilled to have first-hand news about Tutankhamun's tomb.

John didn't pay too much attention to these projects. As long as she was happy, that was all he wanted.

Ena married. He took Lily to the wedding, left her at the Registry Office and told her he would meet her afterwards at a local hotel. Lily told him that Ena had seemed very pleased that she'd come to the wedding, but Percy and her brother, James, had simply nodded in her direction and said, 'Hello.' She'd had no contact with James since she'd left Percy.

'It was quite uncomfortable,' she said. 'Percy was very polite, and we had a photograph taken of the family group. Ena's husband seems nice, too, but I don't think he is very healthy.' She sighed. 'I gave her our address and said I'd very much like to meet whenever she could.'

John smiled. 'That's nice.' He didn't ask about Percy.

When his divorce came through, he asked Lily if she'd marry him.

'Darling, how can I? Legally I'm still married to Percy.'

'Ask him to divorce you. Write to him.'

She got out writing paper and pen and ink and sat at the dining room table. 'Would you post if for me, darling?'

He smiled. 'Of course.'

A few days later she received a reply.

'What does he say?' John asked, hoping for good news.

'He said no,' she replied flatly.

'The only grounds would be your adultery,' John said.

'Yes. And he said he couldn't do that. He wouldn't drag the mother of his children through the divorce courts on a charge of adultery.'

In spite of his disappointment, John felt happy. He'd established a good relationship with David and Piers. His own children were well cared for and seemed happy. He smiled in contentment. *Life is good*.

Nearly every week he and Lily went to a nearby cinema. He loved the dark and the intimacy of being there with Lily. Critical of every film, she always found a fault, either with the costumes or the logic of the script and expounded on the deficiencies as they strolled arm in arm back to their home. John didn't mind. It kept her happy.

***

Percy achieved some measure of contentment pottering in the garden in the evenings and at weekends, but he felt he needed to move somewhere with a smaller garden and easier for Mrs Burton to manage. When Lily wrote and asked him if he'd divorce her, he finally made up his mind. It was time to move from this big house full of reminders of Lily.

He asked Ena to help him look for a suitable house close to his work. She came up to London and found a nice terraced house with a small garden, and then when everything was organised for the move, she returned to help. Fortunately, Mrs Burton was very happy to stay with him.

The move proved quite stressful. Ena helped by selling or giving away a lot of the bigger furniture that wouldn't fit in the smaller house. All the memories of his life with Lily were in that house. The last day, he stood at the front door, not wanting to leave.

'Come on, Daddy!' Ena said. 'Let's see if everything is all right in your new home.'

Mrs Burton had everything ship shape when they reached the new house. His comfortable armchair sat in the parlour, and he was glad to sit down.

'Are you all right, Daddy?' Ena looked at him anxiously. 'You look pale.'

Percy knew she worried about him, and he knew he looked tired. A grey and drawn face had stared back at him from the bathroom mirror. 'I'm fine, darling. Just a bit tired from the move. Don't worry about me. Off you go back to Karl.' He smiled.

Ena nodded and left him, but she seemed reluctant to go.

CHAPTER 15

In March news arrived from James telling them that Lily's father had died. Lily, of course, already knew he'd passed. She and James had scarcely spoken since the Christmas dinner when she'd announced she was leaving Percy.

'The funeral is next Tuesday,' she read, 'in the Catholic Church in Norwood.'

John offered to drive her, but she refused: 'No, it's best not. Piers and David will take me.'

She returned home the evening after the funeral looking pale and shaken.

'Was it very hard, darling?' John enquired.

'Yes, very sad and awkward. I felt like an outsider. And then we all went back to the house. I wouldn't have gone except for Piers and David. George was there, but he didn't speak to me. And then James read out the will, and ...' she burst into tears. 'John, my father left me £25,000! Oh, John, I feel so bad! He'd put a note in to say that although I'd been a disappointment to him, I was still his beloved daughter and he wanted to ensure that I would not be in financial distress.'

John put his arms around her. 'Darling, I will always care for you. Come, sit down, and I'll make you a cup of tea.'

A few days later Lily received a letter from Ena, telling her that she and Karl would be moving to Bournemouth. Karl had been assigned a case there, and they'd found a house to rent. She hoped that John might bring her down one weekend.

John smiled at the news, pleased that Ena had offered an olive branch to Lily. 'Of course. Whenever it suits Ena.'

They travelled down to visit one fine weekend in June, and after a pleasant journey and a drive around Bournemouth, they sat out in Ena and Karl's garden.

'Darling, Ena,' Lily said as they sipped Ena their tea. 'Bournemouth is lovely! Don't you think so, John?'

He nodded in agreement.

'Perhaps we could move here, John? What do you think?'

'I don't think I'd find work here at the moment; the economic situation isn't good.'

'I agree,' Karl, a man of few words, said. 'This is not a good time to be moving jobs. But definitely Bournemouth and Poole are very popular for people in retirement.'

'Yes,' Ena said, 'either of them would be good places to buy property for investment.' She stood and collected the tea things. 'I must go and start the dinner. Do have a look around the garden, Lily.'

Karl got up and helped her. He obviously adored Ena.

John and Lily strolled around, admiring Ena's work in the garden.

Lily suddenly stopped and caught John's arm. 'Darling, I could ask Ena to find a nice house for us, and we can rent it out until you can find work here! I'm certain we'd love to live here.'

He smiled. 'Yes, that's a wonderful idea!' He worried that Lily would fritter away her inheritance on various good causes if it wasn't invested in something.

'Karl seems a good chap,' John remarked on the drive home.

'Yes, but he's not a well man,' Lily replied.

'What do you mean?'

'He has a death aura.'

She'd told John about auras, but he didn't really believe it. He had to acknowledge her healing powers after she'd helped him regain his strength and also fixed little Margaret's legs, but seeing auras was a bit beyond credibility.

'I hope you didn't tell Ena that!'

An ominous silence filled the space between them.

'Well, I was about to, but then Ena started talking about something, so I didn't get the chance.'

Thank God for that.

'I was thinking it might be a good idea to let Ena manage your inheritance. She has a very good head for business and the stock market,' he suggested further down the road.

Lily bristled. 'I'm quite capable of managing my own affairs.'

'I know you are, darling, but you're very busy and don't have time, and it would be an interest for Ena.'

Lily remained silent for a few minutes. 'Perhaps you're right. It would be something for her to do after Karl has passed.'

John blinked, dumbfounded that she could think so dispassionately. 'Hmm,' he murmured.

'I think I'll write and ask her.' She looked at John. 'I won't mention that Karl hasn't long to live.'

'Good idea,' he said drily.

So it was arranged that Ena would take control of Lily's finances. She soon found a house to buy for her and lined up good tenants.

'I told her to go ahead and buy it and that she and Karl could move in and take care of it for me,' she said one evening after she'd spoken with Ena on the telephone.

John thought she seemed proud that she'd thought of the idea. He smiled at her. 'That's a wonderful plan, darling. What did Ena say to it?'

'She thanked me, but said that she and Karl liked to be independent and she'd already organised the tenants.'

A few months later, Lily came up with a bright idea.

'John, darling,' she announced as soon as he came in the door one night. 'I'm going to go to University and study Archaeology.'

Oh, what next? Is this another of her fads? 'That's lovely, darling. How will you manage that?'

'I've been to see the dean, and he said I can start next semester. Now that I have some money, I can pay my way.'

John nodded, glad Ena had taken over her finances. 'What did Ena have to say to that?'

'I haven't told her yet, but it's my money and I can do what I like with it.'

'Of course, darling,' he said to placate her.

However, her adventure into academia didn't last long. She came home one day very annoyed.

'How did the lectures go today, darling?' he asked, raising an eyebrow at her pursed lips and angry red face.

'The lecturers have no recent or interesting ideas. They're just parroting stuff that was written years ago. It's a waste of my time going,' she almost spat the words. 'I know everything they're teaching.' She paced up and down. 'And the other students; well, they're such ignoramuses. They have no respect for someone like me who has been studying archaeology for years.'

He had to stifle a smile. At forty-eight, Lily would seem like an archaeological relic herself to those young students. 'Oh, darling Lily, what will you do? Will you carry on?'

'What's the point? I know more than the lecturers. No. I've decided to stop. I'm wasting my time when I could be making a difference elsewhere. I'm going to concentrate on the environment instead.'

'That's the spirit!'

'Yes. Artificial fertilisers are exhausting the soil. I need to write to the authorities. My spirit guide has warned me. Our future food supplies are in jeopardy.' She strode to the dining room table and started to write to the Prime Minister.

John just sighed.

***

June 1932

    Dear John,

    Just to let you know that I am getting married next month to Ralph Williams. I don't think you know him. So I'll be Mrs Williams when you write to me in future.

    The children like him and he is very good with them.

    Best wishes,

    Vickie

A wave of sadness passed over John. He'd feel awkward going to see his children in Kent with another man there. And he didn't think Lily would like two young children coming to stay. He wrote back wishing her all the best. At least she'd be happily married at last. That thought pleased him.

***

The economic situation worsened. Work was scarce in the North of England. Men started to move south to look for work, and tensions rose between the workers in the South and those from the North who were prepared to work for less money than the men in the South.

John felt his days were numbered at AEC.

'I'll have to look for another job,' he told Lily one night. 'I was thinking of going down to Somerset. Petters in Yeovil are building aircraft, and I think I might be able to get work there.'

She looked up. 'Somerset? There's nothing there. Just cider orchards. Isn't Yeovil where they have lots of glove factories?'

'I don't know about the glove factories, but Petters were making aircraft in the war. They've built the Westland Wapiti, and now they're working on the Westland Pterodactyl.' He smiled wryly. 'I think that will be a bit of a prehistoric monster. But joking aside, I think I'll have to go and see if I can get work there.'

'What about David? His apprenticeship?'

'Oh, he's secure enough. They can't sack him as he's indentured. But he'll have to leave once he has finished his apprenticeship. The same way Piers had to.'

Piers had left after the completion of his apprenticeship and soon found work with the Hoover Company, which had started up in England in 1932. John had been amused when Piers proudly presented his mother with a Hoover vacuum cleaner.

'Mama, look! I have a present for you!' he'd said.

She'd looked at it with curiosity. 'What is it, Piers?'

'Look, I'll show you!' Piers went all over the house vacuuming the carpets, while Lily watched in bemusement.

'I'm sure Mrs Tring will be thrilled,' she said eventually.

Piers' expression drooped, disappointed with her response.

'It's amazing!' John said, trying to express wonder and astonishment.

'Yes, Mrs Tring will be delighted. Thank you so much, Piers.'

John could see that Lily's response wasn't what Piers had expected, but then, Piers' mother had never beaten a rug or tried to sweep a carpet in her life.

***

John returned from Yeovil with a smile on his face. 'Darling, I've got a job there,' he told Lily. 'Now I have to find a house for us to rent.'

'Perhaps I could buy one, John, with the money I have left from my inheritance,' Lily said.

'No, darling, it's my job to support you. You must keep that money. I'll find us a nice house.'

Lily wasn't keen on burying herself in the country. 'Is there a spiritualist church there?' she asked.

'I'll try and find out.'

'Oh!' she cried 'If there isn't one, then this will be my opportunity to start one!'

John frowned and murmured something she couldn't catch.

The idea of starting her own church enthralled and inspired Lily—at last. She'd only had acknowledgement replies to her letters about artificial fertilisers. No one seemed interested in her views on the danger they posed to the environment.

***

John soon found a pleasant house to rent in Yeovil, and he and Lily moved in, along with some expensive antique furniture that Lily had somehow bought. If she kept on like that, she would gradually fritter away her inheritance. Thank goodness she'd bought the house in Poole, and Ena was managing her affairs.

A telegram arrived from Ena with the sad news that her husband had died of TB. It included the time and place for the funeral. Lily had been right about Karl not having long to live. The realisation sent a chill down John's back.

They drove down to Bournemouth for the funeral. Percy looked very pale and sad. Ena kept close to him.

'She has always adored her father,' Lily remarked, 'and he adores her, too.' She sighed. 'I haven't been a very good mother, have I, John?'

He took her arm. 'Darling, you were the best you could possibly be.'

After the funeral, John tried to keep in the background. Ena eventually came over to him and thanked him for coming.

'Ena,' he said, 'perhaps you'd like to come to Somerset for a while, instead of being on your own. There's plenty of room in our house. Any time. I could drive down and get you in the car one weekend.'

She smiled. 'Thank you, John. I appreciate that.'

He didn't think she would come, but, a year later they had a letter from her asking if it would be possible for her to come for a while and perhaps look for work. She was feeling a little bored and lonely in Bournemouth.

John wrote back and said that he and Lily would come for her the following weekend.

They got back to Yeovil to find a letter from David waiting for them. He wanted to know if it would be possible for him to get a job with Petters. He'd completed his apprenticeship and had to leave.

Being well respected at Petters, John had no problem getting David a job, and he moved in as well. Everything finally seemed to be working out. Lily was busy organising a spiritualist church, and with David and Ena living with them, it was like the happy family John had never had.

CHAPTER 16

Mrs Higgins, the woman who came in and did the cleaning for John and Lily, had a room to let in her house. Tentatively, Lily asked her if it would be available for her to rent it for meetings. She didn't want to mention spiritualist meetings, knowing that could generate an adverse reaction. Actually Mrs Higgins didn't care what went on in her rooms as long as the rent came in on time. So Lily established a Spiritualist church and, to her delight, gradually people started to attend. *I wish Leslie was here*, she thought when laying on the sofa after a busy day. *I'd love to be able to talk to him about it and have him attend my meetings.* She looked over at John. He had no interest in Spiritualism, which she found disappointing. She'd thought he was her soul mate, but at least he supported her in her projects.

She sighed and returned to reading one of the several newspapers spread around her. She liked to keep up with all the political news. 'This Adolf Hitler has the world to ransom,' she said, lifting her head from the paper. 'I'd like to meet him to see his aura.'

John looked up from laying the dining table.

'It says in the paper that German Jews will be deprived of their citizenship. I don't have a good feeling about this Herr Hitler.'

He frowned. 'Darling, I don't think many people do.'

'There will be a terrible war with Germany.' Lily's eyes glazed. 'But the real enemy is China. The Chinese will take over the world.'

John looked up sharply, Lily was losing her mind!

Her eyes regained their focus, and she continued, 'And listen to this! All persons wanting to marry must have a medical examination, and can only get a Certificate of Fitness to marry if they're disease free. My goodness, he even has charts of social classes to demonstrate who can marry who.'

David came in from fixing a puncture on his bicycle, and Ena carried in a dish for dinner in time to hear this remark. Ena glanced at her brother.

Like John, she probably hoped Lily wouldn't make one of her crass remarks about social classes. David was going out with a girl who worked at one of the several glove factories in the town, and Ena was seeing a man who was a mechanic at Petters.

John tried to change the subject. 'Dinner's ready!' He smiled at Ena. 'Ena, this looks delicious.'

'Yes, it does,' David said. 'A change from our cooking, eh, John?' He smiled as he spoke. 'I'd better hurry, I've got rugby training this evening.' He looked at his mother and continued loudly, 'Then I'm meeting a girl. Doris. She's a glover.'

Lily looked up. 'A Glover? Is she one of the Yorkshire Broughton-Glovers? By the way, David, I need you to come to my church and take part in a séance on Saturday.'

'Oh, Mother. I don't have time. I only have the weekends off, and then there are matches and training.' He deliberately called her Mother, knowing it annoyed her.

'Nonsense, it's only two hours. You have the psychic gift. You must use it. Now, this Saturday afternoon please.'

'I have a rugby match then.'

Lily frowned.

He sighed and reluctantly agreed. 'Sunday afternoon then.'

Lily had found that her youngest son had the ability to go into a trance and receive messages from people who'd passed, but John doubted Doris's family would approve of or understand his taking part in a séance.

Their cosy family life came to an end at Easter, when David told them he was moving into digs with Doris's sister. She needed the money. Her husband had left her with two young children, and she had to rent out a room. Then Ena announced that the mechanic with whom she'd been going out, Charles Baker, had asked her to marry him. She'd said yes, and they would be moving to Bournemouth after the wedding.

Later that week Lily lay on the settee, reading the daily papers. Suddenly she looked up. 'John! Why don't we go to Berlin to see the Olympics? I could meet this Mr Hitler, and I could read his aura!'

John's shoulders sagged. 'Darling, I don't think you would be able to meet him. He has an army of bodyguards, and I think you'd find it too much, jostling with crowds of people. We wouldn't be able to get priority seating, you know.'

'Perhaps, you're right,' she conceded. She shuffled the papers until she came to the Times and the crossword. 'But we could go and see the Coronation next year. That Wallis Simpson woman! Really! Thank goodness she won't be queen!'

John thought that was far enough away for Lily to have lost enthusiasm by then. 'That's a good idea,' he said cheerfully.

***

Lily didn't forget, however. As the time drew nearer, she started talking about going to see the Coronation of George VI and Elizabeth.

'James's consulting rooms are right where the royal carriage will be passing,' she announced. 'I can go up and stay with him and Phoebe, and we can all watch together.'

John's eyebrows rose. He didn't think Lily had had any contact with James since she'd left Percy, except for when Ena married Karl, and that had been ages ago and had been merely a nod of acknowledgement. 'Oh! Have you been in contact with James?'

'No, but I'll ask Ena to go with me, and she can make all the arrangements.'

'Ena lives in Bournemouth now; that might be awkward for her.'

'Not at all, you can drive me to Bournemouth, and then Ena can get Charles to drive us to London.'

'Hmm, perhaps.' He thought privately that Charles wouldn't go out of his way to do that. *Lazy sod. He's latched onto a good thing marrying Ena.* Neither of them had any time for Ena's second husband.

'I'll write to her now.' She smiled at John.

He ended up driving Lily to Bournemouth to collect Ena and then to the station. He helped Lily into the First-Class carriage for their journey to London, then turned to Ena. 'Thank you, Ena, dear, for doing this; I haven't seen Lily so excited for ages.'

'Well, it's an outing for me too, and it'll be good to see James and Phoebe again.'

'Was it awkward making the arrangement to bring your mother?'

'Not really, Leslie is meeting us at the station and taking us to May and Piers. We'll stay there for a few nights. I think James is happy to have the chance to reunite the family again. And I'll have a chance to go and see Daddy.'

John still felt guilty about Lily's husband. 'Give my regards to Leslie, haven't seen him for ages; May and Piers too.'

'Of course.' She smiled. 'Thank you so much, John.'

He had a sudden thought. 'Do you have enough money for all this, Ena?'

She gave an impish smile. 'I'm using mother's money, John, dear. She's talking about taking us all to The Ritz for dinner, and I don't have that kind of money.'

He smiled and lifted her case into the carriage, then put it on the overhead rack. 'Take care, both of you.' He gave her a kiss on the cheek. 'I'd better go. It'll be dark by the time I get back to Yeovil. I'll see you next week when I come to get Lily.'

They both knew it would be far easier for him if Lily got the train back direct from London to Yeovil Junction. But neither of them would let her travel by herself. Even if Ena put her on the right train and he went to meet her, goodness knows where she'd end up. If she got talking or noticed someone's aura, she'd be just as likely to get off at the wrong station with them while still talking, or miss her stop altogether.

He waved as the train pulled out of the station and, with a sigh, walked back to his car.

The following week, when he went to Bournemouth to fetch Lily, he found her bubbling with excitement.

'It was splendid, darling!'

'How did you go with James?' John hoped the rift in the family had been healed.

'Oh, he was polite, but cool. But I met one of my cousins, Ruby. She was married, but her husband was killed in the war. She has a son. He wasn't there; he's at University. But she's living back with her parents, my Aunt Patricia and Uncle Cecil Porter. She's changed so much, but I suppose we all have. Although she did say that I didn't look a day older than when we met last.' She looked thoughtful. 'I think that was when I married Percy.'

Ena glanced at John and smiled. 'Yes, it was nice to meet some of the extended family.'

***

The following year David paid John a visit. 'John, I'm a bit worried. I'd like your opinion on something.'

Thinking it was probably something to do with his recent engagement to Doris, John smiled, 'Of course.'

'Well, last night I had to go to Mother's séance. I'd rather have gone out with Dorry, but Mother insisted. She wanted me to take over from her. She gets exhausted very quickly these days. Anyway, she went into a trance and was channelling something very frightening.'

John sat down at the kitchen table. 'Go on.'

'Her guide told us to warn the nation about Mr Hitler. He, the guide that is, was talking about a secret meeting in the German Reich Chancellery. Apparently, Hitler is bent on taking over Europe by force. He said that Germany had a 'tightly packed racial core'. I don't understand what exactly that means, but it was central to his ideas. Their population is growing and they need more room, they won't have enough food to feed the nation, and the Aryan race needs protection and expansion. And Germany was flanked by two hate inspired antagonists, Britain and France. I remember that bit particularly.' He paused and frowned. 'There was a lot of other stuff, which I can't remember exactly, but it sounds like Germany is planning a full scale war. It all sounded so logical. John, I'm afraid for Dorry. What will happen? Britain wasn't prepared for the Great War; are we any better prepared now?'

John grimaced. 'I don't know, Dave. Someone high up might be getting worried because we certainly seem to be getting more defence contracts. Perhaps this guide of Lily's was mistaken. No-one wants another war.'

David frown deepened. 'If only you'd been there and heard what Herr Hitler had said. John, it was all so reasoned and well thought out! It was frightening. Who can we warn? What can we do?'

'Nothing, dear boy. For a start, who would listen to your mother? And if she was in a trance, she wouldn't even be aware of what was said. Who else was present?'

'Oh, apart from me, several women and a man. Most of them were there to hear from relations who'd passed, so they weren't interested in stuff about Mr Hitler.'

'Did he say anything about when these hostilities would start?'

'By 1943 at the latest, because at the moment the equipment of Germany's army, navy and the Luftwaffe was nearly complete, and if they waited any longer then the forces of Britain and France would have caught up.'

'Well, that's another six years away. A lot can happen in that time. Come on, cheer up! Stay for dinner. Not as good as Dorry's sister cooks I'm afraid.'

John tried to be cheerful, but he had a deepening sense of foreboding over what David had told him.

***

By 1939 Percy's chest pains had become worse. Short of breath, he struggled to get to work.

'Mr Percy,' Mrs Burton scolded him. 'Look at you! You've hardly eaten any breakfast!'

'Just a bit of indigestion, Mrs. Burton. Not your cooking!' he said hastily.

'And you seem to be out of breath going upstairs these days. Don't you think you should see a doctor?'

'No, no, I'm fine. Just getting old.' Then he suddenly thought that Mrs Burton was his age, too. Embarrassed, he took his hat and coat. 'Better get going; mustn't be late for work!'

I'm too like my mother. No faith in doctors.

It seemed to take him longer and longer to get to work these days; he had to keep stopping to wait for the indigestion pain to pass. He was glad when he reached his office and could sit down.

Eric Swanton had retired several years ago, and Percy had been offered a partnership but had declined. He just didn't have the will or enthusiasm any more. The new partner was Eric's nephew, Bertram.

One morning, Percy collapsed at his desk.

Ena was preparing dinner when the knock came at the front door. Quickly removing her apron, she went to answer it. Her hand flew to her mouth when she saw the policeman. 'Oh! What has happened?' she asked, fearing the worst.

'I'm sorry to tell you that your father collapsed at work this morning and is in St John's Hospital, Lewisham.'

'Oh!' Ena stared at the policeman. 'It must be serious. I must go to him at once!' Tears came to her eyes. 'Thank you, officer,' she said as she closed the door.

'Charlie! My father's in hospital; I must go to him at once!' she cried. 'Charlie! Can you drive me?'

'It's a long way from Bournemouth to London,' Charlie grumbled. 'Can't you get the train?'

Ena gave him a black look.

Sheepishly he looked back at the evening paper he'd been reading. 'I'll take you to the station.'

Ena thought the train journey would last forever. *I should've been to see him more often. Got him to come and stay with me. The Bournemouth air would've been good for him. Better than the London smog.*

At last she reached Waterloo, got a taxi to the hospital and hurried to the entrance. The big door swung open, and the hospital smell hit her. A severe-looking nurse sat at the front desk.

'It's not visiting hours,' she said, indicating the big clock over the desk.

Ena glared at her. 'Men's Ward, please,' she said in her haughtiest voice.

The nurse started to protest, but Ena stared her down.

'Corridor on the right.'

She walked into the men's ward, but a nurse stopped her: 'I'm sorry; it's not visiting hours.'

'I have to see my father, Percy Hedgecock.'

'Oh, of course.' She led the way to a curtained-off bed.

Ena caught her breath when she saw her father. The crisp whiteness of the pillow emphasised the grey of his face.

'Daddy!'

His eyes slowly opened. 'Ena, darling,' he said in a weak voice, but he managed to smile at her.

She took his hand, noticing with shock how thin he'd become. 'Daddy. I didn't know you hadn't been well; why didn't you tell me?'

'My heart, apparently. Been in a bit of pain lately. Thought it was indigestion, didn't want to bother you for that,' he managed to say.

'Oh, how silly.'

He smiled at her. 'Ena, darling, I love you and the boys. Tell them, and tell your mother.'

'Daddy!' Tears came to her eyes.

'Darling, Ena, don't judge your mother too harshly. She's not like other women. She was the love of my life.' He smiled at her wistfully. 'She made me so happy for many years, and she gave me four beautiful children.' He closed his eyes. His breathing stopped but his smile remained.

Ena was heartbroken. Percy was only fifty-six. Too young to leave them. She felt guilty that she'd been so wrapped up in her own life that she hadn't been to see him much in the last year or so. She realised now just how demanding Charlie was on her.

After sending telegrams to David and George, she got a taxi to Piers'. He'd been married for some time, and she knew his wife, May, would welcome her.

Ena and Piers organised the funeral. David and George both came with their wives.

After the funeral they found, to their surprise, that their father had left a small sum of money to be divided between them, and a small legacy for Mrs Burton, who moved in with her sister.

Piers, George and Ena each used their money for the deposit on a house. David bought a sports car, a very expensive racing bicycle and a tandem. When he and Doris got back to Yeovil, they went straight to John and Lily's.

'Mother,' he said as soon as he walked into the parlour where Lily lay on the sofa. 'Dad died last week; did you know?'

She paled. 'No. I didn't know.'

'I thought you would have received some kind of spiritual message,' he whispered as he bent over and kissed her cheek.

Lily frowned. Why hadn't she seen Percy's spirit? Were her powers failing? Were the spirits annoyed with her? 'It must mean he had a peaceful passing,' she said, brightening up. 'I only get spirit visits if the death has been sudden and violent.' Privately, however, she worried that her psychic gifts were waning. She sat up. 'He was too young,' she said. 'Only two years older than me.' That was a frightening thought.

'His heart,' David said. He was sure his father had died of a broken heart caused by Lily. He didn't pass on his father's message that he still loved Lily. 'Come, Dorry, we'd better go.'

'Stay and have some tea,' John said.

'Thanks, John, but we'd better get home. I'm on an early shift tomorrow, and we have to unpack and get organised.

John gave Doris a kiss on the cheek, and Lily waved a limp hand. 'Goodbye, then.' Percy's death upset her more than she showed.

CHAPTER 17

One evening a two months later, John sat at the end of Lily's sofa. He took her little feet onto his lap and gently stroked them. 'Lily, darling.'

She looked up from the crossword.

'I was thinking, now that you're a widow, we could get married.'

She just stared at him.

'I'd get down on bended knee, but you know my knees are not the best.' Embarrassed, he tried to make a joke of his proposal. 'I could make an honest woman of you at long last.'

'I suppose it would be better to marry before the war,' she said eventually. 'There's going to be a terrible war very soon.'

John fell silent. He had to agree that it looked like war was imminent. He tried to bring the subject back to his proposal. 'Lily, I know that on marriage, all you possess would be mine, legally, but I'd never touch your money; you do know that, don't you?'

'Money doesn't matter to me,' she replied.

He thought that was probably because she'd never had to go without anything or work a regular job to make ends meet.

'I understand, but I've always wanted to make you my wife. I've loved you since the first day I saw you, and I'll never stop.'

She put her pencil to her lips. 'Not being married doesn't bother me, but if it makes you happy then, of course, we can get married.' She smiled.

John had to be content with that. He wrote to each of her children to ask their permission, feeling it was the right thing to do. He was fond of them all and didn't want to lose their respect.

Piers replied that it was all right by him.

David came and saw him, thanked him for asking his permission and said that as far as he was concerned, he wished him good luck and every happiness.

George didn't bother to reply.

Ena wrote back that she would be happy for him and hoped their marriage would bring them both joy.

He and Lily married quietly in London in late June 1939. Leslie was his best man, and Ena was Lily's matron of honour.

'Let's go to the Ritz to celebrate!' Lily exclaimed afterwards. John looked at Ena who winked at him. Quietly she put her hand in his and slipped him a small package, then she put her finger to her lips. He put it in his pocket, guessing it contained some of Lily's money. When he looked later he found a bundle of twenty-pound notes.

In the taxi on the way to the Ritz, he turned to Leslie. 'Are you still working, old boy?'

'Well, I've actually resigned.' Leslie grinned. 'I didn't really need to earn money, and I was getting bored, so now I'm concentrating on my own research and inventions.'

'That's excellent!' John felt pleased for Leslie. 'Keep me informed of what you are doing. I'll have to come and visit soon. I don't think we have time now.'

They had a short honeymoon, just a weekend in a hotel near the Ritz—his budget didn't stretch to Lily's preferred venues.

***

Three months later, on 3rd Sept 1939, Britain, France, Australia and New Zealand declared war on Germany. The Bristol Aeroplane Company offered John a job, and he knew the Germans would be targeting aircraft factories for bombing raids. Bristol would be an even more dangerous place than Yeovil.

'Lily, darling, I've been offered a better job in Bristol. I think I should take it. There will be a great need for aircraft in this war, but I'm afraid for you; there'll probably be a lot of bombing.'

'Pff,' she replied. 'I have no fear of bombs. You're as bad as Percy was. He wanted us to move to Dover in the last war. Dover! Can you believe it?'

'I know, but this war will be a lot more devastating than the Great War. Lily, darling, please listen. I think you should go and stay with Ena in Bournemouth until the war is over.'

'What! Stay with that awful bore, Charles. No, John; I'll stay here until you find a house in Bristol. Or I can stay with David and Dorry. They won't be moving, I'm sure.'

John thought that David wouldn't have any option in the matter. Dorry was very close to her family and wouldn't want to move, and Dave's skills would be needed at Westlands. John didn't think David would be pleased to have his mother staying with them for any length of time.

'Think about it, darling. It may be some time before I can find somewhere for us to live. Why don't you move into your house in Poole?'

'On my own? I don't think so darling.'

'But you'll be on your own here when I'm in Bristol, until I can find somewhere for us both, if that's what you really want.'

She looked at him steadily. 'John, I know you will find some-where in Bristol for us. I'm coming with you. I'll get Davey to continue with my spiritualist church and séances. Perhaps I can join the Spiritualist movement in Bristol.' She picked up her book and continued reading. The matter was settled as far as she was concerned.

In March 1940 John finally found a suitable house to rent—a ter-race house much the same as the one he had rented in Yeovil—in Filton, within walking distance of BAC. He organised for their furniture to be moved and a woman, Mrs Brown, to come in and 'do' for them. Lily moved in with David and Dorry for the last week while he got everything sorted out. They were all thankful when John came down to fetch her.

Lily didn't understand the new ration books.

'Look, John, our weekly ration each is two ounces of butter, cheese, and tea, and one egg. One egg! And meat the equivalent of two chops. Really! How will we survive?' She put down the list. 'And now what are you doing with my newspaper?'

John was cutting it into squares. 'I'm making toilet paper.' Pa-tiently he stacked the paper, then made a hole in the corner of the pile with a bradawl and threaded a piece of string through. He smiled. 'We can't get toilet paper any more. I'll hang it by the toilet.'

Speechless, Lily just blinked.

'Come, darling, I need you to help me put the blackout curtains in place.' John held up pieces of black material. 'You hold the material, and I'll put in the hooks.'

Lily nodded, kicked off her high heeled shoes and climbed on a chair. 'Will I have to put these up every night?'

'Yes, before you turn on the light, remember.'

She gave Mrs Brown their ration books so she could get their rations when she was queuing for her own family. Mrs Brown took the books to register them with the appropriate shop keepers. Each day she removed the relevant coupons.

'You'd better keep the book, Mrs Watts,' she said. 'I'll just take the coupons and try and get food for you.'

Lily watched John building a shelter in the back garden. 'Darling, why are you going to all that trouble?'

'Because of the air raids,' he explained patiently. They'd been through all this several times. 'As soon as you hear the siren, you must go straight out to the shelter. Even in the night.'

'I'm not going to get out of a warm bed to stumble out in the cold and dark!'

'Please, Lily. Listen to me. The German bombers can come at any time. The house could be hit, and you could be burnt or killed by flying glass or shrapnel. Please, Lily, promise me you'll do as I say.' He took her by the shoulders and kissed her. 'I couldn't bear it if anything happened to you.'

Reluctantly she agreed. He never felt sure that she actually did go to the shelter when he was at work. At night, if he wasn't on air raid duty and was at home, he just wrapped a blanket around her, picked her up and took her out to the shelter.

***

By the start of summer Lily had grown restless. John was hardly ever home, and she had nothing to interest her. She didn't have anything in common with the women in her neighbourhood; the blackout and petrol rationing meant it was nearly impossible to go out in the evenings; and no one seemed interested in séances or the occult or anything that interested her. She didn't knit, sew or cook, and she couldn't get the books she wanted. Even newspapers were getting scarce, the paper thinner and the news restricted. She felt useless.

Then she read that the ARP had created a Housewives' Service in Bristol and that they had started to help in the blood transfusion depot. She put down the paper and sat up straight. *That's for me.*

When John came home that night, she gave him a hug and announced, 'Darling! I've enrolled in the Housewives' Service!'

John looked at her blankly. 'Housewives Service? Darling, what does that mean? Do you have to go and scrub floors?'

'Of course not! I'll be in the blood transfusion depot. Of course, I'll only be doing paper work at first: there has to be copies in triplicate of all blood donors' registrations and their registration cards, but at least I'll be helping the war effort, darling!' She trembled with excitement.

'That's wonderful!'

'Oh, and there are some women combing pet dogs and using the hair to spin and knit for the soldiers! But I didn't think I could do that.'

'No, the blood transfusion is more your style, darling.' He gave her a hug.

One September day Lily arrived home just before noon, after working at the depot since early morning. She made herself a cup of tea and sat out in the garden, pensively looking at the ugly air raid shelter and thinking what an eye sore it was, when the siren went off. With a sigh she put down the cup of tea and made herself stroll over and get into the shelter.

She lay down and put a pillow over her head in an attempt to block out the horrific noise of the bombers.

***

Aviation archives

  The Filton 'Blitz'

  The airfield was attacked on 25 September 1940 just before mid-day by 58 bombers with fighter escort. The raid was primarily aimed at the Bristol Aeroplane Company's works on the south side of the airfield. One of the air raid shelters on the airfield received a direct hit, five others seriously damaged and during the raid over 200 people were killed. Luftwaffe reconnaissance planes had determined that there were no fighter aircraft stationed at Filton prior to the attack but (Auxiliary Air Force) was moved in from 26 September 1940, flying Mk1 fighters, as a result of this raid.

***

When the sirens sounded, the workers in John's tool room raced to the shelters. John quickly checked that everyone had left, and then took his list and ran out to their shelter. He called the names. All present except the office boy. Cursing his gammy leg, he hobbled as fast as he could back to the tool room, thinking that young Roy must have been in the toilet when the siren sounded. A quick search revealed no sign of him. As he ran out of the building, the bombers came. He threw himself to the ground and covered his head. The ground shook, the noise so unbearable he thought his head would burst. An almighty explosion happened close by. He raised his head slightly and saw that a bomb had fallen right on their shelter, collapsing it. He thought his heart had stopped. It took the bombers only five minutes to wreak devastating damage.

As soon as the bombing stopped and the all clear sounded, he raced to where the entrance to the shelter had been. A horrific sight met him. Bits of concrete had sliced through bodies and heads. He glanced down and saw Roy cowering by the smashed door, which had protected him somewhat. Blood streamed from his head. He snatched him up and made his way to the first aid station.

Shock made him shout at Roy: 'Where were you! I looked everywhere for you!'

'I went back fer me book,' came the shaky reply. 'It's a detective story, and it's me mum's. She'd a killed me if I'd have lost it.'

He left Roy at the first aid station and went back to help remove the dead and injured from the shelter. Of the fifty-five people it'd held, only five had survived, and they had horrific injuries.

Other shelters had been hit as well. He did what he could to help the injured, and then he suddenly thought of Lily. The bombs had been all around Filton. With his heart in his mouth, he hurried back home.

A lot of houses had been bombed. Dust and rubble lay every-where, and people stumbled around in shock. He saw a half house with beds hanging perilously from an upstairs floor. Water gushed down the streets from burst water mains and he smelled gas from a broken gas main.

He sighed with relief when he saw their house still standing, but he'd made Lily promise to go into the shelter. He found it intact and went in calling, 'Lily. Lily.'

She wasn't there.

Panic stricken, he raced back to the house, and looked in every room, getting more and more distraught. *Perhaps she's still at the blood transfusion depot.* Then from the upstairs front bedroom window, he saw her limping down the street, bedraggled and blood stained.

He raced down the stairs and out the door. 'Lily, my darling,' he said, rushing up to her, 'thank God you're safe. What's wrong with your leg; you're limping. What happened to you?'

Lily looked down at her foot. 'Oh, I've lost the heel of my shoe.' She smiled through the grime and dust on her face. 'I'm all right, darling. I was just helping the lady across the road. Look, her house is a ruin. Oh, John, it's the first time I've done anything so useful in so long!' She started to cry.

He swept her up in his arms, took her inside, and set her down on the settee. 'Oh, Lily, darling, I couldn't find you!'

The shock set in only once she'd put her arms around him. He started to shake. While telling her what had happened, he realised that if he hadn't gone to look for Roy, he would've been in the shelter and killed along with the others.

She told him how she'd gone out and tried to help. He took her hands and saw the cuts and bruises. 'Oh, Lily, darling, you were so brave!'

'Nonsense, darling; I just wanted to help.'

When he'd stopped shaking, they went outside and saw what looked like the entire city of Bristol in flames.

The raid also destroyed eight new fighter planes on the aerodrome which had just been completed.

All over Filton people were evacuated due to the dangerous condition of the houses and the unexploded bombs.

'Darling, you mustn't go out until all these bombs have been defused,' he told Lily the next day.

'I'm not stupid, darling. I'm not going to walk into a crater with a bomb in it. And I have to get to the depot.'

He had no time to worry since a lot of the night shift engineers now had to work double shifts to cover for those that had been killed.

Mrs Brown's house had been bombed, and she and her family had been evacuated a few miles away, so they no longer had anyone to come and do the housework.

Lily made a brave attempt at looking after the house, in between her volunteer work, but she had no idea how to go about it.

CHAPTER 18

Early in 1941, John received a letter from Leslie, asking how they were and telling them that his house had been bombed. All his workshop and projects had been destroyed. He'd been on Air Raid Warden duty. A floor beam had fallen on him and broken his left arm while he'd tried to help rescue people trapped in the debris. He was now staying with Mrs Wilson.

'Oh, poor Leslie. He must be devastated,' Lily cried when John read the letter out to her. 'John, he must come here. It will give him a chance to rest and think what he wants to do. I can help heal his broken arm!'

John thought back to the time he'd stayed with Leslie after his plane crash, how incredibly good he had been to him. But he felt a bit jealous about Lily's relationship with Leslie. They had so much in common; they both felt the same way about Spiritualism and Leslie was in love with Lily, too. Would he be able to trust him? Then he felt guilty. He was the one Lily had married. Leslie had been his best friend and support all through the years.

'Yes, of course, you're quite right. I'll write to him at once.'

Two weeks later Leslie arrived in Bristol. John managed to get enough petrol to meet him at what was left of Temple Meads Station.

'Good to see you, old boy.' He gave Leslie an affectionate slap on the shoulder.

'You too, John. Goodness you've lost weight!'

'Must be the rationing.' John grinned. 'You're still a skinny rasher of wind, anyway. Seriously, it's good to see you. Lily is thrilled you're coming. She actually tried to make up a bed in the spare bedroom, and she picked a few flowers and put them in a vase. You're honoured. Check the bed before you get in, she probably has the blankets where the sheets should be.'

Leslie gave a knowing smile.

John put Leslie's case in the boot of the car. 'Is that all?' he asked.

Leslie grimaced. 'All my worldly goods are in that case. I lost everything else. But I was lucky to have been sheltering in the underground station. And at least it's only my left arm that's broken; I can still move my hand.'

Poor bugger, John thought, *all his books, experimental work and electrical stuff gone.*

'Jump in, old boy, just enough petrol to get home. I think I'll have to put her up on blocks for the duration.' He sighed. John's car was his pride and joy.

Within a week Leslie had the house shining and food on the table.

'Where did you learn to cook, Leslie?' John asked one evening after their meal of vegetable stew with a few scarce pieces of meat in it. 'That was delicious. I don't remember you cooking when I stayed with you.'

Leslie smiled. 'Thanks, old boy. After my house was bombed I went to stay with Mrs Wilson, as you know. I had nothing to do all day while my arm was healing, and I was feeling very down and out, just moping around. She took me under her wing and showed me how to cook a few simple things, and how to do washing and cleaning. It kept me busy and stopped me brooding about my losses.'

Lily smiled at him. 'Leslie, you're our saviour!'

The air raid siren sounded.

'Out to the shelter.' John jumped up. 'Bring all your blankets; it's going to be a cold night.'

***

Leslie discovered that Bristol was a ruin. Lily still went to the blood transfusion depot most days, but she grumbled that coal was rationed and the house cold, and she couldn't get the books she wanted. Everyone was tired and hungry. They traipsed out to the shelter every time the siren went off, so disturbed nights became ever more frequent. They never knew if John would come home safely.

However, Lily seemed to enjoy having Leslie with her.

'Darling, Leslie,' she said one day. 'How would I survive without you here?'

Leslie's heart swelled at these words. *If only she knew that being close to her is all I've ever wanted? I know she has never considered me as a lover, but this is the next best thing.* He smiled at her. 'Of course, you would've survived, my dear!'

She smiled. 'I love having you here, Leslie, dear. I hope you're not too bored?'

He shook his head. 'Never.'

***

One evening, John told them that German planes had flown over Filton at lunch time when workers came off shift and gunned them down as they walked along the road.

'It was horrific.' He put his hands over his eyes to blot out the memory.

He thought about what David had heard Lily's spirit guide say about Hitler's speech back in 1937. Mr Hitler hadn't waited until 1943; he'd struck before the allies were able to build up their armaments. Who would've listened to David's story then? Winston Churchill, perhaps. Too late now. He sat down next to Lily. 'What are you writing, darling?' he asked, looking over her shoulder.

She looked up and smiled. 'I've decided to write poetry.'

Oh, not another fad.

'Yes, it passes the time during our tea breaks at the Blood Donor Office. I compose poems in my head.'

John and Leslie just stared at her.

'I've written my first poem. Would you like to hear it?'

'Indeed,' John murmured.

'That would be nice,' Leslie smiled, always the diplomat.

'It's called "Perfection".' She took out a note book and, with a deep breath, read:

'Perfection by Diana Joyce.
The tropospheric layers are mutilated space,
Disrupted atoms therefore must find another base.
Angry at dissection, they evade detection,
Until their plane has met the perfect imperfection.'

She looked up expectantly.

John frowned, puzzled.

'That's beautiful,' Leslie said.

'What does it mean?' John asked.

Lily's beaming smile faded. 'I thought it was obvious,' she replied with a pout.

'And I thought you said you wrote it. Who's Diana Joyce?'

'It's my pen name.'

'Why can't you use Lily Watts?'

'It doesn't sound right, and also I want to be anonymous when my poetry becomes famous.'

'Oh. Right.' John smiled. 'It's amazing, darling! Keep it up! Now, I must go; I'm on air raid duty tonight.' He gave her a quick kiss and nodded at Leslie. 'The dinner was lovely, thanks, Leslie.'

He shook his head as he got on his bicycle and slowly cycled back to the aerodrome. He'd never understand Lily and her fads.

CHAPTER 19

By 1944 John had become more and more worried about Lily. She'd always been like a little doll, tiny and petite and always cheerful, but now he thought she seemed to be getting thinner. She couldn't afford to lose any weight, and she looked pale and dispirited.

'Lily, darling,' he said one evening, 'do you think your volunteer work is getting too much for you? I'm worried about you.'

Lily bristled. 'Nonsense! I'm just a little tired, that's all.'

He had a sudden thought: 'Have you been donating blood again? You're too small; you shouldn't be a donor! I asked you not to!'

She looked a bit shifty. 'I'm fine. I'll just lie down for a bit.'

Leslie also seemed concerned. 'I know Lily has cousins somewhere in Hampshire in the country,' he said. 'Perhaps they would take her for a while to recover her health. Shall I write to Ena and see if she knows their address?'

'Good idea; yes, please do.'

A few days later Leslie said that he'd heard back from Ena. 'She said Bournemouth and Poole are also being heavily bombed, but Lily has cousins somewhere near Ringwood and the New Forest. She gave me the address.'

'That's good,' John said. 'I'll write and ask these relations if they'll take her for a few weeks. If they're happy with Lily going there, I wonder, would you take her, Leslie? It would have to be the train; I can't get petrol, and the car is up on blocks anyway.' John shrugged.

'Of course, I will. Even if you put Lily on the right train, she'd likely start talking to someone, and God only knows where she might end up!'

'Thanks, old boy. Appreciate it.'

'The train might take a long time. We'd have to change at Salisbury and get a bus. But, I agree, it will be better for Lily to go to her cousins. She'll have other company instead of just us, and she must stop donating blood. I can't believe they let her do it.' Leslie frowned.

Naturally, Lily didn't agree, but then when John mentioned the Porters, she remembered that her cousin Ruby now lived there and that they had a big library. When John told her that part of the house had been taken over as a convalescent home for wounded officers, she became enthusiastic:

'I can set up a healing clinic! I'll be useful again!'

John felt she wouldn't even miss him.

Three weeks later he received a letter from Leslie:

April 1944

Dear John,

Just to let you know we arrived safely at Lily's cousins, the Porters. Lily has settled down very well. She seemed pleased to meet up with her cousin, Ruby again. I think she is delighted to find the library here is very comprehensive. She has already visited the convalescent officers. I warned her not to mention spiritual healing at this point, which she seems to have observed. I went with her the first few times to make sure. The nurses are not so keen on her. She seems to float around putting her hands over the wounded soldiers and closing her eyes. You know Lily. I had to tell her not to try any healing until the nurses get used to her, just talk to patients to cheer them up. But, as you know, Lily is not good at normal conversation. She is too keen on educating them on the troposphere ....

They have a big garden here, and hens, so I have been helping out with the gardening work, well, as much as my old bones can take!

I am thinking of staying here for a bit, partly to keep an eye on Lily and partly because I think I am more use here than as an air raid warden in Bristol now that the raids seem to have stopped.

I hope you are happy with that.

Regards

Leslie

P.S. Lily sends her love.

John didn't know quite how he felt when he got this letter, disappointed both that Lily hadn't bothered to write and that Leslie was not returning at once. The house in Filton was cold and lonely without them. He thought he'd better write back to Leslie—and a letter to Lily—but he didn't know quite what to write.

Eventually he wrote about the bomb that had landed the year before that the locals had nicknamed 'Satan'. The bomb disposal team had had to dig down nearly thirty feet to get to it to make it safe. He thought that might interest them. Nothing else of interest was happening, just food shortages, coal shortages, no petrol. He couldn't even get the time off to visit them.

Perhaps sending Lily to her cousins was the worst thing he could've done.

Then he got a letter from Vickie.

Dear John

I'm sorry to have to tell you that Danny was killed in the Battle of Tunisia.

I'm sorry not to have told you sooner. I had a bit of a breakdown when I heard. I'm better now.

Regards

Vickie.

News of his son's death was the last straw.

He was fifty-six years old and felt he'd lived three lifetimes. He went to the cupboard where he kept the emergency brandy and poured himself a glass.

***

The war officially came to an end on the 8th May 1945. At least in Europe. It seemed that not much changed in England. Rationing remained in effect. Petrol was scarce. John hadn't seen Lily for a year, and hadn't had many letters from her. He yearned to see his wife again. He wrote, asking if she would be coming back to Bristol soon. He also wrote to Leslie, asking him about the situation. His reply didn't cheer him.

Dear John

Thank you for your letter. It's so good that this wretched war is over, at least in Europe. But not much seems to have changed for us. And for the brave men returning home from the war, what awaits them? Bombed buildings and no homes to go to, and sometimes no families or friends left either, and everything rationed.

But Lily is well; she seems very happy here, bringing relief to the convalescent officers. And I am very happy working in the garden and looking after the hens, but I think the Porters will be glad when their home is restored to them.

I asked Lily about going back to Bristol, but she doesn't seem inclined to leave here just yet. I think she feels she is making a difference to the suffering of the men.

I don't know what to say, John, perhaps you just have to come here and kidnap her if you can get petrol and get your car going again. The trains are full of returning service men, and not all of the trains are running, due to lines and stations having been bombed.

I will let you know how things turn out.

Regards

Leslie.

John sighed. He wanted Lily. He wanted a normal home life. He wanted peace and certainty. He wanted to come home from work to be greeted by Lily. A nice meal would be welcome, too, but just having Lily would be enough, being able to go to the pictures or for a meal with her occasionally, pottering in his shed, working on his car, knowing she was there doing the crossword or deep in a technical book. He got out his pen and paper to write a reply to Leslie.

***

Leslie had replied to John's letter with a heavy heart. He'd noticed that Lily and one of the convalescent officers seemed to be spending a lot of time together. *Oh, Lily. Don't do this to me again. I won't be able to bear it.*

Gradually the convalescent officers recovered and left the Porters. The few remaining men could get up and walk around the gardens. Leslie often found them wandering around the vegetable garden, and he'd stop for a chat. One morning as he was hoeing weeds in the garden, one of the officers came by.

'Garden looking good, Leslie,' he said.

'Yes.' Leslie stopped and leant on his hoe. 'I heard that a few of you will be deemed fit enough to leave soon.'

'Yes, most of us, except Sheriden. He was in a pretty bad shape when he came: septic scorpion bite, dysentery and bad bullet wound from Burma y'know.'

'Oh? What was he doing there?' Leslie made a show of hoeing a few more weeds and then stopped and leaned on his hoe again.

'Commando; won the Military Cross, but he never mentions it. Good man to have around in an emergency. Tough. He was in the siege of Madagascar too.' He grinned. 'But a bit of a lad, so I've heard.'

'Oh?' Leslie raised his eyebrows, keen to keep him gossiping. He leaned closer. 'In what way?'

'Oh, got into a bit of trouble before the war; family packed him off to Australia. Worked on his uncle's sheep station out there for a couple of years. Only came back because of the war.'

'Bit of trouble, eh?'

The officer looked a little embarrassed—likely conscious that he may have been indiscreet—and made to move away. 'Don't know; with the ladies, perhaps. Better get going.'

Leslie went back to his hoeing. He had a lot to think about.

He heard voices and looked up, thinking he recognised Lily's. Sure enough, she was walking along with that very officer, Sheriden, and he had his hand on the small of her back. Leslie's heart sank.

Lily saw him as they came near. 'Oh, Leslie! Have you met Captain Sheriden? Richard, this is my dear friend, Leslie Carter.'

The two men looked at each other. Richard gave an easy, charming smile and shook Leslie's hand. 'Lovely garden you have here,' he remarked.

Leslie managed a non-committal reply, but feeling the electric air between Lily and Richard left him distraught. He'd felt the same kind of energy when Lily had first met John. *Ridiculous! Lily must be at least sixty, and this Richard looks about thirty!* Handsome and with lots of charisma, he could have the pick of any of the lovely nurses in the wards. *What should I do?* John was a good man, honest and true, and Lily's children thought the world of him. John had better come and get Lily straight away.

With a casual wave, Lily and Richard strolled on.

That night Leslie sat down to write to John. What to say? Dear John, you'd better come and get your wife. I think she's having an affair with one of the officers?

He sighed. *Perhaps I'm reading too much into it.*

Dear John,

I hope by now you have your car back on the road. I think it's time Lily and I left the Porters and came back to Bristol. Most of the convalescent officers have left.

The Porters have got a new gardener. Well, he is actually the one they had before the war; he's come back, and I think he needs the peace of the garden to heal his mental trauma.

Anyway. Let me know when you can come.

Leslie

Things took a turn for the better a few days later when Captain Sheriden's parents came to fetch him. Leslie had kept a close eye on Lily and tried to turn up whenever he spotted her and this Captain together—probably much to their annoyance.

When the Sheridens arrived, Richard introduced them to Leslie and Lily. He noticed the mother looking strangely at Lily. The atmosphere between Richard and Lily, and the way they looked at other, must have been noticeable to her, too.

Richard's father looked at his watch. 'Better get going, Richard. Goodbye, ah, Mrs Watts, Mr Carter.' He nodded at them, and then they were gone.

Lily remained subdued for the following few days.

***

Leslie's letter delighted John. He'd already got his car off the blocks and checked her out. She was running perfectly. He wrote back to Leslie, telling him he'd come the following weekend.

He looked in the mirror. *Hmm.* He'd lost weight, which didn't suit his strong frame, and he looked gaunt and tired. He hoped Lily wouldn't notice.

He arrived at the Porter's the following Sunday morning.

Leslie stood by the front entrance, looking out for him. 'Hello, Wattie! Good to see you, old boy.'

Lily came out and rushed into John's arms. 'Darling! You've got so thin!' She stood back and surveyed him.

'I'll get our cases. We're all ready,' Leslie said, tactfully leaving them.

'Wait! I must say goodbye to Ruby.' Lily ran back inside and reappeared a few minutes later with a plump, middle-aged woman. 'Ruby, this is my husband, John. John, my cousin, Ruby. She has been so good to have Leslie and me to stay all this time.'

Ruby smiled. 'How do you do, John. It's been lovely to have Lily here, and Leslie has been a great help; I shall miss them.' She turned to Lily and gave her a hug. 'Take care, my dear, and safe journey back to Bristol.'

Three hours later they arrived in Bristol.

The bomb and fire damaged city shocked Lily. 'I'd forgotten how dreadful it all was,' she remarked gloomily.

CHAPTER 20

'Perhaps I should go and visit Ena,' Lily remarked one evening. 'We could call and see David and Doris on the way down. And we can look at my house in Poole that Ena bought for me. Do you know, I've not actually seen it?'

Work owed John some time off, so he thought it might be a good idea. He had enough petrol coupons. There were still a few tattered posters around, asking 'Is your journey really necessary?' In this case John thought it necessary.

'I think it'd be lovely for you both to have a few days away,' Leslie said, being his usual thoughtful self.

'Oh!' Lily said, 'but you must come, Leslie!'

John looked at him.

'No, no, another time, perhaps, I have a few things I want to do here.'

John smiled at Leslie gratefully.

'I think we might be passing the Sheriden's place in Hampshire; we could call in and see how Captain Sheriden is going,' Lily remarked casually.

John noticed Leslie's suddenly concerned expression. He frowned.

'I think it would be a good bit out of your way,' Leslie said, 'and I'm sure the Captain is doing well. He probably had a sweetheart waiting for him. Good looking man like him.'

'Oh, no. He hasn't got a sweetheart, he told me so.'

John looked from Lily to Leslie. Something was going on, but he didn't know what. 'I don't think we can just turn up like that,' he said, 'and anyway, I've never met this man, and I think we'll have enough to do if we call to see David and Doris on the way.'

Lily pursed her lips in displeasure.

'Lily,' John continued, 'if you write to David and Ena now, I can post the letters tomorrow on my way to work.' He went to the bureau and got out the writing paper—with paper still scare it was as thin as airmail paper. 'I've saved some old envelopes. I'll glue some paper over our address.'

Two weekends later they left Bristol.

Getting away from work and being with Lily put John in a cheerful mood. He opened the passenger door for her. 'In you get, darling.'

She slid inside, and he tucked a rug over her knees to keep the chill spring air at bay.

Lily smiled up at him. 'This is nice.'

Leslie came to the car. 'I've prepared a flask of tea and some sandwiches for you if you want to stop on the way.'

'Thanks, Leslie. That's so thoughtful of you.' John took the basket and put it in the boot.

They shared a pleasant drive through the Mendips to Yeovil. David had been looking out for them and came out to the road as John parked.

'So good to see you, John!' The two men shook hands.

David walked around, opened the passenger door and helped Lily out. 'Hello, Mother.' He gave her a peck on her cheek.

Lily stood and surveyed him. 'You're looking thin. Are you well?'

'Of course. Everyone's thin with the rationing. Come on in. Doris is looking forward to seeing you.'

Doris stood in the hall holding a young boy in her arms. A curly haired toddler clutched the hem of her skirt.

John gave Doris a kiss on the cheek. 'And this must be Robin.' He indicated the boy that Doris carried.

'Yes, and this is Marilyn.' She looked down at the little girl now hiding behind her skirt.

'Hello, darlings!' Lily held up her cheek for Doris to kiss.

Doris bent down to oblige.

Lily frowned at Robin as if evaluating him. John could see something wasn't quite right about him, but before Lily said anything, he quickly took her arm, and said to David, 'This seems a nice house.'

'Yes, the rent is a lot, but it's close to Doris's parents, and has a nice garden for the children.'

'I have the kettle on; I'll make a cup of tea.' Doris moved towards the kitchen, still holding Robin.

David took John and his mother into the dining room. 'It's a bit untidy,' he said. 'The children make a bit of a mess. And Doris's piece work takes a bit of room.'

John looked around. *That's an understatement.*

'Piece work?' Lily raised her eyebrows.

'Yes, she makes gloves at home. The factory sends a big parcel every week, and she's paid for each pair of gloves she makes. It brings in a bit of extra money. That is, when she has time.' He shrugged despondently.

Lily nodded and started to talk about the levels of Strontium 90 in the soils and what it did to children playing outside.

David glanced at John, who smiled and changed the subject: 'How's work, Dave?'

'Well, you know what it's like being a Rate Fixer, John. Management think you're giving the men too high a rate, and the men think you're not giving them enough time.'

John nodded. 'Yes, it a tough job; you can't win.'

Lily wanted to know what they were talking about.

David grimaced. John suspected he couldn't be bothered explaining to his mother, but John welcomed the opportunity to keep the subject away from that little boy.

Doris brought in the cups and saucers while he tried to explain to Lily. 'The fitters work on an hourly rate. When the rate fixer gets a drawing from the drawing office of a part to be made, he estimates the length of time a fitter should take to complete the job. If the fitter finishes the job sooner than the rate fixer estimates, he's happy, but management aren't, because they're paying for unused time. And if the job takes longer, the fitter isn't happy, because he's not being paid for the extra time he spends.'

Lily nodded. 'So the faster the fitter works and the better worker he is, the more he gets paid and the happier he is.'

'Yes, but the part he has made still has to pass quality control, and if isn't perfect then he has to redo it and not get paid.'

Lily looked at David. 'That must be a very stressful job; you'd be disliked by everyone.'

Davey nodded glumly.

'So why do you stay? Can't you get a job somewhere else? Bristol for example, where John works.'

Fortunately, Doris returned then with the tea pot and hot water, and the conversation turned to the difficulty of getting coal. John realised that David was tied to Yeovil because of Dorry's family. With that handicapped boy they needed the family support.

As soon as he deemed it politely acceptable, he stood. 'Thank you for the tea, Doris. It's been lovely to see you and Davey and the children, but we'd better take our leave now.' He put his hand under Lily's elbow. 'Come, darling.'

On the way out he took David aside. 'Listen, Dave, if you need financial help, please let me know.'

David gave a shaky smile. 'Thanks, John, you're a brick, but we'll manage.'

As soon as they'd settled in the car and had waved goodbye, Lily turned to John. 'That poor boy.'

'Yes.' John nodded. 'Would there be anything you could do to help him? I didn't like to say it to David and Doris; didn't want to raise their hopes.'

Lily shook her head. 'No. He's a mongoloid, and I think he's also retarded.'

John took a sharp breath. 'So nothing can be done.'

'No. It's thought it might be something to do with chromo-somes.'

'Oh.' John didn't have a clue what they were.

'And I think he also has some brain damage.'

John felt thankful that Lily had managed not to make any com-ments about Robin during their visit. 'Apparently Doris went into labour during an air raid and was on her own and just had time to get under the dining room table,' he said. 'Maybe that was a factor in the brain damage?'

'Perhaps.' Lily became quiet, and for a time neither spoke.

Eventually John said, 'What about we stop soon and eat Leslie's sandwiches?'

Lily smiled. 'Yes, we have to get our strength up to face that Charles!'

As soon as war broke out Charles had taken to his bed with a bad back and a cough. Ena, terrified it might be TB like her first husband, mollycoddled him. She did all the work in the house and the garden, and cooked appetising meals for him. John and David thought he was just a lazy sod, who didn't want to contribute to the war effort. They suspected that Ena had gone without food in order to feed him nice meals.

During their brief visit. Charles lay on the lounge covered with an eiderdown. He fluttered a pale hand at them. 'Hello, Lily, John, so nice to see you,' he said in a weak voice.

John felt like slapping him round the head and telling him to get up off his lazy ass and help his long-suffering wife. He managed to restrain himself. 'Hello, Charles, still suffering, I see.'

Charles coughed. 'Yes, try not to make a fuss.'

Lily just looked at him and frowned.

John hoped she'd make one of her usual tactless remarks, but Ena quickly took her arm and said, 'Come into the garden, Lily, and look at my vegetables and roses.'

'I'll come too.' John wanted to get away from the sickbed aura around Charles.

He noticed that Charles's car, which would've been up on blocks during the war, was now down with the wheels on. He turned to Ena. 'Who got Charles's car back on the road?'

She flushed. 'Charles felt better one day last week, so he got it down and went for petrol and took me for a ride.'

He's been doing that for years, John thought with a sardonic curl of his lip.

Ena must have seen it because she said, 'Yes, it was so nice to get out, but he paid for it the next day; he's been in bed since then. He got up especially because you were coming.'

John opened his mouth to say he felt privileged, but then thought better of it. 'Nice broccoli you have there,' he remarked instead.

Soon Lily had had enough. 'When will we go and see my house in Poole?' she asked.

'Well, as the tenants are still there,' Ena replied, 'we can only drive past, but the lease is up next year. I can tell them you're not renewing it. That's if you want to come and live in Poole.'

'Oh, yes, indeed; we do, don't we John?'

John didn't know if he'd be able to get work in the area.

'Anyway, it's not far,' Ena said. 'I usually get the bus, but if John would like to, he can drive us. I've booked you into a nice Bed and Breakfast place near here for tonight.'

Thank, God, John thought. The prospect of having to stay with Charles was more than he could stomach.

'All right, let's go!' Lily said, picking up her handbag.

They soon found the house and drove slowly past. It looked charming from the outside.

'It's lovely, darling!' Lily turned to Ena. 'How clever of you to find such a nice place.'

'Yes, and it's been earning you money all these years,' she replied.

'Has it, darling? That's amazing!'

John couldn't fathom how Lily could be so clever and understand just about anything, but had no interest or idea about finances.

Ena showed them the bed and breakfast house on their way back.

John stopped outside Ena's house. 'We won't come in, Ena. I expect Charles is tired from the effort of getting up and having visitors.' He tried not to sound too sarcastic, but Ena looked at him sharply. 'And your mother is tired too,' he continued quickly. He got out of the car, opened the door for Ena and put an arm around her. 'Thank you, dear Ena. For everything.' He gave her a kiss on the cheek. 'We'll call round again tomorrow before we head back to Bristol.'

***

That winter of 1947 was the worst in living memory.

One morning when John brought Lily her cup of tea in bed, she said, 'It's so quiet, darling. And bright. What has happened?'

John smiled. He put the cup and saucer on the bedside table and drew back the curtains.

Lily looked out. 'Snow!'

'Yes, lovely for now, then chaos!'

Heavy snow fell all over England. The Thames froze, and no trains, supply trucks or buses could get through. The coal shortage caused continual power cuts, and factories and mines closed due to the loss of power. The government told everyone not to use electricity during the day so that essential factories could remain open.

Food supplies, already scarce and rationed, became more difficult to get. Water pipes froze, and the toilet couldn't be flushed. Everyone felt tired, cold and hungry. A lot of men found themselves out of work because the factories closed. Without their father's pay, a lot of children had no food.

At night they went to bed early to save on coal. By the time they walked from the kitchen up to the bedroom, their hot water bottles were no longer hot. Lily and John each wore two pairs of socks, pyjamas, jumpers and cardigans to bed, and then they piled all the coats they possessed on top of the eiderdown.

'Poor Leslie, all on his own; he must be freezing. I think he took a rug to bed with him. He said even his chilblains had chilblains.' Lily shivered.

In the morning John brought her up a cup of tea. 'Sorry darling, it's weak because it's the third time the tea leaves have been used.' His breath came out in a white haze in the freezing air.

Lily wriggled out from her nest of bedclothes and smiled at him. 'Thank you, darling. It's lovely, and it's hot.'

John pulled back the curtains. 'Look, Lily, we have an artwork in ice on the inside of the window panes!' He came over and kissed her.

'Ohh, stop!' She giggled. 'Your nose is freezing!'

John laughed. 'Can I warm my hands, like Eskimo men?'

'Go away...' she mumbled, disappearing under the covers.

Eventually some newspapers arrived showing photos of double decker buses submerged in snow.

'Even Poole.' Lily read out the headlines. 'I thought Bournemouth and Poole were warmed by the Gulf Stream; look here's a photograph of a bus in Poole stuck in a snow drift.'

When the snow melted the country flooded.

John often wondered, like a lot of people, how the country would ever get back on its feet. The lack of building materials and manpower, and the enormous war debt to be repaid to America, which left no money in the public coffers, hampered the rebuilding of the devastated cities and houses.

***

Lily became more downcast as the days dragged by. The snow melted and turned to slush. The frozen water pipes burst with the pressure and now as it thawed water gushed out.

'I should've turned off the water main before the thaw,' John muttered when he came downstairs one morning to find the kitchen flooded.

Lily tried to put a brave face on it, but John could see she wasn't coping. Eventually he suggested that she and Leslie move to her house in Poole. Ena had given the tenants notice and they'd reluctantly left.

Lily immediately cheered up. John wrote to Ena and asked her to organise furniture for Lily. The house in Filton was sparsely furnished with just some pieces that John had made and with the minimum to make it comfortable. Lily had some nice antiques which he now organised a removalist to take.

Lily insisted on buying a car. 'I'll need a car when we move,' she told John one day. 'Leslie will be able to drive me to see Ena, and I'll be able to come and visit you. I'll write and ask Ena to send me a cheque.'

John felt miserable. Not only was he unable to provide Lily with a nice place to live, but he couldn't keep her happy or comfortable. Now she was eager to be gone. That it was his suggestion made it worse.

He was sixty-one. He had another four years to go before he retired. He had some savings, but not a lot. Lily was already sixty-four, but you'd never know to look at her unlined face, youthful figure and bouncy chestnut curls—although John suspected the hairdresser had something to do with the colour.

He didn't want to move jobs at this stage, to go somewhere new just for another four years. He'd stick it out here. At least he knew the score. He felt his work mates liked and respected him, and he got on well with them.

Lily and Leslie finally left the following year, 1948.

'I'll be able to come down and see you every few weeks,' he told her. 'Perhaps Leslie would drive you up to see me.'

'Of course, old boy,' Leslie said, ever willing to oblige.

That arrangement only lasted for a few months.

CHAPTER 21

Lily and Leslie settled into her house in Poole, a bungalow on a rise with a view of the harbour.

Lily sat outside most afternoons after lunch, reading and sometimes dozing off. Leslie occasionally drove Lily to Poole Harbour. One Sunday afternoon as they walked along the front, a voice called, 'Lily! Lily, is that you?'

They turned. A man hurried towards them.

'Richard!' Lily said, overjoyed.

Leslie frowned.

'Lily. I thought I'd never see you again. I left the Porters in such a hurry I didn't have time to get your address.' He nodded to Leslie.

'We thought of calling to see you on several occasions,' she said. 'What are you doing here?'

'Oh, I've got a job here in town, working for an Agricultural Machinery company. I'm their representative.'

'Jolly good!' Lily said enthusiastically.

Leslie suspected she didn't have a clue what that actually meant: travelling around to farmers trying to sell them farm machinery they couldn't afford.

'You must come and visit us. I'm living in Poole now, you know. We were just about to leave for home. Walk back to the car with us.'

Leslie walked behind them, listening to the conversation.

'Where's your husband, Lily, is he here with you?'

'Oh, no, he's still working in Bristol.' She waved a hand dismissively.

When they got back to the car, Leslie noticed Richard regarding it speculatively.

'Nice car,' he said.

'Why don't you come back and have tea with us? What do you think, Leslie?'

What could he say? 'Of course, my dear.' He opened the door for Lily to get in. Buggered if he was going to open the door for Richard.

Richard seemed impressed with Lily's house and the new car. No doubt he assumed her husband a wealthy man—a dangerous assumption.

Leslie made tea. He arranged cakes and biscuits on a tray and took it into the lounge where Richard appeared quite at home, sitting and talking to Lily.

'Mmm, lovely cake,' Richard murmured, helping himself to a second slice.

'Yes, Leslie made it. He's a wonderful cook!' She smiled at Leslie, who was wondering if he should offer to take Richard back to wherever he lived. Maybe he should; at least it would get rid of him.

Eventually he said, 'Would you like me to drop you back home, Richard? Before it gets dark?'

'No, that's fine, thank you, Leslie. I can easily walk. It's only a few miles to my digs.' He stood up and shook Leslie's hand. 'Thank you, Leslie. It was nice to meet you again. I hope we can see more of each other.' He turned to Lily. 'And thank you, Lily. It was such a tonic to see you, too.'

Leslie thought Lily almost simpered. He went to the front door with him. 'Good night, Richard.' *Asshole*.

Richard grinned. 'Good night, Leslie.' He took off at a brisk pace.

Leslie went back into the lounge.

'Wasn't that a pleasant surprise to see Captain Sheriden again?' Lily smiled happily.

'Perhaps.' He picked up the tray of tea things. 'Somehow I don't trust him.'

Lily frowned. 'But he's a very personable man; I didn't get that impression at all.'

'What was his aura like?'

'I didn't see one. Perhaps because of all he's been through in Burma and the war.'

'Maybe.'

'Leslie, do you think I'm losing my psychic powers?'

Ah, that explains a lot—all her discontent and moodiness of the last few years. She was afraid of losing her one gift. 'I don't know, my dear, but perhaps it wanes as one gets older.' He walked out to the kitchen with the tray and left Lily thinking.

Lily wanted to go to the harbour quite often after that. Leslie thought she secretly hoped to meet Richard again.

'Perhaps we should go to Bristol to see John this weekend,' he tentatively suggested.

'Hmm. I think he might be working. Why don't we go to the harbour and watch the yachts?'

He sighed. 'If you like.'

Somehow, they kept bumping into Richard. Gradually he and Lily became more and more familiar with each other. Leslie tried to stay close and tried to bring John's name into the conversation. John came down one weekend, but they hadn't gone to the harbour.

***

That summer Lily came up with her brilliant idea: 'Why don't I buy a boat, Leslie?'

'What for?' Sailing made him seasick, and he didn't like the idea.

'Well, Richard said he'd take us out fishing for conger eel. Apparently, it's good sport and great fun. And you could make jellied eel.' She smiled with enthusiasm.

Great. That's all I need. Doesn't she know I detest jellied eel?

'We need more fun in our lives, don't you think?'

'I think we're happy as we are.' He didn't like the sound of this at all.

'I'll get Ena to send me the money. Richard said he'll choose a nice fishing boat for me.'

Leslie became more and more alarmed. He went to see Ena when he was supposed to be out shopping.

'Ena, I don't like what's going on with this Richard. Your mother has been totally taken in by him. I don't know what game he's playing, but she seems to be infatuated by him.'

'Does John know?'

'No. The few weekends he has been down, we don't go to the harbour, but otherwise she wants to go there every weekend. I'm sure it's in the hope of seeing Richard, and he always seems to be there, hanging around.'

'Oh dear. Perhaps next weekend you'd better come and get me first. I think Charles will be all right on his own for an hour or two. I need to see this Richard.'

The following weekend when Leslie told Lily that he thought Ena would like to come with them, Lily wasn't happy with the idea.

'I think she needs a break from Charles. She never goes out, you know.' Leslie had his response all planned.

Lily reluctantly agreed.

When they got to Poole Harbour, Richard was lounging by the harbour wall, looking at boats. He smiled when he saw them. 'Hello, Leslie, Lily.'

'This is Ena,' Lily said, not introducing Ena as her daughter.

Richard smiled, clearly enjoying Ena's good looks. 'How do you do, Ena.' He shook her hand, then smiled at Lily. 'Look, this is the boat I've selected for you. It's got twin engines, very manoeuvrable. Nice little craft all round. Should get great sport with it.' He smiled his winning smile at Ena.

Leslie assumed from his laying on the charm with Ena that Richard had gathered from Lily that Ena held the purse strings. 'She's very reasonably priced.'

The boat looked enormous to Leslie.

'We can take her for a quick test run. I just have to see the owner over there. I hoped you'd come today.' He indicated a man further along the harbour who was studying them with interest.

I wonder what percentage Richard is getting from this deal...

Richard smiled at Lily. 'Shall I get the keys?'

'Oh, yes! That would be lovely. What do you think Ena, Leslie?'

'Why not?' Ena said. She looked at Leslie.

He hesitated, reluctant to leave the two women he loved most in the world alone at sea with Richard, but Lily looked like a little girl wanting a birthday treat. 'All right then ...'

Richard strode off to get the keys.

Lily turned to them. 'We'll be quite safe with Richard, you know. He was a commando in the war and is an expert on amphibious landings and handling boats. I've told him I want to buy it.' She turned to Ena. 'So I'd like you to take the money out of my bank for me.'

Ena nearly choked when Lily told her how much the boat would cost. 'But, Lily, darling, how often will you use it? You won't be able to use it on your own.'

'I know, darling; I'll give Richard the money to get it, and any time I want to go out in it he'll take me.'

Ena shot a desperate look at Leslie. This was worse than either of them had thought. 'But if you want to go out one day during the week, how will you contact Richard? He's working, isn't he?'

'Yes, but he's his own boss, so he can take me whenever I want, and anyway, he'll be coming to lodge with us soon.'

Ena and Leslie both jumped. 'What!'

'Yes, he has to move from his digs, so I said he could come and live with us.'

Leslie was speechless, but Ena said, 'Does John know?'

'Not yet,' Lily said airily, 'but he won't mind.'

Leslie knew that not only would John mind but also he'd be extremely distressed and angry.

Richard returned, all smiles, and jumped easily into the boat. 'Come on, ladies.'

Leslie looked at Lily and Ena, both dressed in tailored suits with high heeled shoes. *Not exactly boating attire.*

Richard took Lily's hand, but when he noticed her high heels, he simply got out of the boat, bent down, picked her up and solicitously settled her on one of the wooden seats. Then he turned to Ena and gave her a look which made her blush. He held out his hand. She just looked at him. He picked her up and sat her beside Lily, then turned to Leslie. 'Can I help you, Leslie?'

Leslie desperately wanted to say no, but the sight of the rocking boat made him accept his offer. He sat down between Lily and Ena.

Richard nonchalantly moved to the engines. Within minutes they were off and speeding through the water.

'Oh, this is lovely!' Lily exclaimed. 'Don't you think so, darlings?'

'Yes!' Ena agreed, her eyes sparkling with exhilaration. 'It's amazing!'

'Don't you think it's a good idea to buy this boat?'

'I'm not sure,' Ena replied cautiously.

After half an hour, Leslie felt decidedly green around the gills. Richard slowed the boat, turned around and gently headed back to the harbour. Once there, he leapt ashore and made the boat fast, then helped them all out.

'Oh, that was wonderful, Richard!' Lily bubbled with enthusiasm.

'Thank you, Richard,' Ena said, distant but polite.

Leslie simply felt happy to be on dry land.

'I'll return the keys now,' Richard said, too smart to start talking about the boat. 'And then I must head off. I have a lot of paper work to get through before Monday. Hopefully, Fred, the owner won't have sold her before you make a decision. I know there are a couple of people interested.' He turned to Ena. 'So lovely to have met you, Ena.' He took her hand briefly and gave her his dazzling smile. And with that he was gone. A little while later they saw him talking and laughing with Fred.

'I feel so refreshed,' Lily said to Ena with a smile.

'Perhaps you need to wait until John comes down next and talk to him before you make a decision about the boat,' she said.

'Oh, John knows nothing about boats, only aircraft, and anyway, you heard what Richard said, it might get sold to these other people.'

'That's just a salesman's talk,' Ena replied.

'Richard isn't a salesman; he's a representative,' Lily said defensively.

'Same thing,' Leslie muttered.

Lily jutted out her chin. 'Let's go out for a meal. The fresh sea air has made me hungry.'

'I have to get back to Charles,' Ena said, her good mood evaporated. 'Perhaps you'd drop me home first, please, Leslie.'

'Of course, my dear.'

***

The following week Lily and Leslie visited Ena. As soon as they stepped inside, Lily asked Ena to give her the money for the boat.

'It's my money, darling.'

Ena sighed. 'Yes, but I'll have to sell some of your stocks, and now is not a good time.'

'Why not?'

'It's just after dividend payments have been made. Share values have dipped.'

'Well, wouldn't I have got a dividend payment which would make up for that?'

Charles gave a weak cough.

They all looked at him expectantly.

Whatever he was about to say, he changed his mind and just made a 'harrumph' sound.

Ena sighed.'I'll have the money by next week.'

'Thank you, darling. Just have a cheque made out to Richard Sheriden.'

Now Charles did speak. 'So, this Richard has moved in with you, Lily?'

'Yes. His previous lodgings weren't very nice, apparently.'

'So he's paying you rent?'

Ena's sharp intake of breath broke the silence. Appalled that Charles would mention money, Leslie and Ena looked at Lily, waiting for her reply.

Lily glared at Charles. 'Come Leslie. We'd better go. Leslie will come for the cheque next week, Ena.' She stood. 'Goodbye, Charles,' she said coldly.

Ena came to the front door with them.

Lily touched Ena's cheek. 'So common, your husband, Ena.'

Leslie gave Ena a kiss on the cheek. 'She doesn't mean it, my dear,' he whispered in her ear. He suspected, however, that Ena knew that Lily did mean it, and what was worse, knew she was right.

When Leslie went to collect the cheque the following week, Ena said, 'Come and see my garden, Leslie, it's doing very well. Would you like some carrots?'

Once outside, and out of Charles' earshot, she asked how things were working out with Richard.

'Oh, it's not too bad. He helps a lot, not lazy by any means, and always clears the table and washes up. He has offered to cook several times, but you know, too many cooks and all that.' He smiled. 'Try not to worry too much, my dear. John will be coming on the weekend, so that might bring things to a head.'

'Leslie, dear, I saw the way Lily looks at Richard. I'm wondering if she's becoming senile. The way she's behaving is ridiculous.'

Leslie blinked, affronted at the suggestion that Lily had anything wrong with her. 'No, my dear. I think she's just flattered at a younger man taking an interest in her.'

'But he's only interested because she's wealthy!' Ena clenched her fists. 'If she were penniless I don't think he'd bother for a moment.'

Leslie considered this. 'Hmm, I think you're right, my dear.'

Ena surveyed her vegetable garden. Absentmindedly she bent down and pulled out a weed. 'Perhaps you're right, Leslie. My mother was a beautiful woman. She has been admired and adored by men all her life. Lately there has been no-one to pay her any attention. Now Richard turns up, and he's following the same pattern. In her mind it's nothing to do with her wealth.'

'But John pays her attention. He idolises her, and so do I!'

'I know, Leslie dear, but this is someone new and young,' she hesitated, 'and good looking and charming as well.'

Leslie sighed. 'I hope when John comes, he'll see what's happening and throw Richard out.'

'Hmm,' Ena said doubtfully. 'I think I'll write to David, he might be able to talk some sense into her.'

***

When Richard heard that Lily's husband would be coming at the weekend, he suddenly remembered he had to visit his parents.

At least a confrontation would be postponed. Leslie noticed that Richard didn't leave any trace of his presence behind. He had to admit that he was very neat and tidy, and had very few personal things—probably the commando training.

John had been there all day and Leslie was pretty sure that Lily hadn't mentioned Richard to him. After dinner he said, 'So, what do you think of us getting a lodger?'

Lily glared at Leslie.

John started 'What lodger?'

'Oh, hasn't Lily told you?'

'It's only Captain Sheriden,' Lily said casually. 'You remember he was in the Porter's convalescent home when Leslie and I were there. We met him the other day, and he was looking for new lodgings, and as you know they're hard to find, so we said he could come here until he found somewhere else.'

Leslie looked at her in amazement. He'd never heard her be so liberal with the truth before.

'So where is he then?'

'Oh, he had to visit his parents this weekend.'

John looked suspiciously from Leslie to Lily.

'How is work going, John?' Leslie asked to change the subject.

'Oh, the usual.' He smiled. 'Can't wait to be sixty-five when I'll be able to retire.'

Phew. The tricky moment had passed. Leslie had done his duty to his friend by letting him know Richard was there. He didn't mention the boat. No need to distress him further.

They went out in it less and less as the days grew colder. Richard liked to fish at night; he said the eels were more plentiful then. Lily went with him once, but came back cold and shivering and said she'd wait until the warmer weather before she went out again.

'But you go, Richard. I know how much you enjoy it.'

Richard looked delighted. No doubt fishing would be much easier without having to pander to Lily, and more lucrative. Though Leslie hated them, apparently Conger eels fetched a good price.

***

Ena received a reply from David a few days later saying that he, Doris and the children would come the weekend after next. Excited, early next morning she caught the bus to her mother's. She surprised Leslie having his breakfast.

'Ena, my dear! What are you doing out so early?'

'I've just heard from Dave. He and Doris and the children will be coming to stay with you next weekend.'

'Oh, I'd better get the rooms ready,' Leslie exclaimed. 'I hope Dave will be able to talk some sense into Lily.'

'Yes. Well, I'd better get the bus back.'

'No, wait, my dear. Have a cup of tea, and then I'll drive you home.'

Lily came into the kitchen. 'Ena, darling! How nice to see you! I wanted to see you to ask you to make an appointment with your hairdresser for me. I think I need a different hairstyle. This one makes me look old, don't you think?'

Ena suppressed a desire to roll her eyes. 'Not at all, Lily. It's very flattering.'

'Even so, darling, I think I'd like a change.'

Ena sighed. 'All right, Lily. I'll make an appointment for you.'

Lily beamed. 'Now what has brought you here so early in the morning?'

'I just came to tell you that David and Doris and the children are planning to come and stay with you next weekend.'

'That's very nice, but why didn't they write to me and tell me?' Lily pouted.

'I think Dave was going to, but now he doesn't need to.' Ena tried to be diplomatic. She got up from the table. 'I'd better get back.'

Leslie stood and fetched the car keys. 'I'm just going to take Ena home, Lily,' he said. 'Would you like to come with us?'

'No, darlings. I'll just stay here. As soon as possible for the hair appointment, please Ena.' She smiled at her daughter. 'Mustn't waste time!'

***

David and Doris's visit was not a success. Robin screamed and carried on. 'I'm so sorry, Leslie, he's a difficult child,' Doris said. Now eight years old, it was obvious that Robin was more than just difficult. Strangely, he seemed calmer when around Lily, but Doris hovered over him, afraid he might break something.

As soon as they arrived she went around the house with Leslie, showing him the things to put away. 'He's liable to pick something up and throw it at you,' she said, indicating a brass bell on the sideboard. 'That, for instance.'

Marilyn overheard this as she came in with her father, Richard and Lily.

'But Robin is a lot better since Mummy and Daddy took him to see Mr. Edwards,' she said, apparently eager to have something nice to say about her brother.

Silence.

Lily frowned. 'You mean Harry Edwards?'

'Well, yes,' David said slowly. 'One of Robin's hips was out and twisting his spine,'

'Why didn't you bring him to me? I know Harry Edwards is a good healer, but so am I. I would have helped him.' Lily's eyes filled with tears.

Leslie stepped forward and took Lily's arm. 'I think Harry Edwards is perhaps a little closer to Yeovil, my dear.'

'We didn't want to bother you, Mother,' David said quickly. 'You're busy with the boat and settling in and everything.' He frowned at Marilyn, who, puzzled, had gone red with embarrassment.

Richard interrupted. 'David, why don't you come out tonight for conger eel? And bring Marilyn.'

'All right.' Dave smiled, keen to see his mother's boat. 'You'll be good, won't you?' He looked at Marilyn, who nodded.

Marilyn beamed at Richard. 'Thank you so much, Mr. Sheriden.'

Richard smiled at her. 'You can call me Richard.'

She looked at her father, confused at being told to call an adult by his first name. 'Thank you, Mr. Richard.'

Lily swallowed. 'Yes, David, you must go, you'll love it; it's very exciting.'

Down at the Harbour, the water slapped against the sides of the boat. Stars shone in the clear night sky, and the reflection of the harbour lights danced in the water.

Marilyn held tight to her father's hand until Richard swept her up in his arms. 'Come on, my sweet,' he smiled, 'let's get you settled.'

David watched as Richard sat Marilyn down and wrapped a blanket around her.

'Thank you, Mr. Richard,' she said shyly.

He laughed. 'No need for the Mister. Just Richard will do.' He smiled at her and then turned to David. 'She'll be quite safe here.'

They caught a few eels, and then Marilyn vomited. Richard cleaned up the mess without complaint. 'It's all right, sweetie,' he said gently, 'next time you'll be used to it and not get sick.'

When they returned home, the place was in an uproar. Robin had tried to flush a toilet roll down the lavatory, blocking it. He lay on the floor screaming with delight and kicking his feet, and wouldn't go back to bed.

David closed his eyes. He felt sick after seeing the eels killed and now this.

Richard walked in, saw the mess, swept Robin up from the floor and had him in bed before Robin realised what had happened. Then he unblocked the toilet, washed his hands and smiled at everyone.

Lily smiled back, clearly pleased that Richard was making a good impression.

Richard looked around the room. 'We had a great time, and Marilyn was very good. Did you enjoy it, sweetie?' he asked her.

'Yes, thank you, Just Richard,' she murmured, smiling at him.

He joked and laughed, and the atmosphere lightened.

David and Doris returned to Yeovil first thing in the morning. On their way, they stopped at Ena's. Ena smiled, delighted to see them. 'Come in, darlings!'

'No, we'd better keep going,' David said. 'We just called to say goodbye.' He frowned. 'Robin caused a bit of an upset yesterday. But I just wanted to tell you that Richard seems a nice enough bloke. We went fishing last evening, and I took Marilyn. She was sick all over the boat, and Richard was so kind to her. Then when we got back the place was pandemonium with Robin, and Richard had it all under control in no time. Perhaps you're worrying for nothing.'

Ena's eyebrows rose in surprise. 'Maybe. But did you notice the way mother looks at him?'

'Not really. You know what she's like. Always a new fad. This will all blow over.'

Ena didn't look convinced.

'Don't you remember when she had the Phrenology craze?' he continued. 'Went around feeling the bumps on everyone's heads? That didn't last long.'

Ena laughed. 'I remember her peering at people's heads with a concentrated look on her face.'

'Yes, and un-nerving innocent bald men!' David smiled. 'Don't worry, sis.'

'I'll try not to. Now, safe journey home.' She looked in the car. Robin was kicking the seats and pinching Marilyn. ''Bye Doris, 'bye darlings.'

***

Leslie put back the ornaments he'd moved out of reach of Robin. Richard had gone out, and Lily sat quietly in the living room.

'Are you tired, Lily?' he asked.

She gave a big sigh. 'Darling, Leslie. I'm upset that David took Robin to Harry Edwards, instead of coming to me. Have I lost my healing powers?'

He sat beside her and took her hand. 'I don't know, Lily. But healing takes a lot of emotional strength and energy. I think since your time at the blood bank in the war, you haven't regained your health.'

'Mmh. Maybe. But they could've asked me.'

'But would you have been able to say no?'

'Of course not. I've never refused to heal anyone who comes to me.'

'Well, that's probably why David didn't ask you. He knows you're not as strong as you used to be.'

'Perhaps you're right.' She sighed.

***

Leslie found Christmas enjoyable that year. Richard went to his parents; John came down for a few days, and they went to Ena's for Christmas dinner. For once everyone was happy and cheerful. Even Charles seemed a bit less like a spectre. Perhaps things would work out after all.

CHAPTER 22

A new year – 1951. Leslie felt hopeful. At least, he did until the fateful morning when he took Lily her morning cup of tea in bed and, as he approached her room, heard muffled giggling and a man's voice saying, 'Shhh.'

He froze. *Oh Lily!* His hands started to shake. Lily's china tea cup rattled on the saucer. His stomach sank. Slowly he turned and made his way back to the kitchen. He heard a door softly opening and closing upstairs.

He sat down for a few more minutes, waiting for the sick feeling to subside. It didn't. He didn't feel like taking the cup of tea up now. It was probably cold anyway. Eventually he got up and made a fresh pot and took a cup up to Lily. He knocked gently on the door and went in. Lily lay against the pillows looking flushed.

'Ah. Leslie. Good morning; my cup of tea. Thank you, darling.'

He couldn't bear to look at her. He placed the cup and saucer on her bedside table, mumbled something and went out. Back in the kitchen, he sat down and closed his eyes. What to do?

He heard Richard moving around upstairs, but he couldn't face him this morning. He made a quick decision and scribbled a note saying that he'd gone shopping early. He left it propped up against the milk jug on the kitchen table. Lily could get her own breakfast, or Richard could get it for her if he hadn't gone to work by the time she got up.

He felt weary to his bones.

Picking up the keys, his wallet, and shopping bag, he left the house and got into the car. The frosty morning made it hard to start. He tried several times, his heart racing. He had to do it before Richard heard him and came out to help. At last, to his great relief, the motor kicked in.

He drove off without thinking and suddenly realised he was heading for Ena's.

He stopped outside her house and sat for a while. *How could you do this, Lily? How could you treat John like this, and for someone who is only leading you on?*

'Leslie! What's wrong?'

He looked up and saw Ena's face anxiously peering in the car window.

'Come inside.'

He didn't want to face Charles.

She seemed to read his mind. 'Charles is still asleep; he won't get up for another hour or two.'

Slowly Leslie got out of the car.

She took his hand. 'Come. I was just going to make a cup of tea.'

He sat at the kitchen table, silently watching as Ena busied herself with the tea making.

At last she sat down, placing two cups of tea on the table. She put her hand on his. 'What is it, Leslie?'

Tears came to his eyes. 'I think Lily is sleeping with Richard.'

Ena blinked. 'What?'

'I went up with her morning cup of tea, as I always do about eight o'clock, when I heard giggles and muffled voices. I went back downstairs and then heard her door open and close.'

'Oh, Leslie; what is she thinking? Has she gone crazy?'

'I don't know. Perhaps you're right, that she's going senile. I think Richard has been flattering her and making her feel young again. Oh, Ena, whatever will John do. He absolutely adores her; he'll be devastated.'

'She's so headstrong; she won't listen to anyone. We'll just have to be patient and hope it's a passing phase and that she'll see sense soon. What else can we do?'

Leslie slowly nodded. 'You're right. But what about John? This will kill him.'

Ena took his hand. 'No, Leslie, dear. John will be devastated, but it won't kill him.' Sadly, she continued, 'We all have our own road to travel. I don't think there's anything we can do.'

'It's all my fault,' Leslie burst out.

'Whatever do you mean?'

'Your mother met John at my house, and then I was the one who suggested Lily go and stay with her cousins in Hampshire where she met Richard.'

'Don't be ridiculous, Leslie. They were Lily's choices!' Ena frowned. 'Stop blaming yourself, Leslie, you've been her anchor all these years.'

They sat, each thinking their own thoughts.

Eventually Leslie stood. 'I'd better go before Charles gets up and wonders why I'm here so early.'

Ena smiled as she got up from the table. 'Dear Leslie, don't despair. Everything will work out.'

Sadly, he said, 'I love her, Ena. She's my life.'

She sighed. 'She doesn't deserve you, Leslie.' She reached up and kissed his cheek. 'Come any time, Leslie dear.'

He smiled. 'You know that I love you like the daughter I never had, don't you, Ena?'

Her eyes moistened. 'Yes, dear Leslie, and I love you too. Come, start the car before Charles wakes up.'

Just when Leslie thought things couldn't get any worse, a week later Lily came down to breakfast smiling. He'd been taking her morning cup of tea up a bit later, waiting for the sound of her bedroom door being discreetly opened and closed before he went up.

'We must go and see Ena today,' she announced. 'I need to get all my money. I'm going to buy a sheep farm on Exmoor.'

Leslie nearly dropped the egg he was taking out of the boiling water for her breakfast. 'A sheep farm? Exmoor?'

'Yes. Richard says it will be a great investment; the price of wool is going up and lamb is fetching a good price. It'll be a better investment than those old stocks and shares that Ena invests my money in.'

His heart sank. 'Why don't you talk to John about it first? We could go up to Bristol this weekend. You haven't been up to see him for a while.'

'The weather hasn't been favourable; you know that.'

He didn't argue. There was no point. Lily would win every argument.

'As soon as I've finished my breakfast and got ready, we can go.'

An hour later they arrived at Ena's.

She was about to go out. 'Oh! I wasn't expecting you.'

'No, darling,' Lily said. 'May we come in? I need to talk to you.'

Frowning, Ena took off her hat and coat and hung them up. She looked at Leslie for any clues as to this unprecedented visit.

He just shook his head and looked glum.

Lily walked into the kitchen. Fortunately, Charles was still in bed.

'Now, Ena, I want to take all my money out of the investments. I'm going to buy a sheep farm on Exmoor.'

Ena sat down suddenly. 'What!'

'I was just telling Leslie. Wool is fetching a good price at the moment and so is lamb.'

'How do you know?' Ena asked sceptically.

'Richard said it would be a good investment. He knows of the perfect place. South Molton in Devon.'

'So who will run it and do all the work? How many acres? What is the house like? How many sheep will be needed?'

Lily dismissed all these questions with a wave of her hand. 'Richard has done all the research. I can trust him. He managed an enormous sheep station in Australia, you know. He would supervise it all.'

Ena looked at Leslie. He assumed she thought as he did, that Richard would manage it all for his own interests.

'So, darling. If you could organise the money for me as soon as possible.'

'How much?'

Lily looked around and then slid a piece of paper over to Ena. 'That's the price and the name of the solicitor to make the cheque for the deposit out to.'

Ena gasped. 'This will leave you with hardly anything in the bank, Lily.'

Lily shrugged. 'You have to invest money to make money, Ena. I thought you knew that. And anyway, money doesn't bother me.'

'I'll write to John,' Ena stood. 'He needs to know.'

Lily flushed. 'This has nothing to do with John. It's my money. I can do what I like with it!'

'So Richard will be in Exmoor farming and you'll be in Poole waiting to get a return on your so-called investment.'

'Oh, no!' Triumphantly, Lily said, 'I'll be going as well.'

'What!' Ena went pale with shock. 'You'll go and bury yourself in the country? You were bored in Bristol, and you seem to like Poole. What will you do in the middle of Exmoor?'

Lily frowned; apparently she hadn't thought of that aspect. 'I'm sure I'll manage. I can get books and the papers. It's not outer Mongolia, you know!' She stood and smiled. 'Well, darling, if you would just deal with the paperwork.' She blew a kiss at Ena. 'Bye darling ... Come, Leslie dear. We have a lot to organise.' She took Leslie's arm and they left.

Ena walked briskly to the shops, trying to defuse the rising tide of anger building inside her. All the time she'd spent researching and buying and selling stocks and shares for her mother, and now she was going to blow it all on this, this ... She didn't know what to call him.

By the time she got back home she felt more composed. She didn't want Charles to know. She thought he secretly expected they'd inherit a nice fat sum when Lily passed.

A week later when Lily came for her money, Ena said, 'First, I need to see the contract before I give you the money for the deposit. I checked and the solicitor is in Ringwood.'

'Yes, it's Richard's family solicitor, and he has it all prepared.'

Ena stood and looked her mother in the eye. 'Lily, I've been your de facto financial advisor all these years. I'll go to court and challenge this if I don't see the contract and make sure your name is on it.'

Leslie smiled in encouragement.

Lily pouted. 'All right.'

Charles looked from Lily to Ena with a puzzled frown, clearly wondering what on earth was going on.

'Why don't you come with us now, Ena,' Leslie said, 'and we can go to Ringwood. It's not that far. We can see the solicitor and look at the contract, and you can discuss it with them.'

Ena looked at him gratefully for saving her from having to explain the situation to Charles. 'Thank you, Leslie, that would be the best plan.'

Charles started to say something, but Lily forestalled him: 'That's settled then. Goodbye Charles.' With that she picked up her handbag and walked to the front door.

The journey passed in uncomfortable silence with both women fired up, and they had to wait a half an hour before they saw the solicitor, which didn't help defuse the situation. At last his office door opened and he came out, looking from one to the other.

'Jenkins, Herbert Jenkins.' He held out his hand to Leslie.

Leslie shook his hand. 'These ladies are the ones you have to deal with.'

'Oh.' He turned to Lily and then Ena, who stepped forward.

'Good morning, Mr Jenkins. My name is Mrs Ena Baker. I'm here to see the contract that Mr Richard Sheriden has had drawn up for the purchase of a farm in Devon.'

'I'm sorry, but what has that got to do with you?' He frowned and looked from one to the other.

'Quite simply because it is my mother here who is buying the property.'

'Oh no, there has been some mistake. Mr Sheriden is buying the property.'

Ena stared at him. Then she said loudly and very slowly: 'My mother, Lily Watts, is financing this purchase. We have every right to see the contract. Please show it to us.'

'This is most irregular. Client confidentiality and all that.'

Ena's stare turned into a glare. 'If we don't see the contract, there will be no deposit.'

'You'd better come into my office.' He went off to fetch the contract, muttering to himself about irregularity. When he returned, Ena put out her hand for it.

'The Sale of Lower North Radworthy Farm, Heasley Mill, South Molton,' she read, then scanned it quickly for Lily's name. *Not there. How unsurprising.* 'Why is my mother's name not on the contract?' she asked.

The solicitor frowned and drummed his fingers nervously on his desk. 'The purchaser is my client, Mr. Sheriden.'

Ena leaned forward and looked him in the eyes. 'No, you are wrong. My mother is the purchaser. Either her name and only her name goes on the contract or there will be no sale.'

'Please, Ena, darling,' Lily said, 'it's perfectly all right; Richard knows what he is doing.'

Ena narrowed her eyes at her. 'I'm certain he does,' she said dryly, then turned back to the solicitor. 'You will need to contact Mr Sheriden and get this contract amended or there will be no money available.' She stood and raised her eyebrows in challenge.

Herbert Jenkins' mouth fell open. No words came out.

'Good afternoon, Mr Jenkins.' She swept out of the room.

Lily and Leslie had no choice but to go after her.

When they got back to the car, Ena confronted Lily, fuming: 'Can't you see the game Richard is playing?'

'How dare you make me look a fool in front of that beastly little man!' Lily spat out the words.

'Don't you understand? If your name is not on the contract, it won't be on the title deeds. That means Richard will own the farm, and he would be able to sell it, and you would have nothing!'

Lily frowned. 'I'm sure Richard wouldn't do a thing like that; I trust him.'

'Lily! Listen to me! I don't know what's going on between you two, but I won't have you being fleeced of everything you have.'

Lily fell silent and sat sullenly all the way back to Bournemouth, where they left Ena at her house. Lily barely said farewell.

Leslie didn't know what to do.

Back home, Lily threw off her coat and kicked off her shoes. She scowled as she sat at the kitchen table.

He put the kettle on. With his back to her he said, 'Lily—'

'Don't you start, Leslie!'

'Lily, we're all worried; Richard seems to have you enthralled. I'm sure he thinks a lot of you, but it's like he's put a spell on you. Please look at what's happening!'

'What gives you the right to criticise me and tell me what to do?'

'Because I, because I ...' Leslie started to say because I love you, then stopped. 'I suppose I don't have any right.' He looked at the ground. He wanted to take her in his arms and tell her that he loved her, and that John loved her, and that she didn't need this man's attentions. She'd changed from being a beautiful, tender woman into a silly child. *Oh, Lily! What can I do? You're hurting all the people who care for you.* Was she going senile? But she was so alert and intelligent. Perhaps he should write to John. But then, it was none of his, Leslie's, business.

'Oh, Leslie, darling! I just meant I'm tired with Ena telling me what to do all the time, and everyone treating me like a child. I need to take charge of my life.'

He wanted to say that she was indeed behaving like a child, but he didn't have the heart to hurt her. The kettle boiled.

***

Richard was in a cheerful mood when he returned to the office. He'd just sold a tractor and would make a good commission, which didn't happen very often since the farmers had very little money to spare these days. And he was down to his uppers. He'd borrowed to the hilt, and this job didn't pay—he got barely any commission. And in reality, he could do no other work. There wasn't much call for trained killers in post-war Britain.

Luckily things were looking up now that he had Lily panting for him.

He grinned at Jennie, the office girl, who looked up and smiled back.

'Phone call for you.' She handed him a piece of paper from a notepad. 'A Mr Jenkins. Said would you ring him. The number's there.'

Great. Looks like Ena's come up with the cheque.

With a spring in his step, he went into the back office to the phone.

He came out five minutes later, slamming the door and with a face like thunder.

Jennie looked up and saw his expression. 'Bad news, Richard? Anything I can do to help?' She batted her eyelashes at him.

He managed a smile. 'No, no. Just something a bit unexpected.' He took his bag from the table and started towards the door. 'Think I'll knock off now. Sold a Massey today.'

'Good, the boss'll be pleased,' Jennie called after him.

He needed a drink. Just one; better keep a clear head. He headed into the Blue Boar to rethink his strategy.

***

When Richard arrived home that evening, he appeared to be in good spirits. He took off his coat and came into the living room. 'Hello, Leslie, Lily. How has your day been?'

Lily looked at him and smiled. 'Very well, thank you, Richard. Come and sit down.' She patted the sofa.

They chatted about some commonplace matters, and then Richard casually said, 'Did you see Ena today?'

'Yes. She made us go to see the solicitor, to look at the contract, and when she saw it, she was so angry because my name wasn't on it.'

Richard jumped up. 'What! How come? That old Jenkins must have made a mistake. I clearly told him the property would be in your name.'

Leslie looked closely at Richard. He was a good actor, for sure.

'You see! I knew there was a reason for it. Ena was just being fussy.' Lily looked at Leslie triumphantly.

'No, no; she was just being a caring daughter.' Richard smiled. 'You're lucky to have her looking after your interests. I'll ring Jenkins in the morning and sort it all out. Don't worry about a thing, Lily. This is going to be a brilliant investment.'

Lily smiled and turned to Leslie. 'I knew Richard would work it all out.' She remained in good spirits all evening.

The next morning Leslie went to see Ena. She looked pale and drawn. He thought she obviously hadn't slept much.

'Dear, Leslie, how good to see you. I've written to John and was just going out to post the letter. I think he needs to come down and sort all this out.'

Leslie nodded and told Ena what had happened the previous evening.

'That Jenkins fellow must have contacted Richard, and he had time to plan that he'd pretend to Lily that it was all a mistake,' she said, then suddenly turned to him. 'Has Lily thought about you? What will you be doing? Staying in Poole or going to Exmoor with the happy couple?'

'I don't know, my dear. I don't want to go, but I think I must. I have to look after Lily. That's if Richard allows it.' He took a deep breath and sighed. 'I was going to ask you if I should write to John, but you've forestalled me. Shall I post your letter for you to save you going out?'

With a heavy heart he went to the Post Office and then back to Poole.

***

John opened the letter, recognising the handwriting as Ena's. Just the first sentence made him anxious; he thought something had happened to Lily.

Bournemouth, June 1951

Dear John.

I think you need to come down to Poole as soon as possible.

Lily has it in her head to buy a sheep farm on Exmoor and install the lodger, Richard, as manager.

This Richard seems to be exerting undue influence on her. I think he is trying to swindle her out of her money. But he gives the appearance of being very genuine and a nice trustworthy person.

Sorry to bother you, but I think you are the only person she will listen to.

Ena

He put down the letter and sighed. *What next?* He replied straight away to say he'd be down the following Saturday. He also wrote to Lily saying he'd be visiting and was looking forward to them being together.

When he arrived on Saturday, just before lunch, Leslie met him at the door.

'Where's Lily?' John said, impatient to see his wife.

'She's resting in her bedroom.'

John walked up the stairs and gave a gentle knock on their bedroom door. He opened it and peered in. Lily lay on the bed with the curtains drawn. He drew them back, then sat on the bed and tried to take her into his arms.

'Lily darling,' he murmured.

'Oh, John, how nice to see you.' She sat up and smiled.

'Now Lily, what's all this about you buying a farm on Exmoor?'

She frowned. 'Who told you that?'

'Why Ena, of course. She's very worried about you.'

'Nonsense! I'm quite capable of looking after my own affairs. Ena worries too much.'

'What's going on with this farm business? Do you expect me to come and live there when I retire? You know, I have absolutely no experience of farming, darling.'

She sat up straighter. 'John. I'll be moving down to Devon with Richard.'

He frowned. 'I don't understand.'

'Darling, it's obvious to me that it's time we went our separate ways. We hardly ever see each other. We've been drifting apart.'

John's eyes widened. He drew back. 'Lily! What do you mean?'

She studied her finger nails. 'Really, John, you hardly ever come to see me, and when you do you're always tired, falling asleep after dinner; it's obvious you've lost interest in me.'

'What! Whatever do you mean, Lily? I'm working extra overtime to save up for my retirement, that's why I don't come down so often, and I'm tired, Lily. I drive down to see you whenever I can. You could come and see me more often, you know; you have nothing else to do. Leslie is happy to drive you to Bristol.'

When she didn't reply, he sat back and his arms fell to his sides. 'What are you trying to say?' he asked dully.

'It's over, John. I want a divorce.'

It didn't make sense. *I'm not hearing this right*. He got up. 'You're tired, Lily. I'll let you rest and we can talk about it later.'

He left the bedroom, closed the door and leaned against it. His head spun and he felt sick. After a moment to recover, he went downstairs to where Leslie was preparing food in the kitchen. 'Leslie! What on earth is going on? Lily said she wants a divorce.' He sank onto a chair at the kitchen table.

'What!' Leslie swung round from scrubbing carrots at the sink. 'A divorce?' He joined John at the kitchen table. 'Everything is going crazy.'

John frowned. 'Where is this Richard? I'd knock him for six if he were here, make mincemeat of him.'

'I think he's gone to visit his parents, or so he says.' Leslie hesitated. 'John, I don't know what's going on, but I don't like it. Lily's changed. She won't listen to anyone. I think she's completely infatuated with this Richard. I think he makes her feel young and attractive again.'

'My, God, she's sixty-seven! How old is this Richard?'

'I'm not sure, but he can't be more than his mid-thirties.'

'It's ridiculous. Does she seriously think he'd be interested in a woman twice his age? Why that's younger than David, and he's her youngest son!'

'I know. I was hoping you would be able to talk some sense into her.'

John stared into space. His fists clenched, and red patches mottled his face. 'I can't handle this, Leslie. I think I'd best go back to Bristol. If I wait and see this Richard, there's no knowing what would happen. I just want to kill him!' He'd never felt so angry before.

Leslie just watched him with a sad expression.

'You know Lily,' John added, 'once she has made up her mind about something, there's no turning her.'

'John,' Leslie said. 'You can't just let this go. A divorce! What is she thinking of? Perhaps we should go and see Ena and see what she thinks.'

John shook his head sadly. 'No, Leslie. Lily was adamant. If she changes her mind, she knows where I am. I'd better go before I do something drastic. Like killing this Richard bastard.'

'At least stay for lunch?' Leslie said with a hopeful expression.

'No. Thanks. I feel sick. Couldn't eat anything.' He got up from the table and picked up his overnight bag. 'Thank you, Leslie. You're a pal. Let me know what happens. Divorce!' He stumbled out the kitchen door.

***

Leslie shook his head in distress. He didn't want John to leave like this, driving all the way back to Bristol in such a distraught state. But what could he do about any of it? His position was intolerable. He loved Lily, but he hated that she'd fallen for Richard's wiles and couldn't bear what she was doing to John. He sighed. He was seventy-two. Too old to change. He would always love Lily. Just because the person you loved hurt you, didn't mean you stopped loving them.

Mechanically he went about his household chores. Thank goodness Richard had gone home, or where ever he went when he disappeared at weekends. He didn't feel like facing him.

Eventually Lily came downstairs. He hadn't taken her any lunch, so he assumed she must be hungry.

'Leslie, darling! What's for dinner?'

'Well, I was making John's favourite, steak and kidney pudding ...'

'Oh, lovely, darling. And where is John?'

Incredulous, he stopped checking on the water level in the saucepan and turned around. 'Lily, John has gone back to Bristol. He's devastated. He said you want a divorce.'

She sat at the table and looked everywhere except at Leslie. 'Well, there's no point in carrying on like this, is there? I mean, he's in Bristol and doesn't come and see me very often. I'm sure he has another woman there.'

'What!' Outraged, Leslie nearly spilled the kettle of boiling water. He slammed it down. 'John loves you, Lily. He would never even look at another woman!'

She shrugged. 'He's a man. He has needs.'

'What! Oh, that's ridiculous, Lily. Whoever put that notion into your head?' As the words left his lips he had a strong suspicion just who had done exactly that. Then a thought suddenly hit him: Did Lily not see him as a man? A man with needs? Good old Leslie; always there. He felt like a male Cinderella. Bile rose in his stomach. He glared at her.

Lily shifted uncomfortably. 'Anyway, it's for the best. I can't see him settling down on a farm.'

'Lily! Richard is a charlatan. He's manipulating you! Can't you see it?'

Lily glared back. 'I can't believe you'd say such a thing about Richard! He's so kind and helpful.' She reddened. 'He thinks the world of me.'

'He thinks the world of your money!'

'How dare you!'

'Has he paid any rent since he came here?'

Lily stood and put her hands on her hips. Her chin jutted out defiantly. 'No, but then, neither have you!'

His jaw dropped in amazement. 'Who do you think has bought all the food since we've been here? Paid all the bills, electricity, gas, rates, petrol? I have, Lily! I was living rent free, and I thought it only fair that I paid for everything else. And when I stayed with you in Bristol I paid my share too.'

'Oh ...' Lily gazed at him open-mouthed.

'But if that's what you think of me, then it's time I left.' Leslie went back to the stove, turned off the gas, and walked up to his room.

Sick at heart, he wondered what to do next, where to go. Then he thought of John. He'd ask him if he could stay with him until his War Damage compensation came through. He got out paper and an envelope, carefully filled his fountain pen with ink and started to write.

A gentle knock came on his door followed by Lily's voice. 'Leslie. I've come to say sorry. May I come in?'

'Yes,' he growled.

Lily opened the door and came in. 'What are you doing?'

'I'm writing to ask John if I might stay with him until I sort out where to go.'

'Oh, Leslie! Please, please, don't leave me. I'm so sorry about what I said. I don't know what came over me. I can't live without you!'

He looked at the tears in her eyes. He tried but failed to stay firm in his resolve. He nodded. 'What about Richard?'

'I'll ask him to pay rent.'

He knew that would never happen.

She went over to him and put her hand on his cheek. 'Dear, Leslie,' she murmured.

He sighed and stood up. The steak and kidney pudding would be ruined if he didn't see to it straight away.

***

It took a bit of doing, and the delay while the contract changed annoyed Richard, but eventually Ena sorted out the money and Lily signed. Richard became the manager of a farm on Exmoor. A beautiful place with a lovely old manor house. All he needed now were the sheep and the sheep dogs. He brought his grey mare, Geraldine, from his parent's estate and resigned from his job, after a last tryst with Jennie, kissing her goodbye as he told her he'd be lost without her.

He persuaded Lily that they needed several thousand pounds to buy the best breeding sheep and also trained, pedigree sheep dogs. She gave him all her jewellery and some priceless antiques to sell to stock the farm.

They moved in late in the year after he managed to butter up old Leslie to come and live with them. *Stupid old Leslie; he's just a dogsbody, but he obviously adores Lily. Yes, a dogsbody.* He put him in mind of the old Springer spaniel his father used to have.

Now he just had to wait for her divorce to come through. He'd suggested that she sue for divorce on the grounds of desertion. Well, actually, she had deserted her husband, but it sounded like John would go along with the story that it was him who'd deserted her.

Everything was rosy!

He saddled up Geraldine, called the dogs and went to round up the sheep for dipping. He'd managed to find an old codger,

Steven Rudd, living nearby, to help him. That's when Rudd was sober enough.

***

CHAPTER 23

Though sixty-five, John felt eighty. He could retire now. But to what? He'd never felt so dispirited. The day after he left work for the last time, he felt he had to get out of the house. He decided to drive down to see Ena, perhaps call and see David and Doris on the way back.

Ena opened the door and her face lit up with delight. 'Just about to have lunch, John, there's enough for all of us.'

After they finished lunch and the washing up, Charles went to lie down. *The effort of eating was too exhausting for him,* John thought cynically.

He and Ena sat at the kitchen table having a cup of tea. John sighed. 'Ena, I don't know what I'll do, now that I've finished work.'

'I don't want to pry, but do you ever hear from your daughter?' Ena asked tentatively.

John gave another sigh. 'I haven't heard from her for years. I think she resents me for leaving her mother. And I think my mother turned her against me, too. I used to send them birthday and Christmas cards, but then the war and Danny being killed, just made everything so difficult, and I've lost touch with her. When my mother died she left the house to Margaret.'

'Dear John. Look. Why don't you move down to Bournemouth? There's nothing to keep you in Bristol is there?' She paused and looked questioningly at him. 'At least, I don't think so, is there?'

He smiled ruefully. 'If you mean, have I found another woman, the answer is no.'

'Well, I know of a widow who has rooms to let. Her last boarders were a couple, and they've just bought a house and left. It's not far from here.'

He considered for a moment. 'I suppose it would be a good idea to make a fresh start.'

Ena took a sip of her tea. 'Yes, and this lady doesn't drive. She has a big garage where you could park your car.'

He nodded. The idea appealed.

'You'd be close to me, and it's only about fifty miles from Yeovil, so you'd be able to visit Dave and Doris.'

He smiled. For the first time in ages, he felt a bit more optimistic.

'Why don't we go and visit Mary Westover now, and you can think about it. Her rooms won't stay vacant for long.' She got up, and he followed suit.

'No time like the present! All right. Do we have to let her know we're coming?'

'No, she won't mind, she'll be clearing up after lunch.'

Mary Westover impressed John with her no-nonsense attitude, and they liked each other at first sight. She appeared to be about fifty. Her husband had been killed in the war, so Ena had told him.

Mary surveyed the dingy brown paint. 'I'm going to redecorate the rooms before I re-let them—now that we can get paint again!'

They agreed that he would rent the two rooms and the garage from her, and she would provide all his meals and do his washing.

'I could help with the painting,' he said tentatively.

Mary Westover only smiled and shook her head.

When they got back in his car, he became a bit apprehensive. 'Ena! What will I do all day in rooms? I've been so used to doing my own bit of cooking and cleaning, and working all day, how will I pass the time?'

Ena laughed and patted his knee. 'John, you love carpentry, and you'll have a big garage. There will be lots of things you'll find to do, and I'm sure Mary will find a few odd jobs for you, and if pinch comes to shove, I can definitely find things for you to do at my place.'

He felt his spirits rise. 'You're right, Ena.' He smiled at her. 'I'm suddenly looking forward to retirement. Thank you.'

***

Leslie thought it was sickening the way Richard buttered Lily up and she didn't see it. She just lapped up his attentions. She'd bought him a Landrover and a tractor and other essential farm materials, but the place was becoming a disgrace.

The walled yard and stables at the back of the house had turned from a lovely courtyard into a boggy mess of horse shit and dung. Richard didn't seem to do any real work on the place. He just went out on his horse or on the tractor, taking bales of hay to the sheep in the winter. That useless drunkard, Rudd, hardly ever turned up for work, yet Richard still paid him a weekly wage. *From Lily's purse*, Leslie thought angrily. Lily had to sell her lovely house in Poole to finance their increasing debts. *Where did the money go? Best not to think about it.*

Lily's divorce came through, and life went on, until one day, Richard said, 'We're off to Barnstaple for the day, Leslie.'

Then he and Lily disappeared.

Good. I can have a rest.

They came back in the evening with Lily beaming. 'Oh, Leslie, congratulate us! Richard has asked me to marry him, and I said yes.' She wriggled her left hand at him, showing a small diamond ring.

Leslie shot a look at Richard, who had the grace to look a bit shamefaced.

'Had to make an honest woman of her!' he said, trying to make a joke of it.

Initially dumbfounded, when Leslie finally found his voice, he said, 'I hope you'll both be very happy. Have we anything we can drink, to celebrate?' He needed something to soften this latest blow.

'Only some homemade cider.' Richard laughed.

'That will be fine.'

***

Ena told John that Lily planned to marry Richard.

He looked down at his hands and said nothing.

Ena looked at him closely. 'Are you all right, John?'

'Yes, my dear, but you know, I don't feel as bad as I thought I would. I'm happy where I am, and Mary is very good to me.' He looked a bit sheepish. 'Actually, we've moved in together.' His face reddened.

It took Ena a few minutes to understand his meaning. 'You rascal!' Delighted, Ena clapped her hands. 'I'm so pleased for you both.'

John smiled. 'Thank you, my dear. I'll never stop loving Lily, but I'm very fond of Mary and she is so good to me. I'm very happy and contented.'

Ena planted a kiss on his cheek. 'You deserve it, John.'

***

In June 1954, Richard and Lily married quietly in Bournemouth with Leslie and Ena as witnesses. Ena tried to contain her anger.

'It's outrageous,' she whispered to Leslie. 'My mother is seventy, and he's thirty-seven!'

Leslie squeezed her hand. 'Nothing we can do, my dear. Just accept the things we cannot change.'

She managed a smile. 'Dear, Leslie, what would I do without you?'

He smiled back. 'You'd cope, just as you always have, my dear.'

At first Leslie thought things were improving. Richard seemed to be trying his best to make things go smoothly and keep Lily happy. Bright and cheerful, he took Lily to the library in Barnstaple or for drives to Porlock whenever she felt like it.

Leslie tried to help around the house, but he was getting on in years. He felt happy when Richard suggested they get someone to come in and do the cleaning.

***

Yeovil. June 12th 1954

Dear Mother,

I'm sad to have to tell you that Doris has breast cancer. She has had one breast removed and had radiation therapy in Bristol. Now she has to have the other breast removed. No-one is prepared to have Robin, so he has been placed in a home, Manor Park in Stapleton, also in Bristol.

I was wondering if Marilyn could come and stay on the farm with you and Richard during her school summer holidays. She has been a great help to Doris, but Doris is worrying that it is too much for a ten year old to have to cope with. Marilyn was very upset when she saw the huge blisters and scars on her mother when she was washing her. Doris hopes that the blisters and scarring won't be so bad by the time Marilyn comes home.

I hope all is well with the farm and Leslie, you and Richard.
Your son
David

Lily read this letter out to Leslie and Richard at breakfast.

'Of course she must come!' Richard exclaimed.

'Yes,' Leslie said. 'Poor Doris, Dave should have told us before.'

Lily sighed. 'Unfortunately, cancer is still a word people don't want to mention. Yes, I'll write to Dave at once.'

'Tell him we'll drive to Yeovil and get her. Just let us know when Marilyn's school holidays start.' Richard smiled at Lily. 'I'd better get going; we have to get the sheep ready for sheering.'

Lily put the letter down. Her hands fell in her lap. 'A few years ago I would have been able to help Doris. I've lost all my healing powers, Leslie,' she said sadly.

He patted her hand. 'Dear, Lily, you healed so many people.'

'You know there is no hope for Doris, don't you, Leslie?'

For several minutes they sat in silence.

'I'll make a fresh pot of tea,' Leslie said.

***

Marilyn felt thrilled when she heard she'd be going to Exmoor for her summer holidays. She'd just finished reading Lorna Doone and couldn't wait to see the moors.

Doris smiled at her daughter. 'You'll need new clothes. Let's see if there's any spare money. Go and look, Marilyn.'

Marilyn went to the sideboard where the tins of money sat: one for the rent, one for the gas bill, one for the electricity and others for various expenses. She knew there wouldn't be much in any of the tins.

'It's summer,' her mother said; 'we won't be using much electricity. We can use that money and we'll go shopping as soon as I feel a little better.'

Marilyn shook her head. 'I don't need new clothes, Mum! They'll get dirty on a farm. My old clothes will be fine. And I have a summer dress from last year I can still fit into; it's a bit short but that's alright. And I have a pair of shorts.'

Doris gave a smile of relief and sank back in the bed.

When Lily and Richard arrived, Marilyn was already in a fever of excitement. She'd never spent much time with this Grandmother. When she'd asked, her father had merely muttered something about her being a bad influence. Now she had her little bag packed and ready since breakfast. Her father had gone to work very early in the morning, muttering things like, 'Don't take any notice of your Grandmother, and do as you are told and help Leslie ...'

At last the Landrover pulled up outside. Marilyn ran out as Richard got out and lifted Lily down from the passenger seat.

They refused the offer of tea. Lily went to take Doris's hand, but Doris's arm didn't move.

'Mummy can't lift her arm,' Marilyn said quickly.

'The surgeon had to cut into the muscles of my arm to remove the lymph glands ...' Doris said sadly, 'but I can still use my hand.' She turned to Marilyn and gave her a kiss. 'Goodbye dear, and be good and do as you are told.'

Marilyn nodded. 'Mummy, are you sure you'll be able to manage without me?'

'Of course, my dear; I'm improving every day, and I have lots of friends to help.'

They said their goodbyes and Marilyn followed Richard and Lily out to Landrover. To her surprise it had no back seat, just metal shelves sideways over the wheel hubs.

'Jump in, Marilyn. Look here's a cushion to sit on.' Richard handed her a thin piece of wadding.

The journey seemed to take forever, and Marilyn couldn't see the moors very well. The Landrover had no side windows. Her bottom had gone numb by the time they reached the farm, but the beautiful old farmhouse set in a large lawn with a fountain perked her up again.

Leslie fussed over her, making sure she had enough to eat and liked her room.

'It's all lovely; thank you, Leslie.'

He smiled.

'I think you should call me Aunty,' Lily said the next morning. 'I don't want people to think I'm old enough to have a granddaughter.'

Marilyn nodded. 'Yes, Aunty.' The request didn't seem to surprise her. She'd learnt to be diplomatic around Granddad John and his wife Mary when they visited.

She found lots of books to read, which made her happy. It was a luxury to be able to read whenever she wanted. She explored the old house and then went to the big living room. The fireplace was enormous.

'I can stand right in the fire place and see up to the sky,' she said in amazement.

Then Richard came in scowling. 'They're hunting again across our land again.' Dogs could be heard baying in the distance.

'I'll fix them!' He strode into the boot room where they kept the rain coats and boots and came out with a brass hunting horn. He stomped out into the courtyard and blew the horn. Immediately the sound of the dogs faded.

Marilyn watched him with admiration..

Richard returned, grinning while tossing the horn in the air and catching it. 'That put them off the scent.'

Goodness, it's so exciting here, Marilyn thought. *I'll write and tell Mummy all about it.*

Two days later when the master of the hunt delivered a haunch of venison, Richard laid on the charm and made no mention of them crossing his land.

He seemed pleased to have Marilyn for company. She trudged behind him wherever he went and loved the two sheep dogs. Richard told her they'd cost hundreds pounds as they were pure Welsh Collies and had won many medals at sheep trials.

Several days after she arrived, Richard told her they must catch Geraldine.

'She's a grey mare. Sixteen hands. She looks white, but we call them greys,' he smiled at her. They set off with Richard carrying the saddle and bridle. When Geraldine saw them coming she rolled her eyes and galloped away. After spending about twenty minutes chasing the horse, with Richard cursing, he eventually caught her and managed to saddle her.

He leaned over to Marilyn, holding out his hand. 'Come on, sweetie, jump up.

Marilyn looked up. She'd never seen such an enormous animal, except for Rosy the elephant at Bristol zoo. 'I'll walk,' she muttered. 'I'm afraid.'

Richard laughed. 'Okay, but we'll be going a long way. Or would you rather go back to your Grandmother and Leslie.

'No, I'll come with you. But I'll walk.'

He smiled. 'I'll try and go slowly.'

Marilyn thought her lungs would burst trying to keep up and not show she was tired, but by the time the work had been done, rounding up the sheep and dipping them, she was far too tired to walk. Richard lifted her up in front of him, and they cantered back to the farm, the dogs following behind.

Richard grinned. 'We'll make a horsewoman of you yet.'

The next time they went to catch Geraldine, when Richard couldn't catch her after twenty minutes, he threw down the halter with a curse. 'I'm going back for my whip. I'll show her who's boss,' he muttered.

He strode away. Marilyn watched him go. Why was he going for the whip? Was he going to beat Geraldine? She couldn't bear that thought. She took a deep breath and picked up the halter. She had no idea how to put a halter on a horse. Her heart beating loudly, she slowly walked towards Geraldine.

'Geraldine,' she whispered softly, 'Geraldine ...'

The horse looked up, rolling her eyes, and then walked slowly over to her. Marilyn looked up at the enormous sixteen-hand horse —whatever a hand was. Shaking with fear, she stroked the horse's nose, and when Geraldine lowered her head, she slipped the rope around the horse's neck.

Just in time. Richard strode towards them with the whip.

'Well, well, after all, you're braver than you thought!' He smiled. 'This will be your new job in future. Look, I'll show you how to put a halter on.'

Marilyn grinned with pride.

Gradually she became braver and was able to walk Geraldine around the enclosed courtyard. The back of the house made one side, the stables made two sides and a high stone wall created the other side. Between the stables and the house, a low door way led out into the home paddock.

One day Richard helped Marilyn up into the saddle and showed her how to use the reins to turn the horse and dig in her heels to make her go. Thrilled, Marilyn gently put her heels into Geraldine's sides and tried the reins. Geraldine obediently turned and walked around. Richard leaned idly against the wall, watching.

Geraldine started to go faster, and suddenly Richard sprang into action. He raced across the courtyard, snatched the reins and threw himself against the horse's head. 'You bitch!' he roared. 'I saw what you tried to do.'

Marilyn shook.

'I'm sorry, sweetie,' Richard said as he pulled mare around. 'Geraldine just tried to kill you. She was heading for the paddock through that doorway.' He pointed to the doorway. It was slightly higher than Geraldine's shoulder. 'She was starting to break into a gallop. She would've gone under the doorway and you would've been smashed against the wall.'

Marilyn swallowed. 'I think I'll get down now,' she said shakily.

***

Lily liked having Marilyn with them. She got out her books on Egyptology and taught Marilyn about Tutankhamun and the riddles of the Pyramids. She even gave her the little mummy Harold Carter had given her. She talked to the little girl about the troposphere, the planets and all the other things that interested her, and Marilyn seemed happy to listen and absorb all this new information.

Richard also seemed to enjoy having her accompany him around the farm, and Leslie found her helpful in the kitchen.

'What would you like to do when you grow up?' he asked her one day as they washed potatoes in the scullery.

'I want to be farmer,' she announced proudly. 'A sheep farmer!'

When the time came for Marilyn to leave, Lily presented her with a bag.

'These are some books you might like, darling,' she smiled.

Marilyn peered into the bag. She took out an enormous book, 'The Riddle of the Pyramids', and then the others; 'The Elements of Agriculture', 'The Dogs' Medical Dictionary', 'The Thirteen Logical Fallacies', 'The Wind in the Willows' and 'Winnie the Pooh'. She was ecstatic.

'Oh thank you, Aunty!' she said.

'I've written in each one for you,' Lily said.

Marilyn looked inside each book. *Aunty had inscribed each one, and each of them said with love from Granny!'*

After the holiday Richard and Lily drove Marilyn home. Doris was still in hospital.

Dave shook his head at their unspoken query. 'Not good,' he said. 'They had to cut through the muscles in her arm to get all the lymph gland out. They think they have it all, but now she can't lift either of her arms at all.' He gave a sad smile. 'When the doctor told Doris this, she just laughed and said, "Well I'll just have to sit and twiddle my thumbs!"'

Richard and Lily drove back in silence.

A few weeks later, Marilyn had a letter from Lily. And a photo of Marilyn on Geraldine. Richard had written on the back: Quite the best. R.

CHAPTER 24

The farm seemed quiet and empty with Marilyn gone. Lily soon became restless with no real diversions that suited her, and Richard seemed unsettled. It appeared that Richard found it irksome to spend the long winter evenings sitting with two old people, reading and listening to classical music. He needed the company of people his own age. After being used to an adrenaline-charged life as a commando, a quiet life on a remote farm didn't satisfy Richard's needs.

Things went downhill.

Richard stayed away from home many nights. He told Lily he had to see to some lambing ewes or watch out for foxes. She believed him. Or at least, she wanted to believe him.

Leslie knew better. He'd heard the Rudd fellow mumbling something about some girl in the village that Richard was seeing. He'd also overheard some gossip in the village when he'd been shopping. The gossipers fell silent when they saw him.

Things seemed to go from bad to worse. He sometimes heard Lily and Richard arguing.

Late one night on his way to the bathroom he heard them arguing again.

'What kind of companion are you anyway?' Richard said. 'We can't have a joke and a laugh ... and that gigolo of yours ...'

'What gigolo?'

'Leslie! Who did you think?'

'Leslie is not my gigolo! How dare you ...' Lily's voice shook.

'He's always creeping around spying on me ...'

'How dare you say that!' Lily's voice rose, and then Leslie heard her sobbing.

'I'm going out. I can't stand this anymore.' Richard again.

Leslie dodged into the bathroom and locked the door. Just in time. Richard burst out of the bedroom, slammed the door behind him and clattered down the stairs. Leslie stayed in the bathroom until he heard the Landrover start and drive away.

He knocked on Lily's bedroom door. 'Lily? Are you all right?'

'Yes, Leslie. Go back to bed.' He heard her sniffing.

'I'll make you a cup of tea.'

He went down to the kitchen where the kettle always simmered on the Aga, made the tea and took two cups up to her bedroom.

'Here you are, my dear.' He sat down on the little chair at the side of the bed.

She looked terrible: red eyes and nose, and her once-bouncing copper curls now hung limp and bedraggled.

She took a sip of tea and blew her nose. 'Thank you, Leslie.' She managed a wan smile. 'Where will it end?' She sniffed.

In divorce probably, Leslie thought.

The next few months were awful, then one day when Leslie and Lily were sitting quietly after lunch in the big living room, they heard the kitchen door slam. Lily seemed to shrink within herself.

Richard burst in. He looked from one to the other and smiled. 'Nice and cosy, the pair of you. Like an old married couple.'

Leslie just looked at him.

Lily couldn't raise her eyes.

'Well, I've filed for a divorce,' he declared.

Lily looked up, stunned.

Leslie wanted to get up and put his arms around her, but thought better of it.

'I'm citing your adultery with Leslie here.'

'What!' Incensed, Leslie jumped up. 'That's a gross lie. How can you say such a thing? There has never been any kind of relationship between Lily and myself, and you well know it!' he almost shouted.

'Prove it. You've been hanging around Lily ever since I've known her. And I have proof.'

'What!'

'Yes, Rudd came to the house one day to see me, and I wasn't here, he went to the stairs to call out and saw Leslie coming out of Lily's bedroom.'

Leslie and Lily blinked, dumbfounded, and too shocked to think clearly and question how that drunkard Rudd even knew where to find Lily's bedroom and why he'd even come to that part of the house. Richard knew that Leslie always took Lily a cup of tea in bed—at least, when Richard wasn't around.

'Anyway, it's all in hand.' Richard smiled as he turned away. 'Well, I've got work to do, even if you two haven't.' He walked out. A moment later, they heard the Landrover starting up.

Leslie joined Lily on the sofa and touched her hand. 'What will you do, my dear? Will you contest it?'

'What's the point?' she replied wearily. 'I don't think I have any money left to fight his accusations, and anyway, the marriage is over.'

***

It took some time for the farm to sell as it'd been neglected for several years. Most of the ewes had maggots. Foxes had got at the lambs, and the price of sheep had declined. Richard didn't get much for them, but he didn't seem to care—Leslie suspected he'd been squirrelling away Lily's money.

The divorce came through and the farm eventually sold for a lot less than Lily had paid for it. After payment of the debts and the divorce settlement, Lily had just enough money left to buy a small house. Ena looked out for somewhere reasonable.

'The best place I can find for that money is a place in Ferndown. It's a very pretty place, and the house is convenient. It's only ten miles from me,' Ena told them when they visited her.

'That's good.' Leslie tried to be bright and cheerful. 'Thank you, Ena.'

'Yes, thank you, darling,' Lily said dully.

'Well, it'll be good to be finally away from Richard,' Leslie said, trying to cheer Lily up.

He and Lily moved into the new house, and Leslie found it much easier to keep clean and warm than that old rambling farmhouse.

'I haven't been very clever, have I, Leslie?' Lily said to him out of the blue one morning as he took her up her morning cup of tea.

'Oh, Lily, dear, don't think like that!'

'I had a great gift. Did I use it wisely, Leslie?' she asked in a despondent tone.

'Of course you did, my dear. You healed hundreds of people, and helped others with your séances.'

She regarded him sadly. 'Thank you, Leslie. For everything.'

***

One day when Leslie and Lily visited Ena, she took Leslie aside and showed him a cutting from a society magazine. 'Take a look at that.' She gave a grimace.

He put on his glasses and peered at the article: Country Life Magazine, July, 1959.

He shook his head and made a sound of disgust at the photo of a wedding with the caption, 'Richard Sheriden and his new bride, Patricia Wentworth-Smythe'.

Richard had lost no time marrying into society.

'Don't let Lily see,' was all he said.

***

Leslie worried about Lily. She hadn't been well for some time, and he thought she was losing weight. One lunch time she sat up in bed, picking at the food on the tray he'd brought her.

'My dear, don't you think you should see a doctor?'

She shook her head. 'Darling Leslie, there's nothing wrong with me.'

He took away the tray with the uneaten meal on it and later voiced his concerns to Ena.

She simply said, 'You know Lily. She won't be told anything.'

A few nights later, he brought her a cup of warm milk. 'Please try and drink this, Lily.' He sat on the bed and held the cup to her lips.

'Later, darling.' She sank back into the pillows. 'Leslie, I'm so cold. Can you get into bed with me and warm me?'

He blinked. How many years had he wanted to hear those words?' Speechless, he nodded, then put the cup of milk on the bedside table, took off his trousers and woollen cardigan and climbed in beside her. He hadn't realised quite how thin and frail she had become.

Gently he took her into his arms and kissed the top of her head. 'Try and rest, my dear.'

'Leslie.'

'Yes?'

'All my life I've been looking for my soul mate. At first, I thought it was Percy, then John and finally Richard, but Leslie?'

'Yes, my dear?'

'My soul mate was right there all the time.'

He frowned, puzzled. 'Who?'

'Why, you of course, darling Leslie.'She sighed. 'I haven't been kind to you, have I?'

'Shhh, try and sleep. Are you feeling warmer now?'

'Yes.'

He held her gently; she felt so fragile in his arms. With a full heart, he went over and over in his mind what she'd said until eventually he dozed off. He woke a few hours later, feeling cold and stiff and desperately in need of a pee.

He blinked and tried to straighten his arms, then realised that Lily no longer breathed. *My darling Lily*. Tears came to his eyes. He lay there for many minutes, then gently extricated himself, kissed each of her closed eyelids and got dressed.

***

ACKNOWLEDGEMENTS

I'd like to thank the following people, organisations and publications for their help and assistance with this book:

Shirley Gould, for getting me started, for motivating me and for painstakingly correcting my grammar.

Barbara Spense for encouragement and proof reading.

Trish Behan for her amazing contribution.

François Beugels for his input.

Tahlia Newland for her editing skills.

Resources

Oliver Lodge, *Raymond.*

James Dunning, *It had to be Tough: The origins and Training of the Commandos in World War 11.*

Elizabeth d'Esperance, *Shadow Land or Light From the Other Side.*

Richard Roberts, *Saving the City: The Great Financial Crisis of 1914.*

Brian Clacy, *Frank's War in a Thornycroft: An Army Service Corps Diary.*

Ruth Smithers, *Sex Tips for Husbands and Wives from 1894.*

Damien Lewis, *Churchill's Secret Warriors.*

Lorraine Sencicle, *The Dover Historian.*

Harlech Press, *The Poem by Diana Joyce, pen name for Lola Watts*.

Hannah Tinkler, *The Story of the WVS Bristol 1939 – 1945*.

BBC – WW2 People's War - *brssouthglosproject*

AFTERWORD

This is the story of my grandmother, Lola Inez Over. The main contents are factually correct.

Lola's mother was Spanish, I have no idea how she met my great-grandfather.

Richard went on to have two children by his second wife. He died in 1997, aged 80.

I stayed with my grandmother's second husband, John and his third wife, Mary, in Bournemouth during some of my school holidays and they were happy times. The hallway in the house had a coat rack that John made from the wooden propeller of the aircraft in which he crashed. I have fond memories of John. He bought a new car every year, took the engine apart and then rebuilt it. Passengers had to put on slippers to ride in his cars.

I also spent two summer holidays with my grandmother and her third husband, Richard on the farm on Exmoor. Richard was great fun, a daredevil who saved my life when his horse, Geraldine, that I was riding made a bolt for a low doorway in the courtyard. Without Richard's swift action, I would have been decapitated.

Leslie and my Aunt Ena (known in the family as Deans) were constants in my young life. I loved them both and also John. I have the oak cabinet that John made to hold his record collection and vividly remember him playing the scratchy recording of Cavaleria Rusticana that he loved.

In the book, I am David's daughter, Marilyn.

Some names have been changed to protect the guilty.

Stolen Love, Fractured Lives – An incurable, hereditary disease haunts the lives of three generations of women and the men who love them. Add a stolen baby to make a tangled web of lies and deceptions.

***

The Unpredictable Past – When a mysterious man, Will, moves into the house opposite hers, Elizabeth's quiet village life is turned upside down. Their friendship develops when Will helps with researching the involvement of one of her ancestors, Edward, in the last revolution in England. This friendship sets the neighbours gossiping and infuriates Elisabeth's daughter, who is convinced Will is a con man preying on her mother, thus raising doubts in Elizabeth's mind. Elizabeth and Will delve more into the past and attempt to solve the mystery surrounding the death of Edward's son, Edmund. How can Elizabeth find out the truth about Will? Is he who he seems?

***

Seeking Samuel Goldberg — Liesel discovers at her Grandfather's funeral that she has Jewish heritage — a family secret held since the days of Nazi Germany — and learns of her grandfather's unfulfilled quest to find family members missing since the outbreak of World War Two. After an unfortunate love affair, Liesel uses the few clues her grandfather left to try and locate her father's cousins. Her travels bring her much more than she could ever have expected.

If you enjoyed this book please leave a review at your point of purchase, or on Goodreads.com

DISCUSSION POINTS FOR BOOK CLUBS

1. Do you believe in Spiritualism? Have you had any experience of supernatural events

2. Were you aware of the Army Service Corps and the logistics involved in feeding and transporting hundreds and thousands of men and horses to the battlefields of WW1?

3. Do you think Percy was suffering from PTSD when he returned from the First World War?

4. Was Lily heartless in her treatment of Percy and her pursuit of John?

5. Were you surprised by the effects of the bombing in England?

6. Did Lily get her comeuppance by the way Richard treated her in the end?

www.ingramcontent.com/pod-product-compliance
Lightning Source LLC
Chambersburg PA
CBHW031954130726
47904CB00013B/1385